CONTENTS

Shayne Silvers

Knightmare

Nate Temple Series Book 12

ISBN: 978-1-947709-28-7

© 2019, Shayne Silvers / Argento Publishing, LLC

info@shaynesilvers.com

THE NATE TEMPLE SERIES—A WARNING

*N*ate Temple starts out with everything most people could ever wish for—money, magic, and notoriety. He's a local celebrity in St. Louis, Missouri—even if the fact that he's a wizard is still a secret to the world at large.

Nate is also a bit of a...well, let's call a spade a spade. He can be a mouthy, smart-assed jerk. Like the infamous Sherlock Holmes, I specifically chose to give Nate glaring character flaws to overcome rather than making him a chivalrous Good Samaritan. He's a black hat wizard, an antihero—and you are now his partner in crime. He is going to make a *ton* of mistakes. And like a buddy cop movie, you are more than welcome to yell, laugh and curse at your new partner as you ride along together through the deadly streets of St. Louis.

Despite Nate's flaws, there's also something *endearing* about him...You soon catch whispers of a firm moral code buried deep under all his snark and arrogance. A diamond waiting to be polished. And you, the esteemed reader, will soon find yourself laughing at things you really shouldn't be laughing at. It's part of Nate's charm. Call it his magic...

So don't take yourself, or any of the characters in my world, too seriously. Life is too short for that nonsense.

Get ready to cringe, cackle, cry, curse, and—ultimately—*cheer* on this snarky wizard as he battles or befriends angels, demons, myths, gods, shifters, vampires and many other flavors of dangerous supernatural beings.

~

DON'T FORGET! VIP's get early access to all sorts of Temple-Verse goodies, including signed copies, private giveaways, and advance notice of future projects. AND A FREE NOVELLA! Click the image or join here:
www.shaynesilvers.com/l/219800

FOLLOW and LIKE:
Shayne's FACEBOOK PAGE:

www.shaynesilvers.com/l/38602

I try to respond to all messages, so don't hesitate to drop me a line. Not interacting with readers is the biggest travesty that most authors can make. Let me fix that.

CHAPTER 1

I sat atop my mountain, idly regarding the countless miles upon miles of sprawling land far, far below me: from calm, secluded ponds to bioluminescent forests; from turbulent seas of boiling sands to frigid, fingernail-splintering tundras; from oceans of molten stone to fields of glass reeds, and even a monochromatic island with a white mansion, white walls, white *everything*.

But that was long gone now. I'd introduced it to color. And destruction.

Every inch of this savagely breathtaking world was inhabited by multifarious hordes of nefarious, exotic, and alien creatures that could have only been birthed from the darkest depths of a god's nightmare—all majestically malicious and insatiably malcontent.

The less frightening they appeared, the more horrifying they likely were.

And most lucky souls would never discover that the ecosystem, let alone the organisms within, even existed, unless they had their heads firmly tethered in the clouds, wasting away their days by reading strange, fantastical—allegedly fictional—scribbles that had been scratched into dismembered, prehistoric titans known as trees by mad men and women living out their days in voluntary solitary confinement.

Readers of mythology and fairy tales were the only beings with forewarning of the dangers—and beauties—that the world truly had to offer.

Because those gullible souls had technically earned a PhD in Faeology and had a survival guide built into their subconscious mind.

For the non-readers, or readers of more mundane genres, ignorance was bliss—they just didn't know that the joke was on them.

Because the Land of the Fae was very real.

And it had been my new home for...a while now. I'd claimed this mountain for myself—Mount Wylde. My neighbors were succubi sprites, feral fairies, conscious elementals, pitiless goblins, kings, queens, talking trees...

Except none of them dared visit me atop my mountain. They'd tried—in the beginning.

I had dissuaded them. Violently.

I knew that much, but I had trouble recalling any specific altercations. I was fairly certain that I had first come here to recover from a mental malady; some days that thought was nothing more than a vague reverie, leading me to question whether it was fact or fiction.

Because I knew that I had been *born* here.

However...

I had strange dreams of another place—an entirely different world where every moment didn't revolve around the mastery of my instincts, dominance, and power. A different life where I wore a disguise and a different name. A life where visiting the Land of the Fae had been an objective, not an odyssey.

Which story was true? Was my mountain in Fae a *new* home or my *true* home?

Was I Wylde, or someone else?

Maybe *this* was my mental malady—not knowing which life had been real.

One thing I knew for certain—emotions were dangerous for me to entertain, let alone try to control. And dwelling too long on thoughts of that other life threatened to suffocate me with emotions I normally avoided.

Even *acknowledging* this now—that dream of a different life—I felt a storm brewing deep within me, a violent hurricane threatening to rise to the surface of my mind and annihilate everything within one hundred paces. I rolled my shoulders irritably, shaking off the sensation—and the tempting dream—with a shudder.

Instead, I focused on the currents of power curling through the very air as I took a calm, measured breath. The constant ebbs and flows of power were ingrained into every facet of the Land of the Fae—the trees, the creatures, the air, the water. And I could manipulate it, make it dance to my desire.

Life *lived* here, birthed and strengthened by the constant battle of give or take, do or die, kill or be killed.

Any existence that was less chaotic seemed pointless to me. In nature, stagnation was decay, and growth—movement—was life.

What was the point in any other method of living? A life of sedentary suicide? No. Death feasted on the unambitious, those content with the crumbs of mediocrity rather than scavenging for the slightest morsel of self-betterment—in any scope whatsoever.

Those who chose to never challenge and improve *any* aspect of their lives for the better were no different than lambs led to a slaughter.

Power was the answer. The more power one attained, the longer they lived. Power was the key to happiness, and happiness was the art of living.

A sudden burst of wind rustled my hair, whipping up cyclones of snow and grit as it screamed loud enough to send most creatures hissing and fleeing back into their hiding places.

Without moving a muscle, I stopped it.

The wind immediately fell flat, squashed down as if it had only existed in my imagination. It may as well have. I grunted dismissively, the simple flex of power helping to reestablish my sense of self, banishing those errant thoughts of some other paler reality.

Reality *was* my imagination.

Existence was granted only by my approval.

Because on this mountain, I'd found power. I had reclaimed my power here. I wasn't sure where I had lost it, or how, but I'd found it again—like I'd momentarily lost my shadow only to find it had simply been obscured by another larger shadow beside me.

I settled my palm across the staff resting across my lap. *Shadow,* I thought to myself, feeling uncomfortable for some reason. I squeezed the shaft hard enough for part of it to crack and crumble over my knuckles. With no outward movement, I instinctively grasped the dust and reforged it into the very fabric, the very essence, of the staff.

Then I settled it back across my lap, forcing my pulse down to forty beats per minute.

I tried to remain in that zone, knowing that it kept my mind—and thoughts—devoid of all but the most relevant of concerns. That was the lowest pulse rate I'd been able to attain.

Then again, I'd grown bored with attempting to lower it any further.

I'd grown bored with almost every activity or momentary hobby in my time here, as a matter of fact.

My education was advancing, but not at the pace I desired, and thinking of it made me angry, impatient, and bitter. I quickly forced my pulse to slow again, refusing to let my emotions take hold—only danger awaited me on that path.

I needed new adventures, new skills to learn—before I turned into yet another lamb.

I sensed movement to my right and almost flinched in surprise, having forgotten that I wasn't currently alone. My winged unicorn—alicorn, technically—had glanced over at me as if having read my thoughts on boredom. "Never you, Grimm," I murmured, not meeting his gaze. "I'll never be bored with you."

Grimm snorted softly before returning to his meal—a faint wisp of a rainbow, this time. It had been a while since we'd seen any truly vibrant rainbows—as if they knew a rainbow killer now occupied the once solitary mountain.

I could have simply *made* a rainbow for him, but he'd argued that me doing so took all the fun out of killing them. Like breeding cows or sheep and calling their slaughter a *hunt.*

Which made sense.

Domestication was weakness.

Still, the diluted diet—and poor company—made him antsy, hungry, and…cautious.

There had been other visitors, but I couldn't recall them staying for any measurable length of time. One had stayed by my side, but she was a mentor of sorts, a wielder of great powers that I was still struggling to learn—an elusive, fickle branch of power dissimilar to my other methods of wielding power.

But I cared about those visitors. Some of them…

Didn't I?

I risked a glance at Grimm. Yes. I cared about him. If I looked closely enough, I would notice the wings of black smoke sprouting from his back, but they would only become visible to others when he consciously chose to unfurl them. Usually, when it was too late to save themselves from instant death.

It was hard for anyone to hide magic from me now, though. Not after my time on this mountain. *My* mountain. Magic…spoke to me. Sang to me. It was simply a part of me.

I glanced down again, unimpressed by the thousands upon thousands of feet of open air between me and the base of my mountain.

My world.

I sighed wearily.

Maybe someone else wanted it. I was running out of entertainment, and stagnation was a very tempting suggestion at times—even though it meant certain death.

Because all of Fae stretched out before me—all the magic, monsters, stories, fables, and legends told over campfires for hundreds and thousands of years. They were down there, living, drinking, eating, fucking…

And I couldn't seem to remember why I cared about such things.

Like being concerned with the daily schedule of an ant colony.

The metaphor caused a weak bubble of a memory—a rarity for me, lately—to slip past my defenses. I focused on it, curious.

And it slowly began to clarify in my mind's eye. I remembered that the Fae Queens—Summer and Winter—had both sent armies to the base of my mountain, allowing a single messenger to travel to the peak to demand an explanation of my intentions.

And I'd thrown each of them off the cliff—right here, in fact—without uttering a single word, and without my pulse climbing higher than forty-one beats per minute.

Summer's representative had flown further, but Winter's had hit a tent full of fellow soldiers, so it had been a wash, really.

They hadn't sent anyone else since, and had soon departed, leaving me in peace. No. That wasn't right…

I absently scratched at my beard, frowning. "Hey, Grimm?"

He jolted in surprise, not accustomed to hearing me talk twice in less than an hour. He quickly regained his composure and glanced over at me, licking rainbow-colored blood from his lips. The snow beneath his meal was liberally painted in matching splashes of color. His nostrils flared, and his black feathers rose briefly—the red orbs on the tips glinting wetly in the pale sunlight—before the long feathers fell back down to rest against his flesh.

"Yeah?" he asked guardedly.

"Didn't the Queens send more messengers after the first two?"

Grimm studied me thoughtfully for a few long moments before finally nodding. "Yes. They brought written messages the second time, fearing their voices might offend you."

I frowned, shaking my head. I vaguely recalled the exchange. "What did they say again?"

He paused long enough for me to glance back at him. "You didn't read them," he replied cautiously. "You said you didn't care what ants had to say, request, or demand, and that it was better for them if you didn't read anything they'd sent..."

Ants.

That was what had jogged my memory. I nodded absently, shifting slightly in the snow, still only recalling the topic as if it had been a foggy dream from my childhood.

"You want to read them?" he asked, interrupting my thoughts. "I kept them. In case you changed your mind later."

I considered it for about ten seconds before finally shrugging. "Sure." Because I could think of absolutely nothing else more interesting to do at the moment. It was marginally better than stagnation.

"Alice put them inside your satchel," he said, jerking his chin to my right. "I'd offer to grab them, but I don't have thumbs," he said dryly. I turned to see the white-scaled leather satchel beside me, and I frowned, feeling a momentary flash of alarm.

Something about that leather was dangerous. I'd heard numerous people say so, but I couldn't recall any of their faces, or any of their actual warnings. I shook off the thought, reaching my hand into the satchel. Almost instantly, I felt two folded papers. I pulled them out, frowning down at the wax seals of the thick parchments.

One was a blue snowflake.

The other was a golden flower.

I felt a sudden wave of anxiety, but I didn't know why. It wasn't like I was afraid of the Fae Queens, but...some instinct was screaming at me in a muffled voice.

I set the folded letters in my lap, choosing to regain my composure before opening them. I glanced over at Grimm. "Where is Alice?"

Grimm arched an eyebrow at me. "Well, she was sketching over on that rock a few hours ago. Then she suddenly decided to go pick elderberries."

My shoulders tensed of their own accord, something about his answer making me uncomfortable. I couldn't place why, but it felt similar to the danger I had felt from my satchel. "Why did you say *suddenly*?"

Grimm studied me suspiciously. I stared right back, having no idea what I had done that might be construed as suspicious.

He sighed. "Dude. You randomly decided to start taking your clothes off —without giving us a word of warning." He jerked his chin to my other side where I noticed a pile of old clothes sitting in the snow. "You hadn't even pulled your shirt over your head before she noticed and ran away as fast as she could. She tossed her sketchbook into the igloo, snatched up her basket, and then ran that way," he explained jerking his chin behind me.

I frowned, looking over my shoulder at the igloo pressed up against the wall of the mountain—our little home. I saw Alice's sketchbook on the ground, halfway into the doorway, corroborating Grimm's story.

I glanced down to see that he was right about another thing. I was definitely naked. Luckily, the letters from the queens concealed most of my dangerous bits.

"You don't remember any of that either?" he asked, sounding mildly concerned.

Instead of answering, I focused on the letters, scratching at the stubble on my chin with two fingers. "You should probably go check on her. I'll put some pants on," I said woodenly.

He didn't move for a few moments, but I pretended not to notice, turning each letter over as if inspecting them for magical traps. The truth was, I vaguely remembered doing exactly as Grimm said. But only *after* he'd mentioned it. Part of me found nothing wrong with my decision to strip down to my skin, but I was beginning to sense an altogether different voice in my head. It was muffled and distant, but it carried a lot of emotional baggage with it. And that voice was growing louder, and closer to the forefront of my thoughts with each passing second.

"Go. Get. Alice!" I snapped. I had to consciously focus on my words, feeling a sudden migraine coming on—a splitting tension in the base of my skull that threatened to knock me unconscious. And it had all started with that abstract voice.

My tone must have given Grimm cause for alarm, because he was already galloping away from me as fast as he could.

I let out a shuddering breath, relieved to have relative privacy, even if only for a few moments. Long enough to work out this problem in my mind.

"What the hell is happening to me, and where is that voice coming from?" I whispered out loud. And I realized I sounded afraid.

CHAPTER 2

*I*nstead of approaching the problem head on, I took a deep breath and forced myself to relax. Almost instantly, my migraine began to subside. I glanced back out over the ledge, acknowledging the rings of clouds circling my mountain. With a bored flick of my wrist, I morphed them into something more tangible and aesthetically pleasing—an exotic, nude woman lying on her side, smiling at me with a suggestive smolder. It was a flawless rendition of that beautiful, white-haired woman who had visited me here long ago—a familiar face but somehow a stranger. She, too, had been hunting for power—and she'd found quite a lot of it, actually.

I'd offered her more power, but she'd declined. I couldn't currently recall what I had offered her, though. I studied her face and her smile, feeling my pulse quickening, and the muscles below my waist abruptly clenched in a strange manner—and they did so alarmingly fast.

With a sudden, harsh slash of my hand, the figure dissipated, and I let out a soft, shuddering breath. That…had almost given me an emotion—and something else entirely inappropriate.

I couldn't afford one of those again. Not here.

Not wanting to risk looking at the clouds any longer, I glanced down, focusing on the the staff in my lap rather than the two letters. It was as long as I was tall and formed from a stone-like substance. Similar to quartz, with gems of every color embedded deep within so that it shone like a rainbow when the sunlight hit it just right.

I'd been annoyed at frequent—too frequent, for my taste—lightning storms plaguing my camp at the peak of the mountain. I'd used my newfound control of power to set up traps to catch them and solidify them into spires. They'd littered the snow like spears cast down from the heavens —spears originally intended to kill me.

And they had featured a familiar rainbow tint that tickled my memory, hinting at the offender. For some reason, I knew I hated and feared this asshole. I couldn't quite recall why, or who he was, but he was the cause of most of my emotions.

So I kept one of the solidified, rainbow bolts as a reminder. That I would soon need to respond to the motherfucker—

I took a deep breath, walling off the sudden emotion before it could fully ripen.

I climbed to my feet and snatched up my clothes Grimm had pointed out, using the motions of dressing to keep my mind occupied. I tugged on a worn, faded pair of jeans and a long sleeved t-shirt. I didn't see any shoes, so I sat down on a nearby rock so as not to get my jeans any wetter than they already were. The cold didn't bother me, despite being barefoot.

I stared at the two letters in my hand, feeling anxious for some strange reason. Then, with trembling hands, I cracked open the yellow seal and unfolded the parchment.

I cleared my throat, wanting to read it out loud.

"I, Queen Summer, request your assistance in the extermination of Mordred Pendragon. All past grievances will be expunged in exchange for an alliance with Master Wylde Fae."

The words centered me, slightly, as I struggled to comprehend their meaning. Mordred...that was another asshole I wanted to impale on a frozen lightning bolt. How had I forgotten about him?

A noise drew my attention, and I glanced over towards the igloo to see Alice riding on top of Grimm. The two of them watched me cautiously as they slowly approached. Alice was a young, towheaded, slip of a girl, and she was wearing a blue dress with white polka dots. White stockings covered her skinny little legs, and her yellow shoes bobbed back and forth in time with Grimm's gait.

She was Fae, and my responsibility. She was also my instructor in the dance of power. Her mother had died trying to help me, leaving her an orphan. Which was incredibly sad, but you wouldn't sense that from talking with her.

Because she was a Seer, and she had seen her mother's death long before it had actually happened. Alice hadn't forewarned anyone about what she had seen, choosing instead to spend her penultimate moments with her mother in a time-capsule devoid of any looming shadows.

Which meant she had chosen to accept those shadows for herself, refusing to let anyone else help her. Alice was deceptively dangerous, and the wisdom behind those young eyes had tasted a lifetime of the harsh, poisonous bite of truth.

Her mother, Alvara, had tried getting me a very important book and had paid for it with her life. Even worse, she hadn't succeeded. Because—

I took a calming breath, closing my eyes for a three-count, banishing the sudden visual memory.

The sudden *emotion.*

Alvara wasn't the only one to have died to help me.

Pan—

I staggered to my feet, my eyes dancing wildly as I gripped my staff like it was the nearest flotation device in a turbulent sea. That name…

How could three letters cause so much pain?

I squeezed my staff desperately—like it was the last vine on a crumbling cliff—

I gasped suddenly, stars exploding across my vision as I felt an unseen fist squeeze my heart. I ground my teeth at the strength and unimaginable pain of the seemingly innocent metaphor. It had been entirely too close to…*something.*

So, I smothered it, hoping that I would overcome this episode, this abrupt torrent of emotions threatening to devour my soul and send me into a rampage. But I felt my grip, my control, loosening.

Grimm had paused a safe distance away, sensing that something was wrong. I focused on counting the rocks in my immediate vicinity—anything to distract me from those three letters.

I panted hoarsely, the snow around me swiftly melting into puddles as I struggled to harness the foreign emotions roiling deep within me, thrashing about in their eagerness to rise up to the surface.

The other letter, I thought to myself. *Maybe that will distract me.*

I cracked the blue seal, almost ripping the paper in my haste.

"I, Queen Winter, offer you a gift of your choosing in hopes that you lead the Armies of Fae against the Usurper, Mordred Pendragon and his Black Knights. Gift granted upon successful eradication of the False King and Black Knights. Time is of the essence, Lord Wylde Fae."

I grunted, and my shoulders tensed and quivered as the words echoed in the dusty halls of my mind—halls that hadn't heard a verbal discussion in some time. Not one that had done more than ricochet off the exterior walls.

I stumbled, gripping the staff for support.

Wylde Fae...

That was my name.

No.

My *Name*.

And, like an avalanche, more memories came crashing down upon me, drowning me, slaughtering the defenses of my instinct-only mentality.

I shuddered, seeing Alice staring back at me. They were only ten feet away from me now, having closed the distance at some point. They both looked nervous, but also resolved to stand beside me—figuratively. Even though Alice was shivering.

She...*never* shivered, even with all this snow. Something about her blood making her immune to the extreme temperature of my mountain.

No. I shook my head stubbornly.

This mountain, not *my* mountain.

"I..." Clearing my throat was an effort in pain. "I am Wylde Fae," I finally managed.

Alice nodded very slowly, staring deep into my eyes, her shivering slowly receding. "What else?" she asked, gently. Oh, so gently. And...was that excitement in her voice?

I struggled, grimacing as I sifted through the influx of memories—each scalding my soul like a white-hot brand. Without the staff for support, I might have slipped and tumbled down the mountain.

"I am...Nate Temple," I finally rasped, feeling like I'd finally shoved off the blanket threatening to suffocate me—the blanket of memories—of why I was really here on this mountain, of what had happened, of who had died...

Of who I needed to kill.

And an entirely new level of stress, weighing *more* than a mountain, threatened to flatten me. Because he—Mordred Pendragon—wanted to kill all the people I loved. All the people I had forgotten about in my quest for power. My quest for answers in Fae.

I grunted, gaining some measure of internal strength to hold up the mountain of responsibilities slowly settling onto my shoulders. The mountain of responsibilities I had entirely forgotten.

The people I had entirely neglected.

I stared down at my toes, feeling ashamed and confused as it all came back to me.

But one memory hit me hardest of all.

Pan…was dead. Mallory, a man I had grown to love more than my own father, despite his lies.

He had willingly sacrificed himself for me, in hopes that he could help me regain my memories of my life in Fae.

I gritted my teeth defiantly. And I was *not* going to disrespect that memory any longer. I would honor him with Mordred's blood on my bare hands.

I forced my breathing back under control, knowing I was still a little wild around the edges, and that I needed to keep a clear head.

After a few moments of self-reflection, I slowly looked back up, staring at Grimm and Alice. "I'm sorry," I whispered.

Alice flashed me a bright smile and clapped her hands. "You did it!" she cheered. "You went all the way down the rabbit hole and clawed your way back out!"

I felt a faint smile splitting my cheeks, knowing what she had meant. I had needed to spend time here in Fae to regain my memories, to master my origins, my legend. I hadn't known what that would entail, but I definitely hadn't anticipated losing myself in the process.

Alice, on the other hand, had apparently known all along.

But her words rang true. Despite my sudden stress, I felt whole—able to recall everything from my childhood in Fae as well as my childhood in St. Louis. There were no more contradictions preventing me from using either power.

Which meant…

"It's time to get to work," I told them. Another thought hit me, making me frown. Time between Fae and the Earthly realm was not a reliably measurable relationship. Sometimes, a week in Fae could only be an hour back on Earth.

Other times…

A week in Fae could be *months* on Earth.

"How long have we been on this mountain?" I asked anxiously, fearing the worst.

CHAPTER 3

*B*efore either of them could answer, we were interrupted by a strange metallic sound coming from the edge of the cliff. I turned to look but the sound had stopped, and I saw nothing alarming. I frowned warily, waiting to hear it again. A moment later, it continued.

Clunk. Scraaaape. Clunk. Scraaaape.

An icy chill rolled down my spine, and I turned to lock eyes with Grimm. I jerked my chin in a silent command.

Grimm nodded, slowly backing away. "I'll keep her safe."

Alice opened her mouth to protest and then her eyes widened as she pointed over my shoulder at the cliff. I spun back around, instinctively shifting into a fighting stance. I saw a single, black gauntlet clutching the edge of the cliff. I blinked incredulously.

"That's our cue," Grimm muttered, and I heard Alice grunt in protest as Grimm turned and galloped away. I risked a quick glance over my shoulder to see a frustrated and concerned Alice craning her neck to stare at me—wanting to help, but knowing she wasn't a fighter.

I shook my head sternly.

Then they disappeared entirely from view, galloping back down the path where Alice had gone to pick berries.

I turned back to my uninvited guest.

A second gauntlet snatched onto the ledge, and then a black helmet rose over the lip of the cliff. The armored Knight stared at me, his visor firmly clamped down so that I couldn't see his actual face. Then he laboriously pulled himself the rest of the way up and over the edge.

I let him, too impressed to move.

The Knight finally climbed to his feet and, judging by the steady rise and fall of his breastplate, he was panting with exhaustion.

His armor was dented, scratched, and looked beaten to hell, but a large bloody symbol painted his chest, and it was perfectly unscathed. If not for all the wear and tear, the armor would have been breathtaking. Whoever had made it had put their heart and soul into the artistry rather than just connecting thick, bulky plates of metal. I caught hints of beauty here and there, designs etched into the surface, but it was hard to tell with how dark and scuffed the armor now was.

Other than the heavy breathing, he didn't appear to be handicapped in any noticeable way. He still had some fight left in him, the crazy bastard.

"Did you just climb my goddamn mountain?" I asked incredulously. "In *armor?*"

The Knight glanced back over the edge of the cliff, and then stepped a safe distance away before turning back to me. "Nate Temple," he growled from within his helmet, sounding like Darth Vader. "Now I've got you." And then he drew a sword from his back that was longer than my freaking leg.

I couldn't help it. I burst out laughing. I even had to lower my hands to my knees to support my weight as I doubled over. Because all I could think about was the Black Knight fighting King Arthur in that scene from *Monty Python and the Holy Grail.* The knight with infinite spunk who kept on fighting no matter how many limbs King Arthur chopped off his body.

The Knight growled at me, lifting his sword into a ready stance, and a faint thought drifted up through my fog of laughter. He wasn't a Knight.

He was a *Knightmare.*

A Knight was what he had once been under the service of King Arthur. But Mordred had used some form of blood magic to basically brainwash the Knights—as seen by the bloody symbol painted on my foe's breastplate—turning them all into ferocious, powerful hounds who could do nothing but obey their new master. Whether they wanted to or not. I'd helplessly watched Mordred's spell settle over them—watched as the magic corrupted their souls.

Long story short, the once-noble Knights were no longer chivalrous, good, or merciful.

Which pretty much burned up the last of my laughter. I took a deep breath, straightened my body, and then I smiled at him. "I've been waiting for you all day, sweetheart. Come give daddy an iron kiss."

The Knightmare snarled, pounding towards me much faster than his armor should have permitted. Having faced one of these assholes before, I had anticipated his enhanced abilities. Even with all my newfound Fae powers, I wasn't entirely sure how this fight was going to play out.

Knight takes King, or King takes Knight?

At least Grimm had gotten Alice to safety.

And I was *very* glad I'd put my pants back on.

Remembering how magic had reflected right off the first Knightmare I had fought, I spread my arms—and my magic—wide.

My power picked up every foreign object within fifty feet. Stones, logs, blocks of ice, and small trees jumped up from the ground all around us. I loudly clapped my hands together, and every one of those objects flew towards the Knightmare like metal filings to a magnet.

He cursed, managing to swing his sword and bat down a few of the closer, larger projectiles as he tried to bob and weave away from the rest.

So I flung my hand down at the ground, turning the area of melted snow into a sheet of dirty ice beneath him. He slipped and skated, suddenly off balance, right as the majority of the objects hammered into him in a satisfying chorus of thuds and dings, leaving him kneeling on the ice, panting raggedly.

I clutched my staff as I watched him, wondering if I'd achieved anything beyond pissing him off.

He slowly lifted his head to stare at me, and I almost took an instinctive step back. He definitely wasn't down for the count.

I thumped my staff into the ground, and it suddenly blazed with multi-colored light. I gathered that power, condensed it into a tight beam, and sent it screaming at the Knightmare's helmet.

The bar of light was so bright and hot that it tore and scorched the earth, leaving a trail of broken earth in its wake. It struck the Knightmare full on, and it was so wide that it split into two beams that continued on behind him.

I released the power, panting slightly as a dark purple after-image replaced where the bar of light had been—kind of like what happened if you looked too closely at the sun for more than a few seconds and would see a dark orb in your vision for a few moments.

That blast had been hot enough to melt rock into liquid, and it definitely wasn't any form of natural element, so I was hoping it had at least dazed him.

When the after-image faded from my eyes, I saw the Knightmare still kneeling, his helmet smoking and scorched from my blast.

The crazy motherfucker was laughing.

I cursed under my breath. Other than throwing more objects at him, I wasn't entirely sure how to put him down for good. I could maintain my distance and keep throwing different flavors of direct power at him in hopes one would actually have an impact, but that would weaken me while he remained relatively unharmed. I needed a game changer. Something big and powerful that wouldn't bounce off that cursed armor.

The Knightmare slowly lifted his massive sword—in one hand, no less— and pointed it at me. "My turn—"

A white spear struck his sword with a loud *clang*, knocking it clear from his hand. We both spun to see a hairy, filthy, beast of a warrior standing less than a dozen paces away from the Knightmare. My knees buckled as I recognized my savior.

Talon—looking like he's survived a couple thousand miles of hard roads. "Yield." And that was all he said, not even looking at me.

The Knightmare slowly climbed to his feet, squaring his shoulders as if preparing to wrestle. "You climb faster than I gave you credit for, cat."

He took one step before Talon's white spear—his Eyeless—suddenly reappeared in his paw. He thumped it into the ground hard enough for me to feel it in my toes. A warning.

"Yield," he repeated.

The Knightmare took another step, crouching lower as if preparing to lunge in order to close the entire distance in one swift leap.

Talon lifted the gleaming white spear high, and then slammed it into the ground harder than before, causing a concussive blast of snow and grit to ripple outward with an alarming *cracking* sound. "YIELD!" he hissed.

The Knightmare had leapt impossibly high into the air, though, and was already descending upon Talon with both fists raised high overhead as if attempting to squash Talon like a bug.

I flung out a blast of pure starlight, hoping to at least bat him off course, but the searing beam of power simply ricocheted off him and out into the open sky beyond the cliff, scorching a hole through a cloud before winking out.

The Knightmare was only inches away when Talon suddenly disappeared. The Knightmare struck the ground with both fists in a resounding *crunching* sound. I heard a whistling sound from over my shoulder, but the object whipped past me—mere inches from grazing my flesh—before I had time to even flinch. A gleaming sword, crackling with arcs of pale yellow lightning down its length, abruptly tore through the Knightmare's back and out his chest, stopping only when the sword had stabbed deeply enough for the cross-guard to catch on his back.

This, of course, pinned the Knightmare to the ground like a frog on a dissection table, and the fingers of yellow lightning crackled and burned over the Knightmare's armor as his shoulders slumped and he let out a final death rattle.

I spun, following the trajectory of the thrown sword, to find Alex standing on top of a thirty foot boulder that was perched on the edge of the cliff. He stood tall with his hands hanging loosely at his sides. His once-white cloak was now dirty and whipping in the wind like he was some kind of angel of death.

Alex Pendragon, the new King Arthur. I remembered when I had found him here as a stolen child in Fae, fleeing from the Wild Hunt.

From that young boy to a grown man who just single-handedly smoked a Knightmare. They grow up so fast.

And that's when I noticed that the boulder he was standing on was actually halfway from sliding over the edge, and showing no signs of stopping.

Because some idiot wizard had coated most of the ground in ice.

I opened my mouth to shout out a warning when he promptly leapt off the boulder like a freaking ninja, did a double flip, and landed in a one-legged kneel. His fist was buried in the snow to brace his landing, but his other arm was extended out to the side with his hand open like he was a crosswalk guard warning the little helpless wizard—me—to *stop and look both ways*.

The sword ripped back out of the Knightmare's body to zip across the clearing—again, flying entirely too close to my shoulder for comfort—and into his open palm. I stared, stunned, as I heard the Knightmare's body crumple to the ground behind me.

I marveled at the legendary sword in Alex's hand.

Excalibur.

I'd carried it around for a while, back when it had been disguised as the War Hammer my parents had bequeathed to me. The ultimate joke had been to learn that the hammer had actually been the Sword in the Stone, not just an overly ornate hilt attached to a crude stone mallet.

As far as I knew, it was still missing one piece before it would be complete. It had been broken down in order to hide it from any would-be evil villains until Alex could get his hands on it and rebuild the epic sword.

Talon was suddenly standing beside me, tugging me to my feet. Before I could say a word, the filthy feline had wrapped me up in a tight hug, slapping my back with his furry paws as if he hadn't seen me in a few decades. I didn't even care about his filthy beard as I hugged him back tightly.

I was still trying to process how they had managed to climb all the way up my mountain, and how easily they had dispatched the Knightmare. Maybe I needed to get myself a sword. Alex sheathed Excalibur as he stared in the direction of the Knightmare, his face hard.

Talon finally stepped back, smiling at me as he shook me by the shoulders. "It is so good to see you, Wylde," he said.

I smiled back, feeling the same emotion deep down. We'd grown up together, after all. And now I could remember all the trouble we had gotten into in our youth. "Nate or Wylde. Pick your poison."

Talon grinned. "You found your way back, too?" he asked excitedly.

I nodded. "About five minutes before this asshole showed up," I muttered, glancing back at the Knightmare.

Talon nodded, his smile faltering. "He was sent to assassinate you."

I grunted, wondering if I should feel honored at Mordred's dedication. "You climbed a mountain. To save me from a Knightmare."

Talon hesitated before nodding. "Yes and no," he admitted, shifting from foot-to-foot uneasily. Alex was watching the two of us, but his eyes were distant, lost in thought. Talon turned to look at Alex, as if hoping he would explain.

Alex snapped out of his daze to lock eyes with me. "We followed his trail. Going around the mountain to find a safe path up here wouldn't have ended well," Alex said. "For you."

I studied him pensively, noticing that most of the soft edges—what few he had to begin with—had been sanded away. The man before me was every inch the king, even though he currently looked like a scruffy refugee or survivor of the Apocalypse.

There was just something royal about him.

"I see," I finally said, gauging his cool reaction. "Well, thank you." Alex dipped his head a fraction of an inch, taking no pride in his job. It was what it was. Nothing to get excited about.

Grimm suddenly landed directly behind Alex with a heavy thud. He snorted loudly, close enough to shift Alex's shaggy hair. "You should take a step back, boy," he warned.

Alex hadn't reacted to Grimm's sudden landing directly behind him, but his eyes narrowed at the verbal threat.

He slowly turned around to face the unicorn. "Kings don't step back, pony-bitch."

Grimm's nostrils flared and he pawed at the snow with one fiery hoof. Alex suddenly bobbed low and lunged forward to wrap his arms around Grimm's neck in an aggressive blur. My eyes widened in alarm, fearing he was about to suplex my unicorn.

CHAPTER 4

*G*rimm snorted out a series of cringeworthy laughs, and I froze in confusion. Talon rolled his eyes.

"Good to see you, punk," Alex said, sounding happy.

"You too, kid. Nabbed another one, eh?" Grimm growled, jerking his chin at the dead Knightmare.

Alex patted his neck, and finally took a step back. "No other choice," he said with a weary sigh.

I glanced over by the igloo to see Alice standing in the doorway, watching us anxiously. Grimm must have told her to stay back until he knew it was safe. I discreetly held out my palm, telling her to remain by the igloo. She scowled, folding her arms.

"So, what have you two been up to?" I asked, turning back to Alex, not feeling even remotely jealous of his bromance with my unicorn. Really. I didn't.

"Tracking the Knightmares and keeping an eye on Camelot," Alex said, sounding tired. "We think Mordred is finally ready to make his move. My best guess is that he'll target the Fae Queens, first, but I don't know which one," he admitted.

"That's why he sent this one after you," Talon added. "To keep you busy or remove you from the equation."

Alex pursed his lips, and pulled out a small dreamcatcher from his belt.

It was woven from wild vines, and it looked familiar. It took me a moment to recall that I had made it for them.

A way to track the remaining Knightmares in Fae.

Twelve stones decorated the perimeter of the ring at equidistant points, but they were all cold and lifeless. Three of the stones were black with a red dot in the center, symbolizing the Knightmares who had died in the line of duty. One right beside us, another back at Stonehenge, and…wait a minute.

I frowned. "You killed another Knightmare?" I asked, pointing at the third black stone. When Alex didn't answer, I looked up at him.

"No. I did not."

"Then who did?"

He shrugged, staring at me intensely. "No idea."

I thought about what that might mean for a few seconds before sighing. "Well, I guess it's one less to worry about," I said, turning back to the dreamcatcher.

The remaining white stones symbolized the nine surviving Knightmares. Except they featured a blue dot in the center, which instantly made the hair on the back of my neck stand straight up.

Because I hadn't used any stones with blue dots.

And they should have been glowing, along with a section of the web so that Alex could use the dreamcatcher like a compass to track them down. I turned to Alex and found him nodding in agreement.

"The Knightmares have been disappearing on and off for months, their stones growing dark like a snuffed out candle. That mystery death was the first," he said, reaching out to tap the third black stone that I'd asked him about, "and he never returned. But the others would always pop back onto the dreamcatcher after a day or so. That is, until a few days ago when nine of them disappeared at once." He pointed at the dead Knightmare. "He was number ten, the only one left on our dreamcatcher, so we chased him down. Didn't expect him to climb your mountain."

I felt a sudden chill down my spine. "The others left Fae," I breathed.

Alex nodded. "I'm thinking they went to St. Louis. But this won't work outside of Fae," he said, indicating the dreamcatcher.

I cursed. "You need a new dreamcatcher to find them."

Alex shrugged. "That's your shtick, magic man."

"Quickly," I snapped, suddenly feeling restless as I imagined nine Knightmares loose in my city. "Give me something you have from our realm," I demanded impatiently, deciding to cover all my bases in case the Knightmares weren't limiting their vacation plans to St. Louis.

Talon pulled out a flask of Macallan from his jacket, and Alex pulled out an old t-shirt. I reached into my satchel, searching for anything helpful. I found a black dragon scale I had taken from my old friend Raego a very long time ago.

I trotted over to the pile of debris I had used to pelt the Knightmare, and quickly found a wiry root from a stubborn tree. I tore it off and tied it into a circle, holding my hand over it and murmuring a word. I felt the knot tighten as the root obeyed my command.

Fae magic was cool like that. It was much like the exchange of favors among Fae people, you just needed to know how to bribe the elements. I asked the root to do me a solid, promising that it would help me kill the Knightmares who were invading its homeland.

I opened my hand to find a perfect circle, and I quickly tore Alex's shirt into strips, using one to bind the dragon scale to the root. Then I wove a hasty, crude web from one end to the other, eyeing my shoddy work. It wasn't as pretty as the first one, but it would work. I opened Talon's flask and poured the entire thing over the dreamcatcher, soaking the cloth as I murmured another word under my breath.

The new dreamcatcher throbbed in my hands and I glanced down to see the dragon scale smoking, indicating that there were definitely Knightmares back home. Then I frowned, counting the glowing orbs decorating the strips of Alex's t-shirt.

I grunted. "It's only showing seven of them," I growled, racking my brain for some answer that made sense of the discrepancy. I glanced back at Alex's dreamcatcher, hoping to see that two glowing orbs had reappeared to reach our total of nine surviving Knightmares, but it remained dark.

"What does that mean?" Alex demanded.

I scowled. "It means that two of the Knightmares are not in Fae, and not on Earth," I muttered.

Alex growled furiously.

I took a calming breath. "Easy, Alex. We know where seven of them are. That's better than what we knew a minute ago," I said sternly.

He closed his eyes, taking a deep breath. "You're right."

I glanced over at Alice, thinking furiously. I needed to get back home and make sure everyone was okay. Let them know that I was okay. But I didn't want to tow Alice around with me. I had a feeling things were going to get very dangerous, very fast. And I knew the Knightmares had no qualms about abducting a child.

I handed Alex the new dreamcatcher. "Head back to St. Louis. See if you can find out what our friends are up to. I'll meet you there in two hours."

Alex took it, his eyes drifting towards the dead Knightmare as he hung both of the dreamcatchers on his belt.

"Why two hours?" Talon asked, frowning. "Come with us now."

I subtly flicked my eyes in Alice's direction. "I have a few things to take care of, first," I said, low enough so that she couldn't possibly overhear me.

Talon nodded, but his tail began twitching, letting me know he wasn't pleased about my delay.

I turned to see Alex still staring at the Knightmare.

"So...you guys should probably get going," I said, hoping to hurry them along.

"He deserves a proper burial, at least," Alex said, sounding disgusted.

I scoffed. "Um. The dude just tried to kill me. I'm perfectly fine with letting Grimm eat him."

Grimm licked his lips noisily. "Yum."

Alex shook his head adamantly, clenching his jaws. "He was a Knight of the Round Table! He. Will. Be. Buried!" Alex rasped, clenching his fists at his sides. "Even if I have to do it myself."

I stared at him, seriously considering the possibility that I might be the only sane person currently standing on my mountain. And if the barefoot wizard standing in ankle-deep snow was the compass of morality and rational thought, we were all in very big trouble.

"You sure didn't seem too concerned about that first Knight. Remember?" I snapped sarcastically. "The one who killed Gunnar and Talon," I added, pointing at the feline warrior. Talon curled his lip at the memory. I turned back to Alex. "You impaled him on Grimm's horn, and then you used him to play Wheel of Fortune. *That* guy."

"Good times," Grimm sighed nostalgically.

I nodded my agreement. "Then you cut off his hands and mocked him with them. Am I ringing any bells yet?" I demanded, annoyed by his sudden streak of piety. This bastard Knight had just tried to *kill* me! "*And* he was trespassing on my mountain!" I added loudly, throwing up an indignant finger.

Alex slowly turned his head to look at me, and I had to force myself not to take a step back under the intensity of his glare. "I did not know the full story back then," he finally said in a gravelly voice. "I was acting out of vengeance. I was also unaware that I was a vessel for King Arthur's spirit. I am no longer the same man." He glanced down at the Knightmare, and I watched his anger grow deeper—harder, regretful. Then he knelt down beside the body, tugged off the man's helmet, and carefully set it down on the Knight's chest. He pointed at the man's face. "Does this look like a monster to you?" he demanded.

I didn't think that was a very relevant question, because psychopaths could look just as normal as anyone else, so I assumed it was rhetorical as I studied the Knight. He looked...well, he actually looked relieved, as strange as that may sound. And entirely normal. Bearded and hardened, but not a man I would declare a monster.

"You two just spent days hunting him down, and then you helped me kill him!" I argued. "Is everyone forgetting that?"

Talon looked over at me this time. His bearded, shaggy face was hard and frustrated. That face had seen long bloody days lately, and he definitely hadn't had time to bathe. His long fur was caked with mud and blood—the moisturizer of a true warrior. "We came to kill the monster he had become —against his will—not the man he should have been," Talon said. "That is what King Alex mourns. The death of potential. One less Knight he could have saved."

"It's not his fault he was turned against everything he stood for," Alex added, sounding one step away from murder. "He built his entire *life* around chivalry, honor, and integrity. Mordred stole that from him."

I frowned thoughtfully, seeing the situation in a new light. On one hand, they had a point.

On the other hand...

They had *zero* chance of saving any of these men, regardless of who they had once been. Mordred's spell prevented it.

CHAPTER 5

I did feel better to realize that their anger was directed at Mordred, not me. Every now and then, a meteorite of truth hit you in the face, letting you know that you weren't actually the sun in your particular solar system. You were just a forgotten moon behind a forgotten planet.

That was both a crappy feeling, and a crappy metaphor.

It sucked to suddenly learn that it was not all about you.

Alex hung his head, looking sick to his stomach. "This was Sir Bedivere, Nate. Fucking Bedivere! When Arthur was dying, Sir Bedivere was the Knight he trusted to return Excalibur to the Lady of the Lake! And now he has died with Excalibur in his *spine!*"

My eyes widened in disbelief. "Are you sure?" I asked softly.

Alex whipped out a folded parchment from his pocket and flung it at my chest. I caught it with a frown, and then glanced down as I unfolded it. Twelve symbols filled the page, and they were familiar. I had first seen them on the Round Table—one for each of the original Knights.

Except these were inverted, and beneath each symbol was a familiar name. One of the symbols and names already had a crude, bloody *X* marked through it. I took a wild guess and assumed that was the other Knight I had been taunting Alex about earlier—Sir Handsnomore had actually been Sir Geraint. I couldn't recall any specific stories about him, though.

I found Bedivere's name, glanced at the symbol, and then bent down to shift the man's helmet so I could compare the paper to the symbol on his breastplate.

I stood and slowly lowered my hand, letting the parchment hang by my hip. Holy crap. Alex was right. This guy wasn't as famous as some, but I had heard of him. The story I knew about him was that he had been the one to put the dying Arthur into a boat to take him to Avalon.

I glanced over to see that Talon had his lips curled back as he stared down at the dead Knight, and everything about him made me think of an avenging angel. He was the epitome of righteous fury—dead set on making Mordred pay for leading them to this moment.

I hadn't expected to see Talon so invested in Alex's cause, but it was obvious that the cause had rubbed off on him. Alex was staring down at the dead Knight as well, and he was panting shallowly.

An apology felt hollow at this point, but I tried anyway. "I'm sorry, Alex. I hadn't thought about it like that. I just painted them with the same hatred I feel for Mordred, because I don't think any of them can be saved. I don't know how to remove the curse Mordred put on them."

He nodded stiffly. "I judged them prematurely too. At first," he admitted. Talon was nodding as well. "The only solution I can think of is to put Mordred in a shallow grave."

I nodded my agreement. "Okay. I can get behind that one."

"Han Solo?" Grimm suggested into the uncomfortable silence.

I frowned, not following his meaning for a few moments. And then it clicked. I turned to Alex, nodding excitely. "I can put him on ice. When this is all over, we can give him the funeral he deserves." I didn't add that we might have nine other Knights to send off by then—whether Alex liked it or not. And if the third dead Knight wasn't in Fae or back home, I doubted we would ever find him. We would just have to use process of elimination to learn which Knight it was, since Alex's paper only had the one red X on it.

Alex thought about my suggestion, and finally nodded. "I suppose that is better than a shallow grave on a lonely mountain occupied by a creepy, socially bankrupt wizard," he said. I narrowed my eyes at him and caught the hint of a distant grin through the stubble coating his chin.

Rather than snarking back, I dipped my head. He'd earned a little return fire for my callousness. "As my king commands," I said subserviently, bowing at the waist.

He flashed me a genuine smile. "Thank you, Nate."

I glanced down at Sir Bedivere again. "We should take his armor. It's incredibly powerful, and we will need it to stand a chance against the others." Silence answered me, and I looked over to see Alex pursing his lips. "Technically, it belongs to the Round Table," I added. "Maybe we can find a way to replicate it. You can put it in the Sanctorum for now," I suggested, since that was where the Round Table was, and it might appease Alex's conscience.

Alex nodded. "You're right. We can't risk it falling into the wrong hands, so the Sanctorum is as good a place as any. But I don't have to like it."

I nodded.

Talon waited a few moments as if to make sure Alex wasn't going to change his mind. Then he silently went to work on removing Bedivere's armor—as respectfully as possible.

I watched in silence as Alex pricked his finger and crossed out Bedivere's symbol on his piece of paper. He studied the mark for a moment, as if murmuring a silent prayer. Then he let out a tired sigh, and folded the paper back up.

He glanced down with a frown, and I followed his gaze to see the two letters from the Fae Queens. Then he turned to look at me. "You already spoke to the emissaries I told them to send?" he asked, sounding surprised.

I winced instinctively, and took too long to come up with an answer.

"He threw them off the mountain," Grimm said, ever the helper. "Summer flew further."

"Not helping," I growled, shooting him a dark look.

Alex cursed. "Damn it, Nate. We need their cooperation!"

I grunted. "I've been doing just fine without their help," I argued. Then I frowned, only just now catching what he'd initially said. "What do you mean, the emissaries you *told them to send*? You're working with them already?"

Alex shook his head. "I met with them. I demanded their surrender, as well as restitution for stealing me as a young boy."

My eyes almost popped out of my head.

Alex smirked, noticing the look on my face. "I learned how to negotiate from a ruthless professional. Instead of my initial terms, they agreed to work with me against our common enemy—which was what I really wanted all along. A truce, Nate. And I made sure to include *you* in that truce." He took a deep breath, as if trying to calm himself down. "And you're telling me you threw their emissaries off the mountain?" he hissed.

"I know, Alex!" I snapped, knowing I had no excuse. "I'm sorry! But I haven't exactly been in the right fucking headspace lately, in case you hadn't noticed. Why else do you think I'm living on a goddamned mountain in the middle of Fae—as far away as I can get from anyone I care about!" I roared, panting, and clenching my fists.

Grimm was suddenly standing between us, forcing us both to take a step back. "Let's cool down a minute, boys. It's been a shitty day for everyone."

I nodded, forcing my breathing back under control. "Thank you, Grimm."

He snorted. "It's nothing." Once confident I was back in control of my temper, he got out of the way, no longer walling me off from Alex.

I looked Alex in the eyes. "I'm sorry, man. I'll figure something out, even if I have to visit the Queens myself and apologize. I'm still trying to get my head back in the game."

Alex lowered his eyes with a sigh. "I know. I'm sorry, too. Let's just focus on what matters. We're all on edge these days."

Talon had tied up the armor and was dragging it behind him like a dead body. He paused, assessing the both of us. "You two finished acting like children? Because we have work to do in St. Louis."

We both nodded.

Alex walked up to Talon and placed a hand on his shoulder. Much like I could use my magic to Shadow Walk, Talon could simply step out of Fae, and he was able to carry people with him if they were touching him.

"I'll take care of Bedivere for you, and then I'll see you guys in two hours at the Sanctorum," I promised, turning away. I needed to figure out what to do with Alice, how to keep her safe while I went to work. Maybe I could take her to the Armory until everything calmed down.

Alex spoke from over my shoulder. "Be careful in St. Louis, Nate. Last time I was there, I heard there was an assassin looking for you."

I spun, surprised. "Who the hell would hire an assassin—"

A Gateway erupted behind me, and I almost got whiplash spinning back around to face the potential threat.

Instead of snapping my own neck, I slipped on the ice, bounced on my ass with a flash of pain, and then began to tumble towards the edge of the cliff. Alarmingly fast.

I heard several voices shouting at me as I tossed my staff in an effort to use my hands to claw and scratch for some lifeline, but the ice was slick and I found no salvation to slow me down.

Before I knew it, I fell off my goddamned mountain and into the goddamned sky.

Just like the emissaries from Summer and Winter.

"Fucking Karma!" I screamed.

CHAPTER 6

*T*he wind whistled in my ears as I fell through a blanket of clouds, flipping and spinning wildly as I tried to gain some measure of control so I could think of a solution.

I sensed a dark shape in the clouds beside me, but I couldn't make out anything specific, and it didn't try to eat me alive, so that was good. Thankfully, I broke through the clouds a few seconds later, giving me a clear view of the entire Land of the Fae drawing closer to me faster than I would have preferred.

Grimm abruptly swept up alongside me, and I realized that his silhouette had been the dark shape I'd sensed in the clouds. But he didn't attempt to catch me, contenting himself with a leisurely freefall with his Horseman pal.

"Help me, Grimm!" I snapped, trying to reach out and grab him.

He shifted slightly out of my reach, his black shadow wings somehow still able to snap in the wind. "Who's the best fucking unicorn in the world?" he asked calmly, but loud enough for me to hear past the whistling wind.

"You are! Now catch me, you psychopath!"

"That wasn't very convincing," he said unhappily. "Try again. This is a long fall, so you have time for a few attempts."

I cursed him at the top of my lungs, reaching out to latch onto any part of him. I missed, and began flipping and spinning and cartwheeling for my efforts.

"You will tell everyone how majestic I am," Grimm said, "and that I nobly saved your life at the very last moment, risking personal harm to do so."

"Oh, you're risking harm alright," I snarled.

He flared out his wings, suddenly soaring up above me as I continued to plummet downward like a rock.

I cursed again, turning upside down and spreading my arms and legs out like a starfish so I could locate him. I saw him a dozen paces above me, calmly descending just out of my reach.

"I'm sorry, Grimm!" I shouted, hoping he could hear me.

"Who's fucking majestic?" he shouted.

"You're fucking majestic!" I crowed.

He thought about it for a second, and then shook his mane. "Give me a G!" he yelled, sounding like he was trying out for the head position on the *My Little Pony* Cheer Squad.

I gritted my teeth to prevent myself from cursing him out again. I risked a quick glance over my shoulder in order to count how many seconds I had to learn humility—

"Holy crap!" I gasped. I was falling *way* faster than I had thought. I angled my body so that I might glide parallel to the slope rather than striking into the side of the mountain. It might buy me a few more seconds.

Hopefully.

I spun back to Grimm, panicking as I did my best to imitate a flying squirrel. "G!" I screamed.

"Give me an *R*!"

"R!" I shouted at the top of my lungs.

"Give me an *I*!"

"I!" I shrieked.

He was cackling, now. "Give me an *M*!"

"M!"

"Give me another *M*!" he cheered, kicking his hooves happily, making it look like he was practicing a choreographed dance.

"M!"

"What's that spell?" he yelled, and he barely managed to say it through his raucous laughter.

"GRIMM!" I cheered desperately.

"Damn right it does!" he snapped.

And then he folded his wings close to his body and plummeted directly for my face. My ears had popped at one point, likely due to the rapid change in elevation. At the last second, Grimm dipped beneath, preventing me from grabbing onto him. I spun around so that I didn't break my back over his spine, and that's when I saw how much closer to the ground we now were. Trees whipped past us, maybe thirty feet below, but the boulder field was still a little bit further down the slope.

It was at this moment, while calculating distance, trajectory, velocity, probability, and a newfound faith in God, that I was introduced to an upper echelon of pain that mankind had never explored before.

My groin slammed into the engine block of the original single-horse-power motor—my unicorn—at Mach 7 speed.

I instantly lost my breath—and the ability to make any sound louder than a newborn chipmunk's cry. Grimm also gasped in pain at the impact, rapidly descending a few feet before he managed to spread his wings wide and fight against physics. I was sprawled over his back, holding on for dear life, and I was only able to suck in pitiful amounts of air as I tried to recover the ability to breathe.

The tops of the trees were so close that I feared they might actually clip my feet as we screamed over them. But we were so close to the edge of the treeline, and I spotted cushy-looking snow drifts interspersed with the titanic slabs of rock and ice that had fallen from the mountain at some point in the last thousand years.

As long as we didn't hit one of the hard targets, we would only break all of our limbs upon landing. I heard the tendons of Grimm's shadow wings straining and creaking as he tried to keep the tips of the trees from impaling us.

With a snarl of effort, Grimm brought us past the last tree—my foot actually grazing one of the branches on our way by. If I hadn't already been struggling to breathe, I would have let out a sigh of relief.

Naturally, Grimm chose that moment to buck me off his back without any warning whatsoever. As I flew over boulders that were as big as most houses, I cursed myself for ever agreeing to his stupid cheer.

Fortunately, I hit a snowdrift of fresh powder rather than solid ice.

Unfortunately, I blew entirely through it and into another.

This one managed to stop me, and I immediately began clawing my way out from my tomb of snow, since the entrance I had made upon arrival had instantly caved in behind me, and I had already been struggling to breathe.

It should say something about my level of panic that I didn't think of using my magic to blast my way out until my head broke through the surface.

Sunlight kissed my cheeks, and I just stayed there with my eyes closed for a few moments, retraining my body on the use of oxygen. When I opened them again, my first sight was Grimm standing a dozen paces away, shaking snow from his mane and rump. He saw my head poking out of the snowdrift, and scraped a hoof back across the ground, lowering his head towards me without breaking eye contact.

"Majestic," he whispered, drawing out the word so that it stretched out over three seconds. And I realized that his strange stance was a bastardized attempt at a bow.

"You're insane," I whispered, clawing myself the rest of the way out of my snowdrift.

He dipped his head. "You say the sweetest things." I climbed back to my feet, shaking off the snow covering my body. Grimm waited until I was finished before he began prancing about in a bizarre dance, lifting his hooves almost delicately as he spun in a circle like a show pony practicing his steps. Then he stopped, jerking his head at something closer to the base of the mountain. I noticed a red splash on one of the boulders and winced. "That's where you threw the Summer Fae dude. You totally beat his record."

I stared at Grimm, shaking my head. *"Who hurt you?"* I asked, genuinely concerned for his sanity.

He turned to glare at me. "I thought you would be happier," he grumbled. I folded my arms, shaking my head. "That was the most excitement I've had in quite some time," he grumbled. And this time, he didn't sound like he was teasing. I sighed—still not pleased with him, but recognizing that my friends often had to go to drastic measures to prove a point to me.

Although this was definitely a new record for maximum effort.

I let out a breath, lifting my head to look up at the mountain. It...was *really* fucking tall. Taller than any other mountain I'd ever seen.

"Welcome back, Nate," Grimm said, joining me to look up at the mountain.

I frowned over at him. "What do you mean?"

He continued staring upwards. "Call it the Grimm Stamp of Approval—a second opinion that you really are Nate and not Wylde."

"What the hell are you talking about?" I asked, confused.

"Wylde wouldn't have pissed his pants from a little tumble like that," he whispered.

I glanced down, suddenly mortified. Seeing no spots of shame, I slowly turned to level a glare upon my unicorn. "Asshole."

"Made you look!" he hooted, bursting out with laughter.

Despite the adrenaline still coursing through my veins, making me feel twitchy, I found myself smiling along with him after a few moments, shaking my head.

"Wylde would have used some weird Fae magic to stop gravity or something," Grimm said. "So, welcome back, Nate. You incompetent bastard. I missed ya."

I sighed, setting my hand on his back and climbing up. "Thanks, I guess." Once situated, I grabbed onto his mane, glancing up at the mountain. Now that I wasn't worried about immediate death, I remembered why I had fallen in the first place. "Any idea who made the Gateway?" I asked, suddenly concerned for Alice.

"I saw one angry eyeball and decided that voluntarily plummeting to my own death was more preferable than his company. I'm guessing it was your old butler."

I narrowed my eyes. Dean—or as I now knew him, Odin. "Let's go kick his ass," I growled.

"Cool."

And Grimm took to the skies.

CHAPTER 7

G rimm landed in the center of the clearing between two adult figures and Alice. I hopped off his back and called my rainbow staff to my hand. It struck my palm with a meaty *thwack*, but I barely felt it.

Alex and Talon were nowhere to be seen, but Sir Bedivere's body—wearing only white pants and a flowing white shirt—remained where I had left him. The pair must have stuck to our plan, taking the armor along with them. That was good, at least.

Grimm had gone to stand beside Alice—who was clutching my satchel as if willing to die over it. I bit back a grin, proud of her defiance. And I slowly turned to face my uninvited guests, my staff suddenly crackling with power and blinding light. The elements in the air practically purred, begging me to use them in combat.

I think I was smiling as I stared them down. But it definitely wasn't friendly. I had strong feelings when it came to Odin and his betrayal of my trust, and I hadn't exactly defined what those feelings were yet.

He'd helped me, and he'd lied to me. Where that placed him on my trust scale was yet to be determined.

And I definitely hadn't expected his guest, who only served to increase my suspicion.

Odin wore thick gray robes and even had a wide-brimmed, pointed hat on his head, but it was old and bent at the middle so that it flopped backwards. He had a long white beard, and one piercing blue eye. His other socket was covered by a leather eyepatch with metal runes stamped across the surface.

And he was currently holding his own insanely dangerous spear—Gungnir—so I wisely decided not to let go of mine.

Grimm and Alice stepped up to flank me on either side, and they had their *take no shit* faces on, mirroring me.

"You shall not pass!" I growled, thumping my staff into the snow.

Alice let out a surprised giggle, but Odin and the woman just frowned at me, not catching the Gandalf reference. Which was disappointing, because he was wearing the perfect cosplay for it.

In myths, when he appeared in this fashionable ensemble, he was attempting to disguise himself, trying to pass as a wandering traveler. It was actually one of his known aliases—the Wanderer.

But he was failing epically, thanks to his companion. He must have had a family meeting planned, because the person beside him was—

"Freya, meet the bane of my existence, the source of my gray hairs, and… my pride and joy," Odin finally admitted with a faint, begrudging smile, "Nate Temple." Then he glanced at Grimm and Alice thoughtfully. "To clarify, he's the one without shoes. Not the talking horse."

"*Alicorn*, Cyclops. I will also accept Bifröst fixer or Rainbow killer," Grimm growled, scraping a hoof through a muddy puddle, somewhat ruining the threatening impact. "Bitch."

Odin narrowed his lone eye at Grimm, but he didn't rise to the challenge.

The woman *tsked* gently but seemed to be masking an amused grin. There were contradicting stories about Odin's wife—some said he had married Frigg, and others Freya. Some said they were the same woman. Others spoke of an affair. And those were just the top-level theories.

I decided I had more important things to think about—like the Knightmares in St. Louis—than my fraudulent butler's love life.

Freya was stunning, majestic, and royal in every sense of the word. She wore a simple white toga with a bronze brooch over one shoulder to hold it in place. Her golden hair hung freely, trailing over her shoulders and down her back, and although pleasantly curved, she looked to have very little fat on her, maybe weighing in at one-twenty, tops.

And her eyes were sea-foam green. I could sense the raw power crackling within her and, although I couldn't place what kind of power it was, I knew enough to decide that she was likely every bit as dangerous as her husband, the Allfather.

"It's a pleasure," she said, briefly meeting my eyes. She looked... exhausted, now that I looked closer.

"Lady," Grimm warned, sounding amused. "People only say that to Nate one time before things go to hell. Get ready for disappointment. You ain't seen nothing yet."

Odin nodded his agreement, not seeming aware that he had done so. "If you're finished moping about, we have vital things to discuss."

I narrowed my eyes. "I seem to recall a story about you hanging around a tree, moping about, as you call it."

He scoffed. "Oh? If you're wanting to walk a mile in my shoes, would you like me to help stab your eye out, or did you want to do it yourself?" he asked, extending Gungnir.

I wanted to argue, but he had a fair point. So I glared at him instead.

"I've arranged a schedule for you," Odin muttered, withdrawing his spear. And then the two of them simply turned their backs on us, walking towards the Gateway—which was limned with angry green sparks.

I slammed my staff into the ground, allowing more light to illuminate it from within so that it looked like I was holding a kaleidoscope of carnage. "What makes you think I'm going anywhere with you? That *you* have any right to make *me* a schedule?" I demanded in a low, menacing tone. "I'll give you exactly two hours to impress me, Allfather. After that, I have more important things to do," I said, thinking about the Knightmares in St. Louis again.

"Mani-pedi time," Grimm said, chuckling. "Gettin' my hooves done."

Odin glanced over his shoulder—with his one good eye shadowed by the brim of his ridiculous hat—but he didn't stop walking. "More important than helping your best friend, Gunnar? He and Ashley are injured, and their pups might not survive their birth." Then they stepped through the Gateway.

My sphincter tightened and the light winked out of my staff as I dropped it into the mud.

Gunnar and Ashley...

They were having twins. Oh my god. I was going to be a godfather!

Depending on how long I'd spent here, that unqualified promotion could come to fruition in the next five minutes.

Or not ever, if Odin was telling the truth.

Grimm was already scooping my staff up in his teeth and shouldering me towards the Gateway. "Alice has your purse. Go, go, go!"

"*Satchel*, asshole," I snapped instinctively. "What about the letters?" I asked, not seeing them anywhere.

Alice patted my purse—no. *Satchel*. "In here," she reassured me. Then she promptly hung my satchel on Grimm's horn when he wasn't looking. He narrowed his eyes at her, but he must have seen the wisdom in not letting the smallest person in our trio carry the luggage.

I scanned the area for anything else I might need to take or hide, because I was pretty much abandoning the only home I had known for the last... well, however long I'd been living here.

My eyes settled on Sir Bedivere, and I let out a curse. I called up my wizard's magic and buried him under several feet of snow and ice, smothering him like a blanket and concealing him from view. I used my magic to set a boulder on top of the mound so that I could find him later.

Then I grabbed Alice's hand, and tugged her after Odin and Freya. Staring through the Gateway, it sure didn't look like St. Louis. The only other place I could imagine Odin taking my injured friends was Asgard, the home of the Aesir gods—where the Allfather ruled as king.

I felt a momentary thrill at the thought of seeing Asgard for the first time, but it was short-lived as I envisioned my friends in danger.

Another part of me wondered how much time I had before I would be expected to babysit two infant werewolves. It wasn't like I could go fight a war in Camelot with two babies strapped to my back.

That would be inconvenient.

No.

Irresponsible.

CHAPTER 8

J jogged through the Gateway with Alice in tow, ready to see wonders beyond wonders—gleaming palaces in a city of clouds, einherjar taunting each other over a table of mead-pong while Valkyries soared in the skies above. Maybe even a few buxom, lingerie-clad, female dwarves wrestling in an inflatable pool of slippery Jörmungandr drool. The Bifröst twinkling above the pristine city like a brand-new metro rail.

Except…we must have arrived in Asgard a couple of millennia too early because instead of a Norse frat party or an exponentially-advanced, utopian civilization, we stepped into a wildly overgrown, hilly forest that hadn't seen an axe for thousands of years. The lowest sections of leafy canopy were at least fifty feet above our heads.

And it was raining so hard that I immediately thought of the Old Testament cruise line, the *HTV We Noah Guy.*

Torrents of frigid rain struck the leaf cover in a deafening roar, so heavy that dozens of thick streams—like miniature waterfalls—cascaded through it to splash onto the spongy, mossy ground all around us.

Our breath visibly fogged before our faces in dense, opaque clouds, making us look like we were a gang of little steam engines. Alice giggled, clapping delightedly as she began auditioning for the Cheech and Chong reboot, *Puff Puff Don't Pass,* waving her arms through the thick vapor.

Then she began stomping in the puddles, soaking my clothes before I managed to jump clear. Like a startled turtle, my testicles instantly reacted, racing to see which one could retreat back up into my body the fastest.

I hopped up and down, ignoring my sudden shivering as I silently begged gravity to do me a solid and evict the selfish bastards, but it was no use. Like the Jefferson's, they'd moved on up in the world—but to the North side, to that deluxe penthouse in my insides.

Why was this cold bothering me when I'd treated the peak of my mountain like a goddamned nude beach in France?

It took me a few moments to recall one of Alice's first lessons—a way to ignore extreme temperatures, because my Fae magic hadn't helped me by default, only when I was consciously wielding it. Since I wasn't *biologically* Fae, my body wasn't naturally immune like hers, but when my power was in full control, it had begun kicking on all by itself, allowing me to tan in the snow, if I so chose.

But the rapid change in my circumstances—from living full-time in the primitive, Fae mindset to suddenly remembering that I was actually Nate Temple—had jolted me out of my recent habits. It was going to take some time for me to master a healthy balance between the powers and instincts of Wylde and Nate. Not that we were two different people, but we saw and approached the world in two vastly different ways.

Like having two—sometimes opposing—sets of reflexes. Much like...I grunted...PTSD in veterans—going from a war zone where every loud *bang* could herald death to suddenly hearing a loud *bang* back home when someone's car backfired.

So I took a deep breath, consciously willing myself to relax and lower my pulse, giving me back a modicum of self-control.

My pride and joy decided they rather preferred their new accommodations, but at least I wasn't shivering anymore.

I glanced up at the canopy, shaking my head in awe. Up there in the unobstructed rain, visibility had to be less than ten feet, and I idly wondered how this frosty weather wasn't actually hail or snow rather than rain.

It reminded me of the freakish rainstorms I had seen in Miami when I had visited several years ago—except remarkably colder. The weather could turn at the drop of a hat—from clear blue skies to ominous black clouds, instantly raining so hard that drivers on the highway would actually stop, put their cars in park, and then turn on their hazard lights.

Grimm shook his mane behind me, cursing under his breath. I turned to give him a glare for soaking me, but he was too busy staring up at the canopy to notice. He was still holding my rainbow staff in his teeth, and my satchel on his horn. I was simply grateful that his wet dog impersonation hadn't launched the satchel into a puddle or clocked Alice in the head with my staff. Odin's Gateway had also snapped shut, trapping us…wherever *here* was.

"Athgard hath gone to hell," Grimm muttered in a heavy lisp thanks to my staff still clamped in his teeth. He must have assumed the same destination as me.

Freya frowned at Grimm. "Not Hel, Niflheim," she said, in a voice as smooth and reassuring as a caring mother's when her young child woke up in the middle of the night from a bad dream, crying that there was a monster in their closet.

In that example, my personal experiences had been quite different. When I'd woken up from a childhood nightmare or monster in the closet, my parents had both burst into the room with weapons drawn and balls of molten fire in their hands, ready to slaughter some bitch-ass monsters.

Upon seeing no immediate threats, my dad would toss me a wooden sword and, in a somber, deadly-serious tone, inform me that we needed to go on a hunt to make sure the monster didn't return. He would even leave the lights off and let me lead our hunting party in hopes of lulling the monster into a false sense of security.

Illuminated only by the balls of molten fire in my parents' hands, we would check every inch of my room, and then the halls outside, and then a dozen adjoining rooms.

Only now did I realize that by leaving the lights off and making me lead the hunt, they'd really been teaching me to conquer my own fears. To face them with loyal friends at my back.

And it had worked. In short time, I would be grinning like an idiot, because they had turned a startling nightmare into a fun family adventure as we stalked the darkened halls of Chateau Falco with weapons drawn like a trio of hardened heroes ready to make a name for ourselves.

Ten or twenty minutes later, I would crawl back into bed, feeling like a legend, my fear eradicated by my newfound confidence and courage. My parents would then tuck me back into bed, heaping praise on me about how brave I'd been when I'd ripped open that bathroom door, or how stealthily I had moved, and a dozen other silly lies.

Before they kissed my forehead and left, my father would always linger to whisper one thing—staring me straight in the eyes as he spoke. "Temples were born to murder nightmares and monsters. They are terrified—of *you*," and then he would poke my ribs playfully, ignoring my mother's protests. "It's a silly waste of your time to be scared of *them*. Because when a Temple stands up, monsters fall down. So we *always* stand back up, Nate. Always. Temples never *fall*, we just *stumble*. Never forget that."

And I would sleep through the rest of the night like a babe fresh off the nipple. With my wooden sword close at hand, of course.

My parents hadn't tried to tell me everything was okay, that there was no monster, or to dismiss my fears in any other typical, loving, caring way.

No.

They had taken my claim at face value—that I really had woken up and seen a monster—and had then taught me that the only way to banish a monster or nightmare was to remind me that monsters were desperate cowards, only surfacing when their victims were vulnerable and weak. That monsters would flee even a little stick of a boy if he held a modicum of courage.

Because that boy was a Temple, and Temples never fell. They just stumbled.

I realized I was staring at Odin—remembering him as Dean, when he'd joined in on a few of our midnight haunts. He'd been the flashlight guy.

He lowered his gaze, looking guilty—most likely reading my mind and ashamed of the memory. Ashamed of his decades-long deceit.

I grunted, turning back to Freya—banishing both the nostalgic child-hood memories and my anger at Odin. I'd somewhat forgiven him for what he'd done, but seeing him in person…

Apparently, I still had issues I needed to get off my chest. Or maybe my anger was a result of hearing my friends were in danger. Then again, I'd spent a long time in Fae, living a more savage life than a civilized one.

So it took me a moment to process what Freya had said about our current surroundings—and my shoulders instantly tensed with alarm.

Niflheim…

When Grimm had teased about Asgard going to hell, Freya had taken him literally, thinking Grimm had meant *Hel*—the final resting place for those who had died of illness or old age—one of the darker, less pleasant of the Nine Realms. But this wasn't Hel. It was Niflheim.

And I wasn't entirely sure which was worse.

Niflheim was not a spot known for family vacations or a casual stroll through an ancient forest. Other than being a dangerous realm of deadly mist, I knew little else.

And looking around us, I didn't see any mist. None at all.

But in my casual scan of our surroundings, I'd noticed something that concerned the living hell out of me. I managed to keep my face calm so as not to give anything away, but inside, my mind was racing as I pondered what to do about it.

I casually grabbed my Elder-hide Darling and Dear satchel and slung it over a shoulder. Then I took the rainbow staff—*yuck, alicorn slobber*—from Grimm's mouth and thumped it into the ground, feeling marginally better. I swept my gaze across the forested scene to buy myself some more time, still masking my suspicions about Odin and Freya's possible ulterior motives.

Because in addition to what had startled me, there were a few other things that were very wrong with our current situation.

No Gunnar.

No Ashley.

CHAPTER 9

I refocused back on the Norse deities, keeping my face blank as I squeezed my staff, deciding how I wanted to play out the situation.

Odin gripped his spear tightly, as if he was ready to use it, and I wondered just how safe Niflheim was to make someone like Odin feel on edge. Or maybe it was all for show.

"Well?" I asked impatiently. "Lead the way to my friends."

Odin nodded, motioning Freya to join him as he turned around and began walking deeper into the woods. I waited for her to do so, and then motioned for Alice and Grimm to stay behind me.

Then I began to follow the gods.

I rotated my neck from side-to-side, loosening up my muscles as I prepared for the worst, ignoring the rational, prissy, guardian angel on my shoulder. The neighboring angel on my other shoulder wore black leather, smoked cigarettes, and had his own little flask and boombox. He was infinitely cooler.

I glanced around, making sure there were no immediate surprises or dangers—like whatever had first made Odin grip his spear so tightly—and then I gathered up a blast of power, drawing strictly from my Fae abilities in hopes that the gods wouldn't sense it until it was too late.

And then I flung that power towards my target, holding nothing back.

The translucent blast ripped through a stream of falling water, exploding in instant clouds of scalding vapor—betraying the stealth I had intended.

I ignored the startled sounds from my friends behind me, focused solely on the gods before me. Odin gasped, spinning at the last second to face my assault. Freya hissed, sidestepping in a crouch as her hands shot to her hips where she wore a thin belt with a few pouches on either side.

Even though I only saw her out of my peripheral vision for a split second, it was long enough to see her hands hesitate as a baffled frown began to form on her face. But her eyes gripped me like a hunting falcon.

I'd read a relationship book or two, making me quite adept at translating this majestic species' unspoken languages.

One of their strongest unspoken languages was *the look*.

Men could threaten, bludgeon, and maim with a look.

But a woman's *look* was an invisible scalpel. On fire. Coated in sulfuric acid. And it had a default taser function.

That was their *starting* point.

And they leveled up fast, gentlemen.

In fact, I was fairly confident that they'd killed the dinosaurs. *All* of them.

With one *look* from a mildly perturbed cavewoman after a filthy reptile accidentally trampled her flower garden, a figurative meteor had struck the earth and then the majority of the planet had frozen over.

Although her hands had hesitated over her pouches, Freya still had instincts, and those instincts had seen a man doing something incredibly stupid. She hit me with the *look*—an incredibly powerful one—and it was a testament to my epic manliness that I didn't instantly implode into dust motes of eternal shame.

But she'd realized—almost instantly—that I hadn't actually been aiming for her *husband*, which was confirmed about a heartbeat after she hit me with the *look*.

My blast of air snapped Odin's legendary spear—Gungnir—in half. The yellow, smoking stone decorating the blade winked out as the two halves fell to the ground and instantly vaporized. Odin and Freya both stared down at where it had landed, and neither made a single sound. They looked...troubled.

Because I'd picked up on something very alarming about Odin's spear, and I'd done so entirely by accident while scanning our surroundings...

The spear he had been holding had not been the real Gungnir.

"Explain," I said coldly. And if he didn't have a damned good answer, I was prepared to introduce fire to Niflheim.

A whole *Hel-of-a* lot of it.

His spear had looked a great deal like the real Gungnir, but it had been an illusion—a replica.

And all sorts of alarm bells had begun ringing in my mind, giving me a long list of terrifying theories. One in particular had reminded me that Odin had an adopted son, of sorts, and that this son was allegedly the best wielder of illusion magic the Nine Realms had ever seen.

Loki, the God of Mischief.

The problem was, I had no way to verify if Odin was actually Odin, so I would just have to keep a close eye on him.

Odin finally let out a breath, kicking at the ground where his fake spear had landed. Then he was suddenly holding a new one, as shiny as the original, and just as fraudulent.

"Good eyes, Nate."

"It's because I have two of them. They work better in pairs."

He pursed his lips. "That's why I have *five* eyes. Don't forget Hugin and Munin," he muttered, a bit of his fire rising to the surface.

I nodded, having anticipated his retort. "Speaking of, where are Shake and Bake? I've got a hankering for some hot wings."

He took a deep breath, as if trying to center himself rather than allow me to continue baiting him. Having known me my entire life, he was very familiar with my antagonistic tendencies and had long since acquired coping mechanisms. Testing him like this was also a good way to appease my fear about Loki hiding behind an illusion.

"I should have known better than to try deceiving you. I'm sorry," he finally said.

I slowly nodded. "Yes. You should have known better." I paused, waiting a few moments for his tension to subside. "Apology not accepted." The words rang out like a struck bell.

Freya's budding amusement evaporated, and her jaw dropped open in disbelief, but Odin merely stared back at me with one crazily intense eyeball.

"Now, let's skip the mystery and get right to the point, shall we? Why the fake spear, and where are my friends?" I demanded. Then, without looking, I ripped open a Gateway back to Fae behind Grimm, making him hop laterally in startled surprise. "Or are we finished here?" I growled.

Freya's eyes widened even further, and she quickly cast Odin a very nervous look. "Tell him," she said hurriedly. "He would have found out soon either way."

Odin finally hung his head, lowering his eye defeatedly. "No need for that," he said, motioning for me to get rid of my Gateway. I didn't. He cleared his throat. "Gungnir was stolen. And, as you can see, I'm somewhat weaker in power as a result."

I scoffed, still not closing my Gateway. "Why would I believe any of that?" I asked scathingly, trying to assess his power level in order to authenticate his claim.

There *was* something strange about his power compared to any other time I had seen him. It wasn't necessarily that it was lesser, but that it was diluted somehow—like a pale reflection.

Freya suddenly piped in, sounding fed up with our bickering. "He speaks the truth. Gungnir *has* been stolen! It is just one of the reasons we came to you. Now, drop the attitude and come with me. I refuse to let Ashley die, even if I have to drag you by the ear!"

Even Odin arched an eyebrow at her harsh words, turning to look at her as if he'd never seen her before.

Freya carried on, ignoring her husband's look. "Odin spoke very highly of you, but it seems even he can be wrong sometimes. All I see is a willful, spoiled child." She glanced at Alice, her features softening somewhat. "And a beautiful young girl."

"And me," Grimm muttered, sounding mildly irritated. "Don't forget the stunning, magical unicorn who fixed your stupid bridge. Just another under-appreciated government worker making sure your life runs smoothly."

Odin slowly fixed his glare over my shoulder, his eye seeming to crackle with lightning. "After breaking it, eating it, and then *pissing* on it," he growled ominously.

Grimm snorted. "The new one is better. Quit yer bitching."

Odin grew unnaturally still. Freya, for her part, arched an eyebrow so high that I feared it might slide right off her forehead.

Alice was beaming proudly, apparently having only paid attention to Freya calling her beautiful.

For some reason, I didn't entirely like Freya. I had no rational justification for my feeling, but I'd learned to trust my gut.

I bit my tongue from barking back an argument and took a calming breath instead. The faster I got Frantic Freya off her panic wagon, the sooner I would see my friends.

"Fine," I said in a tight voice. "Let's pretend Odin was right, and that I'm slightly more than a willful, spoiled child. What do you expect *me* to do about Gungnir, and what are we doing in Niflheim?" I asked, careful to keep my tone civil.

More civil, anyways. Because they had goaded me here with fear for my friends. Yet now I was learning they wanted a favor. Odin had lost his mojo and somehow needed my help getting it back.

Ultimately, I didn't give one flying fuck about his personal problems, let alone helping him recover his stolen goods. I only cared about my injured friends somewhere up ahead. But my mind still ran with the Gungnir problem, my curiosity getting the better of me.

Was Thor playing tit-for-tat? Odin had stolen and hidden Mjölnir, so maybe Thor had stolen Gungnir in return. Briefly envisioning Thor with Gungnir made my stomach writhe with concern, but I kept my face blank.

Freya locked eyes with me, her jaw clenched tightly as if about to say something that both infuriated and disgusted her. "We need a—"

"Generally," Odin interrupted her in a loud, commanding tone, "*need* will not sway a Temple, especially this one. Let Nate see for himself. Trust me, wife. It is easier. For everyone," he said, shooting me a meaningful glance.

Freya huffed unhappily, but she did nod.

"Generally, that's true," I agreed in a careful tone. But it really wasn't true. Not entirely. For example, my friends needed me right now, and that was trumping my desire to go help Alex and Talon castrate Mordred, cook up some testicle tartare, and feed the delicacy to some horrifying denizen of Fae. When it truly mattered, I could place others' needs above my own.

Odin nodded satisfactorily, his hat bobbing up and down. "We will speak of our own problems shortly, and you will do or not do as you see fit. Whatever you decide, Nate," he said softly. Then he very stiffly turned away, leading us onward.

Freya didn't move, watching her husband with a sad, private frown.

Sensing my attention, she jolted, shot me an accusing glare, and then hurried to catch up with him—although she kept a meaningful distance from her husband, walking parallel to him but not *beside* him.

I arched a brow back at Grimm and Alice, but they shook their heads, not having any helpful advice to offer. Or they were smart enough to not get involved.

CHAPTER 10

I watched Freya as I walked, allowing myself to get a clearer understanding of her mindset. It shouldn't have taken me this long to realize that I was the reason for all of her lonely nights over the last few decades. It wasn't my fault, of course, but I could see how part of her might want to see it that way.

Odin had left her high and dry in favor of working for my family. And here I was, meeting her face-to-face for the first time, and showing absolutely zero remorse.

I felt no guilt or responsibility for that—Odin had married her, not me. He'd made his bed and now had to lie in it. But I could empathize with Freya.

Because Odin had lied to me as well. We both felt betrayed, to some extent. Maybe that was why my gut had initially steered me away from her —not out of any distrust or dislike of her personally, but as a warning to stay away from her since I was essentially salt on a fresh wound.

And yet she was here, helping her husband. No wonder she was short fused with me. This revelation didn't completely change my perception of her, but it wasn't something I could deny either.

I shifted my gaze to Odin, assessing him clinically.

As powerful of a god as he was, he wouldn't have wasted his life working for my parents if he intended me harm. He wouldn't have debased himself for decades, suffering my constant antics, washing my clothes, feeding me, and cleaning up after me. He wouldn't have abandoned his family for my family.

And if I was wrong...

I still had access to all my power. Hell, he'd helped me regain my Fae powers. As I assessed my potential opponent, I grew more certain that he hadn't been lying about being weaker. Was Gungnir the true source of his power? Had losing it really cost him so much? And if so, who now had the weapon of mass destruction?

We continued on in silence, and I realized that Freya had taken the lead. She descended a mossy, sloping decline that led into a tiny, slightly misty, depression—like a miniature valley that was maybe thirty yards in diameter. It was littered with several boulders and stubby, rotted tree trunks, making me think of broken masts from sunken shipwrecks poking out above the oceanic body of mist. The swirling tendrils of fog reached my shins, but it was transparent enough to let me still see the ground beneath. Thankfully, my bare feet didn't slip, but I found myself idly trying to remember if I had packed any spare shoes in my satchel.

As I glanced down to check, Odin cleared his throat from only a pace ahead of me, making me jump. I hadn't realized he'd slowed down. I looked up at him warily, using a suspicious scowl to distract from my flinch.

He dipped his head, silently apologizing for startling me. Then he resumed his march, matching my pace so that we walked side-by-side. "Do you know why your first ancestor chose the prefix *Master*?"

"I've never thought about it," I lied.

Odin hesitated, seeming to read the lie and understand my reasoning. "One should think long and hard on their predecessors. At least to be aware of them—their victories and losses, vices and virtues—lest the sins of the father pass on." He glanced my way, not meeting my eyes but using his peripheral vision instead. "I'm speaking from personal experience, nothing more," he admitted in a low tone.

I nodded after a few moments. "Wisdom is learning from others' mistakes," I ventured.

He grunted. "That it is." We continued in silence for a few more steps before he spoke again. "And wisdom is a luxury many cannot afford. Often, this is because they refuse to carry the right currency, but mostly it's because they are never given the option to buy."

I nodded, a faint smile touching my cheeks at his humility. "Thank you."

He shrugged absently, lifting his head to look for his wife. I realized that she had stopped about ten feet ahead and was watching the two of us with a sad smile. "It's the least I could do," Odin murmured before departing to join his wife.

I watched him walk up to Freya as I silently considered the dozens of elusive questions now dancing through my thoughts. I replayed the seemingly casual conversation, wondering if I had missed something important. The pair spoke in low, inaudible tones—at least quietly enough for the constant rain hitting the canopy to drown out their discussion. They stood before a cozy tunnel of thick foliage at the edge of the misty valley.

Grimm and Alice stepped up behind me, waiting in silence. After a moment, Alice gripped my free hand, refusing to let go. I squeezed back reassuringly, but didn't speak. Odin finally turned to look back at us, pointing a thumb over his shoulder at the tunnel—our apparent destination.

"Nobody move your feet or hands," he warned in a stern, authoritative tone, entirely different than the man I had just spoken with. "Do nothing that could be seen as even *remotely* threatening." Then he slowly turned to face the tunnel. Although I frowned as he began to look—not at the tunnel —but up high.

I slowly followed his gaze to see two pairs of beady black eyes watching us from their perches atop opposite branches just below the canopy. They were eerily motionless; the only sense of life was that they occasionally blinked their eyes.

Cold, unsympathetic murder stared down at us like four gun barrels loaded with armor-piercing rounds of Norse hate.

Hugin and Munin.

Thought and Memory.

Odin's Ravens.

Except I barely recognized them. It only took me two seconds to decide that I no longer had any desire to bring up the Shake and Bake joke.

Because Hugin and Munin were now the size of large dogs, looking as if they each weighed over one hundred pounds—definitely too heavy to perch on my shoulders like they had done once or twice in the past. The comparison of them now versus any other time I'd seen them was almost too shocking to believe—like coming back home from a long weekend to find your pet cat of nine years was now a Saber-toothed tiger. The creatures staring down at us right now were the prehistoric ancestor to the modern-day raven.

Or maybe they had taken a cue from the Ninja Turtles and splashed around in a birdbath of neon-green goop.

Their beaks looked thicker and sharper, and their feathers were longer, beaten, and aged. There was nothing perfect or majestic about these guys. I heard a strange rattling sound, so I peered closer into the shadows surrounding them. They each had a pitted metal band on one foot, and from each anklet hung a collection of bloody human skulls. The skulls even had bits of wet, hairy gore attached in places, and one of them still had an eyeball.

Judging by the faint gleam on their beaks, I was betting I was seeing the remains of a meal they had just finished. Maybe a meal we had just interrupted. I wondered who the unlucky bastards had been.

I had to consciously force myself to lessen my grip on my staff, not wanting to risk provoking them.

I felt the Temple family Crest that was now branded into my palm tingle slightly. Since Alice didn't recoil, I dismissed it as my imagination. And Odin had warned us not to move, so it wasn't like I could check.

Still, I shivered at the possibility that it hadn't been my imagination. Hugin and Munin had been there when I'd first gotten the brand—when I'd discovered the secret Sanctorum inside Chateau Falco. A vast, impossibly located library full of hidden books and other strange wonders.

A library that only Masters Temple could access, I thought to myself, remembering Odin's strange question about my ancestors' choice of title.

One of the ravens let out a bubbling croak, ruffling his huge feathers.

I used to be able to differentiate them by Hugin having a slight chip in his beak, but these raw, mutated versions of Odin's ravens…

They'd been living the cage match fighting circuit for a few centuries, both of them scarred, worn, and beaten. But like a callus, their sustained beatings had somehow only served to make them stronger, harder, and more resilient.

Their battle scars weren't a testament to their inferior fighting skills—they were a declaration of just how many foes the tag-team had slaughtered. And just how powerful those foes must have been to successfully land a lucky shot here and there.

The other raven took slightly longer to react, seeming to focus on me more intently than the others, cocking his head curiously. Then he turned to Grimm, and his feathers ruffled up, seeming to double his size like he was a puffer fish. He abruptly hopped sideways on his branch, belting out a bloodcurdling shriek of his own.

Odin and Freya both let out a sigh of relief, their shoulders relaxing in sync.

Picking up on the gravitas of the situation, I still didn't make any jokes. I didn't say anything, and I didn't move. All I wanted was to get this over with and go see my best friend and his wife. The sober tension from Odin and crew were starting to bother me, making my shoulders twitchy.

Alice suddenly squeezed my hand, and I realized her tiny fingers were practically buzzing with fear. I squeezed back reassuringly.

"They're different than last time I saw them," she whispered, barely moving her lips. "At your house. They're *all* different," she added in a lower tone, her eyes seeming to settle longer on Odin.

I knew she wasn't simply referring to their physical appearance. "Also the same though, right?" I asked in a whisper, thinking of Loki and his powers of illusion.

She nodded minutely. "It's definitely Odin, if that's what you mean. But they were...*muted* before," she said, her gaze unfocused as she stared up at the ravens. "Now..." she trailed off, looking concerned. "They are *overpowered*. Stronger than even I thought possible. Their power lies in their ability to deceive and judge truth. I don't fully understand what I see around him," she breathed, indicating Odin. "But power runs between them like a raging river."

I arched an eyebrow, glancing down at her. She was shaking as she stared at Odin. In a way, her concerns made me feel better. She was confident that it really was Odin. And if she was sensing that they were all connected by power, it was only further evidence that he wasn't Loki. Unless he could pretend to be all of them at once, even mimicking their magical auras...

And just like that, I was back to the drawing board. I shook off my paranoia.

I'd always wondered why the ravens hadn't been more badass. Had they been muting themselves like Alice thought? It would make sense. Dean had been concealing his identity from everyone, so maybe that had forced *them* to appear muted as well—more domesticated—so as not to give away his identity.

So, what exactly was so dangerous about the bird brains? What were they capable of, really?

Looking back up at them, into those cold black eyes, I felt myself shiver slightly. Alice was right. These were not the same ravens that had threatened to shit on Talon at every opportunity, making crude jokes to everyone at Chateau Falco.

"Now we can proceed," Odin said, dipping his head at the ravens individually, respectfully. The ravens had been bouncers, checking our credentials. That didn't ease my paranoia at all. Were they looking for someone, or was all this to protect my friends up ahead?

Freya obediently stepped into the tunnel, following her husband. I waited a few moments before leading Alice and Grimm after them.

I couldn't help but tense my shoulders as I passed directly beneath the ravens, imagining their talons sinking into my shoulders.

As I walked into the darkened tunnel, I found myself wondering why they had looked at Grimm so strangely…

CHAPTER 11

I tried to ignore the ravens silently watching us as we entered the dark tunnel of leaves and foliage that was too thick to see through. With each step, the darkness increased, like we were willfully walking into our own graves, voluntarily allowing Niflheim to devour our souls.

Even still, it was impossible not to notice the sudden crackling of leaves and branches just outside either side of the tunnel walls—the feral growls and the occasional puffs of vapor that blasted through the dense vegetation. It made me think of walking through a dark, abandoned subway with leaking steam pipes while the depthless shadows emitted obvious sounds of malevolent pursuit. Our hunters were toying with us—trying to frighten us enough that we bolted out the opposite end of the tunnel to, in all likelihood, run right into their waiting jaws.

Odin and Freya walked very carefully, almost subserviently, which only served to ratchet my anxiety higher. I gripped my staff firmly, mentally preparing to make a stand and keep Alice safe.

I hoped it wouldn't come to that, but if Odin and Freya looked concerned, I wasn't anticipating a friendly outcome. More like a few pissed-off residents of Niflheim.

And I didn't know enough about this place to determine what kind of monsters they might be.

The rhythmic sweep of heavy wings above the tunnel soon joined the sounds of pursuit from the sides, and I began to feel claustrophobic, wondering if maybe I'd made a bad decision in following Odin and Freya. Then again, maybe Hugin and Munin were chasing off our hunters.

The tunnel curved, revealing a dim light not far ahead. Our destination, and potentially an unwelcoming committee. Almost simultaneously, the sounds of our pursuers stopped—so abruptly that I missed a step. I instinctively lifted my staff across my chest in a defensive guard.

But Odin and Freya pressed on, reaching the end of the tunnel and stepping out into a dry creek bed. I kept my staff in front of me as I followed them out, ready for anything.

The sheets of rain hadn't reached this area, which made the hair on my arms stand straight up. We were surrounded on three sides by a steep ravine of boulders and fallen stones, our only exit back through the tunnel. Unless Odin and Freya intended for us to climb the ten-foot rock piles.

"It's okay. I'm a good climber," Alice said, somehow reading my thoughts. Not in any magical way, but like kids often did when surrounded by adults—wanting to prove their independence and that they could take care of themselves.

But Odin and Freya stood entirely still, not turning to speak to us or explain where we were going next. Grimm neighed suddenly, rearing up on his back hooves. One second later, two wolves the size of small ponies struck the creek bed not five feet away from us, shattering the stones beneath their gargantuan paws, somehow seeming to box us in even though we outnumbered them.

Their lips were curled back to reveal fangs longer than my fingers, and their eyes smoldered with hunger and warning. Waves of power oozed from them, and for some reason, I knew it wasn't magic. I had the almost overwhelming urge to submit to their authority, and I noticed Grimm's legs buckling and shaking in my peripheral vision—as if he was fighting against the same urge.

Or he was scared to death, which was not a typical reaction for the psychopathic unicorn.

Alice had promptly dropped to her rear, sitting down on the rubble-strewn ground, hugging her knees close to her chest.

Which lit a fucking fire inside me. How dare they scare my girl? I gritted my teeth, railing against the enticing urge to submit, and slammed my staff into the stones beneath my bare feet—thankfully, not sharp enough to cut my flesh—as I stared the nearest wolf right in the eyes.

He was massive and ferocious, like *he*—specifically—was the first of his kind—the undiluted, monstrous, prehistoric ancestor to every wolf ever. The first beast to decide he wanted to howl at the moon.

His shoulders were stout and beefy, making a mastiff seem malnourished by comparison, and his paws were a foot in diameter, with long, bone-white claws that sunk into the stone like it was nothing but caked dirt.

Long strands of drool hung from his fangs, and I noticed dozens of gruesome scars across his face and muzzle. Not appreciating my defiant posture and direct eye contact, he hunkered lower, a furious, warning growl bubbling out from his jowls as his mane of fur seemed to bunch up and flare out.

I set my shoulders and took a step closer, slamming my staff into the stone hard enough to create gravel. Knightmares were plaguing my city, Gunnar and Ashley were injured, and then these two overgrown fleabags had chosen to scare Alice.

And now they expected me to roll over for them in some petty dominance game.

I would end their games with one final move.

Check-Nate.

"You're frightening the girl, and I make pelts out of things that frighten the girl," I warned the wolf closest to Alice, not giving one flying fuck who they obviously were.

Geri and Freki, Odin's wolves.

Except, like Hugin and Munin, these two were drastically different than the last time I had seen them.

Almost like I was seeing their Wild Sides—a monstrous, mutated form of one's self that was discovered upon one's first visit to the Land of the Fae. Their id—or primitive, savage side—unleashed.

And this realization actually served to *bolster* my confidence rather than diminish it. Give me a Fae creature and I would give you back a lovingly-packaged, wicker basket of bleached bones. The Fae no longer elicited fear in my heart. Fae was *mine*.

So, I took an educated gamble and opened myself up to my own Wild Side. I let more of that persona—Wylde—creep out, and I distantly realized that I was chuckling, wiggling my fingers around the shaft of my staff in a more versatile grip as I readied myself to play with the prehistoric canines.

The wolf licked his lips hungrily, grinding his paws into the stone as he prepared to pounce.

I stuck out my chin, grinning like a madman. "I'll show you why your descendants now wear collars. How easy it was to teach your kind to roll over—almost like you were *born to submit.*"

He snapped his jaws three times, jerking his head back and forth like a cobra. The other wolf let out a sudden, thunderous bark, and my foe shuddered, instantly ducking his head in an obedient manner.

I had apparently misjudged. The other wolf was the alpha, and I hadn't even bothered to assess him. I'd just focused on the one closest to Alice.

I could tell that my chosen wolf was pissed to be forced to ignore my challenge, but he didn't dare cross his alpha.

And I realized that this was the sensation I had felt. The authority. He really had been trying to dominate me—to let me know that he was second in the line of command. If not for my recent experience in Fae, I was pretty sure he would have succeeded.

I heard Grimm stamp a hoof suddenly, shaking out his mane of long black feathers. I cast a quick glance backwards to see it was now flared out, the red orbs oozing blood, and he had his horn lowered in warning—also conveniently serving to protect his neck.

I knew that wolves and horses had never been the best of friends. Had these wolves been that powerful—to dominate Grimm—or had it been the instinctive reaction of a horse confronting a wolf?

Well, a unicorn reacting to these specific Norse wolves.

Whatever it had been, me standing up to them had somehow galvanized both Alice and Grimm, because Alice was also back on her feet now, clutching a rock in each hand, looking ready to acquire her own pair of wolf pelts—when before, she hadn't even been able to remain upright.

Were Grimm and Alice mirroring me, or had they overcome their fear on their own?

I glanced over at Odin and Freya to see that they were still entirely motionless. They were too focused on the alpha—I wasn't sure which wolf it was, Geri or Freki—standing before them. They hadn't even bothered chastising me for how I had spoken to the beta wolf.

The alpha let out another series of short barks that more resembled the thumping bass from your neighborhood's resident, self-proclaimed badass in his '85 Honda Civic. The car with the loose muffler, faded primer paint, stock rims and tires, and the ridiculous spoiler improperly bolted onto the trunk—a hopeful extra for the unannounced *Fast and Furious* sequel.

The pair of wolves began slowly circling Odin and Freya, sniffing and growling forcefully enough to shift their robes at the sudden clouds of vapor from their nostrils.

There was no light petting, no eye contact, and no slobbery dog kisses. This was a challenge, a ritual. A test similar to what we'd seen with Hugin and Munin.

Odin very slowly extended his hand and the wolves instantly recoiled, snapping their wicked teeth. Freya slowly did the same—careful to make sure the gesture didn't look aggressive.

Both wolves were snarling and sidestepping as they stared at the proffered hands. They looked livid and starving.

What the fuck kind of pet dogs were these guys?

Before I could demand an explanation, both wolves lunged in a synchronized, explosive dash, clamping down their powerful jaws over the extended hands—one wolf for each god.

Blood spurted and both gods trembled, biting back cries of pain.

Without consciously realizing it, I had slammed my staff into the ground again—but this time I let loose a wave of rainbow light that rolled over the wolves like an inferno of air hot enough to singe their fur and scorch their nostrils. All without touching Odin or Freya.

The wolves yelped and whined, dancing back to relative safety—thankfully *after* letting go of the hands in their jaws rather than simply ripping them off.

The smell of singed fur and flash-fried meat hung heavy in the air—not a pleasant mix.

"Back off," I warned them, "before I do something stupid like actually putting some effort into teaching you a lesson."

They narrowed their eyes, licking the blood from their lips as they hunkered low, looking ready to teach me a lesson about disturbing their play time. Then, like they'd abruptly switched personalities, they froze and promptly sat down on their haunches.

"That's right. Who's the alpha *now*?" Grimm sneered.

CHAPTER 12

*G*eri and Freki began panting, letting their ridiculously long, blood-soaked tongues hang out the sides of their open mouths. I blinked incredulously, my pent-up adrenaline suddenly having no outlet.

Alice cleared her throat. "They verified Odin and Freya by blood. It had nothing to do with Nate," she said quietly, shooting a sheepish glance my way. "Although that was very scary, too."

I was pretty sure her assessment was right, because the wolves weren't even looking at me now—they were staring at Odin and Freya, still panting happily as if the last few minutes hadn't even happened.

I narrowed my eyes at Odin, making certain to keep my thoughts veiled as an idea slowly began to form.

Freya produced a powder of some kind from one of the pouches on her belt, and then turned to sprinkle it over Odin's hand before tending to her own. She murmured a strangely musical—yet harsh—word, and the two of them winced at a sudden flare of purple light. When it faded, I saw that their wounds were healed.

Freya's knees buckled slightly, but she righted herself, looking haggard as she took a shaky breath. Odin looked dazed and confused, staring off at nothing. With Hugin and Munin absent, I wondered if he might currently be partaking in a vision quest, using their eyes to scope out Niflheim.

Their reactions made me feel remarkably uneasy rather than reassured.

What the hell was wrong with them? How was a little bit of magic doing them in like this, and why so many precautions?

Freya glanced my way as if to draw my attention, and then she turned to point at the rock wall opposite the tunnel. She closed her eyes, murmuring under her breath, and then she began to draw in the air. Her finger began to glow green, then blue, and then gold, and vines suddenly sprouted out from between the rock walls on either side of where she was pointing, weaving together in the center like they were forming a wicker wall.

And although I could sense power of a sort, I had absolutely no idea where she was pulling it from. It wasn't any kind of magic that I was familiar with.

And it was fucking *loud*. Stone cracked and groaned before cascading down the walls in a deafening rumble, and wood squealed and popped as the vines grew longer and thicker, weaving together with greater complexity. Grimm neighed uncertainly and Alice took a step backwards. Finally, the sounds faded and the vines ceased moving, revealing a masterpiece.

A vine-woven door now stood against the rock wall where Freya was still pointing. It even had a crude handle. Freya's finger began to dim, and I realized she was panting and sweating despite the frigid air.

She opened her eyes and turned to look at me. "We must rest. Grimm and the child may stay here, but your friends await you inside."

My heart began to race at the prospect of what horrors I was about to witness. Locking my friends up behind a secret door implied they weren't healthy enough to protect themselves.

I also wondered if this was actually a prison. A trap.

Were Odin's super-pets acting as protectors or wardens?

Alice set a hand on my wrist, squeezing gently. I flinched instinctively, not having noticed her approach.

"Gunnar really is in there," she whispered, smiling faintly. "And they won't betray you," she said, indicating the Norse crew.

I let out a breath I hadn't known I was holding.

Alice had a thing for Gunnar, having traveled with us in Fae. She'd spent most of her time perched atop his shoulders, weaving yellow ribbons into his hair as she peppered him with a billion questions. She'd flipped the script by seeming to adopt *him* as a temporary father figure. It had been ridiculously cute, even serving to inspire Gunnar that he might actually have what it took to be a good father, and that his fears of failure were entirely unwarranted.

Her gift of sight often manifested in strange ways, like apparently being able to see Gunnar's aura through a magic door. Since she wasn't frowning, he must be relatively safe.

But she hadn't mentioned anything about Ashley...

Geri and Freki began to whine playfully, one of them even rolling onto his back as Alice giggled and bent down to rub his belly. I hadn't even sensed her leaving my side. The other wolf started hopping back and forth, yipping excitedly, and I watched as Alice tried to split her heart equally between the two predators. The wolves were still huge and terrifying, but seeing them resort to puppy-like excitement, I knew Alice was right. She was safe with them.

I noticed Freya was also smiling down at Alice, but her eyes seemed to be seeing something Nine Realms away.

She must have sensed my attention because she blinked rapidly and then turned to look at me. Her smile didn't entirely disappear, but it was noticeably less heartfelt.

Remembering how she likely saw me—as a sort of home-wrecker—I gave her a polite smile and a nod of gratitude for the door.

Rather than returning my smile, she folded her arms behind her back and approached me. She paused a pace away, turning to study the door she had made with her mysterious magic.

"Odin frequently speaks of your friendship with Gunnar. How it is more of a brotherhood, despite your bloodlines," Freya said in a soft tone, still staring at the door.

I nodded, turning to study the door as well. "Yes."

"He said that you even made a deal with Anubis to save his soul..." I glanced over at her this time, frowning. She continued studying the door, speaking as if to herself. "Deals, by their very nature, have terms..."

My frown stretched deeper, wondering if she was implying that this situation was somehow my fault. "Your point?" I asked in a neutral tone.

She sighed, turning to face me. "Are you aware that you have been gone for more than a year?" she asked, not unkindly, but not overly sympathetic, either.

I blinked at her, stunned speechless, and my pulse began skipping erratically as my heart thundered in my chest. One look into her green eyes told me that she was speaking the truth, and that she wasn't pleased about her role as the messenger. Just that she had decided it important enough for me to know—before I walked through the door.

In fact, she looked furious that I hadn't already known, which led me to believe that Odin had willed it, and that his loving wife had chosen to disobey his request. Out of vindictive spite for her husband's wanderings or as a moral duty, I couldn't tell.

Regardless, this was, perhaps, Freya extending me an olive branch.

But I was too concerned for my current friends to consider nurturing a new friendship with Freya. Because the math just didn't make any sense to me.

"I've never had a child or anything," I finally managed, licking my lips as I tried to wrap my head around her statement, "let alone a werewolf pup, but doesn't a pregnancy typically last nine months?"

She nodded ever so slowly. "Precisely the problem. One of them, anyway."

I gritted my teeth in frustration. "So did she already have the twins?" I asked, my patience fraying alarmingly thin.

"The pups have yet to be born," Freya said in a careful tone. She studied me thoughtfully, as if waiting for something. Finally, she sighed, looking mildly frustrated. "Go. See to your friends, and I will see to my husband. Maybe we will both learn the answers to our questions."

And then she simply turned away from me to go check on Odin, who was still staring off into the distance at things only the one-eyed king could see.

Troubled, I strode towards the door, replaying Freya's conversation in my head. Her comments had seemed so carefully chosen that I knew I was missing something, but I was so confused about how Ashley could still be pregnant that it was hard to focus. I knew time passed differently in Fae, but *one year*? That was alarming.

And I'd never heard of a pregnancy stretching three months past the due date. Hell, technically it was even *longer* than three months, since I was basing my math on when they'd had the gender reveal at our impromptu dinner party one year ago.

And what had Freya meant about Anubis and my deal to save Gunnar's soul? Other than letting me know Odin was a gossip, I didn't see how it was relevant for her to mention.

Gunnar and Talon had actually died fighting that Knightmare at Stonehenge—Sir Geraint, apparently—and I'd made a deal with Anubis to bring them back to life in return for—

My heart froze and I almost tripped.

Oh.

Shit.

I'd promised Anubis that I would take out Mordred in *two years*. If Freya was right, that meant I only had one year left to hold up my end of the bargain and kill Mordred.

Otherwise, Anubis had every right to call his loan of two souls due—payable immediately.

Gunnar and Talon would die. Permanently.

I shuddered, feeling like I wanted to vomit. Although one year was still a long time, it was still a deadline.

Even as important as it was to make sure Ashley and her pups were safe from immediate dangers related to her delayed delivery, it was equally important that I get to work on taking out Mordred.

Or else these kids would grow up without a father, and it would be their godfather's fault.

I propped my staff against the rock wall, straightened my satchel, pushed open the door, and stepped inside a pitch-black space.

CHAPTER 13

A cold, gauntleted hand grabbed me by the throat and, to make sure I didn't slip and hurt myself, began to squeeze. Then my unseen host —very courteously—lifted me off my feet, yanked me inside, and slammed me against a wall hard enough to make dust motes fall from the ceiling.

A genuine Niflheim *how the fuck d'ya do, stranger? Happen to be an organ donor?*

I'd definitely received warmer—and colder—receptions.

The door hammered shut behind me, leaving me in pitch darkness and kicking my bare feet in the air like a willful toddler as I struggled to breathe against the cold gauntlet of hospitality around my throat. The particles of dust cloying the air didn't make my already restricted breathing any easier, but life was all about the challenge, and true gentlemen rose to challenges with unwavering aplomb and dignity, as my dad always used to say.

The stone wall was so cold through my jeans that I felt like I was sitting bare-assed on a glacier. The only aspects of my assailant that I could make out were a single, piercing blue eye glinting from a small beam of light that shone through a crack in the door, and the dull shine of a familiar, quartz-like eyepatch.

"Hey, Gunnar," I croaked, unable to let out my breath of relief. "Remember when I lost track of time on that mountain?"

The cold, armored hand threatened to give my neck freezer-burn, and it didn't move a millimeter upon hearing my greeting, making me wonder if my host was actually some other one-eyed dude who liked to choke out his guests.

He remained perfectly still for about five more seconds, and then he sniffed at the air, turning his head slightly. I knew this only due to the movement of the blue eye leaving the thin beam of light from the door, because I still couldn't make out anything else in the darkness.

He suddenly gasped, dropping me back to my heels on the spongy wooden floor. I began rapidly rubbing at my rear with both hands in an effort to ease the biting cold that seemed to have sunk into my actual tail-bone. I didn't want to get a severe case of frost-butt and lose one—or possibly both—of my perfectly curved butt cheeks.

They belonged to St. Louis. I was merely their caretaker.

Before I could say anything, Gunnar wrapped me up in a two-armed bear hug, squeezing me hard enough to make my ribs ache.

And instead of clapping him on the back and laughing, I simply wrapped my arms around him, squeezing back just as tightly.

Because the big burly man was sobbing so softly that I couldn't actually hear it—I could just *feel* him shaking against my neck, his beard quivering like a fistful of tuning forks.

It was a man thing. If the emotion couldn't be heard, maybe it never really happened. It's why men were so fond of high-fives, bumping knuckles, or slapping asses after a victorious athletic performance. Emotions could be secretly transferred via physical contact, so that the enemy—women—could never learn how deep and vulnerable we truly were.

This secret language was called the Man Code, and it had very strict rules. Each method of physical contact also had numerous unwritten—of course—meanings.

High five a little moist? He was sad.

Hug a little too long? He missed you.

The number of pats to the back in a hug were even significant—but they were different from one man to the next, so that they could never be deciphered by any woman.

"What happened, man?" I asked carefully, mentally counting down the seconds so as not to break Rule 57 of the Man Code:

The only physical contact between two Men that can last longer than five seconds are two-armed embraces, and only in one of four specific circumstances: a wedding, a funeral, a hospital visit, or if the Cardinals won the World Series against the Royals. And even then, both Men must embrace a female within ten seconds or suffer a mark against their personal record. Sub-rule: Delayed pats to the back shall restart the five-second countdown, of course. We are not beasts of the field.

I decided that this counted as a hospital visit.

Instead of answering, Gunnar gave me three, slow, powerful pats to the back, and on the third, his hand stayed there, as if making sure I wasn't about to leave again—or maybe to verify that he wasn't imagining my presence.

I opened my mouth to let him know that—although having restarted the countdown by patting my back—he was still dangerously close to violating Rule 57 when his whisper—an additional, altogether different violation of the Man Code—stopped me cold.

"She's dying, Nate. We tried to visit you in Fae and got stuck in the middle instead."

I gripped his shoulders, jumping back in shock.

"Dying?" I hissed. Then I processed the rest of what he'd said. "Stuck? In the middle of *what*?"

He shrugged uncertainly. "The middle of the Gateway, I guess. I don't know how else to explain it."

My mind scrambled, but thankfully, my eyes were beginning to somewhat adjust to the darkness, allowing me to just make out his intimidatingly large silhouette, and that he was facing me with his ears rather than looking directly at me. Werewolves had excellent night vision, so it was a rather strange stance for him to take.

"How long were you stuck?" I asked, frowning. I'd never heard of getting *stuck* in a Gateway. Well, Anubis had once sent his guards after me via interrupting the *destination* of any and all Gateways, but that had taken me to a different *place*. I wouldn't have ever described it as being *stuck inside* a Gateway.

"Six months, Nate. *Six. Months.*" He jabbed my chest with a thick finger, punctuating each word. And he did so while still facing sideways, making it even more bizarre.

I stared at him in silence, a million questions running through my mind.

And I realized I was clenching my fists in unbidden anger, one of his comments striking dangerously close to my heart.

Fae. He'd tried to come to Fae—the place where he had actually *died* in a fight with one of Mordred's Knightmares. Not only had he tried to return, but he'd tried to bring his pregnant wife along for the ride with him! I was panting, and I heard my knuckles cracking ominously.

I'd been freaking out about Ashley and her babies, only to realize that her own husband had *caused* her plight.

Gunnar cleared his throat warily. "What's wrong—"

I cut him off by punching him in the jaw, sending him crashing into the wall. His strange sideways stance had been begging for it anyway. The beam of light through the door showed him leaning against the wall with one hand, wiping blood from his lip with the other. He spat out some blood, rubbing at his jaw as if surprised by the force behind my blow.

"What were you *thinking?*" I demanded hoarsely. "What made you think it was a good idea to come to *Fae?*" I shouted, taking another swing.

He spun and caught my punch in his open hand, his fingers instantly wrapping around my knuckles in an attempt to manhandle me with his superior strength.

"Not today, Lassie," I snarled.

And I immediately lashed out with my other hand to grip his wrist. His eye widened in surprise as I dropped to my rear and forcefully planted my foot up into his stomach. My wrist lock, speed, and momentum allowed me to launch the much larger man over my head and across room. He slammed into the opposite wall hard enough to knock another layer of dust motes down from the ceiling.

The sounds of him grunting as he hit the wall, and then gasping as he hit the floor, were deliciously rewarding. I scrambled to my feet, and then turned around. I heard him wheezing on the ground before I managed to actually spot him in the murky darkness. He didn't try to get up as I stomped over to him. I stopped just out of his reach and glared down, planting my fists on my hips. I was livid. I'd been freaking the fuck out about keeping them safe, and the whole past-due baby mama drama was his fault!

If he hadn't tried taking a Gateway to Fae, he wouldn't have gotten stuck inside for six months.

"Your wife is pregnant!" I growled. "You should have been surrounded by your pack of werewolves at all times, minding your own business! What idiotic fallacy inspired you to take Ashley to Fae—the place where you *died* not too long ago?"

Gunnar looked up at me, spit out some more blood, and then spoke a single word without even an iota of guilt.

"Thor."

I slowly lowered my hands, staring back at him in stunned disbelief. My anger puttered out like a car without gasoline as I tried to make sense of the simple answer. Thor?

Gunnar rolled over and climbed back to his feet. He slowly nodded, staring me down. "Thor came to St. Louis, Nate. He managed to escape whatever hellhole Odin banished him to. I don't know—and I don't care—how, but he came back a few weeks after Stonehenge, and he was determined to kill you and everyone associated with you. Especially Alex," he added with a slight frown. "Something to do with Alex hurting his goats."

My brain made a strange crackling sound and I thought I smelled burnt plastic as my limited, biological hardware showed me the fatal flaw in not agreeing to regular software updates. How had Thor returned so quickly?

A nearby voice cut through my thoughts, seeming to crawl across the floor rather than carry through the air. "Please...stop fighting each other," Ashley asked.

We both wilted at the comment, but I was more concerned at the frailty in her voice. I turned, trying to locate her in the gloom, but all I could make out were a few empty, rickety, wooden chairs pressed up against the walls— a strange place to put them, especially since they faced the wrong way for use. Unfortunately, Gunnar had missed all of them in his fall. I noticed the faintest of glows from a cracked-open door leading to a side room.

Since there was nowhere else she could be, I carefully approached, thankful that everything in the room seemed to have been pressed against the wall like the chairs. Did they not have access to light here? It was obviously intentional since they had formed a clear path through the room. I realized I was focusing on the lack of light because I was terrified of what I was about to see when I opened that door.

"Stop crying over spilled milk," Ashley chided from beyond the door. "You sound like a couple of fuzzy little man babies."

"Big, hairy man babies," Gunnar muttered under his breath, combing his fingers through his beard.

I ignored the Neanderthal, nervously pushing the door open with my fingers one inch at a time. They were shaking from all the imagined horrors flickering through my mind—because the woman belonging to that voice sounded like she was on the verge of death, or in unimaginable pain.

Of course, the door squealed as it opened. Why not make the situation creepier?

I peered into a relatively brighter room—meaning the space was illuminated by a candle that had been purposefully hidden behind a vase on the floor. The vase prevented me from seeing the actual flame on the wick, but I'd been to her house enough times to recognize the familiar, herbal aroma that she claimed was therapeutic.

I was pretty sure that she was the only living soul who held that opinion. The rest had died from inhalation.

I'd dubbed it *Perfumania on Fire*, and no one had argued with me. Well, Gunnar had, begrudgingly, and only after Ashley had given him a very pointed look.

I stared at that obstructed light—only bright enough to prevent me from tripping over my own two feet—wondering how big the room actually was since I couldn't make out all the walls. I recalled how Gunnar hadn't looked directly at me, how tightly he had embraced me, and how the other room had also been devoid of light and furniture.

He'd been using every sense *other* than sight. Why?

My eyes locked onto a small cot backed up against the wall opposite the door, and all thoughts about the room or the darkness fled my mind. Seeing the vague silhouette of the woman occupying the cot, I sucked in a shallow breath and forced myself to approach.

Even in this darkness, I could see how terrible the once mesmerizing woman looked. Ashley was propped up on a pile of pillows, holding her bare—and extremely pregnant—belly with two fragile hands that looked more like bone wrapped in flesh—no muscle or fat to speak of.

If not for her pregnancy, I would have guessed she weighed little more than eighty pounds. At *best*.

Despite the chill, she was sweating, and everything other than her belly looked gaunt, thin, and drained, like she was sacrificing every part of her body to grow her babies. She seemed to have trouble seeing me, squinting her eyes—just like Gunnar.

Two forms suddenly emerged from the darkness on my side of the cot, one of them towering over me in a silent, menacing manner, and the other emitting a low, warning growl. I hadn't sensed their presence at all, which was impressive. The two entered my personal space—a space that wasn't conducive to a long life on the best of days.

And this wasn't the best of days, so I wasn't in a very personable mood.

CHAPTER 14

*G*uards.

I gritted my teeth, knowing they meant well, but after the day I'd had, I wasn't feeling very understanding.

Gunnar let out a low, throaty grumble, and the two guards instantly took two steps away from me.

Still, I sensed they were a heartbeat away from violence if I made any move even *resembling* a threat to Ashley.

A few moments of brittle silence hung heavy in the air as I waited until I was certain they were in control of their actions. That I was in control of my actions. "And who do I have the pleasure of almost provoking?" I asked in a cold tone that I hardly recognized as my own.

"Drake and Cowan," Gunnar said.

I frowned in their general direction, the tension in my shoulders lessening significantly. I knew those two. Gunnar's very own Geri and Freki—trusted lieutenants for his pack of werewolves. Drake was the shorter, scrappier figure, and Cowan was the taller, stronger, silent type.

Both were deadly and competent; their unique skill sets a perfect complement to each other. I snorted, breaking the tension. "At least smile or something, guys. I can't see anything in here."

Drake, surprisingly, burst out laughing. Then he shouldered the much taller Cowan in a teasing manner. And I suddenly remembered that Cowan's skin was practically the color of charcoal.

I winced, abruptly realizing how my words had come across. "No. Wait," I stammered. "That's not what I—"

"It's okay," Cowan said in an incredibly low, baritone. "It's technically true...pasty fairy," he said in an amused, rumbling grumble. And I thought I caught a glimpse of his pearly whites as he flashed me a disarming grin.

I felt a smile tug at my cheeks—relieved to hear that I hadn't offended him—but I was even more grateful he had teased me back. Like a double reassurance that he'd found my ignorant—and entirely innocent—comment funny rather than incendiary, which was rare these days. I turned back to Ashley, shaking my head. This whole situation was bizarre, and I couldn't understand how the pieces fit together.

"Can one of you finally tell me why we're hanging out in the dark?" I asked, exasperated. When no one immediately answered me, I decided to force the issue, speaking in an exaggerated, theatrical voice. *"In the beginning, Nate said, 'LET THERE BE LIGHT'—"*

"No!" Gunnar barked, recoiling.

I froze in the act of dramatically lifting my hand to make a ball of fire. Ashley had turned to shove her face into a pillow and Gunnar had immediately averted his gaze. Drake and Cowan looked suddenly tense, but they hadn't turned their eyes from me. Interesting.

"Okay...no light," I said calmingly. Their reactions had told me the answer to my question. Gunnar and Ashley were blind to some extent, or at least had a newfound aversion to light. Drake and Cowan, on the other hand, were unaffected. I cleared my throat. "I need answers. Now."

Ashley hesitantly peeled her face away from the pillow as if to make sure it was still dark. Then, instead of answering my question, she let out a harsh sob and lashed out with one skeletal hand to grasp mine in an unbreakable iron grip.

Before I could speak, she tugged me closer with surprising strength. Not wanting to risk dog-piling her on top of the cot, I dropped to my knees instead, the tops of my thighs slamming into the bed frame hard enough to shake the whole thing.

But I didn't feel any pain because she had firmly pressed my hand down over her bare, pregnant belly.

My heart fluttered wildly, and all I could manage to do was stare at my hand touching her feverish skin.

And *everything* else in the world simply ceased to matter in a single, never-ending moment as it hit me—*really* hit me.

Ashley was pregnant with my best friend's kids.

Even though it was obvious that she was in severe danger, her health rapidly deteriorating—

I felt two forceful kicks thump against the pads of my fingers, and my heart instantly disintegrated before the resulting dust fell down into my stomach, making me severely light-headed all of a sudden.

I sucked in a shaky, involuntary breath, struggling to blink through a stubborn film of tears. If I had been standing, I would have fallen down. No question about it.

Ashley laughed, squeezing my hand tighter, but I couldn't peel my eyes away from her belly, silently praying that I would feel another kick or two.

Instead, I felt two imagined, steel wires whipping out like lassos to ensnare my heart, eternally binding me to the precious children just beneath the surface.

I was *touching* Calvin and Makayla.

Gunnar and Ashley's twins—named after my parents—were still alive.

For now.

And I had *felt* them!

"My babes *need* you, Nate," Ashley whispered, her voice breaking with emotion. This time, I managed to slowly peel my eyes from her belly, but there was no way I was retracting my hand. Ashley stared down at me, and although I couldn't make much out in the darkness...

Her eyes were twin orbs of white-hot flame—of impotent fury that she was stuck in this bed.

"They *need* their godfather," she growled, and she may as well have punched me in the nose, because my fingers tightened ever so slightly on her belly like I was swearing an oath on a Bible *to protect and to serve.*

No. Something *much* stronger than that.

These two little furballs had me by my very *soul*, and I hadn't even gazed into their *eyes* yet.

I slowly, but resolutely, nodded back at the deadly mother wolf, no words necessary between us.

"Thor hit her," Gunnar said from directly behind me, in probably the coldest voice I'd ever heard. And his words struck me like a bolt of lightning out of a clear blue sky. "She fell on her stomach..."

My vision flashed red and I heard a roaring sound in my ears, followed by a splintering, cracking sound, and then pained curses from the werewolves.

I winced at a sudden source of nearby light, remembering how afraid Gunnar and Ashley had been of any illumination. I traced the source, and found that I was squinting down at my own forearm. My sleeve had bunched up at some point, and golden light flared from beneath my skin—thankfully, my flesh dampened it somewhat—illuminating my veins with molten gold like a glowing root system for a tree. I was panting in confusion because I also realized that I wasn't kneeling beside the cot anymore, but facing a stone wall instead.

I didn't remember moving. Not at all.

And I couldn't see my *hand*—my arm simply ended at the wrist where my glowing-veined arm touched the wall.

A huge, dark hand hesitantly reached out and settled over my forearm as if to shield some of the light. I frowned down at it, wondering why the hand was still dark with the light pulsing from my skin.

I followed the arm up to see Cowan staring down at me. His eyes were wide with concern as he gave me a slow, calming nod. Then he very gently began pulling my forearm away from the wall.

I turned to watch my arm, confused by his gesture, and I blinked to see my fist slowly emerging from *beyond* the rock wall, along with a cascade of grit and gravel and dust. Understanding finally dawned on me. I'd punched a hole in the wall, and I didn't even recall doing it. Nor had I felt it.

I'd mentally *snapped* upon hearing what Thor had done. And I could have really hurt someone. Hurt Ashley...

My shoulders began to shake violently at the thought.

But the imagined horror was abruptly replaced by a deeper, anchoring fantasy. Of Thor roasting alive before me, screaming and begging for forgiveness.

And me smiling as I watched that hope for mercy burn out of his eyes.

Thor...

Although I had no real proof, I was fairly certain Thor had been behind the lightning bolt attacks on my mountain in Fae—however short-lived his petty assault had lasted.

He'd done fucked up, son.

He hadn't simply crossed a line. He'd flown so far beyond the line that he wouldn't be able to see it if he looked back over his shoulder.

Thor...had *hit* Ashley—a pregnant woman. The *mother* of *my* godchildren. *My* family.

And I'd punched a hole through solid rock upon hearing it. I slowly turned to look up at Cowan, shakily dipping my head in gratitude for his help. He was still gently gripping my forearm—but I could sense the tension in his hold, like he was ready to physically hurl me back outside if I snapped again.

"I'm...okay now," I managed in a thready whisper. He held onto my forearm for a few more moments as if to discern for himself whether I was mentally stable enough to remain by his charge, Ashley. Finally, he released his grip, staring down at my glowing skin with awed trepidation.

I turned to see Gunnar and Ashley both facing away from me, averting their gazes from my glowing veins. I shoved my sleeve back down, blocking out the light and plunging the room back into relative darkness.

"I didn't want him to know, Gunnar," Ashley said tiredly, cautiously peering over her shoulder to make sure the light was extinguished.

"He *needed* to know," Gunnar growled, sounding as if he was on the edge of shifting. "*Everyone* needs to know. Because we need the Nate Temple who reacts like *that!*" he growled, violently pointing his armored finger at the large hole in the wall.

Ashley shot me a concerned look, sighing. And I suddenly understood. She'd known how unstable I had become, how easy it was for strong emotions to trigger me. That was why she'd tried to reassure me that her pups were alright by placing my hand against her belly.

And Gunnar had done the opposite, slapping me upside the head with an emotional uppercut.

Good cop, bad cop.

And it had fucking worked, alright.

Even now, I could imagine those two tiny sets of paws pressing into the meat of my fingers as they gave their godfather his first double-werewolf puppy fives.

Ashley had been right, of course. I *was* on edge. Still, something like this...

Yeah. Gunnar also had a point. This situation needed some of that savage, uncontrollable emotion that I had been bottling up for...

One *year*, apparently.

Passion could fuel magic, empowering it exponentially. But twelve months of abstinence was a long enough dry spell to make any predictions on the impending magical fallout from my first foray back into the game more akin to a reckless gamble than any kind of calculable probability.

"Perhaps my husband is now cool-headed enough to explain it all to his best friend—before I fall back asleep," Ashley said with an undertone of warning, even though she sounded like she was about to pass out.

Gunnar grimaced guiltily, nodding. "Of course."

He let out a deep breath to gather his thoughts, plunging the room into a tense, fragile silence.

Which was more restraint than I would have ever been able to achieve in his shoes. Hell, I wouldn't even be coherent if our roles were reversed. My friends would have had to lock me up somewhere that I couldn't hurt anyone—

Somewhere *exactly* like Niflheim. Huh.

I was suddenly very curious how they had ended up here—who, exactly, had chosen this remote destination and why.

Gunnar interrupted my observation, speaking in clipped, precise sentences—as if attempting to keep his own emotions in check. But the rage and utter disgust for the creature who had dared to harm his wife—and possibly his unborn children—was obvious to anyone who knew him well. Probably even to those who didn't.

Gunnar was often a perfect portrait of a balanced life. But right now, he was clenching his fists so tightly that I heard his knuckles cracking and his metal gauntlets creaking. He was alarmingly close to losing his shit and pulling a Nate Temple.

"Like I said," he began, "Thor came to St. Louis a few weeks after Stonehenge, and he wasted no time in threatening or beating down anyone who might know where you, Odin, Alex, or his hammer might be hiding. No one had any real answers, but enough people mentioned Asgard and Fae that he left for a time."

Drake cleared his throat. "We had to physically stop Gunnar from hunting you down in Fae to warn you."

Cowan nodded somberly.

I frowned, thinking back through the foggy haze of my time in Fae. Finally, I shrugged. "There was a brief period where lightning bolts kept striking our camp out of a clear blue sky, but it really wasn't much of an issue. I don't think he ever actually set foot on my mountain," I told them, frowning to myself.

Because...why hadn't he? Sure, I'd been playing with some heavy-duty power, but if Thor was so notoriously, dangerously powerful, shouldn't he have *embraced* that kind of a challenge? Wasn't that one of his most notable tendencies in the old stories? To react first and think later?

I made a mental note to brush up on my Norse mythology before confronting him. It would only take an hour or less to get the necessary information, and that would likely be invaluable in our upcoming fight.

Because I'd decided there was *definitely* going to be a fight. No. An execution.

Gunnar looked pensive, as if he'd hoped for an answer that better explained whatever he had endured. "Thor soon returned to St. Louis even angrier than before. He was blood-crazed, seeming half-drunk with his desire to kill you. And since he'd apparently been unsuccessful in Fae, he started hunting down your known associates, terrorizing anyone who might have something on you that he could use to lure you back to St. Louis."

Gunnar grew silent, his breathing rapidly increasing.

"Faster than I would have thought, his investigation led to me, your old childhood friend."

I leaned closer, clenching my own fists. I didn't need any further motiva-tion to want to kill Thor, but I couldn't help myself. I wanted to make sure I noted every single crime he'd committed, so I could punish him for each of them.

Anything else simply wouldn't do.

I was about to teach the world an abject lesson in judgment—letting the *gods* learn that their capacity for petty violence was nothing compared to the infernal rage of a pissed off *godfather* named Nate Temple.

I realized that I didn't even care if Thor had friends who might strongly object to my decision. I had enough fury to annihilate a whole fucking *pantheon* of godlets right now. If any of them had a problem with that...

Line 'em the fuck up.

"I was forced to flee my pack in order to keep them safe," Gunnar growled. "Otherwise Thor would have killed them all in his search for me. I made a grand announcement where everyone in the supernatural community could see, relinquishing my Alpha status. Then I staged a fight with one of my top wolves so that everyone knew I was gone for good. After I let him win, I walked away, giving up my pack to the new alpha."

My eyes almost popped out of my head at that, and part of my soul crumpled up into a corner, dying slowly. Gunnar had given up his crown for his wife. Even though it had only been a charade, a way to protect as many as possible…wow.

The werewolf king was without a pack.

And I realized that my capacity for violence still had some room to grow.

CHAPTER 15

G unnar continued. "We couldn't risk staying at Falco either. Not with Thor knowing Odin had lived there for decades. Too many people use it for sanctuary these days. Falco keeps them safe, but Thor seemed content to hunt us to the ends of the earth since he couldn't find any of your other friends. Achilles has closed his bar—I heard he now lives exclusively at the Dueling Grounds. In a tent." I arched a brow, stunned. "Raego's mansion was destroyed by a freak lightning storm—everything within the property lines, and not an inch more. The weatherman couldn't shut up about it for weeks. Luckily, Raego managed to flee overseas with his dragons first, abandoning St. Louis entirely," Gunnar said in a flat, clinical tone. "So I wasn't about to let a similar bunker buster lock onto Falco."

I realized I was panting, but Gunnar didn't pull any punches and kept right on going.

"Those are just the highlights. They barely scratch the surface of how bad things really are back home," he added. He grew guarded, holding something back. And as much as I wanted to know what that was, it was blatantly obvious that now wasn't the time to pile on more headaches that weren't directly related to his wife and pups.

"We spent months living like refugees, running from hiding spot to hiding spot, but eventually, we ran out of places to go. And that, of course, is when Thor found us."

I winced. He was right. I'd made so many enemies over the years that I was surprised to hear anyone would risk taking him in—even without Thor banging at their door.

As much guilt as I felt for his story, an insistent part of me continued to repeat another name over and over again in a rhythmic chant.

Odin. Odin. Odin…

Because…this was technically all his fault for stealing—and then hiding —Mjölnir in the first place. Then, in order to keep Excalibur a secret, it had been disguised as a War Hammer that looked suspiciously like Mjölnir— enough to start rumors and draw Thor out to hunt me down.

All without giving me any warning.

In Thor's estimation, I'd stolen not just his hammer, but his father, too. And then I had destroyed the Bifröst. And then his father had chosen to side with me over his son—in front of witnesses.

And the whole goat thing hadn't helped. *Damn it, Alex.*

Then, when he'd come at me in Fae, I'd shrugged him off so casually that he may as well have thrown glitter at me.

I knew that no amount of reasoning was going to get through to the God of Thunder. He'd been a crazy bastard before all of this, so I was betting he was now functioning with a few less screws than usual.

"Despite the obvious dangers and numerous enemies in Fae, they were safer than risking a direct confrontation with Thor. We still had three months before Ashley was due, and Fae could buy us some time—as long as we found *you* before someone else found *us*."

I could sense the frustration in Gunnar's voice. Not just at the situation, but at his inability to hulk out and smash Thor with his bare hands. Not while he was trying to play defense at the same time, keeping Ashley safe. Jesus.

Gunnar lifted his hand to scratch at his beard, drawing attention to his gauntlets. I'd almost forgotten about them, so wrapped up in his story. With a surprised grunt, I realized I recognized them. The armor had belonged to Sir Geraint, the Knightmare who had killed Gunnar and Talon. After I'd brought them back to life, they'd returned the favor, claiming the set of impenetrable armor as a trophy.

Gunnar sensed my attention and nodded proudly, flexing his fist dramatically. I wasn't about to tell him that I'd learned the Knight's name, or how Alex now felt about the whole—

"Odin's ravens found a Knightmare here in Niflheim," he said.

"WHAT?" I shouted.

Gunnar nodded smugly. "They killed him, don't worry. His armor is in the other room if you want to suit up."

I stared at him, shaking my head in disbelief. Hugin and Munin had killed a Knightmare? I suddenly changed my mind about how dangerous the pair were. That had to be the mystery death we'd been concerned about —the third black stone. That was why he hadn't been in St. Louis or Fae. He'd come here. But...why?

Regardless, he was dead now. No big change in the ultimate tally, but it was one less stress to carry on my shoulders, at least. We still had nine Knightmares left for us to deal with, and two of those were still unaccounted for. Were they in another realm, too? If so, why?

"They ate him," Gunnar added, making my stomach curdle. And I suddenly realized why some of the skulls on the ravens' ankles had looked so fresh. One of them had been the Knightmare.

I decided that I would skip the details when I brought Alex the armor. I would just tell him I found our mystery dead Knight. I swallowed audibly. "Where is the rest of this set?" I asked, indicating his gauntlets. "The set from Stonehenge."

"I traded the whole suit to Grimm Tech for some Tiny Balls calibrated to take us to Fae. I told them to find a way to improve the armor, learn how to make something similar, or at least show us a way to break through it. To give us a fighting chance against the other Knightmares still working for Mordred."

Instead of telling him about the one we had killed an hour ago, I leaned forward, suddenly curious. "And?"

He shrugged, lowering his hands. "No idea. They didn't have the armor long before I had to go into hiding. It seems hyper-resilient to elemental attacks. The armor can withstand extreme voltage without transferring the shock to the person wearing it—which is why I stole some of the armor back. I took the gauntlets so that I could at least punch Thor if necessary, and I gave Ashley the breastplate and helmet to protect our babies. I left the rest with them, but that was six months ago, apparently. Maybe they've learned something new since then."

Damn. I'd have to go check for myself, because we definitely needed some better weapons to take down the Knightmares. My magic had rolled right off him earlier, and the only reason Gunnar and Talon had succeeded in killing Sir Geraint was because they'd specifically focused on attacking the straps and buckles holding his armor in place. And they'd attacked two-on-one.

The only other weapons that had been successful in breaking the armor were Grimm's horn, Excalibur, and...I blinked.

Alex had used Sir Geraint's own sword to chop off his hands! How had I missed that? I hoped Talon had scooped up Sir Bedivere's blade when he grabbed the armor earlier. If not, someone would need to go fetch it.

"Did they find a sword with the armor?" I asked.

Gunnar shook his head. "I don't think so."

"Damn." That would have been incredibly helpful.

Something else Gunnar had said suddenly gripped my attention.

I leaned forward. "Tell me about your Tiny Balls." Too late, I heard how it sounded when spoken out loud. Also, Ashley's choking cough made Gunnar growl in a defensive tone.

"They work!" Ashley teased, patting her belly.

CHAPTER 16

*D*rake and Cowan were coughing, hands firmly covering their mouths in an effort to camouflage their laughter.

"Why did they backfire?" I asked, choosing my words more carefully this time. The adolescents quieted down.

Gunnar nodded, clearing his throat. "We were eating dinner around a campfire outside of town when Thor suddenly appeared out of nowhere—similar to when you Shadow Walk, but with a flash of multicolored light, like a rainbow. That's the only reason we survived. The sudden light scared the bejeezus out of us, and we scattered on instinct."

I grimaced, knowing exactly what he was talking about. I didn't have any explanation on how Thor did it—since he wasn't a wizard—but Gunnar's description was exactly how I would have explained his method of travel.

"Drake and Cowan kept Thor distracted while I tried to get Ashley into her breastplate so we could flee."

"Uzis," Drake growled, sounding as if he was smiling nostalgically.

"Shotgun," Cowan murmured, sounding like he felt obligated to come clean.

Gunnar nodded gratefully. "They saved our lives," he admitted. I arched a brow at the unlikely pair and gave them my own nod of appreciation. That was hardcore. Cover fire on the God of Thunder? Ballsy.

Gunnar finally continued. "We tried to escape in the confusion, but the breastplate slipped loose. Thor pounced on the opening, knocking her down to the ground, right onto her belly…" he whispered, panting raggedly.

"With Ashley lying unconscious on the ground, we were ripe for the picking. I couldn't fight Thor and keep her safe at the same time. So…I threw down one of the Tiny Balls, scooped up Ashley and jumped through. Right as he hurled a strangely-colored lightning bolt at us."

I winced, reading between the lines. Gunnar had turned his back on Thor to be a shield for Ashley as they escaped.

"I don't know if it was a design hiccup or if Thor's lightning broke the Gateway, but we landed in a blindingly white world just before the opening winked shut behind us."

I let out a shaking breath, wanting to destroy something with my bare hands. "Blindingly white…" I repeated, studying him nervously. "Literally blinding?" I whispered incredulously. "Is this permanent?"

Ashley interrupted tiredly. "We're not blinded, just hyper-sensitive to light. Odin and Freya don't think it's permanent, but they admit they can't be certain. Gunnar—ironically—seems less sensitive to light than I am, but maybe that's because he already misplaced one eye so had less to lose."

Gunnar growled at his wife's jab. "I'm not three months past due."

"Technicality," Ashley murmured groggily.

"*Factuality*," Gunnar growled. Then he turned to me. "The only way I can think to describe it is staring directly at the sun, but there was no heat. And we couldn't really *move*. Almost like we were trying to walk underwater or through mud. It was all slow motion." He looked frustrated, trying to find the right words. "I remember it taking sixty seconds to be able to move my head enough to look down at Ashley in my arms. We couldn't have been there longer than five minutes before everything shattered."

I stared at him, shaking my head. On an academic level, I was fascinated, but on a personal level, I was horrified. I'd never heard of anything like it.

"I tried opening my eye but I couldn't see anything," Gunnar whispered. "So…I called out to Odin—to his wolves, Geri and Freki, for help."

I arched an eyebrow, entirely caught off guard. Gunnar had called *Norse-One-One*? My suspicion had led me to assume Odin had *conveniently* found Gunnar and Ashley. This changed things.

Kind of. We would just have to—

"No one expected *us* to show up," Cowan rumbled, making me flinch.

Drake nodded. "We hadn't seen Gunnar or Ashley since the night they disappeared. But to us, it had been *six months* of hiding and running from Thor, not five minutes of a rave."

Cowan winced at his partner's phrasing, but nodded at the facts.

"Everyone thought they had died, but we knew better. Unlike the rest of the pack, we were still bonded to them. So we encouraged the rumors, and kept our heads down, knowing they would return at some point."

I nodded approvingly. "Clever."

He shrugged. "Then, two hours ago, we were getting drinks in a bar, laying low in East St. Louis—"

I coughed, especially upon seeing Cowan's sudden guilty flinch, which he tried to cover by shifting from foot-to-foot.

I managed to keep a straight face, knowing exactly which kinds of places that served drinks in East St. Louis. "Of course," I agreed. "Libations are important."

"I didn't say lubrication!" Drake snapped very quickly.

"Libations are drinks," I said, trying not to burst out laughing.

"Oh. Right. Well, we were just laying low."

"Laying low," Cowan agreed, stiffly.

"Anyway," Drake snapped defensively, "I was buying a drink for a nice, young, Ukrainian, college student—"

"Anastasia," Cowan interrupted. "At Hustler—"

"I can't remember where we were," Drake cut in hurriedly, shooting a murderous glare at Cowan's attempted assistance, "but *Anastasia* was telling me her troubles when I suddenly felt my bond to Gunnar practically screaming at me. I dropped my drink, slapped some cash down, and we jumped in our truck."

Cowan nodded somberly. "We didn't even get Anastasia's phone number," he murmured.

Drake coughed, staring daggers at his partner. "We *really* need to work on your sidekick skills," he muttered under his breath, before turning back to me. "Anyway, we sensed Gunnar had returned, and that he was close—just on the other side of the bridge—and that he was in pain."

"We found them under the Arch, of all places," Cowan added. "When we arrived, we saw Odin and Freya picking up our Alpha and his wife and..." he trailed off uneasily.

Drake spoke up. "We may have overreacted, not realizing they were allies. Until we saw Odin's wolves. They were gloriously terrifying," he said, sounding as if he was speaking of his childhood heroes.

I grunted. They hadn't impressed me all that much.

"Once we realized we were all on the same side, Odin said he knew a place where Thor might not find us—at least until we figured out our next move." And he shot a finger gun at me, clucking his tongue. "Hello, Mr. Next Move."

I frowned, turning from one face to the next. "I feel like I just watched an impersonation of those guys in *Half Baked*."

Drake and Cowan folded their arms unhappily, and in sync. I turned my back on them with a sigh, thinking over the story. "Odin sent for me?" I asked, frowning.

"I did," Gunnar said. "Once we settled in here, I told Odin we weren't going anywhere else until someone brought you here."

"To be fair," Ashley cut in dryly, "I believe it was your lady wife who refused Freya's help until we had a chance to speak with Nate."

Gunnar nodded. "That's what I said."

Everyone turned to stare at him.

Finally, he sighed, waving a gauntleted hand. "Fine," he muttered before folding his arms stubbornly, mirroring Drake and Cowan.

Ashley was smirking at her husband, and I couldn't help but wince. Because her smile stretched her already gaunt face so thin that it looked like her skin was on the verge of tearing.

She turned back to me. "I allowed her to do a cursory check to make sure I wasn't in immediate danger before I commanded them to find you."

I glanced down at her belly, unable to make the math work. "You don't look six months pregnant, like when you went into the Gateway. And if six months passed you by, why aren't you *twelve* months pregnant?" I asked rhetorically. "Because right now, you look like you're somewhere in the middle, like you might be ready to go any minute," I said as kindly as possible. "Shouldn't you have already delivered?" I asked uneasily.

She nodded. "That's what concerned Freya—the time discrepancy of my pregnancy. She believes that my body was in stasis in that other place, and that it is now attempting to catch up—that six months of development are going to happen in a rapid, painful, fast-forward. A *special delivery*, as it were," she added in a lame attempt at humor.

My eyebrows threatened to jump right off my forehead. "How quickly are we talking?" I asked, feeling panicked.

Gunnar grunted. "No idea, but my hair has grown an inch since we arrived." I blinked at him incredulously, unable to make my mouth work. "Which is why we wanted to talk to you. To get a second opinion, if you will."

Part of me very seriously considered walking back outside to kill Odin. If he thought Gunnar and Ashley had died six months ago, why hadn't anyone come to tell me? Unless…they had also known Gunnar and Ashley weren't dead—just like Drake and Cowan.

I narrowed my eyes at Gunnar. "You are asking what I think of Odin? Do you mean the man who created this whole mess in the first place? Thor's *father?* I don't think you need to ask me how I feel about my dear butler," I growled. "We already know he's a talented liar."

"So…you don't trust him?" Gunnar asked, sounding troubled.

I cursed, waving a hand violently. "I don't know, Gunnar! I'm just pointing out the facts."

Gunnar nodded, his eye flicking towards Ashley. "She's too weak for a natural birth, according to Freya. She's barely hanging on as it is."

I winced, really thinking about the biology of the whole situation. Mothers ate more food while they were growing, and that was stretched out over *months.* For Ashley to catch up so rapidly, she would need to eat significantly more than most mothers. To match the number of calories a pregnant mother would eat in three months, and to do so in a fraction of the time…

It was no wonder she looked so frail. The twins were literally killing her. And that wasn't even taking into account whatever the broken Gateway might have done to her. Or Niflheim, for that matter. Or what complications that Thor's initial blow to Ashley—and her falling down on her stomach—might have caused.

No wonder Freya had seemed so frantic.

I turned to Gunnar, trying to mask my concern. Because I had absolutely *no* idea what to do.

CHAPTER 17

*A*shley coughed weakly, and I had to force myself to keep a straight face, hearing the rattling sound in her lungs. "My shifter blood gives me heightened healing, so that's helping a lot. But Freya is still concerned about nutrition and calories—that I won't be able to feed my babies…" she trailed off, letting out a heart-wrenching sob.

I grimaced, feeling sick to my stomach. "I understand," I said softly. "That was my first thought, too."

She nodded, struggling to regain her composure. "She's amazed that I'm still alive, and with Thor obviously hunting us, it's not safe for me out there. She isn't just my doctor, Nate. She is also my bodyguard, as are Odin and his pets."

I growled angrily, liking that even less. But it made sense why they'd been so super-charged. Odin had commanded them to cut loose in order to keep Ashley safe.

That was something, at least.

Drake and Cowan also growled, their feelings hurt.

She waved a hand, indicating the pair. "For all intents and purposes, Drake and Cowan were banished along with us. No one knows where we went—but you are not the only one lacking in the trust department, Nate," she said dryly. "We have Drake and Cowan—and a fistful of Tiny Balls—"

I did laugh at that, but quickly muffled it. "Sorry."

Ashley rolled her eyes. "What I'm trying to say is that we are not relying strictly on the Norse. There are too many suspicious coincidences—not even counting the fact that Thor has also been causing problems for Odin in Asgard. We brought our own guards, and told Odin and Freya that we would only accept their help if you approved it."

I frowned, wondering what kinds of problems Thor had with Asgard. Then the rest of her words hit me. I froze, opening my mouth silently like a fish on dry land.

She was literally leaving the ultimate decision of her care up to me? I had assumed that she'd meant it figuratively—that they wanted to talk to me before *they* decided what to do. That was an incredible show of faith, and a level of responsibility that I didn't think I could accept. Because if I guessed wrong...

I shuddered. I would never—ever—be able to forgive myself. I would never be able to look them in the eye. Guilt would crush me. Definitively.

I finally cleared my throat, staring at her. "You can't ask me to do that, Ashley," I said in a low tone, staring down at her belly—at the two pups inside. The ones I had high fived. "I'm not a parent. I'm not qualified to tell you what to do. I can give you my best guess—which will be backed by every piece of knowledge I have about the players involved, but—"

"Which we will then use as the basis of our decision," she challenged, cutting me off. "Calling it what it really is—your decision—is a great burden, but I can't lie to you, Nate. I don't know what else to do, who else to trust. You're always the one to weather us through the storms." She flung out a hand, pointing at Gunnar. "You brought him back from *death*, Nate! Who *else* do we have to make decisions like this?"

I shook my head in denial. "That was just—"

"You know Odin—and Dean. The good and the bad. And you're objective. You're not related—"

I snarled, instantly furious. "Not *related*?" I roared, making the three male werewolves jump in surprise. I heard claws snap out, but I didn't care. "Woman, those kids are as much mine as they are yours, regardless of *blood*. I will crush the world myself if it would keep them safe!" I shouted, making the very walls shake dust down upon us. Ashley was smiling at me, licking her lips satisfactorily. I was panting, and my skin felt like it was on fire. I knew that beneath the clothes, my skin was likely flaring with golden light. I didn't care about that right now.

All I could think about was keeping those two little pups safe. My helpless, innocent, beautiful godchildren. I didn't even care that Ashley had been poking at me on purpose.

"I think…" Drake said very softly, drawing every eye in the room, "that is exactly what she is trying to say." I glared at him, grinding my teeth.

"Right now, I can barely stop myself from shifting," he said. "I'm giving it everything I've got, and I'm humble enough to admit that you fucking terrify me."

Cowan nodded rapidly, his jaw locked shut and his shoulders shaking from the urge to shift and protect Ashley—from *me*.

Drake continued. "Even knowing you're on my side, on her side, my every molecule is fighting to make me shift because you are just too fucking dangerous, man. To know that you are on our side only matters to my brain, but my body only sees a threat that would take all three of us to even *survive*."

He turned to Cowan.

"What about you, big guy? You see any chance of the three of us taking him on and winning? Or is even survival a fool's gambit? A whisper of a hope?"

Cowan cleared his throat, not hesitating. "No chance. I agree entirely. If it wasn't for my oath to Ashley and Gunnar, I would go for a walk. Right. Now." He turned to look at me, wincing apologetically. "Just to get away from the power slamming into me from your emotions. I feel like I'm standing before a storm."

And I realized his legs were locked into a semi-squat and his hands were balled fists. He wasn't exaggerating.

"He's actually kind of a pushover once you get to know him," Gunnar rasped through gritted teeth, obviously lying. He met my eyes and gave a brief nod.

I took a deep breath, dialing down on my rage. And the male werewolves visibly relaxed in a chorus of gasps, looking as if they wanted nothing more than to pass out on the floor.

"More importantly," Ashley said in a stern voice directed at her husband, "Gunnar needs you, and *I need him*." A faint sob escaped her lips. "Calvin and Makayla will need their fathers. Both of them, even their habitually tardy, scarily-powerful, fairy godfather." She smiled weakly. "I need you to teach Makayla your emotional fire. Your passion. If she adopts even half of it, I'll curse you until my last breath," she admitted, shaking her head. "But I'll *bless* you for it, too. Because she will *need* it. You will show her what a *real* prince is. Not one of those flawless, lifeless, Disney figures, but a man who knows his wild side, a man who knows his flaws, a man who has defeated everything that has ever gotten in his way—even, and especially, his own *self*!"

Her voice rang out, and I saw she was shaking weakly.

Gunnar took a step closer, but she flung up her hand, halting him. He obeyed, clenching his jaw.

Then she turned those fiery eyes back to me. "And you better teach Calvin how to slay monsters and swoon women. How to become his own darkly just prince. A man in command of his demons. A man who holds their leashes draped over his forearm, daring them to try escaping as he sips a cocktail and flirts at the bar."

I nodded eagerly, feeling a strange, anticipatory smile split my cheeks at the thought of me spoiling the twins rotten. "Yeah, Gunnar only knows how to slay, not swoon."

He scowled in my general direction—a few inches off, to be honest.

I turned back to Ashley. "Okay. You want me to teach Thor a lesson since you're both blind and worthless." Gunnar growled instinctively, but I patted him on the shoulder, letting him know it was a joke since he couldn't see. "I'll clean up this mess the only way I know how—by making an even bigger mess for them."

She smiled, letting out a breath of relief. "You always do. Even when everyone else doubts, you always pull through with some miracle. Some last-ditch effort to turn the tide." She studied my general vicinity intensely for a moment. "You are our last hope, Nate. Your best friend needs you…"

I felt a tear fall down my cheek. "Defiance," I whispered, reciting the word that signified a promise woven into the soul. I said it for myself, but Gunnar growled his acknowledgment. It was a promise that I would keep them safe, no matter what.

Which meant I had some trash to take out. Thor first, and then Mordred, because both were threats to Gunnar and Ashley and their kids. Thor, directly, and Mordred, indirectly. Because if I didn't make good on my promise to Anubis, he would demand his two souls back.

Gunnar and Talon would die.

I shivered at an unbidden thought. I'd also just met two new souls ready to enter the world—Calvin and Makayla.

I shuddered at the macabre thought, deciding Ashley and Gunnar had enough to worry about without me bringing up the Anubis situation.

I nodded stiffly. "I'm going to go find out the good doctor's intentions. Right the fuck now."

Gunnar glanced in his wife's direction. "Sleep, my sweet. Don't mind the screams you're about to hear."

She mumbled something so softly and lucidly that I wasn't sure she was even awake, but her dazed words set my heart on fire.

"Screams..." she murmured groggily, "like sweet lullabies are the agonized cries as the blood of your enemy sprays the skies."

Yeah. Whether that was an actual quote or some super-pregnant-mother-level of darkness, I wasn't sure.

Either suited me just fine. I had my theme song. Now to go talk to Doogie Howser about his house call business.

"Wait here, Wulfric," I said, dusting off my hands to reveal a flicker of the glowing ichor in my veins—the substance that signified me having the power to kill a god. I'd thought I'd used it all up or that it had faded away without use, but to see it suddenly appear now...coincidences could sometimes work in your favor. "I intend to light him up, and you can barely handle a nightlight. I'll have answers in less than five minutes. Or I'll have a body for you to put on a pyre."

He didn't seem happy about me excluding him, but I felt better knowing he was here to keep Ashley safe. And he'd done enough already. I began striding out of the room, clenching my fists open and closed. I made it to the door before I paused at a random thought. Then I turned to glance over my shoulder.

"Does anyone know what day it is?"

"I think it's Saturday," Cowan answered. "Why?"

I smiled wickedly, turning back to the door. "Good. That means tomorrow can be a new holiday. Thor dies on Bloody Funday." And I followed it up with a dark chuckle straight from my heart.

He already had one day of the week named after him—Thursday. I would give him another—and hope that he didn't pull a Jesus on me, rising back to life three days later for a rematch.

The werewolves growled excitedly behind me as I made my way to the exit.

I was still counting the three-day thing absently, wondering if that would make Thor rise back to life on a Wednesday or a Thursday. Wednesday was named after Odin. Maybe I should just kill both of them and make a back-to-back holiday just to be certain.

Either way, I would wait by Thor's corpse just to make sure.

First, it was time to deal with Thor's daddy and get some gods damned answers from the damned Norse gods.

CHAPTER 18

I strolled outside, letting the door slam shut behind me.

Everyone turned to stare as I walked a few paces from the door and stopped. Even Odin, who had finished his astral ride-along with Hugin and Munin, or whatever the hell he'd been doing when he'd zoned out.

I ignored them, and took a calming, meditative breath. Then another.

Then, I glanced over at my rainbow staff, scratching my chin thoughtfully. Finally, I shook my head and turned to find everyone fidgeting nervously.

Except for Alice. She was sitting on the ground with her arms wrapped around her knees, her chin buried into the crook of her elbow. I knew her well enough to know she was grinning toothily but concealing it from view. Being a Seer, she had noticed what was really going on in my mind, not just what I was physically projecting.

The theatrics.

What I was physically projecting was still genuine, but for reasons not so obvious at first glance. I had secret, ulterior motives as well—just like everyone else in my life. Because I was sick and tired of being the only one not hiding secrets. They wanted to play games? Fine. I could play games, too.

Starting right now.

I considered my plan for a few silent moments before turning to face my target. "Hey, Odin," I called out. "A word."

Odin nodded warily, absently waving off Freya's open concern with a tired, long-familiar gesture. He had taken off his pointy hat at some point, but I didn't see a bag of any kind to indicate where he had put it. Odin had long, wavy silver hair, and it was tied into long, thick braids on either side of his head. The ends of the braids were capped in melted silver with unknown runes stamped into them.

Freya folded her arms and shot me a flat, nervous look as Odin made his way over. She definitely assumed I was up to something, meaning she was either wiser than I thought, or overly judgmental. Either way, she was the smarter of the two for it.

Thankfully, Gunnar hadn't argued to join me for this. It would have really killed my vibe to have my one-eyed, service werewolf stumble and fall—since he now needed his own service animal. Gunnar was also prone to volunteering himself as my moral conscience at the worst imaginable times. As Odin approached, my mind ran through Gunnar's story about the broken Gateway, Thor, Mordred, the ravens killing a Knightmare in Niflheim, and everything else that had happened in my absence.

Odin finally reached me, and I studied him for a few tense moments, not speaking as I considered how many problems we faced thanks to his meddling. But how Odin had *also* gone out of his way to help my friends when they'd been in very real danger.

There were just so many things I wanted to say to him...

I hauled back and punched him right in the nose as hard as I could, since I was a devout student in the Tao of Fisticuffs. The old adage that actions speak louder than words was hard to refute when foreign knuckles were indenting your internal hard bits.

I felt cartilage crunch beneath my knuckles, but my face remained as cool as a winter pond at dawn. Odin, on the other hand, staggered back, clutching his nose in shock.

I stared down at the fresh blood dripping down the back of my hand. Then I feigned surprise upon seeing the golden light peeking out from my wrists beneath the cuffs of my shirt. I grunted, rolling up my sleeves. "Would you look at that," I said as if talking to myself, but loud enough for everyone to hear. "Looks like the godkiller is back for an encore."

Geri and Freki lunged forwards instinctively. Both Freya's frantic shrieks for them to restrain me and Odin's stuffy-nosed commands for them to stand down were ignored by the powerful killing machines. They saw only that their master was in pain, meaning the time for half-measures was over. Without looking at them, I flung my hands out like I was shaking water from my fingertips.

And unseen webs of air struck their legs like bolas, tripping them, trapping them, and then sending them crashing and tumbling to the ground—their own momentum turned against them.

"Science," I said dramatically, wiggling my fingers as the wolves skidded faces-first across the rubble. The hog-tied wolves finally came to a stop, and instantly began snapping their teeth at the unseen bonds. I grunted at their persistent efforts. "Good luck with that, pups."

Then I reared back and punched Odin again—in his good eye—even harder than my nose-breaker. The god cursed, stumbled, and started to fall —and his wife and wolves began to howl. I courteously caught him up in a cord of air and lifted him back upright like I was a concerned citizen.

Except I was actually a Bad Samaritan and waiting with an uppercut to the god's chin that knocked the poor bastard clear off his feet and had him horizontal in the air. The force of the blow even tore away his eyepatch, slingshotting it directly at Grimm—who somehow managed to catch it on his horn. My murdercorn let out a triumphant cheer like a bachelor catching a bride's garter at a wedding.

I shook my head at the odds, and then heard Odin's back strike the ground behind me. Judging by the loud expulsion of breath, it had knocked the air from his lungs. I turned around to see him lying on the ground, staring dazedly upwards with a now partially swollen eye, gasping to catch his breath.

The god's face was a mask of blood.

And the godkiller laughed—a raucous, merciless sound that mocked the stunned silence of the dusty creek bed.

Because the godkiller was learning, adapting, evolving.

No one—except perhaps Alice—realized the true importance of what was happening right now. Which made it all the more effective—on so many levels.

Although a very loud, insistent part of me wanted to continue the show —pummeling Odin into a can of Spam—beating down a god in front of others was actually the smallest benefit of what I was currently doing. Was it rewarding and fulfilling?

Ohmygodkiller, yes.

Not my ultimate purpose, though.

My true intent had been to put both the god's resolve and strength to the test. Dean would know and understand why I was beating him down.

Odin, on the other hand, was more likely to get angry and respond to my disrespect with hyper-violence.

I needed to know which mind was controlling this meat suit—where this god truly stood, and what his ultimate motivations were. The cold, bitter, bloody truth.

And I also needed to know his strength—why he appeared to be running on a low battery.

"Heh." I chuckled, studying the god's blood painting my knuckles. "Battery," I murmured under my breath, smiling briefly at the double entendre. I needed to understand the truth—what was really going on here—because my friends' lives were on the line.

And nothing spoke the truth like knuckles to the teeth.

The wolves were snarling, actually chewing—and crushing—the loose stones that littered the ground in their attempt to break my bonds. It was futile, but it was entertaining to let them think they had a chance—to watch their hope slowly bleed out following each failed escape attempt.

Freya cursed, whipping her hand into her pouch to scoop up some magic powder. I couldn't have any of that nonsense.

Not knowing what she was actually capable of, or where she drew her magic from, I instinctively tapped into my Fae magic to call out to the skies above, introducing me to the currents of power residing high above this strange realm.

Almost instantly, I found an impressionable, adolescent bolt of lightning living within a perfectly white cloud. So I dared it to run away from home and come down to Niflheim to see if it was brave enough to kiss a goddess' fingers.

Luckily for me, the adolescent lightning bolt was bored and prone to mischief, so it eagerly accepted my challenge.

The concussive blast struck Freya's pouch with a blinding flash—obliterating it—and sent her flying ten feet. The explosive power even ripped her toga free from her shoulder.

Even Grimm cursed in surprise, eyeing the white clouds with concern—since none of them had looked stormy. Alice squealed, darting behind the potty-mouthed pony to hide.

I silently thanked the teenaged lightning bolt and then urged it to go back home before it got into any more trouble.

Then I turned to check on Freya. I didn't feel guilty about striking a woman. Not even remotely. For multiple reasons.

Primarily, it was impossible to look at my world with that kind of innocent bias or misplaced courtesy. These two beings were *gods*. The male and female identity was way too simple of a category to limit them to. Unlike with humanity, gender didn't matter in the slightest.

Because gods could do impossible things like giving birth to themselves, sleeping with swans and horses to conceive bizarre animal-human hybrids, and all sorts of other sordid, deviant acts—which pretty much contradicted any arguments trying to sort them into such limited definitions as *male* or *female*.

It was akin to having a problem with hitting redheaded gods but being totally cool with hitting blonde-haired gods. Utterly ridiculous.

In fact, gods would frequently try to use their sex—both figuratively and literally—*against* mortals.

I'm talking to you, Zeus and Aphrodite, ya' kinky weirdos.

And besides, most goddesses knew of a man's deeply-ingrained, almost instinctive penchant to avoid physical confrontation with a woman—and they would shamelessly exploit that weakness faster than a man could whimper *Lorena Bobbitt*.

In summary…

Gods. Were. Not. Like. Us.

And we humans needed to be careful about how much of a leash we gave the kinky deities.

So, I had chosen to hit Freya as hard as I hit Odin. Maybe even harder—that lightning bolt had been eager to impress.

Freya scrambled to her feet with a stunned look—her hair sticking straight up, and her scorched, dangling toga strap revealing an impressive display of perfectly smooth, curved flesh. I noticed this out of my peripheral vision, simply wanting to make sure she wasn't about to attempt another attack. I wasn't an ogler on the worst of days, but I definitely never ogled another man's wife. Not *knowingly*, anyway.

But it was fair to say that I was an avid art enthusiast, always eager to broaden my horizons on the aesthetic of the human form—strictly for academic furtherance.

Geri and Freki continued to rage against their unseen restraints, snapping their teeth and snarling at me. I dismissed them with a flick of my wrist that sent them sliding back another ten paces. I noticed Odin climbing back to his feet, so I crouched and spun, kicking to sweep his legs out from under him. The timing was perfect, and he grunted at the unexpected attack before striking the rocky ground hard enough to gasp—again.

I crouched over him, and waved my glowing arm before his bloody face. Deep purple bruises painted the flesh below his functioning eye and his nose was a crooked, flattened ruin. Where his other eye had once been was a scorched, melted crater—the scars seeming to gleam with golden flakes of metal deeply embedded into the pale tissue.

I'd have to ask him about it some other time.

Because what I had in mind was an altogether different kind of conversation.

CHAPTER 19

I cleared my throat. "It's come to my attention that your son, Thor, is an asshole of truly epic proportions. In fact, he gives honorable assholes like me a bad rep. Hitting a pregnant woman is a death sentence if I'm within a one-hundred-mile radius, but that distance rule doesn't even apply if it happens in my city. And the sentence changes to slow torture if that woman is my best friend's wife."

He nodded stiffly, ignoring the blood pouring from his nose. He did glance pointedly at the ichor glowing in my veins—the ichor I had earned by killing my first goddess, Athena. "You should probably do something about it, godkiller," he growled. Then he shifted his attention to my eyes, letting me see his conviction and utter lack of emotional response for condemning his son—no fear and no anger.

I narrowed my eyes. "Don't try getting into my head, Odin. This is not a game to me. If I'm willing to do this to you, the man who helped raise me, just *imagine* what I would do to Thor."

Again, Odin showed no emotional reaction other than firm conviction —judgment.

I tried to keep a tight rein on my fury, but I was getting caught up in my own theatrics. I'd been hoping to learn something useful—to find some emotion to manipulate when it came to their son. Because I was definitely going to kill Thor, and it was always helpful to know who might take particular offense to that. Parents were usually a sure bet.

But it sure seemed like these parents had never learned the word *unconditional.* Which was surprising. Even if upset or furious about his son's actions, it was hard to believe Odin had no qualms about me killing Thor. Deep down, a father had to feel *something* for his *son*, right?

Maybe I hadn't disrespected him enough.

"Fight me!" I shouted at him, punching him in the ribs. He wheezed painfully, coughing a few times, but he didn't try to escape or fight back.

"He can't!" Freya screamed, sounding torn between fury and fear —of me.

"Of course he can!" I snapped, not breaking eye contact with Odin. "He just needs to let his fingertips kiss his palms, and then throw his knuckles at my face." I shot her an arctic glare, slowly showing her the motion with my fist. "Like this." And I punched him in the good eye—again—rocking his head to the side this time.

He gasped, but still, he didn't fight back. His hands rested at his sides, his fingers loose and utterly relaxed. They hadn't even twitched when I hit him —I'd been watching closely.

"No!" Freya begged. "He *can't!*" she repeated, sounding desperate as she enunciated the last word. "He's giving all his power to the ravens and wolves. Thor is attempting to take Asgard for himself. We are on the run, too!"

She didn't verbalize the word *fool* at the end of her shriek, but her tone had screamed it.

I blinked, turning to stare down at Odin. He nodded tiredly, confirming Freya's claim. "I wasn't going to tell you, knowing you would instantly be suspicious. I was just going to get out of your way and let you handle Ashley's assailant however you so choose," he admitted, his swollen eye flicking towards the vine door where Ashley and her retinue of werewolves waited. "With my throne in limbo, killing him is my prerogative but..." he trailed off, twisting his head to the side to spit out some blood. "I wanted to give you a gift to make up for...well, everything," he said, averting his eye.

And I sensed the genuine shame residing there.

A less cynical person might consider this a sweet gesture, but to me, it just felt like a setup. I could tell that he fully meant what he'd said, but that didn't mean he didn't have other, perhaps more important, reasons to let things play out this way. Unspoken benefits.

I mentally ran through the scenario: Thor challenges Odin's crown, I swoop in and kill Thor, giving Odin back his throne. I'm immediately branded as Odin's enforcer—the Catalyst, Nate Temple, the godkiller, was Odin's personal hitman.

It was too convenient—like every successful con.

But Odin's admission also lined up, and...Odin hadn't once fought back as I beat him half to hell. I frowned at a new thought. Gungnir was missing. Perhaps Odin was impotent without it, and just happened to hear about the attack on Ashley—since they'd only returned a few hours ago.

Otherwise, Odin should have already solved the Thor problem. Gungnir was obviously a big part of whatever was going on. I didn't suspect he was necessarily impotent without it, because he'd supersized his pets just fine.

Had he done that to protect himself or to increase the number of guards over Ashley?

Altruism or self-preservation?

I studied him for any hint of deception, watching as his injuries—ever so slowly—began to heal. Except it was almost at the speed of a shifter, not a god's self-healing abilities. Was he healing slower as a result of his own weakness or was it due to my godkiller inflicted wounds?

"I don't believe in coincidences," I finally told him.

He sighed, sounding frustrated. Then he tonelessly recited every suspicion that had just run through my mind. Once finished, he paused long enough to spit out some more blood before meeting my eyes. "I don't particularly care what you believe," he said dryly. "Either way you want to look at it, Ashley will die without my wife's help. Freya is an incredibly talented healer, but even her skills might not be enough to save this pregnancy."

I gripped him by the shirt, clenching his robes in a fist, considering hitting him again. This time for fun.

Freya piped up in a lecturing tone. "She—"

"ENOUGH!" I roared, flinging out my hand. I hummed a single tone and the air solidified around her, although I left her the ability to move freely, if she so chose.

Let me explain.

My humming tone had surrounded her with translucent bars of air that were stronger than steel and sharper than a surgeon's scalpel.

And the points were kissing her flesh.

So I had given her the gift of allowing her to suffer the consequences of her own actions. Something I felt all gods needed to learn.

She stared at me with wide, horrified eyes, doing her best not to breathe too deeply. "Quiet, Freya," I said in a much calmer tone. "I don't like to repeat myself, and I don't remember asking for your opinion. Your husband and I are having a disagreement. I didn't start this disagreement. He did. I'm just here to finish it. You have a problem with that, then you have a problem with your husband. Not me. Right, Odin?" I asked.

His shoulders slumped and he nodded warily, obviously concerned for his wife. "Yes. Freya, dear, please stand down. I brought his ire upon my shoulders. I don't blame him for his actions right now. In fact, I believe I deserve worse."

"I'm happy to hear you say that, *Dean*." I leaned closer, lifting him up a few inches by the collar of his shirt. "Really," I whispered. Then I released him, slamming the back of his head into the ground.

Freya let out a soft breath. "O-okay."

I hummed a different tune and the trap of invisible spears evaporated. I didn't turn to look as she let out a deeper breath of relief. I also sensed her hurriedly retying her toga.

"And to clarify," I began, looking down at him, "there are no rules in war. You would do the same or worse in my position, correct?"

He nodded with a faint smirk, revealing his bloody teeth.

"Cool. See how much easier this is when everyone cooperates?" I asked with false cheer.

Freya was silent, but her eyes were white-hot nails pressing into the back of my neck. I wasn't too worried about it.

I studied Odin, thinking furiously. "So you siphoned your power to your pets because no one can track you that way?" I asked, wondering if I should believe his claim or not.

He nodded. "Yes. Direct use of my power might attract unwanted attention." I didn't respond, choosing to maintain my doubtful glare. "The power Freya must use to heal Ashley will leave her weak and vulnerable. It might even kill her. She needs protection and, possibly, some of my power in order to remain strong enough to deliver Ashley's pups. I and my pets can hopefully funnel that power into her without Thor noticing."

I glanced over at the tied-up wolves, pointedly and silently letting him realize how easily I had ensnared them. "Guards," I said flatly, obviously unimpressed.

Odin scowled back at me. "You're different," he argued defensively. "You're a godkiller."

"Speaking of your esteemed guards, where are the ravens?"

"Deterring nosy residents from this place and watching out for any new Asgardian arrivals in Niflheim."

I arched an eyebrow, wondering why he hadn't mentioned the Knightmare they had killed. "You expecting company? I thought you said Niflheim was safe..."

He locked eyes with me. "Nowhere is safe, especially not Niflheim, and especially not when Thor is on the hunt. They killed one of Mordred's Knights a while back," he added, "though they never learned why he was here in the first place," he finally admitted. "Niflheim is simply safer than any other place I had access to on short notice. We've been hiding here for some time," he said, jerking his chin at Freya.

"Until we gave up our hut to your friends, of course," Freya said, and her tone was more concerned than critical.

I found myself wondering if the Knightmare had been hunting my friends or Odin, but a sound from the vine door drew my attention. I looked up to see Gunnar and the other werewolves standing in the open doorway not ten feet away. Ashley had a cloth wound around her head, covering her eyes, and Drake and Cowan each had a hand resting on her shoulders, supporting her.

The Knightmare's breastplate rested on the ground beside her, and she held the helmet in the crook of her arm.

Gunnar also had a cloth tied around his head, covering his eye. He stood apart from the others, and in that darkened doorway, wearing the Knightmare's gauntlets, his big barrel chest heaving steadily, he looked like a man ready and willing to break the world.

Drake and Cowan stared wide-eyed at the bloody Odin—and me kneeling over him with bloody fists. They looked disgusted, letting me know—too late—that they'd heard enough of the conversation to paint me as the big, stinky asshole.

"I never wanted to intrude," Ashley said. "Nate could take us to the Armory, since I'm *certain* he feels *terrible* for overreacting. Even if he had the right intentions. *Right, Nate?*"

In case anyone was wondering—and I'm talking to the dudes, here—it wasn't actually a question. It was as much of a warning as the *click-clack* of a sniper loading a round into his war boner.

And even with her head covered, Ashley's *look* was still better than Freya's could ever hope to be.

I stared at Ashley, surprised that I hadn't considered the Armory. Then I remembered all the dangerous, ridiculously powerful artifacts and weapons stored there—the items I was supposed to keep hidden from all peoples. Taking Ashley to the Armory would mean me also granting Odin and Freya —two peoples—access to the no-people-place.

While I left to hunt Thor down like a rabid dog.

Two gods left unsupervised in a supernatural nuclear weapons cache. Then Ashley spoke up, sweetening the deal.

"But I will only go to the Armory if you take Gunnar with you, Nate. The two of you will hunt Thor to the ends of the earth. I wish to hear his cries before I hear the cries of my own babies."

I cursed under my breath, feeling an icy shiver roll down my spine at her tone. "No offense, but Gunnar won't be of much help in his current condition," I said, not pointing out that Gunnar had shifted his attention, using the sound of my voice to better lock onto my location.

Proving my point.

Gunnar stepped forward. "That won't be an issue," he growled, facing me. He looked and sounded as calm as I'd ever seen him—and as if he'd been expecting my argument.

A coordinated assault, the bastards. "Please tell me how that's not an issue," I said dryly.

He nodded. "I want to become a Horseman, brother."

Alice gasped. I just stared back at my best friend in stunned disbelief. Well. I hadn't expected *that*. My satchel suddenly felt very heavy under the strain of the three Horseman's Masks concealed within.

Ashley was nodding, but Drake and Cowan looked like they were about to throw up. So, they hadn't been informed of Gunnar's plan. Interesting.

I opened my mouth to argue, and that's when I noticed a horizontal column of roiling black clouds at the edge of the horizon, miles away—a steamroller of darkness as wide and long as a skyscraper on its side.

But it was approaching fast.

Well, shit.

CHAPTER 20

I stared at the impending storm, knowing it couldn't mean anything good. Maybe it was common enough in Niflheim—like the fog I had expected to see when first arriving here. Although *fog* seemed like a weak, watered down explanation for such a titanic force of darkness.

Everyone stared at the distant storm with varying levels of trepidation, but no one screamed *Thorzilla!* before bolting for cover. So I took that as a somewhat favorable sign.

It looked like we had a while before it would become a real concern, anyway. Finally, I turned to Gunnar, weighing my options. My very crummy options.

I'd inadvertently been roped into forming a second band of Four Horsemen: Hope, Despair, Justice, and Absolution. I'd taken Hope for myself but had yet to give the other Masks away—knowing the hefty price tag that came with the job.

Most likely, a target on your back and a discounted price on your future bodybag.

Because the world already had the Biblical Four Horsemen: Death, War, Conquest, and Pestilence. And when there were two teams, it usually implied a confrontation was imminent.

So, I'd been reluctant to pass out team jerseys, not wanting my future brothers and sisters to die as a direct result of my shitty gift. Gunnar, the big idiot, was obviously not thinking clearly. He was soon to be a dad, and he wanted to accept a freaking Mask? I'll admit that I had considered him for a Mask—until he'd gone and humped Ashley into submission.

On the other hand, the clock was ticking. Bad things would happen if I didn't hand out them out soon. My own Mask was severely damaged from fighting Mordred, and I was fairly certain it wouldn't be wearable until I finally handed out the remaining three—because they were designed to work in groups of four, drawing power back and forth from each other.

Still...

"No, Gunnar," I finally said, shaking my head adamantly. "I won't let you do that."

He was silent for about five seconds—typically a good negotiation tactic. Not on me, though, and not on something like this. "With Ashley safe in the Armory, I can finally fight back. *We* can fight back," Gunnar argued, sounding eager enough to lick his lips. "I want a Mask. Now. I'm finished waiting for you to ask. This will make me a better protector."

Ashley was nodding her head. "If not Gunnar, then who?" she demanded. "You two were *born* for this. And you know—whether you want to admit it or not—that Gunnar will stand beside you even *without* a Mask. Denying him this will only serve to put him in a weaker position when you need him most."

I shook my head, wanting to hit something. She was right, but that didn't make her solution viable. Glancing down at Odin, I sighed, and then climbed to my feet. He'd been so silent that I'd forgotten he was there.

"Can I have my eyepatch back?" he asked in a flat tone as he climbed to his feet.

I thought about the question and finally shook my head. "It's Grimm's now. You'll have to ask him—and you will abide by his decision." I turned to my unicorn. "Hey, Grimm?"

He had been slowly swinging his head in circles to twirl the eyepatch around his horn. "Yeah?" he asked, slowing down so that the eyepatch stuck to his nose with a wet *splat* as he looked at me.

"Don't give it to him."

"Cool." And then my unicorn resumed twirling the eyepatch around his horn.

Odin muttered something under his breath, but quieted when I glanced back at him. He turned his back on me, scowling at the distant storm. I watched him for a moment, making sure he didn't see any malicious portent in the weather. He kicked a few rocks, muttering under his breath about his eyepatch, so I left him to pout.

I turned back to Ashley, considering her argument—which had been entirely true. Gunnar *would* be by my side, even if I commanded him to leave.

"No. His most important job is to be your husband—"

"NO!" she snapped furiously, making Drake and Cowan stiffen in surprise. "His number one *job* is to be a *role model* for his *children*. That is the new pathway to my heart. I already know he would lift the world for *me*. Now, I need to know that he would destroy the world for his *children*. Calvin and Makayla need to know what their father is capable of." She paused, gritting her teeth. "The *world* needs to see what Wulfric is capable of. That the Randulfs will *never* be fucked with—gods or otherwise will cower in terror at the sound of Wulfric's howl. Period."

Damn it. She'd expertly flipped the dad argument on me. Not that I necessarily agreed, but I didn't entirely disagree either. We both had solid points.

I turned away from Ashley, having a difficult time staring at the savage, frail, pregnant woman and keeping my focus. I knew there was a war on the horizon, and it was apparently a war to end all wars. In fact, I'd heard it called the End War and the All War.

The Omega War, I thought to myself.

I abruptly stiffened, realizing I was staring at Alice—and her face was as pale as milk as she stared back at me with a similar look of shock. Where had that thought come from? Had we just communicated telepathically? It almost felt like someone had whispered the phrase to me, because I knew I had never referred to the upcoming fight as the Omega War, and I was confident that I hadn't read it anywhere.

She quickly averted her eyes, so I lowered mine in hopes that we didn't draw attention from the others. I didn't want anyone knowing about her gifts. Some already did, but the fewer the better.

"I've already chosen my Riders," I lied, somehow keeping my face blank.

His face grew darker and he took an aggressive step towards me before Ashley placed a reassuring hand on his forearm. He shuddered and relaxed his shoulders.

Somewhat.

He still gave off a desperate, power-hungry vibe, which was completely unlike him. I briefly considered what would happen to his pack—hundreds of werewolves—if they were led by a Horseman.

And then I remembered that he had abandoned his pack to protect them from Thor. The four werewolves in front of me were his new pack.

Ashley spoke up, her voice as clear as a struck bell. "Fine. But Gunnar still goes with you. To keep you safe."

I grunted, wanting to laugh out loud. "He had one eye to begin with, and even that one is now half-blind. I'll be lucky if he's operating at twenty-five-percent."

Freya spoke up, changing the topic. "This Armory," she said, drawing every eye. "It is safe?"

Ashley nodded. "Safer than any place I know."

Unfortunately, I had to agree. Not that I was voting for it, but she was right. Only specific invitation would let someone in, so as long as they didn't open the door for Thor, they would be as safe as babes.

But me letting someone in gave them the ability to potentially take weapons out—which was not acceptable. I'd have to lay down some heavy rules to even consider it.

Freya shared a long, silent look with Odin—who was no longer watching the storm. He finally nodded, and whatever they had decided, it seemed to bolster his spirits somewhat. Freya turned to Ashley and Gunnar, a smile of anticipation on her face that made me decidedly uneasy.

"Then we have a solution. My husband will temporarily cure Gunnar, and we will go to this Armory. I will be able to care for Ashley without looking over my shoulder every two minutes."

I narrowed my eyes. "Cure Gunnar? Just like—"

"How?" Gunnar demanded, looking suddenly eager.

"Make an offering to Odin," she said. "Honor him." Then she slowly turned to me. "And in return for these noble gifts we provide, you will kill my son and try to find Gungnir," she said, hitting me with the *look*.

I burst out laughing this time, shaking my head in disbelief. "Oh, is that all? You sure you don't want me to pinch Heimdall's ass as well?" I blurted, shaking my head. "And unless you have some kind of direct lead on Gungnir, forget about it. Mordred is my next priority," I said, choosing not to elaborate on the risk to Gunnar's soul if Mordred didn't die soon. Ashley had enough to worry about already.

Not liking my response, Freya gave me another *look*, and this one was...*lookier*. It still didn't compare to Ashley's *look*, though.

I noticed Alice murmuring under her breath, and I turned to find her studying Freya's *look* entirely too studiously for my liking. I hurriedly stepped between them, shushing her back.

She was way too young to learn that kind of power. She was already enough of a handful. Case in point, she kicked me in the ankle. Hard. I ignored the willful little demon spawn. And Freya's *look*.

Gunnar turned to Odin, cleared his throat, and then spoke in an authoritative voice. "I demand your help, Allfather."

I winced at Gunnar's choice of phrasing—which had definitely not honored Odin nor implied an offering.

Odin did not respond.

I turned to check on him, and then blinked to find he was staring off at the storm again, his eye entirely silver now—even the white sclera. And his face was slack, like he had fallen unconscious.

Thunder rumbled ominously, like a long, hungry growl. The hair on the back of my neck stood up as I realized that the steamroller of black clouds had covered a third of the distance. Much faster than I had originally estimated.

"Call me crazy, but I don't like the weather in Niflheim," Drake said nervously, staring out at the storm. "I suggest we head to the Armory sooner rather than—"

Gunnar took an aggressive step forward, cutting Drake off, and the Wolf King didn't look remotely pleased by Odin's silence. "I swear that my pack will follow all the old traditions," he growled. "We will show you honor, Allfather. My pack will worship the old ways. Worship *you*, Odin. But you must first honor *me*—now—or I will not have a pack to honor you with!"

"I'm pretty sure that's not what Freya meant," I mumbled under my breath. Proving my point, Odin still did not respond.

I felt a tugging on my shirt and glanced down to see Alice studying each face before her, looking as if she had just come to understand the meaning of life.

"Gunnar is right," she whispered adamantly. "This is *supposed* to happen."

I scowled angrily. What good was a seer if she only saw things you didn't want her to see? I took a deep breath, closing my eyes for a slow three-count. Finally, I opened them, accepting that the only thing my arguments would accomplish was to delay the inevitable.

Who Gunnar prayed to was his business, but I would never let him hear the end of it. He had chosen to worship my butler, after all. I definitely still had some questions that needed answers, though.

Odin suddenly snarled, snapping out of his daze to grip his knees with both hands. He was shaking. "Thor," he cursed, pointing up at the approaching storm. "He is hiding within the storms of Niflheim. If I hadn't thought to check with Hugin and Munin, I might have missed it entirely," he snarled, sounding embarrassed at his failure. "He must have sensed me healing myself. Gods damn it all—I didn't think that was strong enough for anyone to notice!"

CHAPTER 21

Freya shot me a very dark look, as if to make sure that I understood that Odin wouldn't have had to self-heal if I hadn't beaten him so severely. That the inbound Thor was my fault.

I ignored her—very pointedly—by studying the black clouds. The thunder was a constant, rolling growl, and fingers of lightning tickled the land as it crept towards us.

Odin's eye momentarily shifted to that chrome-like silver and then back again. "Thor knows we are in Niflheim, but he still searches for our exact location. Hugin and Munin will try to mislead him, but he knows their games well. We might have five minutes." Odin abruptly turned to Gunnar, as if only just now hearing the werewolf's request. "I agree to your terms, Wulfric."

"Before Gunnar does something he regrets," I said, butting in, "I want to hear details."

Odin nodded, keeping his eye on Gunnar. "I funneled almost half of my power into my wolves. If Geri and Freki agree, I can temporarily bond you to them. They already see you as part of their pack, which is no small praise," Odin said meaningfully, and I recalled a time when I had caught Gunnar having a private conversation with Odin's wolves. I'd asked him about it, but Gunnar had told me he wasn't allowed to discuss it. Curious…

Was their pack relationship similar to how Odin's ravens were on my family crest?

Odin continued. "You will see as they see, and your strength will blossom with the addition of theirs. They will remain by your side like ghostly specters, empowering you, but they will not be able to act in the physical realm until the bond is broken. I will still have the strength to aid Freya with your pups but doing this will leave me weakened—less capable to protect your wife," Odin explained. "But with the Armory to protect her..."

I slowly turned to Geri and Freki. Odin's wolves were no longer struggling, but were instead staring at Gunnar very, very intently. Almost hungrily.

"Do you accept?" Odin asked.

Gunnar was already nodding. "We have Drake and Cowan to help keep my wife safe. Defense will not win this battle. Thor must die. Nate and I will make certain we kill your son, Allfather."

"What did you mean by *temporarily*?" I asked, picking apart his explanation.

Odin remained focused on Gunnar. "Twenty-four-hours. If your wife doesn't give birth on her own in that time...Freya will need my full strength for our best chances at delivering your pups."

"No rush to sell your soul, Gunnar," I urged, not entirely sure that swearing such a committed oath to Odin was worth such a short-lived gift. "Think of your kids."

Gunnar faced me squarely, gritting his teeth. "*I. Am!*" he snarled. He took a slow breath, unclenching his jaw and dialing back the murderometer. "Do not stand between me and my decision, Nate. I gave you an alternative, which you refused to consider. As a result, *this is going to happen.* Unless you have suddenly changed your mind about giving me my rightfully-earned Horseman's Mask, then stop stalling. Each breath brings Thor closer to my wife and unborn children."

I sighed defeatedly, and then weakly motioned for him to proceed. Because he was right.

Gunnar turned to Odin. "I accept your terms. Let's do this, Allfather."

Ashley nodded. "If it gives my husband the strength to disembowel Thor, that will suffice."

Odin dipped his head to each of them, showing no paternal instinct for Thor's demise. None whatsoever. It was enough to make me want a hug.

Alice, the all-seeing little whelp, suddenly wrapped my leg in a hug, squeezing tightly. I sighed, mussing up her hair playfully. "Thanks, Bones."

She beamed up at me before taking a step back.

I gauged our shot-clock, mentally preparing myself for Thor's arrival in less than five minutes. "Hurry the hell up, Odin. We don't have all day, you lazy bastard," I said, pointing upwards, because the black cylinder of clouds blanketed the whole sky now. "And for the record, Hugin and Munin suck at distractions."

Odin rolled his eye, and Freya frowned at me as if I had spoken in tongues, not catching my rapier wit.

"Come forth, Gunnar," Odin commanded officiously. "Let them bite each of your wrists. It will hurt. A lot. You must remain standing."

Gunnar took a confident step forward to meet his fate.

He almost ate it on the second step, his ankle rolling on a loose stone. I slapped my forehead, muttering under my breath. Gunnar remained upright, tore off the cloth around his eyes and, with his lone eye clamped firmly shut, he awkwardly shuffled over the rubble.

I sensed Freya frowning at me, but I pretended not to notice.

I considered telling her that her hastily retied toga was crooked, but thought better of it. Barely. Instead, I walked Gunnar over to Geri and Freki, pausing as I glared down at them. "I know a shifter bear veterinarian in Kansas City. She's never neutered a wolf, but she's always open to new experiences."

They curled their lips up at me, but Gunnar placed his palm on my forearm. "They have done nothing wrong, Nate," he said in a calm voice, sensing how close I was to the edge of my resolve. Although he didn't say it, we both knew how to get him out of this bond with the wolves.

Give him a Horseman's Mask.

But...I just couldn't do it. He was my best friend, and he was about to be a dad. He'd already died once when I'd let him get into a fight that was well above his pay grade.

I wasn't doing that again.

He'd been in my non-Fae life for about as long as I could remember, going back to my earliest, fondest, childhood memories.

I could still see young Gunnar hopping out from our treehouse with a wooden sword, battling unseen pirates while taunting their captain— laughing as he cockily threatened to chew off the captain's peg leg if he didn't surrender.

Someday...

I wanted Gunnar to recreate that pirate adventure with his own kids. If anything happened to him, I didn't think I could do as good of a job at teaching them how to be pirates.

Because...

Pirates wore eyepatches, man. He was halfway there already. There was no question that I would step in as their godfather and play pirates until the timbers were shivered, the sun set at our backs, and we found all the hidden treasures, but...

Figuratively, his boots were too big to fill. And I would never be able to even *fake* the size of his heart.

Because I was born to scare monsters, not inspire kids.

And Gunnar was *born* to raise little heroes, god damn it. It was his special purpose. And every part of me screamed that giving him a Horseman's Mask right now would ruin all of that.

I hung my head, let out a breath, and released my magical restraints from the wolves. They jumped to their feet, backing up a few paces.

Gunnar faced them without fear and began slowly peeling off his gauntlets. He handed them to me without looking, and said, "Step back, Nate," in a bold, eerily calm voice.

I accepted the gauntlets with a grunt, shot the wolves one last glare, and then followed Gunnar's advice, taking a few steps back. Not wanting to drop the gauntlets, I shoved them into my satchel, checking on the clouds again.

I watched, transfixed, as Gunnar extended his beefy forearms like he was doing nothing more dangerous than visiting his tailor. His eye was scrunched up to avoid even this level of dim light, but the quartz eyepatch that was fused into his skin glittered like a night sky full of stars, reflecting the flickering lightning in the dark clouds above us.

His jaw was completely relaxed.

No one moved, but everyone held their breath. Without warning, the mythical wolves lunged, simultaneously clamping their massive jaws down over each of Gunnar's forearms.

He grunted but stood firm. The wolves clenched their jaws tighter, jerking their heads like dogs do when wrestling over a toy in a game of tug-of-war—and Gunnar was the prize.

Blood spurted from Gunnar's forearms, dripping down the wolves' fangs and muzzles, splashing down to the rocky ground.

And Gunnar stood tall.

Ashley gasped lightly, cocking her head as she fidgeted with her hands—likely smelling the fresh blood in the air but obviously unable to see anything. Alice was suddenly beside her, hugging her and squeezing her hand. Ashley's face crumpled as she sagged against the door, freeing her supporting hand to clutch Alice closer.

She was going to be the best, scariest kind of mom.

A low growl slowly began to bubble up from Gunnar's lips as he tugged back against the wolves, countering their movements—almost as if he could sense their lulls before they could.

But he didn't try to break free or escape. His boots remained firmly planted in the now bloody stones.

Geri and Freki's muzzles were liberally splashed with blood and I felt my rainbow staff slam into my hand from across the clearing, crackling with popping arcs of electric, multi-colored light. I'd subconsciously used my magic to retrieve it—obviously concerned by the amount of blood painting the trio.

The wolves squeezed their jaws and I thought I heard bones crunching. My staff flared as wind whipped around us, the air practically screaming. Alice was clutching Ashley's thigh in a tight hug while Drake and Cowan did their best to shelter the woman and child.

I turned to Grimm, shooting him a meaningful look. I murmured two words under my breath, mouthing them slow enough for him to read my lips through the raging storm.

He nodded carefully, scraping one of his hooves across the stone in three exaggerated motions.

I nodded, confirming his follow-up request.

We'd done quite a bit of combat training in Fae—there had been nothing else to do when I wasn't practicing my Fae magic, and we'd come to the brilliant conclusion that a Horseman should probably know how to work with his horse, especially when it was too loud to talk—like a battle.

I turned away from Grimm, cupping my hands around my mouth—

careful not to drop my still-glowing staff. "This is taking too fucking long!" I shouted, loud enough for everyone to hear.

The storm was practically on top of us now, making it appear like night had abruptly fallen. Bolts of lightning began to strike down all around us, surrounding the area in a cage of electricity. And they didn't fade away, proving beyond a shadow of a doubt that it was unnatural.

Odin was rocking back and forth on his heels, supported only by Freya's hands on his shoulders. Her eyes were wide and panicked as she stared up at the skies, knowing full well that she and Odin were in no position to battle their son, Thor—especially since their lovely son apparently had his sights on Asgard's throne.

I hadn't been able to process that little tidbit yet, baffled by the sheer number of pies Thor was jabbing his fingers into.

Laughter rumbled out from within the rotating, horizontal column of black clouds, and I was about a millisecond away from incinerating the wolves from the inside out with starlight when Gunnar roared loud enough to make my ears pop.

Louder than even the screaming wind and lightning and godly laughter.

"I. AM. WULFRIC!" he roared, and then he squatted, jerking his arms down and back, yanking the attached wolves along with him at the moment their footing was the least stable. I saw the flesh of his forearms tear, but he didn't react to the pain.

He was too busy exploding upwards and forwards in a lunge, swinging his arms—and the wolves—ahead of him.

Geri and Freki whipped forward, directly towards each other. Their heads cracked together with a resounding *thunk* and they released Gunnar, stumbling and tripping before falling to their sides, their eyes spinning wildly.

My best friend was panting, illuminated from behind by the sporadic bolts of lightning like he was some crazed blood demon, his forearms shredded with gaping tears. His fists were flexed, emphasizing the thick veins pulsing beneath his tanned skin, and his teeth were squeezed together so tightly that he was on the verge of shattering them.

Whatever this ritual entailed, it apparently still wasn't over yet.

"God damn it!" I cursed.

Thor took my suggestion literally.

A bolt of lightning as thick as an ancient oak slammed into the creek bed, sending rocks flying in every direction.

CHAPTER 22

*L*uckily, the bolt connected about a dozen feet away from Gunnar's side. Gunnar didn't even flinch, too focused on Geri and Freki before him. He continued to mutter under his breath as if unaware of the shitstorm that had just touched down. Freya was still supporting the dazed Odin, but her eyes were as wide as saucers.

Because, like me, Freya was aware of the wild, savage, giant of a man stepping out of the light. Thor's long, greasy, red hair and knotted, chest-length beard looked to be stained with old blood and white ashes, and it was held together in places by an assortment of mismatched silver bands, giving him a primitive, tribal flair, *a la* Jack Sparrow meets ZZ Top. His face was scarred, and his eyes flickered with lightning.

Thor was smiling, his eyes locked onto his father, Odin, and Freya. Thor didn't appear to realize his father was mentally checked out—or that anyone other than his parents were present—as he began to gloat. "Oh, how I've missed you, Allfather. I would never have thought to come here if I hadn't suddenly sensed the *strangest* thing—"

He cut off, finally realizing they weren't alone. First, he jerked his head towards Gunnar and blinked in surprise. That's when it hit me—Thor probably hadn't known that Gunnar and Ashley had survived. If I'd had any doubts, the sudden hungry smile confirmed it.

Damn it all.

Like Odin, Gunnar wasn't paying any attention to our new guest, staring down at the wolves instead.

I waved my hand to get Thor's attention before he did something stupid. "Hey, buddy. I've got a hankering for some goat milk. Help a brother out?"

Thor's cheeks reddened as he turned to glare at me. "My, my, my…" he said, shooting a quick glance around to see who else was at the party. He smirked wolfishly at Ashley and her retinue by the vine door before turning back to address me with a malevolent grin. "And the bastard step-brother I never got to know! What a surprise to find you three together. I thought I already put down the dogs months ago. I do believe that this just became my favorite day, ever. I get to kill three birds with one stone."

"Listen," I said, waving a hand at him. "We're in the middle of this super cool ritual, and you're totally interrupting. So just stick your thumb up your ass for a minute, stand still, and look pretty. I'll let you know when we're finished, *brother*."

Thor's cheeks purpled, no longer amused. He locked his rage onto Gunnar like a heat-seeking missile. "Mangy cur," he growled. "Looks like I'll have to put the bitch's bitch down, again. I've always fancied widows. Like a well-trained horse, they've already been broken in."

And a bar of lightning erupted from his palm.

I lunged between them, slamming my rainbow staff into the ground, taking the full force of Thor's attack into my staff. The golden light in my veins flared, making me look like a disco ball. Multi-colored lightning ricocheted in a dozen directions, and I made sure to direct one so that it struck Thor squarely in the groin in the patented Temple Testical Taser—currently still in the exploratory phase of R&D at Grimm Tech.

Okay. That was a lie. But I had spent a lot of time playing with lightning while in Fae, finding unique ways to modify it, adding my own spin to it so that it was no longer *just* lightning.

Spiked with a little bit of Fae strangeness, it became something altogether different than mere electricity. In fact, I knew how to give it a numbing effect, so that whatever it struck went entirely limp.

So, Thor was going to need a pinch hitter if he had any bedroom plans over the next few days. Which was why the God of Thunder yelped, jumping up and clutching his crotch in surprise that lightning had somehow harmed him in the most personal of ways.

Show me on the doll where Nate touched you.

The shock was also why he didn't notice Grimm's huge unicorn ass looming over his shoulder, directly behind him. Or the pair of hooves kicking out towards the back of Thor's head at the apex of the god's vertical leap.

Grimm's hooves struck Thor in the back of the head hard enough to decapitate anyone other than a god. Paired with me simultaneously swinging my rainbow staff like a golf club at his shins, resulted in Thor—with his mouth wide open in a sudden scream of outraged pain—flying face-first into the rubble at mach-two speed.

Thor hit the stones teeth-first like a lawn dart.

I couldn't believe that our first attempt at using one of our rehearsed battle tactics had worked—one designed for a scenario in which I had fallen off Grimm's back and into a melee battle, about to be clobbered by a stronger opponent.

Donkey Punch was a success. It had worked better than any of our practice sessions, making me realize that we truly were a duo to be reckoned with.

That even without all my powers, I was still a Horseman.

Grimm was more professional about our success, already having galloped over to the vine door where Alice stood with Ashley, Drake, and Cowan.

I, on the other hand, had continued the momentum of my staff, swinging it high overhead, and then slamming it down on top of Thor's skull just as he was trying to get back up.

He grunted, his face cracking back into the stones with a cringeworthy *crunch*.

"More cowbell, bitch!" I shouted, my golden veins casting a circle of warm light around me.

An imagined vision of Ashley lying on the ground after Thor had first attacked her materialized in my mind, and I instinctively kicked Thor in the side of the head with my heel, screaming at the top of my lungs. Remembering what Thor had just implied about Ashley and a broken-in horse, I decided to thrash him again with another heel kick.

"Hurry the fuck up, Gunnar!" I snapped, keeping my eyes on Thor as he swayed groggily on all fours.

"SUBMIT!" Gunnar snarled in a primal growl that didn't even sound human, and I risked a quick glance to see that his forearms were beginning to sprout white fur, and his chest was doubling in size.

Odin's wolves abruptly let out a combined whining sound, lowering their muzzles to the rocky ground, their eyes still a little wild around the edges from their wolf-cussion and the arrival of Thor.

Then they simply evaporated like smoke in the wind, and Gunnar gasped, rising up on the balls of his feet like he'd had a surprise prostate exam party.

Gunnar glanced over at me—and I jumped back a step at the storm of rippling chrome now quivering across his iris—just like I'd seen with Odin when he'd been communicating with his ravens. Gunnar hesitated at the look on my face.

Then he seemed to realize that he had his eye open and that he wasn't cowering from the light blazing out from my veins. And a slow grin split his cheeks. He glanced down at his forearms, shaking the blood off methodically—they were already beginning to heal, but I knew such deep wounds might take a little while to completely recover.

He didn't show any pain from broken or crunched bones, so maybe I had imagined that sound. Or Gunnar was insanely more badass than I had previously thought—and that was a high bar to meet, let alone surpass.

Odin stared at Gunnar, his face incredulous—as if he hadn't believed it would actually work, or that something unexpected had happened. Then he simply collapsed, his legs giving out under his weight. Freya squawked, catching her husband at the last minute.

Gunnar seemed to finally notice Thor on the ground for the first time. His teeth elongated into massive fangs, and lethal, quartz claws ripped out of his fingertips.

No matter how badass Gunnar was, he couldn't kill a god. At least, I wasn't going to let him attempt it.

"Gunnar!" I snapped, frantically pointing over his shoulder—trying to shout over the sounds of crackling electricity that likely signified Thor was regaining his senses behind me. "Odin's under attack!"

Gunnar spun, claws out, already half-shifted into his colossal, bipedal werewolf form. But Odin wasn't in any danger other than perhaps bringing Freya down with him if he fell the rest of the way to the ground.

Before Gunnar had time to catch onto my deceit, I reared back and kicked him in the tailbone as hard as I could. I simultaneously ripped open a fiery Gateway on the other side of Odin and Freya—the portal leading to a space just *outside the entrance* to the Armory in Chateau Falco. I'd save their lives, but there was no way I was letting them inside the Armory proper before establishing ground rules.

Gunnar snarled at the force of my kick, but he hadn't been expecting it. He slammed into Freya and Odin, sending the three of them through the Gateway in a tangled sprawl.

Two semi-transparent wolves—like ghosts—immediately leapt through after them. Geri and Freki. If I hadn't been staring at the Gateway so intently, I might have missed them.

I closed the Gateway before any of them got any bright ideas, and then I spun to face Thor. Luckily, he was still on all fours, shaking his head as he spit out gobs of blood and even a few teeth.

I tee'd up and swung my rainbow staff as hard as I could, clocking him in the jaw hard enough to hear his teeth crack together and see blood spray up into the air.

I quickly turned to check on Grimm's evacuation to see Ashley already astride the unicorn with the breastplate and helmet covering her belly. Alice sat behind her, doing her best to support the pregnant werewolf. Drake and Cowan stared from me to Thor with wide, panicked eyes. I could tell that they weren't necessarily afraid of fighting, but that they were afraid of not knowing what they were expected to do—protect Ashley by fleeing with her or martyring themselves to buy her enough time to escape with Grimm and Alice.

I gave them their marching orders by ripping open another Gateway just outside the entrance to the Armory—a few dozen paces from where I had deposited Gunnar, Odin, and Freya, so that Gunnar didn't try to jump back through to help me fight Thor.

Drake and Cowan stared from Thor to the Gateway, still uncertain how to react—because fleeing with Ashley meant abandoning me. I flung out a hand, hurling a bar of air at them to knock them through the Gateway before they chose to do something nobly idiotic.

Grimm leapt through after them, and I yanked it closed, leaving me and Thor all alone.

I let out a sigh of relief, turning to face the God of Thunder. I tugged off my satchel, dropping it to the ground as I watched him climb to his feet. He wiped a beefy forearm across his bloody mouth and beard, keeping his head down as he spoke. "Oh, you're going to pay for that, boy. I was *really* looking forward to killing them. You only delayed the inevitable. They—and you—are *mine*." Finally, he lifted his head, locking eyes with me.

I smiled a dark smile, lifting my arms out to either side, inviting him to strike me in the chest. He narrowed his eyes suspiciously, not rising to the bait.

I lowered my arms, thumping my staff gently into the ground, as I used a little bit of magic for dramatic effect.

Thin, spidery arcs of electricity began to crackle out of my staff and onto my arm, in every color imaginable. They began to crawl upwards, and then across my torso until dozens of them coated my body like writhing, arthritic snakes.

And everywhere they touched, my shirt began to smolder and burn in an angry array of orange and red lines, breaking the fabric down into glowing embers that flaked away and were immediately whipped up into the stormy, windy air.

And as my shirt burned to nothing, leaving me only in my jeans, the golden veins covering my chest and arms brightened, practically pulsing with a violent hunger to rip a god to pieces.

Despite the darkness from the black cloud above us, the glow from my body cast plenty of light for me to see. As did fingers of Thor's own lightning suddenly stabbing down all around us, surrounding us in an electric cage. I threw up a dome that encompassed the entire area from rock wall to rock wall, not wanting an errant bolt of lightning to strike me from behind.

I blew the God of Thunder a kiss. "I missed you in Fae."

He smiled a humorless, bloody smile, opening his mouth to speak.

And I burst out laughing, pointing at him with my free hand. "Red Rover, Red Rover, send some dentures on over!" I hooted.

Because Thor was now missing his two front teeth.

Thor closed his mouth self-consciously, his face turning purple with rage.

Perfect.

CHAPTER 23

I whipped my head to the left and then the right, cracking my joints to loosen up. Thor watched me, his anger fading to what appeared to be wariness as he studied the golden veins covering my chest and arms. I knew that my eyes also glowed golden—at least they had when I'd killed Athena.

Thor's thinking face more resembled a man in the throes of constipation than one who had a spark of intelligence blossom to life. Regardless, his raw strength more than made up for his intellectual shortcomings.

At least I'd gotten everyone far away from the blast radius, and I'd managed to keep Gunnar out of the fight—since his Tiny Balls were programmed to send him to Fae, not Niflheim.

Now, I just had to hope that my assorted powers were enough to put him down for good.

Just because I had the strength to kill a god didn't mean I was able to kill *this* god. It just put us on relatively equal footing—where my attacks could actually cause real harm.

Like a fight between two run-of-the-mill humans. You could say that either human was equally *able* to kill the other, but that didn't mean they would succeed. They just had the *ability* to do so. The actual victory came down to their prowess in the art of combat.

The first time I'd fought Thor, I hadn't fared very well. Granted, I'd been suffering from all sorts of power hiccups back then as a result of my inexperience with my Fae magic.

I'd fixed all of that, now.

But would it be enough?

So far, I'd gotten in some very lucky—and cheap—shots on Thor. But now it was one-on-one, with no distractions.

Except...

I frowned. For a god who had come to Niflheim to kick ass, he seemed to be remarkably unprepared.

Firstly, he didn't have a weapon at hand. Obviously, I knew he didn't have Mjölnir, but he'd at least carried a knife the first time I met him.

Secondly, he wore a plain, rather ordinary, leather belt—definitely not what I had expected of his legendary power belt, megingjörð, which supposedly doubled his strength.

Thirdly, he wasn't wearing his iron gauntlets, Járngreipr, but those were designed to help him handle Mjölnir, so that was understandable.

Thor was known for always having these three critical possessions with him. Yet he didn't seem to have *any* of them. Had Odin stolen *all* of them?

Thor wore the same primitive furs and leathers as the last time I'd seen him—definitely nothing fancy enough to imply he was the up-and-coming King of Asgard. It didn't take much of an imagination to mistake him for an angry homeless man.

"I will find them," he growled, interrupting my train of thought. "I will hold them in the palms of my hands and laugh at how tiny, pathetic, and worthless—"

"I didn't come here to listen to you sweet talk your testicles, Thor," I cut in, having no idea what he was actually referring to, and not particularly caring enough to find out. He'd been a raging, incoherent son-of-a-bitch the first time I'd met him, and Gunnar's explanation that he'd seemed blood drunk in St. Louis hadn't raised my expectations that anything close to resembling an intelligent conversation was going to occur here in Niflheim.

His face darkened at my comment, and a thick, crooked vein suddenly bulged over his right temple. It was so hard to take someone seriously after you knocked out their two front teeth. Although I wanted nothing more than to immediately put him in the morgue, I needed to get his take on current events first. Otherwise I would lose the opportunity for good.

Because I wasn't entirely sure I could trust Odin and Freya. Something about their actions was just...off.

So, to manipulate Thor into giving up something useful, I needed to keep the brute angry. My specialty. "I was hoping to see your goats again, man," I began. "I still remember the last time I saw Tanngnjóstr and Tanngrisnir—when Alex picked them up by the legs and threw them at you. You accidentally *stabbed* one of them—"

"ENOUGH!" Thor roared. Spittle flew from his mouth and frothed around his lips like he had rabies. He glanced down at the satchel at my feet, his eyes hungry.

I sighed, using my foot to slide the satchel behind me. "I don't have Mjölnir, Thor. Never did." I knew reassuring him was pointless, but I didn't want him making a grab for the whole satchel—I had important shit in there.

"Just curious, but if Mjölnir's been missing for so long, why are you only now interested in recovering it?"

He snarled, clenching a fist at his side. "I've been searching for *decades*, following Mjölnir's trail throughout the Nine Realms. Odin passed it to someone, who passed it to someone else, who passed it to someone else..." he waved a hand, implying many more handoffs. Then he stared at me. "The last person I found to have had it in their possession was Calvin Temple, but he died before I could have a talk with him," he growled.

I tried to keep the shock from my face. My dad had helped hide Mjölnir? But that meant...shit. Maybe I really *did* have Thor's hammer lying around somewhere. Like in the Armory.

I shrugged, keeping my face neutral. "The first time I heard it was missing was when you showed up outside the bar," I told him.

Thor stared at me for a few moments in complete silence, as if trying to catch me in a lie. "Then I hear that you, Calvin's son, had acquired a new hammer, and that you were the new *Master Temple* of your *Beastly* fortress, Chateau Falco."

His enunciation clearly told me he knew about Beasts.

I shrugged, sticking to my guns since he obviously thought I was lying about Mjölnir. "That hammer you saw actually ended up being Excalibur. And you were there when I first found out that my butler was really Odin. I was fooled just as much as you," I admitted, not bothering to hide my own anger. "He lied to the both of us."

"So you say," he growled. "Yet he was just here, and you saved his life."

I rolled my eyes. "I was demanding an *explanation* from him, you fucking moron! And I hadn't gotten it yet, so I put him on a shelf for me to question once I clean up *this* mess," I lied, hoping my staged anger would throw him off course.

It worked, because he scratched at his beard thoughtfully.

"Think about it for a second. If you have even a sliver of common sense stuck somewhere in that pungent face blanket of yours, you've done a little research on me..." He nodded almost imperceptibly. "You've heard— whether you believe it or not—of all the people I've killed and defeated. All the beings Odin might have *helped* me deal with over the years. But he didn't. Which was fine until I learned that he *could* have helped me with them. I detest liars, Thor. Truly. Almost as much as I detest cowards, like you."

Rather than bristle at my accusation, he seemed to stop breathing, his eyes glazing over as he processed my words.

"You're...not a Master," he finally said, scratching at his beard again, looking thoroughly confused this time.

I frowned right back, wondering if he was even dumber than I had given him credit for. "Of course I am. We just talked about this, remember?"

The look on his face made me wonder if he actually had forgotten calling me Master Temple a few moments ago. He appraised me like I was some kind of exotic creature he'd never encountered before. I arched an eyebrow, hoping he realized how insane he sounded.

Maybe he really was drunk.

Although it looked more like he was having some kind of internal epiphany. I ran back through my comments, wondering if I had used too many syllables.

I was beginning to realize that Thor made your average brute look like Einstein. Maybe I could just riddle him to death and watch his head explode.

I couldn't imagine being so ignorant. Not knowing what everyone else was talking about when they said simple things. That would be the worst kind of life.

"You've got to be kidding me," he finally breathed. "How did everyone miss this?"

"Miss *what*, you crazy hairball?"

But he didn't seem to hear me. I watched as his demeanor began to change. His eyes began to dance with lightning—literally—but through that power, I saw a frantic madness lurking deep within. He was on the edge, and I couldn't tell if it was from a passionate hunger or a deep fear. The symptoms for either were very similar.

"I know what you are, Temple. Even though you try to deceive as cleverly as Loki. I'm not afraid of you," he said, his eyes flicking to my hands. "You will not ascend."

At first, I assumed he was talking about my mysterious Catalyst power. But the longer I considered his words and body language, the more I began to doubt my theory.

I frowned at the intensity in his eyes. Then I followed his gaze to see Odin's blood still painting my knuckles. "The godkiller thing?" I asked, showing off my glowing veins.

"Some spell from my mother," he muttered.

I rolled my eyes. "I got this when I killed Athena. Some called her a Goddess of War, but she was kind of a disappointment if I'm being totally honest." I paused, glancing over at him. "Say, you're a god of rain or something, right?"

"Thunder!" he boomed, accompanied by about a dozen bolts of lightning that deflected off the protective dome I'd put up—the dome that hadn't seemed to concern Thor in the slightest. Which…was also strange.

I lifted a finger, nodding. "That's right. *Thunder*. All bark and no bite, as many say."

The cloud above us rumbled ominously—and impotently.

I let him see how unconcerned I was, but my mind was still digesting his strange comment from a few seconds ago—about knowing what I was, that I wouldn't ascend, and that I wasn't a Master, despite him calling me Master Temple moments prior. Maybe he was referring to how I didn't have a Beast riding my shoulders—that I was a fraud for using my mansion to bond my Beast.

"The fact that you're not afraid of a godkiller tells me how ignorant you are," I said, giving up on trying to understand his earlier statements. "Friendly advice. You're a god, so you should probably be at least a little bit afraid. Odin was, and he knew how to take a hit better than anyone I've ever met. Maybe that's why he wears the crown."

Thor had looked momentarily confused until my last statement, which made him narrow his eyes dangerously. "Odin won't be King for much longer."

I appraised him from boots to beard with a doubtful frown. "You can't honestly think you're fit to be King of Asgard. Look at you," I said, waving a hand at him. "You're as batshit crazy on the inside as you look on the outside."

Thor hawked up some nasty concoction from his throat region and then spat out a bloody gob. "The Aesir were not pleased about Odin's long absence. Like a dutiful son, I stepped in to rule. It turns out, his crown fits my head just fine. I've been a great king."

I doubted that. In fact, I was betting any accomplishments he may have celebrated were more likely delayed results from one of Odin's prior decrees.

"When he returned without Gungnir, no one believed his story. Without his spear to verify his tale, the Wanderer learned that he had wandered too far." Thor laughed at his own joke, obviously quite pleased with himself.

I paused, studying his face. "Is that why you stole Gungnir from him? Jealousy? Revenge? To turn Asgard against him?"

He scoffed, shaking his head. "If I knew who took Gungnir, I would offer them a gift. Thanks to their thievery, I am now Asgard's golden boy," he said, smiling. "Soon it will become official," he said, and I noticed a flicker of self-doubt cross his eyes.

I glanced down at the golden light in my veins. "Looks like Odin found a real golden boy to replace you—and he had to travel all the way to Midgard to find me. That's gotta hurt."

He grunted toothily. "I have already made peace with my father's poor judgment. The fact that he lost Gungnir only proves that he was no longer fit for a crown. That's good enough for me. Time is on my side."

I was more concerned with the fact that I didn't sense an undertone of pride—like I would expect from the actual thief. That was troubling. If not Thor, who had stolen Gungnir? And then another thought hit me.

"Who helped you get back from wherever Odin sent you?" I asked, wondering if it might be the same person to have stolen Gungnir. "Was it your brother, Loki?"

Thor's reaction caught me entirely off guard. I had expected anger, or a poor attempt at denial.

Instead, he blinked. And then roared with laughter. "Loki has been locked away in that cursed book for *centuries!*" he hooted. "I doubt even *he* could find a way out of the *Bioloki*," he added, "if anyone even knew where to find it—"

He cut off abruptly, and his posture locked rigid. He blinked several times, opening his mouth wordlessly as if surprised by his own admission. I arched a brow, curious.

"You are not a god," Thor said very slowly, appraising me from head to toe. "How was I able to openly say that if you are not a god?"

And he sounded deeply troubled.

I knew gods were often limited in how much they could share with mortals, so a very queasy sensation settled in the pit of my stomach.

Did it have something to do with me being a godkiller? Had I earned some kind of godly security clearance?

Was that what he had meant about me *ascending*?

Unfortunately, this didn't help me understand the rest of what Thor had been talking about. Loki was trapped in a book? The *Bioloki*? I recognized the second half of the word as his name—Loki—but what did the prefix mean? It had kind of rhymed with *biology*, but I'd definitely never heard of it. Maybe it meant *the biography of Loki*.

Seeing the suspicious frown growing on Thor's face, I decided it was time we wrapped up this reunion.

Thor's reign of terror ended here.

Now.

CHAPTER 24

"*I*'m glad we have the chance to talk, Thor. I was hoping to learn why you still had a problem with me after you realized I didn't have your stupid hammer. How instead of confronting me like a man, you bravely decided to terrorize innocent citizens of my city. Then you took it a step further by attacking a pregnant woman," I took a casual step forward, thumping my staff into the rubble. It crackled with multi-colored light. "But you knew where I was, Thor. You came for me in Fae, and when I beat you like the little bitch that you are—with you still not brave enough to even show your face—you ran away. I kept a souvenir so I would never forget how cowardly you are," I said, eyeing my rainbow-colored staff. "Recognize it? Used to be one of yours."

I thumped it back into the ground, watching his eyes. They hardened upon seeing the staff. "You expected me to face you in Fae, where the very realm submitted to your power? Where Arthur's bastard and his Blood Knights raise an army for war? You think I've lived this long without learning the futility of fighting a man on his own land? How would that be a fair fight?"

I scoffed, surprised he'd been honest enough to admit it out loud, but my disgust at his instant excuse was even greater. "Thor, you have never—ever —let yourself enter a fair fight. Because you're a fucking coward. You only attack when victory is certain. You live your life around your legend because you simply don't understand…" I spat on the ground. "Legends are *made*, not *born*. Anyone who tries to force their own legend only ends up diminishing it."

He snarled defensively. "That depends on who writes the history."

I smirked, nodding. "I'm actually a bit of a historian. And I like to debunk shit. You see, I'm not just a godkiller. I'm also a fraud-killer. I want you to know—before I humiliate you, and then your corpse—that not even your *name* will survive the shame I'm about to heap upon you. Every single 'victory' you've accomplished will be accompanied by at least two contradicting, embarrassing claims. The real story of Thor the Toothless will echo for eternity. Your name will either be forgotten or ridiculed. Forever."

He was panting with rage, and multi-colored lightning crackled over his knuckles. "We're not finished, Temple—"

"You're right, Toothless," I interrupted, sensing he was about to make a run for it. "Your pain is only just beginning."

The multi-colored light began to trail up Thor's arm as he took a step back, confirming that he was definitely trying to make a run for it.

What the hell? He'd been terrorizing my city for a year to find me, and now he was just going to run away?

I lunged with my staff, striking him in the gut.

He grunted and his colored lightning latched onto my staff, puffing out almost instantly as if it had grounded out. Thor gasped incredulously, sputtering something nonsensical in a foreign language as he stared at my weapon. I was just as startled, but I masked it better.

I swung my rainbow stick wide, sweeping at his legs in hopes of knocking him down. But he took the blow like a champ, making the staff rattle in my grip hard enough that I almost dropped it.

Then Thor's boot was lunging for my stomach in a powerful pushing strike to force some distance between us. Not knowing why the staff had bounced off him without much effect—and since he didn't have a weapon—I dropped it to even the odds, sidestepping his attack as I caught his boot in the crook of my elbow.

His eyes widened to see me abandon my weapon, which meant he missed spotting my leg trap. He was also too slow to stop my other elbow from hammering down onto his kneecap. My veins flared brighter as his leg *cracked* loud enough to make me wince at the imagined pain it had to have caused.

Thor bellowed out in agony.

I lost my grip on his leg in his frantic attempt to escape, inadvertently giving him a second to hop back on one functional foot.

His eyes were wild around the edges as he stared at my glowing veins—and how they had flared brighter the moment I managed to hurt him.

I gave him a slow, predatory smile. "Fear me, boy."

Thor took one last look at my satchel before the multi-colored lightning suddenly encased his entire body—faster than I could react—and he winked out of existence like a popped bubble.

I growled angrily, taking a step closer. "FIGHT ME, COWARD!" I screamed, loud enough to make me feel dizzy and lightheaded.

Silence answered me. I stood there, shaking my head in disbelief as I fought down my vertigo. I truly couldn't believe that one hit had made him flee. Surely, he wasn't actually that much of a weakling to run at the first taste of pain, even if it had been a hyper-extended knee.

I'd been taunting him mercilessly while we talked, but that had really just been to get into his head and stir things up. Maybe that had been more effective than I had thought.

Or maybe his real weakness was fear, and he hadn't put true stock in my godkiller claims until I'd actually injured him.

Still…

He was supposed to be a *god*, for crying out loud. The Mighty Thor was really just a mighty chump.

An opportunist who was high off his own legend. Like the jock in high school realizing that he'd already lived out his glory days—but only after he came back to town for his twenty-year reunion wearing his old letterman's jacket and saw that everyone else had moved on—having tucked their old jerseys into a box in the attic at least a decade before.

Whereas he'd been polishing his old trophies and medals the night before the reunion.

I remembered how Alex had fought Thor without any apparent effort, and he hadn't been a godkiller. True, he had his own strange power source tying him back to King Arthur, but I hadn't anticipated this sudden turn of events.

Not after hearing how terrified everyone in St. Louis was of the God of Thunder—Raego fleeing town, Achilles closing his bar, Gunnar and Ashley abandoning their pack. Thor had spent the last year hunting me, terrorizing my allies, and he'd done a good enough job that they had all abandoned St. Louis in one form or another...

For him to finally confront the source of his rage, and then to almost instantly run away at the first taste of blood made no sense at all. I was missing something, and I was determined to get to the bottom of it.

I briefly considered chasing him down. Based on our conversation, I had a very good idea where he might have fled, but I had no idea how to get there, and I knew Alex and Talon were already waiting for me.

Then I thought of Ashley standing unprotected outside the Armory when she really needed to be tucked into a bed for Freya to keep an eye on her. She could go into labor any time now.

I also knew Gunnar would have some harsh words for me after I'd kicked him through the Gateway and deprived him of the chance to fight Thor. With a weary sigh, I scooped up my staff and satchel, and was about to leave when I remembered the Knightmare that Odin's ravens had killed and eaten—and the suit of armor left behind.

I grumbled loudly—since no one was present to hear me whining—as I walked up to the vine door and opened it. I entered, using a ball of flame to light my way, and immediately saw it tucked up against a wall. I frowned dubiously. It looked really freaking heavy. Unfortunately, I didn't see a sword beside it—something we really could have used in our upcoming fight with his brother Knights. I didn't recognize the symbol on the front, but I could figure that out when I met up with Alex and Talon.

My mind began to wander with thoughts on how to duplicate Alex's paper of symbols—how to make it so that crossing off a symbol on one would simultaneously cross off the symbol on the duplicate.

Essentially, a magical drop box folder—only tangible.

It would make it easier to split up and keep track of who was dead and which armors we'd retrieved.

Since I'd seen Talon lug that other set of armor off my mountain, I let out a resigned sigh and got to work. I grabbed a spare blanket on a side table and began setting all the—surprisingly light—pieces into a pile so I could fold up the blanket and move them all at once.

It took me a few minutes, and then I made one last check of the building —since I now had light to see—for the Knightmare's sword. As I searched, I pondered Thor's strange comments again, shaking my head. I found no answers, and I found no sword—empty-handed on both accounts.

I lugged the pile outside, and then ripped open a Gateway just outside my old lady's secret treasure trove.

The entrance to the Armory in the lower levels of Chateau Falco appeared in the center of the ring of sparks.

I could feel Falco vibrating even through the Gateway. It reminded me of a puppy excitedly wagging her tail against the trashcan when her owner returned home after a long day—loud enough to wake the neighbors.

I smiled at an absent thought. A shirtless billionaire lugging a pile of scrap metal into his mansion.

CHAPTER 25

I entered the large hallway outside the Armory with a smile. "I missed you, Falco," I murmured under my breath, lugging the blanket of armor behind me.

The very walls quivered, pleased to have her Master back home.

"That is incredibly unsettling," Drake said, shaking his head as he warily eyed the ceiling. Cowan noticed my attention and gave Drake a firm warning elbow.

Grimm walked up to me and took the corner of the blanket in his teeth, pulling it to the side for me—where Ashley's helmet and breastplate were already propped against the wall. I dipped my head in thanks. He knew where it needed to go. I briefly took stock of the rest of my ragtag crew of miscreants and malcontents.

Odin—having apparently recovered from the strange ritual with his wolves—had Gunnar pulled to the side in a private conversation. He still had dried blood on his face, and I was pleased to see his nose was still crooked. I didn't see the ghostly wolves anywhere, but that was expected. As if rehearsed, the two one-eyed men turned to look at me, and then slowly separated as if they hadn't been talking about anything important.

They had just coincidentally finished their private conversation the moment I arrived. Right.

"Friends don't keep secrets, and secrets don't keep friends," I told them with a stern look. Neither reacted in the slightest.

Alice clapped. "I *like* that one," she whispered to Freya. Odin's wife nodded absently, placing a comforting hand on the child's head. Yet her eyes were locked onto me with unmasked trepidation.

Her other arm was wrapped around Ashley's shoulders in a protective, concerned manner. Ashley still had the cloth tied around her head in order to protect her eyes from light, so she could have been sleeping for all I could tell. But she definitely belonged in a sickbed—if not the Emergency Room.

I decided to move forward on the presumption that everyone was lying to me—whether consciously or not remained to be seen. Everyone had their own agendas. Since I constantly found myself discovering new secrets that usually made my life more difficult, I decided it was about time I grew a bit more cynical and started assuming the worst in people—that they were either dishing out incorrect answers or lying to me for some unknown reason.

It made my life easier.

I cleared my throat. "Okay, kids. Ashley needs a bed, and she needs it ten minutes ago. So I'm not negotiating here. I'm telling you how it's going to be so I can take care of mama wolf. Questions can wait."

Ashley smirked weakly beneath her blindfold.

"You want inside my treasure room, there are rules. Anyone caught breaking the rules gets to die. Zero tolerance. I am the only god in the Armory, *capisce?*"

I was really only talking to Drake, Cowan, and the Norse crew, despite what I'd just said.

Drake and Cowan shifted their postures slightly. Nothing suspicious, just revealing a healthy fear—knowing full well that I meant what I said. But I also saw the resolve in their eyes. They would do anything for Ashley and Gunnar.

Odin and Freya shared a long, significant look, but finally turned to nod at me. Their hesitation was expected, because they knew the death sentence also applied to them—gods. This was one of the joys of mortality, and it was an acquired taste. *Here, there be a godkiller.*

I held up a finger. "Rule number one. No talking to Pandora unless she talks to you first. Even then, you give a simple answer to her specific question. The only other reason to talk to her is to ask for her help in something specifically related to caring for Ashley. You need a towel or something, you may ask her. That's it."

Everyone nodded.

"Rule number two. Touch nothing. Even if you find Gungnir being used as a coat rack," I added, knowing that it would mess with Odin.

They all nodded.

Odin spoke up after a few moments. "No one is here for your Armory, Nate. Ashley was the one to suggest coming here, if you recall."

I grunted and pointed a finger at Freya. "I don't know her very well, but she looks like a shoplifter. That's called profiling."

She squawked indignantly, but Odin placed a comforting hand on her forearm. "My greatest failure is breaking Nate's trust," he said in a guilty voice. She huffed, nodding in understanding. "A close second is failing to teach him tact."

This time he shot me a reproachful look—something Dean had done at least a dozen times a day, and I found myself grinning.

"That boat sailed long ago," Gunnar agreed, smiling.

"Final rule. Do not invite anyone inside. Period. Underscore." Again, they all nodded. "Now, we're going to go around the class and verbally swear—by your name—to abide by those three rules. You break an oath like that with a wizard, and you might just lose whatever Freaky powers you have—godly or not."

The nods were less jovial this time. And I stared each person in the eye as they swore their oaths on their names. I knew it wasn't perfect—there were always loopholes—but it was better than nothing.

Even Gunnar and Ashley swore the oath, but I think it was more to set an example. They were already family, and had already been inside the Armory, so it hadn't been necessary.

"Let's see what Pandora has to show us," I said.

"The way I remember it, she often shows quite a bit," Gunnar mumbled. Ashley slowly turned her head to face her husband, and I saw his shoulders wilt guiltily, even though she couldn't see him.

I burst out laughing.

"She does, does she?" Drake asked, staring at the door—having missed the nonverbal warning Ashley had given her husband.

Cowan elbowed him sharply, shaking his head ever so slightly. Drake cleared his throat, scuffing his boots on the ground. "Well, that sounds unprofessional, if you ask me," he said lamely. "Very unpro-fessional."

I rolled my eyes, still chuckling.

I turned to face the large, impenetrable wooden doors behind me. They were decorated with a full-sized carving that featured a woodland scene with a pond, a wolf, an owl up in the trees, and fish swimming lazily in the pond. And they were all alive so that it looked more like a *Nat Geo* special—just in wood rather than digital format.

As I stepped up to the door, the wolf calmly walked to the forefront of the carving and sat on its haunches.

With a final sigh, I reached out to pet the wolf. He whined happily under my touch, and his fur felt absolutely real. As if my touch had been a gentle breeze introduced to the woodland scene, the leaves rustled faintly, and tiny ripples danced across the pond.

The doors began to open, and everyone stared in wonder.

I turned to Grimm, speaking low so as not to draw attention. "Can you drop off my recycling and then stand guard out here? I won't be long."

"*We* won't be long," Gunnar corrected in a menacing growl, having crept closer to eavesdrop on me.

I nodded impatiently. "Yes. We," I corrected.

Grimm pawed his hoof on the ground. "Rules of Engagement?" he asked, eyeing the hallway.

I thought about it. "I can't think of any reason someone would be down here, so you can give one warning before you maim and incapacitate. If they fight back, gratuitous pain or murder."

"Sweet," he said, licking his lips. "Hurry up and make me a Gateway then, Rider."

I nodded, throwing up a portal to the Sanctorum for him. "It will close in five minutes," I told him, tying off the Gateway to do just that.

And everyone crept closer as the doors split down the middle, opening up into a vast, sandstone hallway wide enough to drive a truck through.

I ignored the stunned gasps of my guests and entered the threshold to find Pandora standing there, smirking at me. "Oh, Master Temple. I've missed you so. I must say, shirtless is a good look on you."

I grinned fondly. "Hey, Hope," I said, recalling the old nickname I'd once given her. Part of me idly wondered about that—how I'd chosen to call her Hope before I knew anything about becoming the Horseman of Hope.

I'd chosen the nickname because Hope was rumored to be the last item in Pandora's Box—after the plague of horrors that would first escape. I also wondered if she had known the coincidence beforehand, because Pandora was wicked, violently loyal, cosmically intelligent—able to read minds, and all sorts of other—

"Why do you block your thoughts from me, my Host?" she asked, blinking slowly, looking mildly hurt.

I stared at her, my own mouth open as I struggled to find an answer. Finally, I arched a brow, actually happy for the good news. "That's great."

She shook her head, looking decidedly uneasy. "I don't think it is. I think it's rather dire, as a matter of fact. Typically, only gods can keep their thoughts private. You are not a god, but you are becoming a large, powerful target. The Catalyst in you, perhaps..." she trailed off, warily.

I felt everyone watching me thoughtfully, but no one spoke.

"It is a pleasure to meet you, Pandora," Freya said, "but perhaps you can find us a bed for Ashley. I wouldn't be surprised if her water broke in the next few minutes—Help!" she suddenly gasped.

"I've got her!" Cowan growled, just as I heard a weakened moan and a sudden thud. I spun to see Freya on the ground with her legs sprawled out below Ashley as if she'd tried to cushion her fall. But Cowan, true to his word, had beaten her to it. He had dropped to his knees—the source of the thud—to catch Ashley in both arms. She hung limply, one of her arms dangling on the floor, whimpering weakly.

Freya was eagerly patting Ashley's cheeks, looking frightened.

Gunnar instantly rushed over to take his wife from Cowan—with a territorial growl of warning. Werewolves. Even their *thank yous* were prickly. Cowan dipped his chin submissively as he carefully handed Ashley over.

Pandora wasted no more time on pleasantries. "Hurry!" she snapped, spinning on her heels and motioning for us to follow her down the hall. "We must get her into the healing pool, now. A bed will have to wait. She is so weak at this moment that I fear she might not wake if she falls asleep." She glanced over her shoulder. "You, girl, fetch me the satchel on the table near the balcony. Nate grab the platter of fruits and cheeses!"

Gunnar snarled protectively and bolted after Pandora. I heard him talking to Ashley loudly, telling her to hold on and to be strong.

Odin and the werewolves trailed behind him like a security detail.

I grabbed Alice by the wrist and heaved her onto my shoulders. Then I ran to the balcony area and spotted the satchel on the table. It was brimming with glass vials and a few bundles of dried herbs.

I scooped it up—and the platter of food beside it—and jogged after the sounds of racing feet, careful not to spill the food.

I remembered the healing pond well. I usually just called it the hot tub, though. Pandora had christened it with Alex at one point—some sort of ritual related to him becoming the vessel for King Arthur's soul. I hadn't known that at the time. I'd thought I'd accidentally given Alex the best gift in the world—a chance to sleep with Pandora and give him some vitally necessary power that he'd need in order to keep me safe some day.

So, Alex had quite literally taken one for the team. The most self-rewarding, altruistic sacrifice I'd ever heard of, the smug bastard.

The two had remained close since, but they both made it sound very casual. Friends with occasional benefits. Strange, but I didn't have the mental energy to get involved in my friends' love lives.

Alice urged me on, but I didn't need any encouragement.

CHAPTER 26

*I*t had turned out that us menfolk were not welcome in the hot tub, or even in close proximity to it. So the men had retreated back near the balcony, leaving the girls to care for mama werewolf. Before we'd been booted out, I had heard Pandora mention that the pool might help with Ashley's vision injuries, so that was a plus.

I had taken Gunnar's gauntlets from my satchel—having forgotten to include them in the pile of armor Grimm had taken away for me—and returned them to him. My style of fighting wasn't conducive to freaking armor, and I wanted to give Gunnar every shred of added protection I could, because he didn't stand a chance against Thor, even as strong as he was. And whether I liked it or not, I knew Gunnar was going to stick by my side, wanting to go wherever the fighting was the most dangerous.

Which was a problem. My primary goal was to make sure he made it home to see his kids when this was all said and done. I knew Gunnar's boost in strength and sight—thanks to his spectral wolves—would only last twenty-four hours, so time was of the essence.

Gunnar wasted no time putting the gauntlets back on with a satisfied growl. I would let him fantasize to his heart's content, but I would be the one to put Thor into the ground. Gunnar could piss on Thor's ashes for all I cared.

I hadn't wanted to leave without getting an update on Ashley, so my patience was very thin. I figured Alex and Talon were already waiting for me in the Sanctorum, and I desperately wanted to hear what they had learned about the Knightmares in St. Louis. What they were up to and if we needed to prepare a defense for Chateau Falco.

So, left to our own devices, we had done what men do best—we'd been arguing and drinking. Well, I had been arguing with Odin. Drake and Cowan had wisely chosen not to get involved in the conversation, focusing instead on their drinks.

Gunnar, of course, was doing neither. Instead, he was pacing back and forth, punching his armored fist into his armored palm each time he turned around—his thoughts solely for his wife, and maybe skinning Thor alive. *Clang! Step-step-step-step-step-step-step. Clang!* If I tried very hard, I could almost see the two wolves curled up on the floor beside Gunnar, sleeping on the job. It wasn't like they had much else to do. They were just batteries for Gunnar right now. And eyeballs, however that worked.

I wondered if I was able to share my powers like Odin had with Gunnar. That would be incredibly helpful. Then again, I wasn't a god, so I doubted it. Pandora's comment about no longer being able to read my mind haunted me for some reason, but I banished it.

I turned away to glance around the open room, avoiding looking out at the sand swept desert beyond the balcony. It made me feel uneasy to stare out there. I didn't know why. It was just so desolate and final. Nothing lived out there—a direct contradiction to the life within the Armory.

I had let the silence stretch for the past five minutes as Odin and I regained our composure after screaming at one another. Okay. I had been screaming at him, demanding to know why Thor had inspired so much fear in St. Louis, but had been such a pussy when I confronted him. How Odin had used my dad to hide Mjölnir. Odin had given me no answers or very vague answers, hence the screaming.

In the last five minutes, I'd thought back on my interactions with Odin. I'd been rude, physically beaten him up, and then screamed at him. And...he was acting like an adult dealing with a toddler.

So. As angry as I was, I decided it was time to mature a little and use this new method called courtesy and respect. Even if I had to fake it. And I didn't need an audience.

I glanced over at Drake and Cowan. "Why don't you guys go see if the girls need anything. Offer to get a bed ready, bring them water, anything helpful. If you don't offer it, they're going to storm in here any minute and demand to know why you're lazing about while they do all the work. It's the only way to beat the enemy."

Cowan nodded thoughtfully and Drake stared at me as if I'd just performed a miracle. The two of them left, murmuring softly to one another as they made their way to the healing pool.

"That was cruel. You just sacrificed them," Gunnar grunted, momentarily drawn out of his thoughts.

I smirked. "It will build character." Even Odin smiled at that, shaking his head wistfully. "Where are Hugin and Munin?" I finally asked him in a calm, gentle voice. I hadn't seen the ravens since Niflheim—and it wasn't like they needed to stand guard there anymore. Not with us having come to the Armory.

"Doing what they do best," Odin said. "They will be of no use inside the Armory."

Gunnar resumed his pacing, oblivious to our conversation. I knew all he wanted to do was check on Ashley and then go kill Thor. I didn't disagree, but I knew we needed to meet with Alex and Talon first. Gunnar only had twenty-four hours before his wolf battery pack ran out, after all.

I nodded my agreement. "I was actually thinking they could be of use against the Knightmares—like that one they ate in Niflheim six months ago," I said casually, taking a wild gamble—because Alex had said that Knightmare disappeared a while ago.

I sensed Odin stiffen and I knew I'd scored a win, but I didn't look over at him, choosing to walk around the room with my staff and now-empty glass as I ran over his nonverbal answer. That was the same time Thor had attacked Gunnar and Ashley, but I still couldn't fathom how it tied together, so I decided to keep digging. I set my glass down on a side table.

"You never found a sword with the armor? Or learned what he was doing in Niflheim? You have to admit, it's kind of strange."

Odin shook his head. "He wouldn't say a word, and Hugin and Munin tried *very* hard," Odin replied in a flat tone that sent a shiver up my spine.

"Where is the Bioloki?" I asked, thinking back on Thor's strange slip-up —how he'd been able to mention something that was supposed to be secret. Because Pandora had also hinted that my mind was no longer an open book. It wasn't hard to guess that they were related.

Odin had gone entirely still. "Why?" he asked, not even bothering to demand how I knew that word.

I shrugged absently. "Entertain me," I said, my mind desperately trying to connect at least some dots. Thor had mentioned a few other strange things as well, but I wasn't going to give Odin that kind of information—not until he gave up some answers of his own.

Because I'd somehow found a loophole into their godly gossip club.

They were no longer prevented from saying certain things to me, and that could come in handy.

Of course, I was also very aware that if gods learned this about me, it would make me even *more* of a threat.

Odin shook his head. "It is safe," he said. "And it has nothing to do with this. Forget you ever heard it."

He watched me intensely for a moment, looking overly concerned as he debated something internally. I let him stew, wondering what he would decide. This new tactic was working way better. Who would have thought?

"Be careful, Nate," he finally said in a soft voice. "Events are spinning wildly out of control. Freya and I have some gift for prophecy, the turning of events, and even we find that we are looking at pale silhouettes of a future that may or may not be. We can't discern what comes next. We are not trying to hide anything from you, we are trying not to distract you with worthless information. Because you seem to be doing just fine by yourself, believe it or not—"

There was a sudden pounding on the door—as loud as a hammer.

THUD...THUD...THUD!

Gunnar exploded into his seven-feet of gargantuan werewolf—his Wulfric form—snarling loud enough to make my ears pop. I stared at the door warily. Even knowing Grimm should have been out there, I doubted he would have knocked like that unless it was an emergency.

Or maybe Thor was out there, and Grimm was dead. I jerked my chin at Odin, telling him to get behind us. I no longer needed him to answer doors for me—and potentially get killed by whomever waited on the opposite side. I needed him to focus on taking care of Ashley.

I didn't want two gods dying today.

As if the thought had been a spark to a flame, my golden veins suddenly flared to existence. I wasn't sure if that was a sign of danger or if my blood had gotten excited about the suggestion. We were about to find out.

Odin obeyed in silence, but he made no effort to leave. Drake and Cowan burst into the room in their four-legged werewolf forms, snarling at the door as our visitor banged again, knocking dust from the rafters.

THUD...THUD...THUD!

I glanced at Gunnar. Surprisingly, the gauntlets still fit his significantly larger claws. I grunted. That was handy, no pun intended.

But it wouldn't be enough to keep him safe. I couldn't risk losing my friend, so I prepared a bit of magic to knock him out of the way in case he got too excited.

Despite my concern for him, and my respect for his power, I couldn't help but admire him. He was the true Alpha of St. Louis, no matter what anyone said or thought. Only a true king could abandon his crown for his people.

And I'd never met a werewolf stronger than Gunnar. On the other hand, I'd met many werewolves who had briefly believed they were stronger than Gunnar.

I hadn't ever visited their graves, though. There hadn't been enough of them left to bury.

"Everyone get out of the way."

They stepped to the side, forming an arc with me at the center.

With a blast of magic, I yanked the doors open and threw a shield up between us.

Grimm stood in the opening with Talon on his back. Talon held his spear in his fist, and had obviously been using it to pound on the door. It looked like my two hours had come and gone.

Everyone let out a sigh of relief. "Could you have knocked any goddamned louder?" I muttered, lowering my shield.

Talon locked eyes with me, lowering his spear. "They followed us here. Hurry."

It took me a moment to process his words. "The Knightmares? All of them?" I gasped, my heart suddenly racing.

Talon shook his head. "No. Just three." Like that made any real difference. "We chased them all over town, but I think it was just a game to them. There was no pattern to it. I think we were set up."

I gritted my teeth. "And now they are here. Yeah. I think you're right. Mordred is trying to divide us. Confuse us. He thought I was in Fae, so he sends his Knightmares here, knowing you two will follow."

"Exactly," Grimm said. "So, let's get moving. Alex is facing them all by himself right now."

My eyes widened. "Oh, shit."

And that's when I sensed it. I could feel the walls from the hallway outside the Armory shaking and groaning.

Falco, the Beast inhabiting my mansion...

Was screaming.

Gunnar took two steps and lifted up Drake and Cowan by the ruffs of their necks—one in each armored claw.

"Your lives before hers!" he roared, his drool spraying their muzzles. They whined in submission, their ears folded back, and their tails tucked between their legs. But their lips were curled in an obedient snarl.

Odin spoke up as Gunnar dropped his lieutenants to their paws. "Go! There is nothing left for you to do here. We will care for your wife."

"No one can get inside the Armory, Gunnar," I urged. "She's safer than anyone in here. Safer than Alex right now."

Gunnar roared, his chest heaving as he settled a murderous glare towards the door, staring beyond Grimm.

I ripped open a Gateway in the hallway. A vibrant, manicured lawn appeared on the other side, and I was sprinting before I considered what might lay on the other side. I was first to leap through, gripping my rainbow staff in one hand. My friends shadowed me, prepared to preach the Gospel of Falco to the unenlightened heathens on the other side.

The first lesson in our religion was death.

Slow, excruciatingly painful, death.

CHAPTER 27

The first thing I realized was that it was cold as hell outside.

I knew this because I had suddenly acquired the ability to make etched glass artwork.

Using my nipples.

Since I had forgotten to put on a shirt or shoes.

The next thing I noticed was that three Knightmares were on my property, about thirty paces away, striding forward with their weapons out.

Alex faced them squarely, holding Excalibur in front of him, and looking as calm as can be.

They all turned to look at me and my crew at the exact same time.

"Get off my lawn," I growled at the Knightmares, my staff suddenly rippling with rainbow light. Grimm snorted indelicately and took a pointed step away from me, eyeing the light out of the corner of his eye with immense disdain. I pointedly ignored my rainbow-hating unicorn.

Chateau Falco rumbled unhappily behind me—a warning.

Three Knightmares against Alex was not a fair fight, no matter how badass he was. I glanced quickly at Grimm, eyeing his horn with a sudden grin.

"Go even the odds, boys," I growled, remembering how his horn was *also* strong enough to break their armor.

Grimm had been snooty about my rainbow staff, and I just didn't need that kind of negativity in my life.

He didn't even hesitate, galloping towards the threat with a pissed off Talon on his back. I noticed a two-handed sword on Talon's back, and I felt a flicker of hope surge within me. Maybe he'd picked up Sir Bedivere's blade after all—another weapon capable of piercing Knightmare armor.

That meant three weapons for three Knightmares.

They thought they could lead my friends on a wild goose chase, then come to my house and expect an easy fight? They were about to have a very bad day. I would pummel them with magic, distracting them while—

A bolt of lightning slammed down out of the clear blue sky, blasting a shallow crater into my lawn and startling the bejeezus out of me. Thor leapt out from within, glaring furiously at Chateau Falco.

I heard swords striking swords in explosive *clangs*, and I cursed under my breath. Looked like we now had two groups to deal with.

Gunnar, of course, saw this as a positive development. He flexed his hairy forearms eagerly, clenching his gauntlets as he eyed the man who had hurt his wife.

Gunnar was smiling, somehow. His massive wolf head and ridiculously long teeth turning his maw into something to inspire horror movie directors.

"So, *this* is where you took my father," Thor snarled. "He hides. Again! I hope you received your answers, Temple, because Odin dies today—"

Gunnar had closed the distance, hauled back his claw, and used every single muscle in his gargantuan body—as well as the ghostly powers of Geri and Freki—to punch Thor in the side of the head with a crackling *zap* from the gauntlets.

Thor flew, rolling and stumbling into a bush—and then through it.

I glanced over at Gunnar, arching an eyebrow. I sensed the spectral wolves at his side, hunkered low and snarling.

Thor had climbed to his feet behind the bush, and he was already striding back towards us, drooling with fury. Twigs and leaves stuck out of his head and beard, and I noticed a faint cut on his temple. That was it. Gunnar was panting heavily as he stared down Thor. "This ends here. Now," Gunnar snarled.

Thor squared off against him, not afraid, but impressed by Gunnar's strength. "You're scrappier than the last time we met," Thor growled, rubbing his knuckles together to create static arcs of electricity that crackled and popped loudly.

My skin was still glowing with golden light, and I wanted nothing more than to tear him to pieces with my godkiller strength. But...seeing how happy Gunnar was, and how he had actually managed to hurt Thor—even if only just a little—I decided to let it play out for a few moments. Gunnar could get his appetizer of revenge, and if the date looked to be going poorly for him, I could step in with the bill.

No credit cards. Payable in blood and teeth only.

Gunnar thumped his two armored fists together, his shoulders bunching forward. Although Thor was huge, Gunnar was significantly bigger, hairier, and looked infinitely more terrifying.

Still, they seemed evenly matched somehow.

The two began circling each other, lifting their fists to settle things the old-fashioned way—dukes up and beards down.

I glanced back at the others, wondering where I was best suited to help. I didn't dare leave Gunnar alone with Thor, but I wanted to make sure Alex and Talon weren't down for the count. Not that I could do much about it if they were, but I could use my magic to pull them to safety—long enough to get a breather.

Talon was a whirlwind, spinning his white staff like a propeller as he darted back and forth, and under, his opponent's slower swings of the sword. He struck hard and fast, CLANG! CLANG! CLANG! Although loud and obviously powerful, Talon's strikes did little more than make the Knightmare stumble before resetting his posture and going back in.

Alex was paying tribute to the Three Musketeers, spinning and twirling acrobatically as he went strike-for-strike with one of the taller Knightmares. "Fight it! Mordred is using you!" Alex shouted. "You are better than this!"

The Knightmare snarled back from beneath his helmet. "We do not break our oaths!" he growled back, swinging his mighty sword. Alex leaned to the side and the Knightmare's blade slammed into the earth in an explosion of dirt and grass. "The Summer Queen will soon be dead, and Winter's Queen will follow. Then there will be no more armies to stand in Mordred's way. You have already lost."

Excalibur blazed brightly, shining like mercury and flickering with golden light, but he didn't land a fatal strike.

Almost as if he was purposely refusing to harm his foe.

Damn it. That was a losing strategy, no matter what his heart told him. The only way to turn these guys back was to kill Mordred, and if Alex was showing a weakness like this, it didn't bode well for his future.

I flung a few haphazard blasts of air at his foe, giving Alex an opportunity to strike as the Knightmare batted my magic away. Alex calmly stepped back, shooting me a flat look.

"You can't save them all!" I shouted at him.

"I can try," Alex snarled, turning his attention back to his foe. For his part, the Knightmare stared at Alex for a moment longer than he should have, but then doubled down on his efforts.

Damn it.

Grimm cursed loudly, and I saw him hobbling away from his opponent. "Did you just punch me in the ass?" he demanded. The Knightmare held the offending fist out to his side and shrugged. Grimm lowered his head and scraped his hoof against the grass murderously. "I did not consent to that."

And then he exploded forward. The Knightmare stumbled back a few steps, trying to predict Grimm's movements, but the unicorn juked to the left and then the right, tripping his opponent up. Grimm took the opportunity to lunge for the opening, and I watched as he head-butted his foe's bicep, his horn piercing all the way through the Knightmare's armor. Then he whipped his head upwards, hurling the Knightmare high into the air.

Grimm snorted, calmly repositioning himself as he gauged the parabolic arc of his foe's downfall. In perfect timing, he reared back and kicked the Knightmare directly in the chest just as he was landing. The Knightmare's sword slammed blade-first into the grass, but he flew into the huge white tree on my property—the tree that was technically a Gateway to the Elder Realm.

Carl had left to go back home on urgent business, although he hadn't told me what that business was. That had been back before I fought Mordred at the Dueling Grounds, and the tree had been silent ever since.

Instead of the typical bark look, the tree more resembled a huge, white snake standing vertical. It even had scales and was warm to the touch.

The Knightmare struck the tree with a meaty thud and crashed to his ass. Grimm took one look at the sword, and then grabbed the hilt in his teeth.

The next thing I knew, he was charging, giving me an entirely new take on the Knightly pastime of jousting.

He looked like a triceratops with only two fucks left to give—missing one horn—as he raced towards the Knightmare. His foe looked dazed, clutching at his wounded arm as he struggled to regain his feet.

At the last moment, the Knight looked up at the sound of the galloping hooves and managed to dive to the side before either the sword or Grimm's horn could hit him.

Grimm veered so as not to headbutt the tree, but the sword sunk halfway into the trunk with an explosion of...

I blinked.

Red blood.

That couldn't be good.

An errant finger of lightning grazed my ass, making me jump and spin back to Gunnar and Thor, who were bobbing and weaving as they tried to land a solid punch on each other.

Thor struck with the power of lightning, his fists crackling and popping and shooting out sudden fingers of electricity whenever he made contact— which was what had just hit me in the rear. Except Gunnar somehow always seemed to catch the strikes on his armored fist or to bat the attacks aside at the last moment. And the resulting fingers of lightning hit him with no effect. He was either ignoring the pain, or the gauntlets were protecting more than just his hands.

Gunnar's counter game was strong, though, because Thor's face was bleeding more than it had been a few moments ago. And I could tell the God of Thunder was very annoyed by that.

I was pleased to see that Thor had regrown his teeth in the last hour.

Because Gunnar's sudden punch to the god's mouth looked hard enough to knock them right down his godly throat.

CHAPTER 28

The God of Thunder rocked back and flung his hand down at the ground, blasting Gunnar's feet with lightning. Gunnar, not having expected it, was hurled backwards a dozen yards in an impromptu cartwheel.

He jumped to his feet a few moments later, his eye a little wild around the edges, and his fur was sticking straight out, making him look like a mutant Pomeranian.

Thor took that moment of reprieve to spin towards Chateau Falco again, ignoring me completely. I frowned at that, wondering if I had a *Doctors Without Borders* badge on my ass—some explanation as to why Thor wasn't picking a fight with me. Just like in Niflheim.

I glanced down at my glowing chest and grunted. Well. Okay. Maybe he'd started to believe the whole godkiller thing.

Thor glared openly at Chateau Falco. "ODIN!" he roared. "Come outside right now or I will blast this place to rubble like I did to that den of reptiles!" he screamed.

Raego. The motherfucker was talking about Raego.

Before I could show him how I felt about that, Thor flung out a hand towards Chateau Falco. A spiraling bolt of lightning, looking almost like a crackling, baby tornado, reached down to strike my ancestral home.

A tiny black cloud that I hadn't noticed hovering over my mansion intercepted the electric storm and simply gobbled it down with an audible gulp. I gasped, feeling a smile tug at my cheeks.

Ruin! Falco and Kai's Baby Beast!

Thor stared speechless at the sudden change in forecast. Welcome to Missouri, where the weather changed at the drop of a hat.

Ruin zipped down to us, pausing to hover about five feet from the gaping God of Thunder.

"Did you just try to hit my mother?" Ruin asked in a cold, murderous whisper. Right now, he was a deceptively small black hole filled with the bottomless, irrational rage of a seven-year-old.

He didn't wait for Thor to respond.

He belched.

And the exact same blast of lightning Thor had tried to use on my mansion—Ruin's mother—struck Thor right in the gut. He flew past us at lightspeed—of course—and knocked down all three Knightmares like metal bowling pins before he slammed into the white tree with an expulsion of breath.

Oh, and more blood.

I didn't know if it was his or from the tree, because the hilt of the Knightmare's sword was still embedded in the trunk, oozing blood in a steady, alarming downpour.

I glanced over at Ruin. "Thanks."

He bobbed up and down, seeming to shrug. "No one hurts my mother," he said as if he was announcing the End Days. "I tried to help Alex, but he told me to come help you two instead," he admitted in a friendlier tone.

I frowned at that.

Gunnar—still looking like a deranged Pomeranian and shaking his head —finally reached us as we turned back to Thor. The Knightmares were already climbing back to their feet, and immediately began backing away from Thor.

Thor looked at them, and then the sword sticking out of the trunk. He yanked it out, ignoring the spurt of blood, and then lobbed it to the unarmed Knightmare with a chuckle.

I froze. What the hell?

The Knightmare caught the blade, and then the three of them simply disappeared. Alex, Grimm and Talon squared off against Thor.

Thor ignored them, turning to me with a look of undying hatred. "Odin will die by my hand. Only *then* will I come for you two. You cannot keep him safe from Thor, the God of Thunder!"

Rainbow light suddenly erupted over his body, and he disappeared.

Gunnar howled in outrage.

Alex, Talon, and Grimm finally made their way over to us, sheathing their weapons and scanning our surroundings as if expecting a surprise attack.

Alex glanced down at his dreamcatchers absently. The one with the dragon scale—representing our realm here—was devoid of lights, but the Fae dreamcatcher now showed seven orbs, and they were all concentrated in the same spot.

"They're all gone now," Alex said, letting out a breath. He shook his head in frustration before approaching Ruin. "Thank you, old friend."

"Of course. When he attacked my mother…" Ruin trailed off, sounding emotional.

"You did well. Can you keep an eye on everything out here? Make sure no one else shows up? I need to speak with Nate in private."

I was staring at the tree, my back to Ruin. I shook my head, not knowing if this was a good development or if we were about to have an army of Elders—a race feared by every pantheon and supernatural group I had ever met—on my lawn.

And whether they would be friend or foe.

I glanced over at Talon beside me because his tail was twitching, and he was sniffing at the air, facing the front gate to Chateau Falco.

His tail abruptly shot up, bushing out like he'd been zapped, and I had about a millisecond's warning before he spun and tackled me to the ground.

I grunted, looking up to see Ruin hovering over me. "That's strange," he said, stretching out a misty limb to withdraw an inky marble from his center mass.

"Bullet," Talon snarled, crouching over me protectively. Everyone began to make threatening sounds pursuant to their flavor of monster.

I flung up a long, curved shield in the direction Talon had been staring, making it large enough to cover us all as I climbed to my feet. I peered closer to see what Ruin held. Because it didn't look like any bullet I'd ever seen.

In fact…it looked like a black marble.

I cursed in recognition. It was a prototype from Grimm Tech, even sporting the logo for my company on the side.

"It's worse than a bullet," I growled. "We're leaving. Now."

I scooped up the marble on a thread of air, careful not to apply any pressure or drop it. Then I ripped open a Gateway and stepped into the Sanctorum, not even bothering to wait for my friends—although they hopped through right after me, looking angry.

"I will try to find them, Nate," Ruin told me from the other side of the Gateway, sounding ashamed.

I waved a hand absently. "Not your fault, Ruin. It was a cowardly attempt, and I bet they're already long gone. But it wouldn't hurt to keep an eye out, like Alex suggested."

Seeing that everyone had made it through, I let the Gateway wink shut and began pacing back and forth in the Sanctorum.

"What is it, Nate?" Alex asked, eyeing the floating marble.

Instead of answering, I turned to Grimm. "Go back to the Armory and guard the door." I flung open a Gateway to send him straight there since he didn't have hands to open his own doors. He nodded, hopping through.

I let it wink shut, feeling marginally better. I had no reason to think anyone could get inside the Armory, let alone that they could even make it that far through Chateau Falco, but I knew it made Gunnar less twitchy to give Ashley another guard.

This black marble had changed things.

I stormed over to the old desk and ripped a piece of paper off the pad of customized stationary. *Master Nathin Laurent Temple* and my family crest stretched across the top. My parents had loved their strange, pointless spelling of my name, which was why I'd chosen to go by *Nate* instead.

I patted my pockets and let out a curse. Of course I didn't have a phone on me. There were no towers in Fae. I reached into the drawers and pulled out a cheap burner I had stashed there for an emergency. Luckily, it turned on when I hit the power button. I tapped through the settings, found the burner's phone number, and scribbled it down on the piece of paper. Then I added the words *CALL ME!* and underlined them.

Then I stepped back until I found a wide-open space devoid of rugs or furniture, and dropped the paper on the ground. "Step back," I told everyone, because they'd followed me, trying to figure out what I was doing.

They obeyed and I took a few additional steps back. Then I took a few more, just to be safe.

I lobbed the black marble at the paper and flung up a shield in case I had been wrong. The marble struck the marble floor and shattered in a puff of black smoke that almost instantly sucked back in on itself.

When it was gone, so was the paper.

"What the fuck?" Gunnar snarled. I turned to see he had shifted back and was fidgeting with the final button of a pair of spare jeans he must have grabbed from the nearby dresser. I kept it stocked for just that reason—shifters were hard on wardrobe budgets.

Now, two dudes without shirts or shoes were in the house, and he made it look so much cooler. His oblique muscles had oblique muscles.

I stared down at the burner phone, scowling impatiently.

It rang, and I had to force myself to wait for the second ring so as not to appear desperate. I flipped it open. "You missed," I said, by way of greeting. "Do you work for me?" I demanded, gritting my teeth. Because that black marble had never been released to the production team. I had quickly seen the potential risks for misuse.

Hit someone with that glass ball and you could send them wherever you wanted. It Shadow Walked the target without their consent.

My Tiny Balls, for the most part, at least gave the person a choice. When they broke, they opened a Gateway and you could choose to step through or not.

Of course, they could also be used for harm—like a grenade. Toss them directly at someone and the resulting Gateway might just rip them in half.

But these black marbles—Abductors, as I had called them—could be used to bring someone directly into a trap. A cage, or any other kind of supernatural prison cell—the ultimate kidnapping tool.

The voice on the other end spoke calmly and rationally, and I found my anger dissipating, replaced by suspicion and doubt.

"How do I know you're telling the truth?"

Their answer made me smirk.

"Thanks for the tip, I guess. I'll wait to see how it all plays out."

I hung up the phone, staring down at it thoughtfully. Truth or lie?

"You going to tell us what the hell is going on?" Gunnar repeated.

I thought about it. "I think I have a guardian angel. Or an overly honest abductor," I admitted. I turned to Alex. "I think that was the assassin you warned me about, but she has a different story to tell."

"Which is?" he asked warily.

I thought about it and then waved a hand dismissively. "These things happen. It's nothing to get worked up about."

CHAPTER 29

*W*hen it became abundantly clear that I was not going to elaborate on my phone call with my mysterious, would-be abductor, Alex and I traded brief stories, giving each other an update on everything we'd run into in the last few hours.

Alex looked exhausted, but acted just as anxious as I felt, refusing to sit down for more than two minutes, subconsciously fondling the dream-catchers hanging from his hip. The Fae dreamcatcher still showed seven Knightmares congregating in one location.

Suspiciously close to Queen Summer's palace, just like the Knightmare had told Alex when they were fighting outside.

So we caught up very quickly, hitting just the highlights.

Talon and Gunnar had listened in silence with grim, brooding faces.

Talon just wanted to go back to Fae and find a way to kill Mordred.

Gunnar just wanted to go kill Thor before his bond with Geri and Freki failed him.

Alex, although relieved to hear we had solved the mystery of the third dead Knight, hadn't been pleased to hear about Odin's ravens eating him. And he hadn't known of any reason for Mordred to send a Knight to Nifl-heim in the first place. We did find out that the Knight had been Sir Gaheris —one of King Arthur's nephews.

I'd heard his name before, but that was about it.

In similar fashion, I hadn't been pleased to learn that the Knightmares who had come to St. Louis had been toying with us, leading Alex and Talon all over town on a wild goose chase. The only logical explanation I could come up with was that Mordred had indeed sent them here as a distraction, so he could set up whatever he was planning outside Summer's castle. Or maybe because he had needed Alex and Talon out of Fae for a little while—reasons unknown, but probably not good.

Alex sat down with a huff, kicking his feet up as he processed my story. He looked exhausted. I didn't point out that he had sat down in his rightful chair, because he didn't seem to notice.

King Arthur's old seat.

"At least Mordred isn't holed up in Camelot any longer," Alex grunted. "If his Knightmares' location is any indication."

I grunted. "Might be a trap."

Alex nodded. "If he's in Camelot, we'll have to go there by foot." I arched an eyebrow, frowning. "He's placed wards surrounding Camelot so that he can immediately pinpoint any sudden arrivals. Like you, would be my guess. Doesn't want you sending an army right onto his front steps."

I cursed under my breath, realizing Shadow Walking and Gateways were now out of the question.

Mordred had set up alarm bells.

Talon absently batted a plastic cup off the table, his tail twitching. It landed on the rug beneath his chair.

Gunnar glanced down with a frown. Then he picked it up and set it back on the table, murmuring something to Talon, who was fixated on the armor and didn't seem to notice Gunnar's help or that he'd even spoken.

Gunnar shrugged, leaning back in his chair.

A few seconds later, Talon swiped the cup back off the table, not even seeming aware that he was doing it. Gunnar frowned at him, and then bent back down to pick it up again.

I burst out laughing. Cats were dicks, always knocking crap off shelves and tables for no reason at all. "Well played, Talon."

He frowned over at me, blinking several times as if he'd been dozing. Then he noticed the cup back on the table and narrowed his eyes. "I do not like it there."

Gunnar frowned at the cup as if it were a philosophical question, not following along. I laughed harder. Especially since neither understood.

Cats and dogs, man. Cats and dogs.

Alex was preoccupied, studying the two full suits of armor laid out on the floor a few paces away. The breastplate, helmet, and gauntlets Gunnar had borrowed from Grimm Tech sat beside them, an incomplete set.

Alex absently scratched at his beard, a slight frown on his face.

Time for me to be the asshole.

"I know you don't want to hear this, Alex, but you need to hunt them down," I said, gently but firmly. "They are too dangerous. It could be a trap, but if they're laying siege to the Summer Queen…"

Alex nodded grimly. "The two of us against seven," he mused, sighing tiredly. He didn't complain. He didn't need to.

The odds sucked. And the only thing I could do to help balance those odds was to give Thor a Viking funeral. With him gone, Ashley would no longer need protection. I could get Drake and Cowan to join me in Fae. I could reach out to my contacts—Raego, Achilles, the Minotaur, and everyone else who had fled St. Louis when Thor came to town—and ask for their help. To pay me back for ridding them of the god who had chased them from their homes. Gunnar could even get his werewolf pack back. I could bring them *all* to Fae. An army of my own.

Except…that would take time. A lot of it. And with the dreamcatcher letting us know that Mordred's Knights were already locked onto the Summer Queen, we didn't *have* any time.

I frowned at another bleak thought.

None of those allies had the ability to dent or even scratch a Knight's armor. They could go up against anyone else Mordred had in his army, but the real problem was the Knightmares.

And the only way to defeat them without bloodshed was to kill Mordred —who was likely *surrounded* by said Knightmares.

Those poor bastards who had been bonded against their will, wanting nothing more than to be good, just, noble men. And they'd been corrupted by a tyrant king—a man dead set on tarnishing his father's name because his daddy hadn't loved him enough, or something just as petty.

Alex didn't want to kill the Knights. He wanted to save them. He would do what was necessary, but he had made it abundantly clear that he didn't like it. Because he saw what they had once *been*, not what they had *become*—

I blinked, Alex's misguided faith giving me an idea.

Then I slowly turned to glance at the armor. Without a word, I stood from my chair, made my way over to the suits of armor, and knelt down between them. I set my hand on one of them, feeling it out with my Fae magic. *The armor came from Fae*, I thought to myself. Avalon was supposedly a realm within Fae—although I'd never seen it.

And Merlin had been a wizard.

Technically, I had the same qualifications—on paper, at least. I knew how to use both magics—Fae and wizard. I closed my eyes, focusing on that strange Fae magic, and I delved deep into the set of armor—just like I would any element of Fae. Because everything had a soul, of sorts, in Fae. Rocks, sticks, vines, stars, you name it.

So I reached deep and introduced myself to the oldest part of the armor, focusing on its origin, its creation—the set of armor as a whole, not just one individual piece.

What it had once been, just like how Alex chose to see the Knights.

And I almost had a heart attack when it answered back in a gruff, no-nonsense hum. Licking my lips, I internally bantered back and forth, asking how it had been formed and why, who had made it…

Basically, I asked it to tell me its life story.

And it obliged. Hell, it was *overjoyed* to talk about the glory days. I even had to redirect it to focus on specifics, because this armor was a talker. Then again, it had been locked away inside Stonehenge—like all the others —for the past few centuries or longer.

The strangest part of all was that Fae conversations like this happened almost instantaneously. Because the item didn't answer individual questions. I simply thought at it, and it thought right back.

So the whole thing took maybe a minute or two. Three, tops.

I opened my eyes, blinking. "Huh. They're parasites."

CHAPTER 30

*a*lex glared at me. "They are *men*, Nate. *Good* men—"

I waved a hand, placating him. "No. Sorry. That came out wrong. Give me a second," I said, scratching my head as I tried to process what I'd learned, and how I might translate it for Alex in a way he could understand. "Okay. The armor. It's…symbiotic. That's why Mordred cursed it. The armor works hand-in-hand with the man, influencing him."

"Why didn't the gauntlets turn me into an evil asshole, then?" Gunnar asked, stroking his beard.

I shook my head. "You're thinking of it as just a gauntlet. If I cut off your hand and gave it to Ashley, would she love that hand as much as she loves you? Would it make her laugh? Tell her jokes?" I said, waving a hand to indicate a billion other examples. "The hand is just a piece of you. All those pieces of you formed together are what she loves. The whole package—and yes, insert adolescent joke," I added, before anyone could derail me. "The armor is like that. It's stronger as a complete unit—like a family."

"United we stand," Alex murmured pensively, nodding.

I shrugged. "I would have gone with *All for one, and one for all*, personally," I said, smiling as I remembered his sword-fighting outside. "If these are cleansed, you should be able to put one on," I said, trailing my hand down the suit of armor. "You would get all the benefits without being brainwashed. In fact, *you*—not the *armor*—will be the one holding the leash. Nothing like Mordred's Knightmares."

Talon's tail twitched, and Gunnar leaned forward excitedly.

"Why?" Alex asked. "If it's so easy to turn the armor against the Knight, why would they risk wearing them?"

I held up a finger. "Ah. But it's *not* easy to turn them. Remember, the only reason Mordred's plan worked at Stonehenge was because he was technically the only living Pendragon when he woke up the Knights and made them swear their oaths. Arthur's spirit hit you too late to stop the *men* from swearing fealty," I said gently. "And *then* Mordred used the Blood Curse on the armor to double down. So, in a way, he turned them *both—man and armor*."

I clapped excitedly, shaking my head. Because I also knew how they had originally been made. Enough of an idea to grasp the concept, anyway.

"I'm amazing. Suck on that, Merlin," I crowed, slapping my knee.

Everyone stared at the two suits of armor dubiously, knowing that if I was wrong, they'd become an evil overlord—a Knightmare.

"How do we remove the curse?" Talon asked.

My brain had already been pondering that, ever since I realized I could communicate with the armor.

The original armor had been blessed by both Arthur and Merlin.

I turned to look up at Alex, who was scratching his scruff again like he had a case of the fleas. I glanced down at my own appearance—a ragged wizard wearing only a pair of faded, unclean jeans. "Fuck it." I turned to Alex. "I'm going to need some of your blood."

Gunnar and Talon perked up, staring at the two of us more intently. Alex didn't even hesitate as he stood from his seat and knelt down beside me. He drew Excalibur enough to reveal part of the blade and then cut his palm. I nodded, and then leaned over to slice my own palm on Excalibur, praying to tack on some extra credit points for sticking to symbolism and tradition. In case I royally screwed this up.

I took hold of his wrist, moving it so that I could easily access it. "Hold it there. Don't move. Might as well close your eyes and think chivalrous thoughts," I added. I took a few moments to memorize the two inverted symbols on the suits of armor beside me.

Then I took a deep breath and closed my eyes.

I only had two examples of chivalry to go by—one literary, and one living.

Thomas Mallory's book, *Le Morte d'Arthur*—The Death of King Arthur.

And Alex Arete-Pendragon-Temple, the man. Yes, I chose to include a hyphen with my name. I had adopted him, after all—saving him from the Fae Courts in their Changeling operation when he had only been a young boy.

I'd earned the right.

And *Arete* had been his real name, long ago, before the Fae stole him. Which was a curious coincidence. Arete had several debated translations or meanings attached to it, but they all funneled into one definition, in my opinion.

To be the best possible form of a thing.

And it was also on my family crest.

I focused on my Fae magic—everything I had surmised from my *talk* with the suit of armor. How and why it had been made.

And I also tapped into my wizard's magic, opening myself up to it completely. I let the two streams of power meet at an angle, like two great rivers. They struck with incredible force, hard enough to create figurative white-water rapids in my mind.

I gritted my teeth, trying to hold my tentative grip on my magics while I split my mind to define my examples of chivalry—Alex Pendragon-Temple and Thomas Mallory.

A faint thought floated down the stream of my imagination, finding perfect harmony and serendipity with the fact that the author I'd chosen as an example had the last name *Mallory*—just like the god who had given his life for me not too long ago. Pan, a man I looked up to as the best father figure I had ever known.

If Gunnar could become half the father Mallory had been, he would be twice as good as any father in existence. Since regaining my memory of my childhood in Fae—and learning how invested Mallory had been in absolutely every facet of my life—I knew he hadn't been a perfect dad or man.

But he'd been perfect for *me*. And that's all that mattered.

It was beautifully poetic, and thoughts of him settled my tentative control firmly in place so that I no longer felt any strain in my mind from trying to hold it all together.

Just like Mallory had held me together—in life and in death.

I love you Mallory. This one is for you. I'll try to make you proud, I thought to myself.

Then I got to work.

I focused back on Thomas Mallory and what I had read of his Code of Chivalry. And then I tried to marry that with what I'd learned from Alex, making a new hybrid of sorts. I recited these beliefs—not to instill them *into* the armor, but to use them like a scalpel to scrape *away* the curse currently painted upon them.

Obviously, I took my own beliefs out of the equation so as not to tarnish the noble virtues with my vices.

To never initiate outrage nor murder.

To never betray those people and values closest to you.

To never be cruel.

To be honorable and merciful in equal measure—even to your enemies.

To grant help to those in need.

To never force yourself upon—or take advantage of—others, especially those who look up to you the most.

And others. I included them all—some not even as words, but as ideals or examples I had seen Alex display in his everyday life. Again, I didn't force these into the armor—I used them like a chisel to scrape away the graffiti Mordred had perverted them with.

To bring the suits of armor back to their roots—to what they had *once been*, not accepting what they had *become*.

I opened my eyes and stared down at my hand. I squeezed my fist to make sure the blood was flowing freely, and then I slapped my palm over Alex's, merging our blood together.

Alex and Nate.

Arthur and Merlin.

And Mallory, I thought to myself.

A low hum—like bass from a speaker—abruptly filled the air in the Sanctorum, and the purple-flamed torches illuminating the space flared brighter with a sudden *whoosh*.

I smiled absently as I closed my eyes and rubbed both of my hands together, mixing up our blood. I made sure to liberally cover the tips of both pointer fingers, and then I placed each of them on a different set of armor.

In my mind's eye, I imagined the symbol as it had first been drawn by Arthur and Merlin, not the inverted curse.

And my fingers flew, tracing over Mordred's curse with new blood.

As my fingers moved, I felt the inverted symbol fade away. The moment I completed mine, there was a faint *pop*, and I knew they were both gone—not just Mordred's curse, but the original symbol as well.

Leaving the suits of armor as blank slates.

And the rivers of power inside me suddenly surged, flooding the banks. I held on for dear life, my entire psyche vibrating at the unbelievable strain of holding it all together. The blackened armor burned, peeling away to reveal something new and virginal. I gritted my teeth, grunting in pain as I fought for this. To give Alex something he could use to make his corner of the world a better place.

A gift from father to son.

And Mallory, my own stand-in father, helped me hold on just a little bit longer. I shook as I imagined the black continuing to peel, burn, and disintegrate away from the armor. My grip on my powers, even with Mallory's imagined support, began to slip.

And then I visualized that fateful day that haunted my dreams.

Mallory holding onto that cliff before the end, and me holding onto him as tightly as I could. How I would have given *anything* for him to hold on just one.

More.

God.

Damned.

Second.

So I did that. Holding on. One second at a time.

And then another.

And another.

And another.

Until I knew that the black color was gone, and I was finally able to let go. I fell back, lost in unconsciousness before my body ever touched the floor.

*I'm proud of you, boy...*Mallory's voice echoed in my mind.

And that made it all worthwhile.

CHAPTER 31

$\mathscr{I}$ woke to find Alex's face close enough to mine for us to touch eyeballs. I recoiled and he jumped back. I groaned, rolling onto my side and shakily pulling myself up to a sitting position.

Alex was there, gripping me by the shoulders. Then he was hugging me tightly. "You did it!" he whispered.

I was still trying to wake up, so I simply sat, trying to remember what had happened. Slowly, it began to come back to me. I glanced down to see a pristinely white suit of armor. My eyes widened, and I weakly shoved Alex back to look on my other side. That one was white as well.

And neither had Mordred's symbol painted across the front.

"I did it," I breathed. "I'm fucking Merlin..."

Gunnar grunted. "Like a broken clock, you are." I slowly swiveled my gaze to find him grinning at me. He nodded, silently congratulating me. I nodded back.

Then he was reaching out to help pull me to my feet. The room spun dangerously, and he quickly guided me over to a chair, sitting me down.

When my vision cleared, I took stock of everyone in the room. Alex and Gunnar were watching me with concerned looks, but Talon...

I cleared my throat. "Go ahead, Talon. Try it on."

He flinched as if I'd goosed him, jerking his head away from the armor to stare at me. Then he took a step back, his tail twitching. "I couldn't. My place is beside you, Wylde. I'm only helping Alex until he finds others. I've just been doing what needed to be done."

I knew what Talon really needed was for me to let him go.

I arched an eyebrow at him, smirking. "You've been by my side forever, Talon. You literally died to save me not long ago, and that's not even taking into account all the times you *tried* to give your life for me," I said, smiling. "Maybe it's time you give your life to *something* instead. A cause that *you* value."

Alex watched him, not moving a muscle. Gunnar held his breath.

Talon stared down at the armor, breathing heavily through his nose. "I… am no Knight," he finally whispered.

"Talon," I said firmly, drawing his attention. "This is a higher calling. Not just watching out for me, but for an entire city. Think about it! You're the *only one* with the experience to teach fledgling Knights how to become a warrior *and* manage their Wild Sides in Fae. Literally you. You're the guy, Tal," I said, smiling proudly, and hating myself for giving him away.

He stared back at me in surprise, his eyes wide and dilated like one of those sad kitten memes.

"I'm not sure I can think of a better person for the job. I've seen the look in your eyes. You want this. Not out of any obligation or duty, but for all the right reasons. And you know Fae better than any of us. Alex is going to need that. The other Knights are going to need that. They're going to need *you*… Sir Talon the Devourer. And Alex is going to need you to keep him out of trouble. Out of danger," I added, solemnly.

Because I remembered what my parents had said about how important Alex was going to be some day. How important he would be to me. I didn't know exactly how, but my parents hadn't been wrong about very much in their many schemes.

Talon shuddered, not even realizing he was purring. And I saw a single tear fall and sink into the fur just below his eye. He dipped his chin, momentarily at a loss for words. But the gratitude in his eyes was unmistakable. "Thank you, Wylde," he finally whispered.

I dipped my chin back at him. He slowly turned to look at Alex, as if needing to verify that he wasn't dreaming.

Alex nodded without hesitation. "It would be my honor, Talon. I've seen your courage, bravery, and dedication over this past year. It's inspiring. Nate is right. I can't think of anyone better."

And then he drew Excalibur.

Talon knelt down before Alex, not breaking eye contact.

Alex gently settled Excalibur on each of Talon's shoulders, and then the top of his head. "I dub thee Sir Talon the Devourer," he droned officiously, biting back a smile. "Rise."

Talon did, and he was beaming from ear-to-ear. He glanced down at one of the suits, his smile beginning to fade as he only just realized how much smaller he was than the previous owner. I grinned, waiting.

The armor began to quiver and hum, and then it simply disappeared. I burst out laughing at the stunned look on his face. He spun to me, horrified.

I'd already surmised something like this happening. "I think it's like your spear," I told him. He frowned, and then closed his eyes.

Suddenly, he was decked from paws to neck in white armor, perfectly fitted to his frame, and his spear appeared in his gauntleted paw. The sight of him in the regal armor made my breath catch. The entire setup began to glow and then it flashed one time, bright enough for everyone to turn away with a hiss of surprise.

After a moment, I glanced back and grinned. A blue cat's paw marked his breastplate, just as another one bloomed into existence on the Round Table, replacing its predecessor. I hadn't even thought to check the Round Table.

"You look like a solution in search of a problem," I told him. He grinned, nodding.

I knew that Talon's spear now had the strength to tear through a Knightmare's armor. I inspected Talon's new get-up, shaking my head wondrously. I didn't see any gaping holes from where it had previously been pierced by a blade or Odin's ravens.

Talon's armor puffed out, and he stood before us just like before, except he had a big old grin on his face. "I'm a Knight!" he exclaimed, purring loudly.

I shot Alex a grin, leaning in to whisper, "Maybe you should read up on the whole knighting process. Rituals are important, man. I'm a wizard. I would know." And then I pointedly glanced down at my professional wizard's attire.

Alex laughed, brushing a hand through his hair. "I thought I had a little more time before I would actually have to do that. I didn't know you were going to get me my first set of armor *today*."

"Two sets," I clarified, glancing down at the unclaimed armor. "You should probably put one on as well. You two are going to need every advantage you can get against Mordred and his seven Knights," I said, jerking my chin at the Fae dreamcatcher.

Alex considered that for a moment. "It doesn't feel right," he finally said. "These are for my Knights. I'll get my own armor later. Maybe you can even help."

I thought about it for a moment and, despite hating his decision, I finally nodded with a sigh. Alex was right. Something about it really didn't feel right, even though I wanted him to wear some kind of protection.

Dads, right?

Alex slowly lifted his head from the spare set of armor, settling on Gunnar. "Hey," he mused to the werewolf, catching his attention. "Crazy idea, but…" and he pointedly glanced back at the armor.

Talon purred louder. Gunnar stared down at it in silence, and my shoulders began to twitch, waiting for his response.

"You have earned it," Alex said. "You and Talon were the first to kill one of the Knightmares. It's fitting that you two would be my first Knights. All I ask is that you consider it."

And then Alex took a step back.

Gunnar remained silent. Then he slowly—incredibly, ridiculously slowly —turned to me, arching an eyebrow. And the message was clear.

How about a Mask instead?

I tried to keep my face blank. Part of me wanted to punch Alex right in the mouth for him trying to poach *both* of my best friends, but…

I had refused his request for a Mask in hopes of keeping him safe. As a result, Gunnar was now a free agent. I'd already given up one best friend to Alex's new Round Table.

Could I really let go of both of them?

All I had to do was give him a Mask.

Gunnar saved me from answering by clearing his throat and turning back to Alex. "I need to focus on my wife right now, Alex. But the gesture means more than you know. Let me figure out all of this father business, first. Ask my wife what she thinks. Because when I commit to something, I devote my all to it."

And then he gave me a pointed, sidelong glance. It was the equivalent of five eyes—two from each of his spare wolves, along with Gunnar's lone eye. A not-so-subtle jab that he wasn't just talking about Alex's offer.

He was reminding me of his true desire for a Horseman's Mask.

Talon cleared his throat, eyeing the dreamcatchers with a frown. "Two more lights just appeared."

Alex's eyes widened before he grabbed the dreamcatcher for Fae. He snarled, and I managed to get a closer look. Talon was right. There were no longer seven Knightmares in Fae. There were nine.

Our mystery travelers had come home. And they were all in the same spot. "You two should go. Now."

"What about you?" Alex asked, checking his gear to make sure he had everything he needed.

I gave Gunnar a considering look. "We can't team up with you until we kill Thor. He's obviously dead set on killing Odin, which will bring him too close to Ashley for my liking. I vote we give him a *decease and desist order*. Personally."

Gunnar grinned wolfishly. "Not what it's called, but your version is better."

"We'll meet up with you as soon as we can," I said.

Alex nodded. "Just hurry. I know time moves differently between here and Fae—and lately it's worked out so that time is faster there than it is here. So five minutes of us fighting in Fae could be five hours here," he said, shrugging. "What I mean is that you have time. Just don't take too long, or we might not be alive when you get there. Feel free to send friends," he added dryly. "We'll keep them busy as long as we can."

"Which will now be longer, thanks to this upgrade," Talon said, his eyes seeming to glow as he clenched his spear.

I nodded. "If I can, I'll send Grimm to help you out."

Alex's shoulders loosened. "That would be a huge help." He glanced at the burner phone on the desk. "I don't know what games you're playing with her but be careful. Maybe she was the assassin, maybe she was something the Knightmares set up."

I nodded. "I don't intend to hang out in St. Louis for very long."

Alex shrugged. "I just want to make sure you get me some armor before you keel over, old man."

I grunted, glancing over my shoulder at Gunnar. "Kids these days."

Alex rolled his eyes. "Say hello to Thor's goats for me," he said with a dark grin—totally unchivalrous.

I chuckled. "Deal."

I traded grips with him, and then Talon. "Give them hell," I said, turning away. "We'll be there as soon as we can. Right after we pay our electric bill."

CHAPTER 32

$\mathcal{I}$ Shadow Walked us to the room in the Armory with the balcony —picking a corner where I doubted anyone would be standing.

"No babies yet, but the healing pool is working," Pandora said from over near the balcony. She wore a sheer, practically transparent toga that showed a scandalous amount of tan side-boob and ended just above her knees, making the whole setup look more like a negligee. She had a long leather strap folded over her forearm. I could sense that it was powerful, but everything in the Armory was powerful.

Gunnar strode forward eagerly, smiling excitedly.

Pandora smiled warmly at his reaction. "She looks healthy again and her sight is recovering, although I advised her to keep the bandage on until we are certain. Head just around the corner and you will find her room guarded by one of your wolves."

Gunnar forgot all about Thor, bolting from the room.

I smiled, walking over to her. "Thank you for helping, Pandora," I said, leaning back against the balcony beside her. I set my rainbow staff on a nearby table.

"I would be of little help without Freya," she admitted. "I can help sustain life, but I know nothing of bringing new life into the world."

I nodded distractedly, finding myself thinking back on the strange phone call with my would-be abductor. I had kept the burner phone in my pocket, just in case she called back. Her story had been almost too prepos-terous to believe, but a small part of me wondered if that also made it too preposterous to be a lie.

Either way, it pertained to me, not anyone else. But I was interested to see how it played out. Soon.

I sighed, deciding to take this moment of reprieve to formulate a plan to deal with Thor. I'd seen Gunnar kick serious ass against him—but that had been with the gauntlets, which we'd agreed to leave behind. Even with Geri and Freki's added strength, I wanted Gunnar better protected. A thought came to mind, a very dangerous one. I sat on it, debating it internally.

I knew there would be no time for me to replicate the armor cleansing ritual in the middle of a battle, so nothing had changed, really. Other than me improving our defenses. We needed offense, though.

Just then, Odin entered the room, saw us, and made his way over.

Inwardly, I cursed. I'd wanted to ask Pandora about my idea, but I didn't want to do so in front of the Allfather.

Odin was hiding something from me—something that seemed to bother him greatly. I could see it on his face whenever he thought I wasn't looking.

So I decided not to tell him anything about Alex or Sir Talon. Or Thor, for that matter. All he knew was that Talon had shown up earlier to warn us about Knightmares attacking Chateau Falco. Thor had shown up later.

"How is your lady wife? Does she have everything she needs?" Pandora asked politely.

Odin dipped his head. "Yes, thank you. Freya has never been one to let destiny remain unchallenged," he admitted with a faint smile.

Pandora's lips thinned. "The Seiðr." It sounded like SAY-der.

Odin nodded. Noticing my thoughtful frown, he turned to me. "Freya was one of the Vanir, and when she came to me as my wife, she introduced us to a new magic—the Seiðr."

I didn't immediately comment, because I'd heard all sorts of stories on exactly how Odin had taken his wife but calling him out on it wasn't going to get me anything useful. "What is it?"

Odin thought about it for a few moments. "It is best described as an original form of witchcraft. Freya can use rituals to divine futures, heal the sick, control the weather, find hidden things," he said, waving a hand. "It can also be used for more nefarious purposes, of course, much like any power."

I thought about it, nodding. That did sound an awful lot like witchcraft.

Divining futures, performing rituals, making potions…and he wasn't lying about those practices working just as well for nefarious purposes.

There was a reason witches got a bad reputation several hundred years ago. Not all were bad, of course, but enough of them had used their powers for all the wrong reasons, attracting all the wrong kinds of attention.

"You are no slouch at Seiðr, Odin," Pandora said, and it wasn't a question.

Odin shrugged. "True, but Freya is definitely the stronger between us. I know enough to help her do as she must. I wouldn't know where to begin without her."

"That is because you have a tiny man-brain," Pandora muttered. The best part of her jab was that I knew she hadn't even meant it snarky. That was just how Pandora was. "It must have been *your* brilliant idea to take Ashley to Niflheim. You understand that it almost killed her, yes?" she demanded, and there wasn't even a *hint* of civility in her voice this time. "Gods hiding out in Niflheim. What a genius idea," she snapped.

I arched an eyebrow, turning to Odin. "*Excuse* me?"

Pandora nodded. "The mist dampens a god's power, potentially nullifying their abilities. The very atmosphere is toxic to them. It has lesser effects on mortals, but it definitely didn't help Ashley."

And the hair on my arms jumped up. "So *that* was why Thor was such a chump!" I cursed, pounding my fist into my palm. The ichor in my veins flared brightly, drawing Odin and Pandora's attention.

Pandora snorted incredulously. "That would be like tying up Thor's arms and then pointing a gun at his forehead!" she hooted. Odin grimaced, averting his eye. Pandora's laughter died down as she glanced at my glowing veins. "Be careful how open you are with that, my Host," she warned. "It is best to hide it. No use announcing you have the power to kill a god before you get close enough to actually do the deed."

I frowned at my veins. "How do I turn off the light show?"

Pandora smiled warmly and turned to place her hand on my shoulder. "Take deep breaths," she murmured, closing her eyes. I followed her direction and closed my eyes. "Relax and think of something other than killing a god. Remember a happy thought."

It was a lot harder than it sounded. Kind of like when someone told you not to think of a purple elephant.

After a few moments, I focused on my childhood memory of playing pirates with Gunnar in our old treehouse, Chateau Defiance.

"Good," Pandora breathed, gently squeezing my shoulder. "Strong emotions pertaining to a god makes your ichor glow. You must remain in control at all times, because even the *presence* of some gods will make it shine. You do not want to announce this power until you are ready to use it."

I slowly opened my eyes, nodding in understanding. It was only when I'd been actively hating on some gods that my blood had begun to glow. When I was pissed about Thor and also when I'd been pummeling Odin in Niflheim. "Just being near a god will make me light up?"

"Without you dampening it, yes. If you are in control of your thoughts, or engrossed on some other topic, your veins will not glow. Once you gain proper control, you will be able to turn it off and on at will," she said, answering my next question. "Just practice."

I slowly loosened my restraint, thinking back on Thor. And my arms immediately began to glow.

I turned to Odin. "I'm sure you were just about to tell me all of this. It was on the tip of your tongue, right?"

He stared back at me, lowering his brow. "I don't often go about telling irrational young men how best to become more irrational. There are consequences to killing a god. Having the ability is only a fraction of the story. Knowing when and how best to kill a god is the real power. Because killing a god stains your soul, marking it indefinitely. Remember, gods judge your soul when you die, so killing one of them doesn't just wash off after you take a shower. Why do you think Anubis was so interested in you? Why do you think we are *all* so interested in you—both your enemies and your potential allies?"

I grunted, having figured as much long ago. "The Catalyst. That's what this is all about, isn't it? My parents somehow saw this coming and prepared me for it."

Odin was silent for a few moments. "Perhaps. Not in any clear way, though. You've...rather made a mess of things while somehow still managing to stay on track."

"I believe he's done an exemplary job, given the associates he was forced to work with," Pandora said, staring directly at Odin.

I remembered that both of them had made promises to my parents—

things they would do to help me, but that they were not allowed to tell me about.

Pan had also made promises—and he had made good on them, sacrificing his life to help me regain my Fae magic. Were these two also tasked with such thankless, bleak jobs?

I didn't currently have the empathy, let alone the mental endurance, to ask them directly. I already had enough to worry about with Thor. Knowing that he really was as powerful as everyone claimed, and that I really should have killed him in Niflheim when he had been weakened by the mist only made me angrier, and my arms began to glow.

Gunnar entered the room as if summoned by my desire to kill Thor.

Cowan and Alice walked a few paces behind him. As one, they all froze, noticing my glowing forearms. Their eyes flicked to Odin, assuming the glow meant that I'd been beating him up again.

Not for a lack of desire, I thought to myself.

Pandora cursed loudly, suddenly staring down one of the distant hallways—the opposite direction from Ashley. Then she spun to me. "Why is Callie Penrose inside the Armory?" she demanded.

My eyes widened, caught entirely off guard. "I have no fucking idea!" I hissed, turning to stare at the hallway in question. One thing I knew for certain, I didn't want Callie finding out that we were all here—that Ashley was on the verge of giving birth, and that Gunnar and I were about to go hunt down Thor.

I didn't want to risk bringing her into my world of trouble, because if she had any idea how crazy things were here, she was the kind of person to offer her help—and she wouldn't take *no* for an answer.

"You have to get her out of here, Pandora," I urged, not even caring how Callie had found her way inside my Armory—or how she'd done so without using the front fucking door.

Pandora had gone very still, her eyes distant. "I think she wishes to speak with *you*..." she said absently.

I shook my head adamantly. "No way. Not with all of this going on," I hissed, blindly whipping my hand out to indicate the buffet of problems already on my plate. I think I flicked Odin in the eyeball because he suddenly cursed.

Pandora glanced down at the leather strap over her arm, nodding after a moment. "I can stall her for five minutes, but I cannot deter her."

I cursed, trying to think of an alternate location. Somewhere remote—"Fae. Send her to my mountain in Fae!"

Pandora nodded, already walking away to intercept Callie. "As you wish. I would hurry, though, because I believe she came here to murder Hope. And she brought a friend."

Alice gasped and Gunnar growled.

I blinked incredulously, trying to process her words.

Then I snatched up my staff as I spun to Alice, ignoring the stark frown on Gunnar's face, and prepared to use my magic to open a Gateway. But I hesitated, realizing how stupid that would be. Callie would sense it.

Talon had once explained how easy it was to hop back and forth between Fae, and I had cursed him for how easy he made it sound.

But I'd practiced it a lot with Alice on my mountain in Fae. I still preferred using Gateways, but I had the ability to *will* us to the mountain. So, I motioned for Alice to join me as I raced past Gunnar towards the door to the Armory, where my unicorn was standing guard.

I motioned for Alice to grab the wrist holding my staff as I tugged the door open with my other hand. Grimm's horn was suddenly an inch from my face as he gave me a warning snarl. I open-palm slapped him on pure reflex, making him snort in shock. Before he could do anything else, I grabbed him by the horn and willed us all to my mountain in Fae.

Grimm was cursing the moment we arrived.

"Payback, you majestic jerk," I muttered, alluding to my no-trust-fall down the mountain earlier. I rounded on Alice. "Hit the music," I said, pointing at the bluetooth speaker beside our igloo, "and make a big loud distraction—something that will give us a good idea of where her head is at. It needs to be in full swing in about five minutes. Got it?"

She pursed her lips, thinking furiously. "I have an idea."

"Good. Catch Grimm up to speed. I'll be right back. I need to go get a feel for Callie."

"I literally have no idea what we're talking about right now," Grimm muttered, "but even I know that was wildly inappropriate."

"A feel for her *state of mind*," I snapped. "I'll come back to join you right there, so keep that space clear," I said, tossing my rainbow staff to mark an area on the far side of the igloo—our home for the past year.

They nodded, and I willed myself back to the Armory.

Gunnar jumped as I appeared right beside him. "What the hell?"

"No time," I muttered. "I'll make this quick, but we can't risk bringing Callie to St. Louis. We have enough people to worry about as it is, and if she sees Ashley in her current state, she will want to help."

Gunnar opened his mouth to say something stupid like *that would be great, Nate!*

"I'm not going to let that happen," I said sternly. "Now hide."

Gunnar motioned for Cowan to join Odin around the corner and out of sight. Then he studied me silently, as if trying to read my thoughts.

Because I knew part of him was very agreeable to Callie watching over his wife while the two of us went to deal with Thor and Mordred. But he was smart enough to also know that Callie would not stand for sitting around in the make-shift hospital.

She would want to join in on our fight.

And he knew me well enough to see my true purpose—that I didn't want Callie risking her life for our fight. He knew this, but the reaction on his face troubled me. It was not a *smile* of understanding.

It was a *grimace* of understanding. Of disappointment.

I didn't have time to wax philosophical, so I turned my back on him and ran to where Pandora was intercepting Callie. Maybe I could overhear a snippet of conversation to give me an idea on how best to deter Callie Penrose. And what Pandora had meant about her coming to murder Hope.

The last time I had seen Callie, she'd stepped out of some silver glowing door—a door that hadn't been there a moment before—to visit me in Fae. And she'd been an entirely different person than the Callie I knew—hopped up on some kind of crazy power that rivaled most gods, and she'd been looking to acquire more. Maybe I was about to find out what that had been all about.

There was every chance that Callie was no longer Callie.

And I wasn't about to bring someone like that near Ashley and her inbound pups. The look on Gunnar's face was probably a result of him thinking I was being overprotective of her.

He had no idea that I was quite possibly being overprotective of *his kids*.

CHAPTER 33

I followed the distant sound of voices until I came to an intersection with a longer, wider hallway. I knew if I stepped around the corner, they would see me. This was as close as I could get without being detected.

I was careful not to bump into any of the tables or shelves full of price-less artifacts lining the walls as I found a narrow spot between two—likely highly dangerous—chests. I nestled myself into this cozy cleavage of carnage and tried to steady my breathing so I could hear the faint conversation.

I craned my neck so that my ear was as close to the corner as possible. The voices were obviously a ways down the hall, but the echo effect on the sandstone helped. Since echoes worked both ways, I resigned myself to listening in silence.

Maybe Pandora would dissuade Callie from this murdering Hope busi-ness. Knowing Pandora, I didn't count on it. I hardly ever took her words at face-value anyway. That phrase could mean any number of things, no matter how ominous it sounded.

She chose to word things in ways that were designed to get under your skin. Or, hell, it could be literal. I was about to find out.

One of the voices was male, but I recognized the other two as Callie and Pandora.

"Did you help Nate's parents do this to me?" Callie asked in a tone that sent a chill down my spine. *My parents?*

"I always do as I'm told," Pandora replied.

Silence answered my librarian.

Pandora finally sighed. "Know that Calvin and Makayla Temple did their best—what they thought was best," she said, obviously talking to me just as much as Callie. "Always. No matter the cost. They always took the path less traveled, and that has made all the difference…"

"Yes or no, Pandora?" Callie repeated, sounding annoyed.

As much as I wanted to jump out and demand an explanation about my parents, I knew this would be my only chance to hear something like this. Perhaps since I wasn't the one asking questions, Pandora was able to speak more openly than usual.

"Yes. I helped Calvin and Makayla…*after* they helped me. Gave me new purpose. Gave me shelter. Protected me from the world of embers and sparks. I had hoped those would fade away one day, but I was wrong. So, so wrong…" she said, sounding haunted and afraid.

Back when I had first met Pandora, I'd granted her freedom as payment for her help. But she had returned very rapidly, terrified of *embers and sparks*.

I had come to assume that she had been referring to the Syndicate—a shadowy group of black hat wizards—but she'd mentioned it a few times *after* I had eradicated them, turning their members over to the Academy of Wizards. I gritted my teeth upon thoughts of the Academy, for entirely different reasons.

Pandora continued. "I'm not sure Nate ever caught what I meant when I told him Excalibur was around here somewhere. It's almost like he forgot I ever said it…Solomon's *Temple*, Nate *Temple's* Armory," she explained. "Kind of obvious they would be connected, right? It's amazing no one saw that coming."

I frowned because Alex already had Excalibur. And then I processed the rest of what she had said. Was she implying that the Armory's neighboring landlord—Last Breath Holdings—was Solomon's Temple? I knew that Callie had recently discovered she was an descendent of King Solomon, but how had my parents gotten tied up with him?

"Anyway," Pandora continued. "I'll keep this here until you're ready to deliver it yourself. After you finish murdering Hope."

"I don't put much stock in fortune cookies," Callie said firmly, and I let out a soft sigh of relief. "I need to see Nate."

"Why do you seek Nate Temple?" Pandora asked after a long pause.

I smiled as Callie considered the seemingly simple question, not falling for Pandora's bait. "I fear for my friend."

"Fear..." Pandora mused. "What a delicious sentiment. But remember, Callie, if we leave our toys on the shelf too long, sometimes they get picked up by others. Or wither away under a blanket of dust and broken dreams of what never was."

Something about that last comment tugged at my own memories, but I couldn't place it.

"I would never leave Nate on a shelf. Not willingly," Callie said.

"What do you call leaving your toy alone on a shelf for a year?" Pandora asked softly.

"I learned the secret of life. The meaning of it all," Callie finally said. "It cost me a year."

I frowned thoughtfully. Callie had also been gone for a year? Coincidence or design? And if by design, who was the architect?

"That's a slippery piece of knowledge isn't it? How long did you grasp it?" Pandora whispered eagerly.

"An eternity. A heartbeat."

"What did it look like?" Pandora pressed, almost too softly to hear.

Callie sounded sad as she answered. "A broken man and a vapid little girl, holding hands before the end of the world," she whispered.

Pandora clucked her tongue. "Ah. That's a good one."

"What did it look like to you?" Callie asked, sounding curious.

"A box," Pandora said, her voice strangely flat.

My eyes shot open at that. Pandora had seen the secret of life, and it had looked like her infamous box of horrors. Good lord.

"I told you..." Pandora said. "Yours was a good one."

"I thought I came here for advice, but now I grow concerned for Nate, which is—"

"You came here for love," Pandora said, cutting her off.

Callie thought about that for a second. "I guess you're right."

My heart may or may not have done a flippy-floppy thing.

"Remember, eventually we all end up killing that which we love most."

And then my heart had a seizure, my good vibes electrocuted by the defibrillator of doom—Pandora.

"Not this girl," Callie said firmly.

"So, you are no longer here to murder Hope?" Pandora asked, sounding disappointed. "That's unfortunate."

I blinked. Who in the hell's side was Pandora on?

"I've already told you I've learned to not put too much faith into words," Callie muttered. "Gods cast riddles like men throw dice—to gamble, to cheat, and to play games with human lives. I'm no gambler."

The mystery male made an approving sound, but Pandora and Callie were quiet for a few moments, likely eyeing each other warily.

Then Pandora gasped, as if coming to some sudden realization. "You read the Omegabet..." she breathed, sounding stunned. "Oh, dear."

"Just a little..." Callie admitted sheepishly.

I frowned. What the hell was the Omegabet?

"And they thought *I* was dangerous," Pandora finally murmured. "Wordplay is not inherently wicked, and it is not only used to gamble, cheat, or play games. Sometimes it is the safest—and only—way to share secret knowledge, requiring the student to earn the right to the lesson. To the Seeing." She seemed to place special emphasis on that last word, as if making sure I overheard her, but she continued talking before I could give it much consideration. "Much as a sword can murder or absolve, grant or take power, justify or decapitate. Words are weapons, child. Much sharper than any blade or magic." She paused, sounding as if she was purposely trying to enunciate her next point. "Sometimes words mean *exactly* what they say. Even if you do not yet have the capacity to realize it."

Silence stretched for a few moments. "I mean Nate no harm whatsoever. In fact, I would rather the world burn than raise my hand against him."

Atta' girl, I thought, smiling faintly.

"Oh, child," Pandora said sadly. "You will raise your hand against him. Never promise what you cannot do. I already warned you that mankind always ends up killing what they love most in life. You will find Nate at home, but he is lonely."

I almost bolted to my feet, panicking. What the fuck was she doing?

"Why is Chateau Falco empty?" Callie asked, sounding concerned.

"Chateau Falco will never be empty, my sweet. Nate is home, with friends, but all alone. He's stuck in a dream, searching for a nightmare, crying as he laughs."

My scalp tingled, realizing how close she was to telling the truth, even if Callie didn't catch it. "What are you talking about, Pandora? I really need to make sure he's okay," Callie demanded.

"I just told you he is not okay," Pandora snapped. "He struggles to find the end of the story. Only you can give that to him."

"I need to see him," Callie said sternly, and it wasn't remotely a question.

Silence answered her. I heard a door open, and I frowned, wondering if they had left. Then I heard it close, followed by the sound of knuckles knocking on the wood. The door opened again, and I heard whistling gusts of wind pouring into the hallway, along with the familiar scent of Fae snowflakes—spicy cinnamon and fresh-cut cucumbers.

"There you go," Pandora said. "I'll leave it open for when you're ready to leave. If you decide you *want* to leave." She giggled.

I was going to kill her. First, talking about me being insane, and then trying to set us up for a little sexy time. I had a god to kill.

I heard footsteps approaching, and immediately jumped to my feet, backing away. "Remember," Pandora called out, sounding much closer. "Blades cut both ways, sweetie. Sometimes what you hear isn't what you hear. What you think isn't what you think. Killing is often just a balance. Wordplay, right?"

Then she began singing to herself as she skipped closer to the corner where I'd been hiding. "Bah, bah, black sheep have you any wool? Yes, sir, yes sir, three bags full. One for the Master..." she trailed off suggestively, and I felt my cheeks heat up, knowing she was probably giving Callie a significant leer over my familial title. Then she was skipping again, continuing her song. "One for the dame, one for the little boy who lives down the lane..."

Pandora let out one last giggle before skipping around the corner and coming into view. She saw me, smiled brightly, and continued skipping right on past me, clutching that strange strap of leather she'd been carrying around. It looked like a limp sword sheath.

I blinked, remembering she had mentioned Excalibur to Callie.

"That's your cue," she whispered on her way by, and I realized I didn't have time to question her.

I considered her song thoughtfully, knowing that Pandora rarely did anything without a purpose. But for the life of me, I couldn't pick up on any subtle meanings behind the lyrics. Her emphasis on *Master* reminded me of Odin's random interest in my familial title when we'd spoken back in Niflheim. I knew that the word *dame* had two definitions. The most popular was an old crone, but another was the female equivalent of a knight...

I heard Callie's voice, but I was too far away to make anything out.

I did hear a heart-stopping, feral yowl, though, making me doubt Callie's friend had been human at all.

I spun around to find Pandora smirking at me. "Your landlord is a big fucking lion named Last Breath," she said dryly. "Have fun."

I cursed, and then closed my eyes, trying to regain my composure. Hearing Callie speak with heartfelt emotion behind her words was already a vast improvement over the last time I had seen her—walking out of that silver door. Back then, she'd been cold, heartless, and utterly unsympathetic.

Although I was glad to see she was past all of that, it didn't make my current situation any easier.

If this was the old Callie, then I needed to be very convincing in my effort to turn her away. Which meant I needed that cold, Fae side of me. The one who didn't waste much time on feelings. I needed to keep Callie away—and that meant I needed to be heartless.

Especially if she was so concerned for my well-being. To save her from danger, I needed to be a raging dick.

Anything less would likely sweep her into my battle with Mordred and Thor—putting her in very real danger. I took a deep breath, and then willed myself back to my mountain in Fae, committing myself to pissing off the girl who I so desperately wanted to see naked.

It was ingenious plans like that, when said out loud, that made lesser men turn away from careers in professional wizardry. But wizards were made of heartier stock.

A wizard's life was tough, but awesome. Most of the naked people we saw were trying their best to kill us. *But...*

We still got to see naked people.

It was one of those glass-half-full or glass-half-empty personality questions. So, unless you wanted a career as a wizard...

Don't piss off the people you want to see naked. Start there.

After all, wisdom was learning from other's mistakes...

CHAPTER 34

I stepped onto my mountain to find that it had transformed into an insane orgy of war fueled by the sultry battle cries of Katy Perry, because Alice had successfully turned on the bluetooth speaker outside our igloo. Thank the gods for solar powered chargers.

Dozens of snowmen filled the area. They consisted of three spheres—one each for the head, the body, and the base—and as soon as they saw me appear out of thin air, they decided that they each personally wanted to kill me. They began zipping across the clearing in zig-zagging motions, scooting across the snow like they were imitating the Silver Surfer.

Then, they began *earnestly* trying to kill me. Grimm raced around the clearing, stabbing them with his horn and laughing like a lunatic. Alice, of course, was nowhere to be found.

I cursed under my breath as I scooped up my staff, promising myself that I would have a very stern talk with Alice about her definition of *distraction*.

Blue splashes of color coated the snow in dozens of places, and I realized that the animated snowmen had been filled like jelly donuts.

I gripped my staff angrily and readied myself to murder these cute little snowballs. Maybe Callie and her lion friend would take one look at the carnage and postpone their urgent need to talk with me.

So I had to make it look authentic.

To that effect, Alice had made sure that I would need to work for it. Because I almost lost an ear to a carrot nose grenade before I managed to fling up a shield at the last second. I had initially thought they were just illusions—glamourie—but Alice had apparently gone all out, taking a stab at grammarie—the art of making things *be*.

As I lunged out with my staff, I felt a release of pressure as I decapitated a snowman. In a way, it was therapeutic to cut loose and fight. And within moments, I realized I was actually laughing, imagining Thor's ugly, hairy head on each snowman. I swung my staff like a baseball bat or a spear, depending on the situation, but either way I killed without mercy.

And...I'd apparently needed this intervention.

I didn't bother looking for Callie and her lion. They would follow the sounds of mayhem and find me soon enough. Right now, I needed them to find a man on the edge of madness, consumed by an inner hunger that was impossible to sate.

I let my wild side come out to play.

I impaled an airborne snowman with my rainbow staff, and then swung it like a bat to decapitate a trio of snowmen behind me. I was laughing as the wind and snow whipped at my hair, and soon I felt the warm spray of blue blood hitting my cheeks.

Balls of fire suddenly lit up the night in several different directions, screaming and hissing as they tore through rows of snowmen.

My humor faded somewhat as I looked up to find Callie laughing as she hurled magic at the snowmen. I watched her, transfixed for a few heartbeats, watching as her white hair reflected the light from the snow. She was simply stunning. Then I noticed her friendly lion, Last Breath.

My landlord was biting the head off a snowman.

Except...he wasn't a typical lion. He was more like a leonine version of Gunnar's Wild Side—a bipedal monster lion. He was white, too, just like Callie's hair. He was slightly smaller than Gunnar, but that meant very little in their weight class.

Since Callie had started throwing magic, I threw a few fireballs of my own as I kept Callie and her kitty in my peripheral vision. And I began to lay waste to the snowmen as if it were a competition between us.

Stick arms, blue blood, and exploded carrot noses littered the once immaculate clearing, but I pressed on until the last of the snowmen were dead or trying to crawl away with their blue guts spilling out behind them in long, vibrant blue smears.

Grimm took great pleasure in calmly trotting up to each of the wounded and stabbing them with his hooves. He finally dispatched the last snowman with a snort and turned to stare at Callie and the lion, lowering his horn in a silent warning.

Callie let out a cautious breath, her smile slipping, and waved tentatively at Grimm.

My unicorn maintained his glare, only shifting his head to keep the lion in his sights. Callie lowered her hand and let out a shiver. Not out of fear, but out of how cold it was up here. Her breath fogged up before her, reminding me that not everyone had my immunity to extreme temperatures.

I yanked my staff out from the ground, shook off some blue slush, and then turned to stare at them. I kept my features cool and blank.

Last Breath murmured something to Callie, keeping his startlingly blue eyes on us the entire time.

It was a, dare I say, cold reception.

The sounds of Katy Perry rolled over the scene of death, and I noticed Grimm absently bobbing his head up and down with the beat. I also noticed the rock I had used to bury Sir Bedivere, having forgotten all about him until that moment.

"Hey, Nate," Callie said.

I wasn't entirely sure what to make of the snippets of conversation I had overheard in the Armory. And then there was this lion guy. My landlord, Last Breath.

I settled on the basics, keeping my voice gruff. "Hey."

Her smile slipped. I could tell that she wasn't necessarily afraid, but that she was very cautious in her assessment of me. In fact, she looked like she was discerning the best way to domesticate the wild animal before her.

Last Breath dipped his head politely.

Grimm snorted, scraping one hoof at the snow in front of him in a not so discreet warning. "Who's the pussy—"

I heard a sound, and flung up a hand, instantly cutting Grimm short. The two of us turned towards the igloo, waiting. Alice hopped out a moment later.

Alice still wore her cute little blue dress with white polka dots, her long white stockings, and her shining yellow flats that definitely weren't appropriate for the top of a mountain. For anyone other than a Fae.

She silently turned off the music and swept her piercing blue eyes over the field of snow goons—now just blue slush, hunks of coal, orange grit, and amputated stick arms.

She curled her lips and threw her hands in the air, looking frustrated. "Great. Now we're going to have Bumblenuts circling the mountain in an hour."

I barely bit back my laughter in time. Bumblenuts? Where had she come up with *that* one? I shot a glance at Callie and Last Breath, fearing that they would call her out on the obviously made-up name.

But they didn't.

Alice's eyes locked onto Callie and she blinked. Then they latched onto the lion and they rapidly switched to ecstatic glee. "Kitty!" she shrieked before sprinting towards him. She'd done the same thing with Gunnar. I wouldn't have been surprised if this part was unscripted. He was noticeably uncomfortable with her unexpected glee, and I had to fight to keep my face blank rather than burst out in laughter. Especially when I saw Callie's beautiful, heartfelt grin—a sight that threatened to melt my currently icy heart.

But I maintained character, relieved that Callie and her friend had fallen for our hastily-staged falsehood. I studied her pensively, and it didn't take long until I felt a weight slowly lift from my shoulders. She really had found her way out of that dark place she'd been in.

As if Alice's arrival had been a white flag, the tension in the air lessened and I motioned for Callie to join me by the fire pit. It was circled by stumps, boulders, and a heavy log—plenty of seats for the four of us. Callie sauntered over, smiling.

Last Breath handled Alice's exuberant affection well, allowing her to pet and tug on his mane. He even suffered her relentless chattering with an amused but helpless look on his face. "My werewolf friend, Gunnar, is bigger than you," Alice said. "Have you ever considered putting ribbons in your mane? Because I'm probably definitely going to put ribbons in your mane." I kept my smile to myself as she peppered him with more questions in a constant stream, barely pausing to take a breath. "Your name is Last Breath?" she asked. "That's a terrible name."

"Some call me Richard," he suggested, feigning offense at her blunt decree.

Alice considered that for a moment before spewing out a new stream of questions. My attention was pulled away as Callie joined me beside the firepit. She blinked at the azure blue flames—one of my personal favorites from my time spent here. It had taken a while for me to make fire that could be cold rather than hot. This one was both.

And it was ever-burning. I'd been toying around with making a lamp out of it, but that had been harder than I'd initially thought. I'd heard of someone making one, though, somewhere.

The trick was to use chips of glacier for the coals, and icicles for the kindling. After that, it continued to 'burn' all on its own.

Callie sat beside me without speaking, simply staring into the flames with a wondrous look on her face. It took every ounce of willpower not to reach over, grip her chin between two fingers, and kiss her until her toes curled.

The problem was that both sides of me—Nate and Wylde—agreed on this course of action, vehemently, for entirely different reasons.

Wylde—my Fae side—was primitive. If he saw something that he wanted, he took it.

Nate—my Earthly side—was fighting his own heart not to kiss those sweet, plump lips. Something I'd done once before, but not for nearly long enough.

So we sat in tense silence. I knew she was hesitant about how savage I seemed, and I was struggling against my very healthy desires. Desires that had been practicing abstinence for way too long.

At the same time, I was doing this for her own good.

Maybe if I said it enough times, I would actually believe it.

CHAPTER 35

I let out a breath as I shifted in my seat. Then I leaned forward to poke the fire with my staff, imagining a bucket of frigid water—cold enough for me to actually feel—pouring down my pants.

I sensed Callie eyeing my staff and then sucked in a breath at the adolescent translation. *Not today, Satan!* I told myself.

"Lightning bolt," I said out loud, answering her unspoken question. "We set lightning traps since we're up so high," I explained. "And…we don't like lightning very much," I added in a grim tone, trying not to think too closely on Thor and what I wanted to do to him—or else my ichor might start glowing. "Anyway, the bolts freeze when they hit our traps. I kept this one as a reminder to keep one eye on the sky." Then I grunted and let out a harsh, cold laugh at the joke.

Keep one eye on the sky, like Odin.

Callie slowly nodded, obviously not catching the joke, but trying not to discomfort me. "It looks kind of…pretty," she said.

I nodded, hating myself for playing this game with her, even though it was just to keep her as far away as possible until I took care of the drama on my plate. "This one hit a…rainbow I made," I said stiffly, realizing I'd been about to say Bifröst—which would have led to all sorts of questions I didn't want her asking. I quickly set the staff down beside me, out of her sight.

"You chose a hell of a time to visit. But that should be the last attack of the day," I assured her, realizing that it was technically true.

I sensed her reading my body language, my tone of voice, and probably a million other things I wasn't consciously aware of. Callie was like that—able to read a person down to their soul with only the slightest morsels of information to go on.

Which was why I needed to overact my part and get her out of here. If she stuck around long enough, she would catch onto my game. Or at least know I was lying—which would make her wonder why I was lying. And that maybe she needed to visit St. Louis to help.

Alice saved me by skipping up to the fire, tugging Last Breath behind her by the paw. He was very careful not to make direct eye contact with me, which was for the best, really. Alice scrutinized Callie, cocking her chin as she pointedly stared at Callie's forehead. Callie visibly squirmed, even though she hid it well. She gave Callie a long, appraising look from top to bottom, seeming like she was using her power as a Seer to assess Callie's intentions or secrets. I wasn't sure if I liked where this was going, but I couldn't stop her without making a scene. Callie would probably just yell at me for yelling at Alice.

"I'm Alice," she said abruptly by way of introduction. "Nate took me on an adventure. We had a fairy tale story with backwards dragons and knights. Have you decided what you're here to do?" she asked sweetly.

Callie blinked at her onslaught. "Yes," she finally answered, looking as if something had just clicked in her mind. I began to think that maybe I should have left Alice back in the Armory.

But it was too late for that now. Last Breath studied the two attentively.

I folded my arms behind my head to lean back against a stump, feigning amusement in hopes that Alice would change the subject. Now.

"Why are you wearing Demonskin?" Alice asked. "You're supposed to be royalty. It's confusing. Unless this is a masquerade ball." She turned to me, frowning. "This isn't a masquerade ball, is it?"

I had to force myself to turn back to Alice and shake my head. "Not that I'm aware of." Try as I might, I didn't notice anything strange about Callie's appearance, and I'd never heard of Demonskin.

"How do I take off my...Demonskin?" Callie asked, looking very interested in the answer.

Alice frowned. "It's not my Demonskin. How would I know how to take it off? It's tied to your soul, and *that's* about as tangled up as I've seen in a long time. Worse than his was." She shot me a long-suffering look, and I realized I was grinning at her dedicated little act of showmanship—because showgirlship just sounded wrong. Alice turned back to Callie, looking as if she didn't know why she even bothered asking me things. "You must have big family problems to go to such great lengths."

I could tell that the simple statement cut Callie deeply, although she hid it well. "I'll try to take care of that," she said softly.

"Your forehead is dusty," Alice pressed. "Royalty should keep their crowns clean," she said, eyeing Callie's forehead again.

I coughed into my elbow, trying not to laugh at Alice's attempt to get Callie the hell out of here. A few more questions and comments like this, and I thought Callie might just run back to Kansas City for an *appointment she'd forgotten to cancel.*

This time, I thought I knew what Alice was talking about. Callie had an unseen brand on her forehead—written in Enochian script. But I quickly buried the thought, realizing it would lead me down a path I didn't want to think about right now.

"I'm not sure how to clean it, Alice," Callie replied with a thoughtful sigh, seeming to have also read between the lines of Alice's comment. I remembered Pandora mentioning *toys collecting dust on a shelf.* And *crown* was another term for *head.*

Except Alice hadn't heard any of Pandora's conversation with Callie, which meant that she was definitely *seeing* something, and seeing it *correctly.* Last Breath's gaze continued to bounce back and forth between the two females like he was watching a riveting tennis match.

"You don't *clean* it," Alice said, sounding exasperated. "You must *dominate* it. Like he did. His shines like the sun, now."

I blinked. "I have a tattoo on my head, too?" That was news to me.

Alice nodded absently. "Different, but the same language as hers. But you have so many other problems going on," she huffed, gesturing in my general vicinity without actually looking at me, "that I wouldn't worry too much about it."

I shot her a dark frown, even though she wasn't looking at me. I really should have left her home.

"It seems being royalty is harder than I thought," Callie said.

Alice sniffed. "We haven't even gotten to the royalty bits. Those are just the lady bits."

I coughed violently into my fist.

Alice casually picked up a snow goon's head and set it in the kettle over the fire to boil. I grimaced distastefully at her theatrics but regained my composure before Callie or Last Breath noticed. "I'll make some tea for you. Can't have a decent reunion without some tea. Right, Nate?"

"Right, my lady," I said seriously, hoping she would wrap this up in the next few seconds.

Alice very carefully set four stone cups down beside the fire. She glanced at me and pointed to one. I nodded, having no idea what she was doing but pretending I did. Then she turned to Callie, pointing to a different cup. It felt like some form of ritual.

The smile that split Alice's cheeks upon Callie's return nod made me wonder what the hell Alice was up to.

She then glanced at the other two cups, shook her head, and stood to her feet. "Kitty and I will be in the igloo. Grimm will leave to scout the camp borders and search for threats."

I'd almost forgotten about Grimm, but I suddenly realized that he was standing directly behind Last Breath, looming menacingly. He snorted, shifting the lion's thick white mane. "And slaughter them mercilessly." Then he took off to the skies, obeying Alice without question.

I felt a faint whisper of Fae magic from Alice, but when I turned back, she was already tugging Last Breath away by the paw, leaving Callie and I alone with the four cups. Two of the cups now held tea—courtesy of the Fae magic I'd just felt Alice use. "Be careful with her, Nate," Alice teased over her shoulder. "She's seen the Omegabet. *You* haven't seen the Omegabet."

I watched her, scratching at my jaw, wondering again what this Omegabet was. "Sometimes, she says things that I can't even begin to comprehend," I murmured to Callie, deciding I could show a little bit of honesty. "She's been teaching me Fae magic. There is a lot to learn. And a very steep learning curve."

Alice scoffed, hearing my whisper even from across the clearing. She glanced back at me from over her shoulder. "You are only taking twice as long as I feared. Which is quite good, considering my mother gave up all hope with you." She turned to Callie, scrunching her nose. "Speaking of hope, I would appreciate you saving the murder until after tea."

Then she slipped into the igloo with Last Breath, leaving me all alone with my would-be murderer.

CHAPTER 36

*C*allie was already leaning away, holding up her hands in an innocent gesture and shaking her head reassuringly. "Wordplay," she assured me.

I tried to consider the statement from all angles. I studied Callie's face, searching for any hint of deception. Callie gave me a hesitant but warm smile.

She slowly reached down to pick up the cup of tea Alice had indicated for me, and then handed it over. I accepted it, idly wondering how Alice had used her Fae magic to make tea, of all things. Callie took her own suggested cup, leaving the two strangely empty cups beside the fire. As she sipped her tea, she studied the empty cups thoughtfully, like they were a puzzle.

I sipped my tea as I watched her, recognizing the familiar taste from our tin of tea leaves in the igloo. What was actually going on here? Alice wouldn't have put on that show if she wasn't trying to tell me something. She would have just taken Last Breath into the hut, giving me the opportunity to find a way to get Callie out of here, pronto.

So why had she said those things? And what was up with her funky tea ceremony involving four cups, two of which were empty?

"Alice asked if you knew what you were here to do…" I said softly, choosing the less incendiary of Alice's statements rather than her parting comment about murdering hope.

"About some things, I'm conflicted. About one thing, I'm convicted," she admitted, pointedly refusing to look at me.

"What are you conflicted about?"

Callie smiled for some reason. Was it because I'd asked about her inner conflict rather than her conviction?

She let out a breath, and I could tell that she was choosing her words carefully. "I have something I need to talk to you about, but I can't do so right now." I frowned, opening my mouth to press her on that, but she held up a finger. "It's not that I don't *want* to tell you, it's that it would require time I don't have." I nodded, considering her words. I didn't have time either. Callie took a slow breath and closed her eyes, as if preparing to say something difficult. "And it would take an objective, non-emotional mindset that you don't currently seem to have. It would detract both of us from our current…battles," she said, settling on a word. "You with Mordred, and me with Kansas City."

I studied her thoughtfully, definitely not pleased, but I was forced to admit she was right. My chosen facade of acting savage had worked better than I had thought. It would only make me look crazier if I suddenly began to defend my sanity. "I…think you may be right," I finally said, biting down a healthy dose of vile humility. "To be honest, this is about as clear-headed as I've felt in quite a while. Which means I'm clear-headed enough to realize how much further I still have to go."

Callie smiled, letting me know that she wasn't passing any kind of judgment. "Thank you."

"Why even bring it up if you didn't want to talk about it?" I asked. Because my mind was racing with possibilities. Was she talking about my parents? How they had apparently meddled in her life as well? I would have to be very careful that I didn't accidentally let slip any of the things I had heard in her private conversation with Pandora.

She didn't immediately answer, focusing her gaze on the fire. "We have both suffered too many lies from those we care about. I have this information I need to share with you, but neither of us can afford to discuss it yet. In my opinion, choosing not to let you know I have this information feels exactly the same as an outright lie. I figured the only way to be honest was to let you know I have it, but that I'm not ready to talk about it yet. Otherwise, if you found out later and thought I had hidden it from you…" she shuddered, and my heart shriveled to see that she actually looked afraid.

"I wouldn't hurt you, Callie. Jesus—"

She gripped my hand suddenly, cutting me off. I froze, my fingers tingling at the unexpected physical contact. I felt like a teenager at his first dance.

"I know you would never hurt me, Nate," she said in a gentle tone. "It's just that…I couldn't bear knowing you thought I had lied to you. So, an unpleasant middle-ground is better than nothing."

I studied her in silence, struggling to keep my emotions—and hormones —in check. Callie turned back to the fire, releasing my hand.

"Thank you, Callie," I finally said. We sat in silence for a time, the fire crackling between us. "And what are you convicted about?" I finally asked, averting my eyes so she didn't feel like I was interrogating her.

She stared at the fire for a long while. I let her, wondering if I was about to dislike her answer. She finally turned to me, her voice bold and without regret. "I want to see it."

I tensed, my eyes widening. I felt a frown creeping over my face, not entirely sure we were talking about what I thought we were talking about. What—I realized, with a flutter of surprise—I *hoped* she was talking about. I opened my mouth, but she cut me off.

"I want to see it," she repeated in a firm, even bolder tone.

I studied her silently. "Why?" I finally asked, fishing for clarification.

A deep smile slowly stretched across her cheeks, making her eyes seem to sparkle. "I need to make sure it matches my boots."

I sucked in a breath, growing very still. Her boots were magical and could sense demons. They could also change forms with a thought. The elusive Darling and Dear made quite a vast array of magic-imbued leather items. I thought these things in a fleeting second, because I knew that her boots could match *anything* she chose to wear.

She nodded, slowly pointing at the satchel she had gifted me—also a Darling and Dear product that was seemingly bottomless and made from Elder hide and black dragon scales. I'd been told—by an Elder and a black dragon—that those were impossible materials to work with.

I continued to study her, not moving. Seeing the gleam in her eyes, I knew several things. She believed she had earned this. That she needed this. And a part of me knew that this was the only way I could protect her from afar.

She wanted a Horseman's Mask—one of the three inside my satchel.

I'd already told her the costs of becoming a Horseman, and until now, she had maintained her distance. I had subconsciously taken that as a denial, but thinking about it from a new perspective...

That was how Callie typically operated—digesting new information in private, and never letting others see what she was truly thinking.

Later, she would often surprise everyone with an extremely in-depth argument for her position, since she had taken the time to process every variable given to her.

Like a master at Chess. You might see them sitting there for a few seconds, and then you might see them quickly move a piece on the board. In basic terms, they had moved a Bishop.

But if you had the ability to see the neurons firing in their brain as they calculated five or ten moves ahead before moving that Bishop...you might just die of inadequacy, realizing that you were subhuman when compared to this person.

Callie was like that, in a way. And I'd almost overlooked it. Seeing her now, with the steadfast gleam in her eyes...

This wasn't a request for a Mask. We were already at the ritual ceremony. And when it boiled down to it, I had only one part left to play. My judgment.

Without speaking, and without breaking eye contact, I reached inside my satchel and grabbed the first thing that came to mind. My heart raced wildly as the coin hanging from my neck seemed to throb, sensing my contact with its sibling.

The Horseman's Mask of Despair. The same word that Alice had alluded to—the one branded onto Callie's forehead in Enochian script.

I pulled out the white stone Mask, marveling at how it seemed to glitter like sunlight striking fresh snow. Just like her hair had done when fighting the snowmen. I stared down at it, feeling a smile creep over my face as it purred eagerly in my palms, agreeing with my choice. Part of me felt guilty, because I had denied Gunnar this same opportunity. Not this Mask, specifically, but to become a Horseman.

And here I was, giving it out to a girl I had kissed and wanted to see naked. *Maybe I should have gotten a second, more objective, opinion,* I thought to myself.

Because when Gunnar found out about this, he was going to kill me. Slowly. Possibly even make chew toys out of my bones for his pups.

I shook my head at the fleeting thought, knowing that despite my feelings for Callie, this felt *right*. And *final* in some strange way that I couldn't accurately explain. I held it out for her.

Callie extended her hand as if anticipating an electric shock upon contact. Instead, the Mask of Despair abruptly snapped to her fingers as if magnetically attracted to her blood. She gasped in surprise, and then her eyes shot wide open, almost rolling back into her head.

Shit.

Then her shoulders slumped, and she let out a shaky breath, her eyes locking onto the Mask in her palms. I felt it purring even from here, perhaps even stronger than it had in my own hand. And I felt a cord of power snap to life between us, rejuvenating me like a shot of espresso.

In some ways, her Mask was similar to mine. In other ways, it was entirely different. The interior of the Mask was a sort of crystal, looking sharp and jagged with veins of silver streaking throughout. She ran a finger over the interior, appearing uneasy about the comfort factor.

I smiled, forcing myself to remain patient. Because I had gone through this before with my own Mask of Hope.

She gasped as her finger brushed through what probably felt like velvet. The interior stuck to her finger as it moved, attempting to latch onto her fingertip—again, like a magnetic attraction. She shivered.

I chuckled knowingly. Mine did the same thing. "Creepy, right?"

She nodded but seemed unable to peel her eyes away from it. "Despair," she breathed.

I felt the purring sensation increase, as if the Mask was responding to her voice. She turned it over in her lap, inspecting the front with a sudden smile of approval. In this regard, our Masks were noticeably different. Hers was a highly detailed, beautiful woman's face—not too unlike Callie's actual face. A ragged bandage covered the eyes, and from beneath the bandage, three rivulets of silver streaked down the surface from each eye.

Six tears for the Sixth Horseman?

I was smiling for altogether different reasons, though. I had known for a long time that this Mask would ultimately end up in her hands. Well, that it had been designed for her. Because we had experienced a shared dream where Callie had appeared in the flesh, her face looking very much like this Mask, complete with the silver tears and bandage over her eyes.

So Gunnar's situation was very different.

I hadn't known whether or not she would accept the Mask, though. Primarily, because I'd offered it to her once before, back when she'd been the power-hungry woman who visited me in Fae, arriving through that strange silver door.

She'd been looking for power, and I'd offered her the Mask of Despair, knowing that Callie was born for it. Except…that woman hadn't been the same Callie. Not even remotely.

So I had always known that some part of Callie had not wanted to become a Horseman—and I was only just now realizing that it had been eating at me from within. However, seeing her holding the Mask now…

I knew that I had found my first Horseman, leaving me only two more Masks to hand out.

One thing that I hadn't noticed before caught my attention. There was a slight indentation on the forehead of the Mask—a horizontal crescent moon with points facing upwards. It was not the same symbol I had once seen branded onto Callie's forehead. What did that mean?

She set it on her knees, finally looking back over at me in silence, her face neutral. I began to twitch nervously, not knowing what she was doing.

"What are the rules on workplace romance?" she finally asked.

CHAPTER 37

I blinked. Then, before I consciously realized it, I was standing upright. "I know the boss. I'm sure he won't mind..." I said carefully.

"Good," she purred, and a wicked grin slowly split her cheeks. "Because that would have been a deal breaker."

I could tell by the determined look on her face that she hadn't chosen the Mask for this reason, but that it was a benefit she didn't want to give up in *exchange* for the Mask. And that it may have even been a reason she had stayed away from the topic for so long. That she hadn't wanted to choose one over the other.

Inside, this made me deliriously happy.

Callie lifted the Mask in her hands, gauging its weight. Although it looked dense, I knew it was no heavier than a light t-shirt.

"You can change its shape," I said. I touched my necklace and it instantly transformed into a dark charcoal Mask with a single golden streak down the center. The gold streak, resembling a bolt of lightning, was actually a fracture rather than a cool design feature. I was slightly disappointed to see that the fracture hadn't magically healed after giving Callie her Mask. Maybe I really would have to hand out all four before mine would heal. As I looked at my Mask, I sighed. The Mask of Hope was almost plain in comparison to the Mask of Despair.

The leader of the New Horsemen had the lamest Mask.

Then again, the stone of my Mask was so dark that it was almost hard to point out any specific details other than that it was a man's face. I turned it back into a coin and smiled. "Just imagine what you want it to look like," I said.

Callie's eyebrows furrowed in deep concentration. In a sudden curl of vapor, her Mask shifted into a familiar-looking silver butterfly charm.

Just like the one I had once given her. Back when we first kissed.

In fact, she reached into her pocket to pull out said charm, comparing the two with a nod of satisfaction.

"You're going to have to teach me how to use it," she said, grinning down at the butterfly charms.

I grimaced slightly at her statement, trying to think of the best way to explain the usage of the Masks. "There's kind of a learning curve. I can share my experiences and help you as best as I can, but I think each Mask is entirely unique. They seem to adapt to the user's abilities or inclinations. At least that's what mine has seemed to do. Each seems to have its own personality. It might be best for you to figure it out on your own, rather than me limiting you by telling you what to do. You aren't an extension of me, of Hope—"

"I'm Hope's counterpoint," she said softly, interrupting me. "Despair and Hope, two sides of the same coin. We are each other's murderer," she said, smiling faintly.

I kept my face neutral, but not to hide any feelings of surprise. Because I wasn't surprised. I was proud. Regardless of how clever she was, I hadn't thought Callie would come to that conclusion for some time yet.

"I had...hoped that was what Alice meant, but only because I've spent a lot of time around her recently and know how she thinks."

She nodded, but her eyes were far away, and I could tell she was debating something in her mind.

After a few moments, she glanced up at me. "You know...and I'm just spit-balling here, but it might be a good idea to take this training seriously. Go somewhere secluded. Very secluded, mind you. Just to be safe. And we will need food and drinks. Shelter. And no one knowing where we are. You know, so we don't get distracted. Because training is important. Very important—"

I burst out laughing at her rapidly blushing cheeks. She wasn't being as subtle as she thought. "Deal. We will...dedicate ourselves to this training."

She beamed, her eyes glinting in the sunlight. "It would be a good time for us to talk about things, too. Rather than these brief meetings, we could get into bigger topics. Like the one I brought up earlier..." she said, her smile fading.

I nodded, forcing myself not to demand answers. Gunnar was on the clock, and for all I knew, Ashley might already be having her babies. "I think I would really like that, all scandalous insinuations aside," I teased, smirking at her blush. "I think sitting down with you and just talking would be fascinating, believe it or not." And I meant it.

"Of course it would," she said, sniffing pompously.

"Out of curiosity, who told you to murder hope?" I asked, because she hadn't sounded surprised when Pandora said it, making me think that she'd heard it before.

"A lot of people," Callie admitted uneasily. "Including Pandora. Others didn't necessarily say it outright, but now that I think about it...they might have been saying the same thing in a different way, and I just never caught it."

I grunted, not wanting to take the time to grill her on it. Because that would lead to longer conversations about what the hell she'd been up to lately. I realized that neither of us had brought that up. No talking about our days at work. I had a good reason. Maybe she did, too. Which meant that if I heard her story, I'd probably feel inclined to go help her out with her problems.

Just like she would with mine in St. Louis.

Which was exactly the problem.

I smiled at her, keeping my thoughts from my face. "Welcome to my life. Someday, maybe you'll have a crazy mountain of your own."

Callie smiled, sweeping her gaze across the scenery as she pocketed her silver charm—not her Horseman's Mask. "Maybe a beach," she said, rubbing her arms. And that suddenly reminded me that I was wearing only jeans—no shirt or shoes. And she hadn't commented on why I wasn't cold. She'd ogled a bit, even though she had tried to hide it. I'd done my fair share of ogling as well, but I had to use more imagination.

"In a very general way, how do I use the Mask? Some kind of ritual or spell?" she asked.

I smirked, shaking my head. "Just slap it on and hold on for dear life. It might not fully wake up the first time. I used mine a few times before it really opened up."

"You say that like it's alive..."

I pursed my lips thoughtfully. "It is, in a way. I brought it to life with some of the Nine Souls from Hell." Callie blanched, looking mortified. I waved my hand emphatically, realizing that it had sounded way worse than I'd intended. "Don't worry. They aren't tainted by demons or anything. I technically *fed* the Souls to the Masks, so if anything, the Masks *ate* them."

Callie pointed her toes at the Masks, and a look of relief washed over her face. I remembered that her boots could sense demons, so her quick test actually made me feel a lot better.

She held up her disguised Mask, meeting my eyes. "Things are going to get wild soon. We will need these more than you know."

I read between the lines, curious about what she had discovered—what she wanted to talk to me about later. "Come back whenever you're finished in Kansas City. We need to do some talking. And *training*," I said, drawing out the word with a grin.

She nodded, but her eyes were thoughtful. "Pandora told me I had to come back anyway. I need to deliver something to someone for her."

I waited a few seconds to see if she would elaborate on the sheathe Pandora had been holding. I hadn't had the chance to ask her about it, but was betting it was the last part of Excalibur—although I had no idea what any of that had to do with Callie.

"I...would like that, Callie." Just to be safe, I tried to think of something else to say to make sure she didn't ask for my help or come knocking on my front door with a bottle of wine and a *Netflix* t-shirt in a few hours.

A man could dream. Sue me.

As incredible as that would be, I couldn't afford the risk. "I would offer to come help—if you needed it—but I might cause more damage in my current state. I need to finish clearing my head."

She smiled at me, her pearly white teeth reflecting the light from the snow around us. "You already helped, Nate." She held up the Mask meaningfully. "I've got it from here."

I spotted Last Breath poking his head out from the igloo—with Alice doing the same a few feet below him. Callie waved at the pair, letting them know we were finished and that it was time for them to leave.

They hurried over, and I couldn't tell who was more anxious. Last Breath—to escape the tiny terrorist—or Alice. I grinned, pointing a finger at the dozen or so silver ribbons tied into his impressive mane.

Callie laughed, shaking her head.

"I'll be back. Soon," she said, just as Alice and Last Breath reached us. Alice grinned at the charm in Callie's hand, giving me a nod of approval—and perhaps a subtle hint that I should have done the same with Gunnar. Then she tapped her forehead, pointed at Callie's forehead, and gave her a thumbs up.

Callie nodded with a faint smile.

"Give them hell," I said, smiling. It was time for her to go, before I changed my mind and asked her to join me. Two Horsemen against my enemies could cause some very real damage. But what if she experienced something like I had where her Mask broke?

Also, I couldn't ask her to step into such a dangerous fight as a fledgling Horseman.

Even knowing this, something about her was just infectious. Grimm landed near the igloo with an explosion of blue slush. He was chewing on something that seemed to still be alive. It struggled weakly in his jaws. From where I stood, I couldn't tell what it had been.

I froze at a sudden thought, and then spun my attention from Grimm to Callie. "Wait. You don't have a horse! It's kind of a requirement."

Callie studied Grimm thoughtfully. I saw the exact moment that some idea crossed her mind, but it was obvious she didn't intend to share it. "I'll figure something out," she said with an amused shrug.

Then she was motioning for Last Breath to follow her back to the still open portal that led back to my Armory. She seemed to be invigorated.

Was that from the Mask?

From spending time with me?

Or maybe it was just Callie—one of the many reasons I so enjoyed spending time around her.

I waited for the portal to close behind them, knowing we couldn't very well go back into the Armory at the same time. We needed to give her a few minutes to exit.

And I really wanted to find out how the hell she'd become my assistant landlord.

CHAPTER 38

I scooped up my satchel and turned to Grimm the moment we were in the clear. "I need you to go help Alex and Talon. They're squaring off against nine of the Knightmares somewhere near the Summer Queen's Castle. Even if they have a Fae army at their backs, none of them can hurt a Knightmare like you can," I said, pointing at his horn. "Alex and Talon will do an admirable job, but they need aerial support. Maybe you will see something they can't."

He studied me suspiciously. "Swear to call me when shit hits the fan?" he asked.

I smiled, nodding. "Always."

"I'm serious, Nate," he said in a tone I'd never heard him use. He sounded afraid. Concerned. "I need you just as much as you need me. Perhaps even more. You gave me a purpose, man. Brought me out of the Dark Lands near the Dueling Grounds. That…" he trailed off, sounding embarrassed. "That wasn't a good place for me. This Horseman gig, though…I feel important again."

I stared at him, surprised he hadn't cursed for such a long string of words. But I was more surprised to hear him opening up to me. I'd always known these things about Grimm, but he'd never had to say them out loud. For him to suddenly think he needed to…

"I promise, Grimm. I need you more than I can put into words. Because none of my cars can fly." He narrowed his eyes murderously. "And they also can't stab annoying things with their head," I added, smirking. "We are brothers, Grimm. I won't leave you behind. I promise. I want to have my own pair of eyes up there instead of relying on Hugin and Munin, and whatever tidbits Odin decides to share."

He studied me for a long moment, and then dipped his head. "Deal, Horseman. Call me when you need me. Until then, I'll get a better look at everything than the ravens could. Then I'll go to Alex."

And then he took off into the sky.

I watched him for a few moments, his silhouette growing smaller as he flew further away. Finally, I shook my shoulders to mask my concern for my friend.

Alice was frowning up at me, looking sad. "Why did we lie to her?"

"I don't want Callie involved."

"But she's a Horseman now."

I grunted. "Not even ten minutes old and you expect me to drag her into my nightmares? No way. I think she's busy anyway. And I have enough people to look after already," I said, mussing her hair.

She hissed, jumping back a step.

I squatted down in front of her. I had questions about some of the things she'd said to Callie—like the Omegabet—but I had much more pressing agendas on my mind, and none of my questions would matter if I didn't figure those out first.

"I need you to put your game face on. Things are going to move pretty fast from here on out, so I want you to keep a discreet eye on everyone in the Armory," I said, touching my eye meaningfully. "Let me know if you *see* anything you think I need to know."

"I always do, Nate," she said in a soft voice.

I nodded, straightening back up. "Thank you. Welcome to my mad world, Alice," I said, holding out my hand.

She clasped mine, unwavering. "We're all mad here," she said.

"Truer words," I mused. Then I squeezed her hand and willed us back to the Armory.

We appeared back in the Armory in the room with the balcony. And again, I found Pandora sitting by herself.

She slowly turned to look over at us, smiling without any hint of surprise. "It worked. Callie left hours ago."

I blinked, frowning. "We left her less than five *minutes* ago."

Pandora nodded absently, as if my comment was of no concern.

But it sounded like one of those other concerns. The big ones.

Pandora turned to Alice, smiling conspiratorially. "Can you go see if Freya needs any help? She could probably use some rest, too." She saw the concerned look on my face and shook her head. "No pups yet, but Freya has been watching over your friend like a hawk. She won't do Ashley any good if she's too exhausted to function."

Alice glanced back at me and I nodded. "Thank you, Alice."

She left quickly, pumping her little legs as fast as she could without actually running.

Pandora climbed from her seat, straightening her toga. She appraised me thoughtfully. "You need to get cleaned up. You are covered in snowman blood. Follow me."

I frowned, wondering how she knew the blue blood had come from snowmen. But she was walking away too quickly for me to do anything but chase after her.

I caught up with her just as she rounded a corner. I matched her stride, spotting the door to the healing pool at the far end of the hall. As luck would have it, we also passed Ashley's room. Drake and Cowan stood guard, both looking up as we rounded the corner. Pandora paid them no mind, focused only on the door to the healing pool.

They appraised me, then Pandora, and wicked grins quickly split their cheeks as they did some basic math. They both flashed me a congratulatory thumbs up. I shook my head sternly, silently telling them it was not what it looked like.

It did not help my case that I was wearing only jeans or that Pandora looked like Pandora.

I sighed, telling myself there were worse rumors to be whispered.

We reached the healing pool, and Pandora ushered me inside, closing the door behind us.

"You ride to war, yet you have no one to wash your back."

I blushed suddenly. Okay, maybe Drake and Cowan had been right.

"*Watch* or *wash?*" I asked, hoping she had misspoken.

"This librarian does it all," she said, smiling as she took a step closer.

CHAPTER 39

I blushed. Me.

"Pandora, what are we *really* doing here?" I asked, holding up a hand. Because I didn't believe the flirting was her true purpose.

Her smile slowly faded. "For many reasons. One was for you to bathe. But I also have things I must tell you, my Host. I had hoped to relax you, first."

I nodded, feeling better about the whole situation. "I'm plenty relaxed," I reassured her.

She arched a dubious brow. "Everyone knows that to be a lie."

I waved a hand dismissively. "Well, everyone is a liar. Talk."

She took a deep breath, nodding as if to gather her courage. "You must be careful, my Host. Even Hope can die," she whispered.

I frowned, wondering if this was like Callie saying she needed to murder Hope—which had actually meant her *becoming Despair.*

"The events happening in Fae are stressing time to an alarming degree. I have never seen anything like it."

I frowned. "You mentioned that I've been gone for hours, but I was only in Fae with Callie for maybe an hour."

She nodded. "And that was just you *speaking* with Callie. The other stakes in Fae are much larger. Queens and Kings ride to battle, and everything can change in a blink. It is straining time. The more momentous the event, the greater the time slippage. That is my theory anyway."

I followed that train of thought, growing alarmed. "What will happen when I fight Mordred? Or if one of the Queens dies? Or if Alex dies?"

Pandora was silent for about five seconds. "I have no idea. I can see the current distortions if I look, but I cannot predict what will happen in the future. Perhaps days or weeks could pass here. Or we could all die instantly of old age."

I gasped, staring at her.

She sighed defeatedly. "I just wanted you to be aware. I know it's not something you can do anything about."

I thought about the Hourglass in my satchel. If it was ever time to take a risk, this was it. I'd fought Mordred too many times already. This was going to be the end. Period. And if I was ever going to give away something powerful, Pandora was the most credible person I knew.

She ran my freaking Armory, after all.

"Maybe I *can* do something about it...." I pulled out the Hourglass my parents had given me—the one that could lock down time between Fae and the earthly realm. It could also speed up or slow down time. It was like a master switch. I handed it over to her.

She accepted it with both hands, treating it as if it was made of porcelain. "I'd forgotten about this," she whispered reverently.

"If you notice that time is getting out of hand, you can use this to control it to some extent. But *only* if things get out of hand. There might be benefits to time moving slower here..."

Pandora thought about that, and then sucked in a breath about two seconds later. "An army. There could be time to build an army."

I shrugged bleakly. "I'm not sure there would be *that* much time, but enough to gather up a few friends at least."

She nodded thoughtfully, setting it down near the wall where it couldn't fall over.

"How did you know about the snowmen?" I asked, indicating some of the blue blood splashed over my arms.

In answer, she walked back to the door and threw the deadbolt, making sure we wouldn't be disturbed. This simple act really put things into perspective for me. But then Pandora really, *really* put things into perspective for me.

"Your parents gave me this," she whispered as she walked closer to me in slow, serpentine steps. She reached up and pulled the brooch off her toga, letting it fall to the ground.

"Whoa," I said, lifting up my hands and trying to keep my eyes on her face—which was incredibly difficult with all that tan flesh swaying at me like the friendliest of hellos.

She drew closer, actually pressing her breasts and hips up against me, pinning me to the edge of the pool. It was only then that I realized that— although she'd seized an added benefit—she hadn't been trying to make a move on me. She held the small metal brooch in her hand, and she was trying to show me what was inside it. I'd been so busy trying to look at only her face that I'd missed it.

I blinked at the open brooch—more of a locket, actually—but it was empty inside. I frowned. "I don't see anything, Pandora," I told her, trying to block out the pleasant view in my peripheral vision.

Which was hard since said view was pressed firmly against my bare flesh.

Pandora frowned. "When I look inside, I can see what my host sees," she whispered. "So that when I am all alone here, I know that he is safe. That he hasn't abandoned me. That he will come back home."

I stared at the brooch and then at her. On one hand, that was incredibly kind of my parents to give her such a gift. But on the other hand…

"My parents gave you a Nanny Cam?"

She frowned, not catching the reference. "Hope can see Hope," she explained. "But I've only used it when I was worried for your safety. I watched you often on your mountain," she admitted in a soft whisper. "I watched you fight Pan," she added, a tear falling from her cheek. "I miss him dearly…"

I cleared my throat forcefully, biting back my own heartache at her unexpected comment. "Me too, Pandora," I admitted sadly. "I had no idea you had this," I said gently. "Some might call it a curse."

She straightened her shoulders. "Knowledge is pain. I have taught you this before. In this very room, to be exact."

I nodded, remembering. She was talking about when she'd helped Alex, paving the way for him to later become the vessel for King Arthur's soul.

"This is how I saw your snowmen. And how I will watch time between the realms while you are away."

There were a million warnings I wanted to give her, but I realized how arrogant it was for me to assume I knew how to handle objects of power better than Pandora. If she had wanted to end the world, all she had to do was go play with her collection in the Armory. This was just a drop in the bucket compared to what she already managed.

"Now, you must clean up," she said sternly. "You look like a vagrant."

Without further warning, she yanked my satchel over my head and shoved me backwards, hard enough for me to drop my staff in the process. And I fell into the healing pool, pants and all. It wasn't deep, so I was instantly able to set my feet and breach the surface. "Hey!" I snapped, laughing as I wiped water from my eyes.

I stared down at my forearms and blinked to find that all the blue blood was simply gone. I checked the rest of my arms, then my chest. It was all *gone.*

Holy crap. One quick dip into the pool had instantly cleaned me.

I was so amazed that I didn't even process the flash of tan flesh in my peripheral vision until it was too late. Pandora ducked her head under the water, and I felt my jeans sliced off from the hip to the ankle as efficiently as a master fisherman deboning a fish.

"Pandora!" I shouted, covering myself with both hands and sitting down on the underwater bench near the lip of the pool.

She flung the ripped jeans, and a freaking knife, outside the tub. Then she rolled her eyes at me and stretched her arms out wide on the opposite side of the tub, giving me some pleasant things to feast my eyes upon.

Listen. I'm a healthy male. And I'd been living on a really cold mountain for a really long time. My testosterone reminded me, painfully, that we had not been working together as a team for quite a while, and that it was time to prove my loyalty. Right now.

I fought it down, noticing that I was gripping the wall of the pool.

Pandora grinned wickedly. Then she shrugged as if to say *suit yourself.*

We sat together in companionable silence, and I finally began to relax, the healing pool actually serving to rejuvenate me, refreshing my energy and revitalizing my mind. I hadn't necessarily felt tired, but now I felt like I wouldn't be able to sleep even if I tried.

I had a lot of things I wanted to ask Pandora about, but I knew I would sit here for a long time listening to her answers. And I had enough questions for *hours* of conversation.

However.

Even though Fae might have a time flux issue, my beef with Thor did not. And Gunnar had a limited window to use Geri and Freki.

But I deserved five minutes, at least. If for no other reason than to clear my head and think about everything I'd learned. I spent my time thinking long and hard about Odin and Niflheim. About whatever secrets he was obviously keeping from me.

After my five minutes, my thoughts drifted back to Gunnar, knowing that he was probably freaking out about my long absence in Fae. And that Drake and Cowan had probably ratted me out, spreading their filthy lies about the hot tub and the librarian. I sighed, glancing over at Pandora. "Do you have any towels? A robe?" I asked.

She shook her head, smiling eagerly.

I frowned, noticing my satchel on the far side of the room.

"You, um, cut up my pants."

"I sure did," she said, biting back a laugh. "What a shame." She flashed me a suggestive grin. And then she drifted towards the front of the pool, propping her elbow on the lip and settling her chin into her palm, fully intending to have a front row seat when I climbed out.

I sighed in resignation. Then I climbed out of the pool, pointedly ignoring the appreciative sounds from behind me as I strode across the room. I reached into my satchel and pulled out some dark jeans and a white shirt. Perfect for making the God of Thunder my bitch.

I pulled out another shirt to use as a towel, and then I began tugging on my clothes, feeling like I was going out on a date. It had been a long time since I'd had a warm bath.

Once I was dressed, I reached inside again, hoping to find a pair of shoes. I smiled as I pulled out a pair of socks and some old boots.

I sat down, tugging them on as I looked up to find Pandora still watching me from the pool. I figured now was as good a time as any to ask her opinion on an earlier idea of mine. "Is it okay if I borrow a few things?" I asked. "From the collection."

Her smile stretched wide. "Of course. Go crazy."

And I found myself grinning as I climbed to my feet, gathering my things.

"Thank you, Pandora," I said, throwing back the deadbolt and opening the door.

"I'll see you soon, my Host," she replied. And now I knew it meant much more than a polite farewell.

It was a literal fact.

CHAPTER 40

$\mathcal{I}$ had dropped off my satchel in the balcony room, deciding it would only get in the way. I'd taken a small item from inside, but that was it.

I walked on through the Armory, using my rainbow staff as a walking stick as I considered my conversation with Pandora. As I walked, I studied the deadly items on the wall, dismissing them for various reasons—either I didn't know how they would directly benefit us, I didn't know what they were, or I wasn't sure if Gunnar knew how to use them. Because I wasn't shopping for me.

I finally found Gunnar in a side room, staring at the Nemean Lion Cloak hanging on the wall. That relic brought back old memories. Gunnar and Ashley had both worn it before, gaining incredible strength to fight off some Greeks.

That felt like it had happened in another life.

I sighed, shaking my head as I gripped my rainbow staff. Gunnar didn't react to my presence. He'd probably scented me from down the hall, being a werewolf.

"You finally ready, or do you need to take off for another six hours," he said in a frosty tone. "Did you have fun with Callie?"

I winced. I hadn't known I had been gone *that* long. Since there was no way in hell I was going to tell him about Callie and her Mask yet—maybe not ever—I jerked my chin at the lion skin. "Pandora thinks time in Fae is more skewed than normal. Big events impact it more than others. She's concerned about it."

Gunnar nodded to himself. "Makes sense. So what was so *impactful* about your time with Callie?" he asked.

Crap. "Why don't you tell me why you and Odin are so buddy-buddy?" I fired back in a calm tone, referring to their secret conversation outside the Armory.

"He was concerned about you. Wanted to make sure you didn't overlook Thor or underestimate him. And he was showing me how to use Geri and Freki," he admitted with a shrug. "Your turn."

"Instead of discussing my relationships, how about we do Odin's bidding. You think that thing will still fit your new dad bod?" I asked thoughtfully.

He slowly turned to look at me, a smile creeping over his face. "Tell me you're not joking…"

I waved a hand at the Nemean Lion Cloak, encouraging him—and glad the distraction had derailed him.

He snatched it off the wall and threw it around his shoulders. Then he pulled up the hood and rounded on me. "Rawr!" he said playfully.

I grunted, rolling my eyes. "Wulfric is way scarier."

He gave me an easy shrug. "Then imagine *Wulfric* wearing it."

"Nah. I'd rather imagine Thor shitting himself when *he* sees Wulfric wearing it."

Gunnar grinned eagerly. "Let's go before some naked librarian walks by and distracts you again."

I grimaced. "Drake and Cowan. Those bastards."

Gunnar shrugged. "I know better. They don't. Which makes the teasing so much more fun."

I sighed. "It will probably make Pandora laugh," I admitted.

"Where are we going, exactly?" he asked, his humor fading as he prepared for the task ahead.

I smiled, rubbing my hands together. "That's where I'm hoping you can help. Otherwise we need to go ask Odin, and I'd rather not see him right now. I have some things I'm trying to work out in my mind about his story. Some things just don't add up. And, call me old-fashioned, but I find it distasteful to ask Thor's dad directions for this particular road trip—to kill his son."

Gunnar grunted. "And you can't hold your temper around him."

"And that," I admitted.

"So? Where are we going, and how can *I* help?" he asked, sounding puzzled.

"Can Geri and Freki help us get to Asgard? Or is that also distasteful?" I asked, frowning.

Gunnar looked up at me sharply. "You're kidding. Asgard?"

I shrugged. "Thor mentioned that he wasn't stupid enough to attack me in Fae where I held all the advantages. Made me think he might feel safe at home."

Gunnar grinned from ear-to-ear. "So you want to wallop him on his home turf, in front of his allies, proving a point."

"Hell no, man. I want to wallop him on his stolen throne, in front of all his people. To kill him on his own seat of power."

Gunnar snarled eagerly. "Oh, I *like* this plan." Then he glanced down, staring at where the wolves must be. I couldn't see much this time, but I did catch a faint, repetitive blur. Were they wagging their tails? After a few moments of silence, Gunnar looked up at me and smiled a terrible smile. "They can take us, but I'll have to drive."

"Get us close. I don't feel like walking far or meeting the locals. The throne room should suffice."

Gunnar arched an eyebrow. Then he burst out laughing, straightening out the back of his Nemean Lion Cloak as if it wasn't fitting him properly. I grabbed his forearm and took a deep breath, unaccustomed to sitting in the passenger seat.

My world exploded with rainbow light.

❧

*G*unnar—via Odin's wolves—earned five stars on their Norse ridesharing service. We landed about a dozen feet from a colossal golden throne. All I noticed was that it was expensive and that it was empty.

The rest of the throne room, however, was not.

Traveling by rainbow power must not have been that uncommon, because as I spun around to make sure we weren't about to be dog-piled by a fleet of Valkyries, I saw a bunch of boring members of the court congregating near food tables on one side of the huge room.

Gunnar and I stood in the heart of Asgard, between parallel rows of thick, soaring, marble columns that led, fifty feet away, to a set of double doors that were at least thirty feet tall.

The members of the court—probably gods and demigods—were eating legs of turkey and other finger foods as they listened to a familiar asshole seated on a chair by the table of food.

None of them noticed us. At all.

I walked up a set of steps that elevated the throne above the floor level of the rest of the room. The platform was a large square shape, and at each corner, a life-sized statue of a god stared outward, regal and majestic. I noticed Thor, Freya, a one-handed man, and another beefy guy. In the center of the platform, stood the tall-backed golden throne. I walked up to it and sat down, kicking my boots up on one of the arms.

This was just ridiculous. Where were the guards? And how could they be so unperceptive?

Gunnar walked up to stand beside the throne, glancing about anxiously. I thought he was looking for threats until he turned to me, pursing his lips.

"You see a bathroom anywhere?"

I blinked at him. I craned my neck, searching, and my eyes locked onto one of the statues. I grinned, pointing. Gunnar nodded. "I normally wouldn't do this, but I think I'll make an exception today," he said. "An exception for *him*."

I nodded, turning my attention back to the crowd of Asgardians, really hoping one of them would turn around.

Gunnar pulled up the hood on his Nemean Lion Cloak, and then began to piss on the side of Thor's statue.

Still, no one turned around. Instead, they listened as Thor began to bitch and moan about one of my favorite subjects.

Me.

"Nate Temple has disrespected Asgard. He has used dark magic to brainwash Odin—"

I burst out laughing.

The crowd spun to look at us, surprised to realize they were not alone.

Their looks morphed to stupefied disbelief to see just how disrespectful two St. Louis boys could be when they felt slighted.

"Hey, Thor," I said, waving.

The crowd parted and Thor slowly walked out from behind them, staring at me incredulously. His face began to darken.

And *then* he saw Gunnar finish his business, shake it twice, and put his tools away.

"Okay. Much better. Now it's mine," Gunnar said, walking back up to me and sitting awkwardly on one butt-cheek on the arm of the throne. He locked eyes with Thor. "Woof." I grinned at the canine territory reference, giving Gunnar a high five.

Thor spun back to his people, pointing a finger back at us. "You see? He is a demon. He mocks all of Asgard—"

"Hey, Thor!" My voice rang out over his. "Shut up," I said calmly. "I love Asgard. I just have a real problem with people who hit pregnant women." I pointed a thumb at Gunnar. "But my friend is probably going to address that topic in more detail here in a minute or two. You see, Thor's target was his wife."

Gunnar gave them a slow, murderous nod.

I saw Thor's shoulders bunch up angrily, but he pressed on. "I admit he even kidnapped *me*, taking me to Niflheim where he knew he would finally have a chance to kill me. I bravely escaped—"

"THOR!" I bellowed, making many of the crowd turn to look. "Tell them the truth. How you came to Niflheim of your own volition, and how I swatted you down like the little bitch that you are."

My words rang out, and the crowd began demanding answers from Thor, looking disgusted. Because if anyone else had said such a thing, while sitting on Odin's throne, they would have been torn limb from limb.

Thor shook his head. "LIES! I would never—" But his words were drowned out by the crowd as they shouted questions on top of questions.

"That man is blessed by Odin, I tell you! I can feel it!"

"Did you attack his wife?" another demanded, sounding appalled.

"They are sitting on Odin's throne! Do something, Thor *Odinson!*"

Gunnar calmly stood and walked over to Thor's statue, inspecting it pensively. Then he pulled something out from behind his back beneath the cloak.

I gasped as he lifted a strange hammer high above his head in one beefy arm. His hood fell back to reveal his long blonde hair, and with that hammer held high…

Gunnar was the epitome of what Thor *should* have been.

Then he brought it down with his full strength on top of the statue.

One blow.

CRACK!

The sound echoed through the room, silencing everyone as Gunnar's strike pulverized the statue in a cloud of white dust and falling rubble.

I stared at the hammer in his hands, trying to process the scene like everyone else in the room. Gunnar spun the hammer in the air, catching it by the hilt. He looked up to find everyone, including Thor, staring at him in stunned disbelief.

Where the hell had he gotten *that?*

"Heard you've been looking for this," Gunnar said casually. "Step right up, God of Thunder. Step. Right. Up."

Thor began panting, shoving Asgardians out of his way in his haste to approach the throne. He stared, wild-eyed at his hammer, visibly shaking.

"MJÖLNIR!" he bellowed in outrage, lifting his hand out as if he could grab it, even though he was still twenty feet away.

CHAPTER 41

I wisely climbed to my feet, because I suddenly saw guards slipping in through the tall doors on the opposite side of the room.

I watched as Gunnar closed his eye, his muscles suddenly bulging as if from some great force was trying to tear Mjölnir from his hand. Thor was trying to call it back to him…

And Gunnar was resisting.

Making the whole scenario look like an arm-wrestling match.

I heard Gunnar's knuckles crack at the strain, but the hammer didn't budge. I kept a close eye on the guards, but they seemed just as transfixed with the spectacle as everyone else, lowering their weapons in shock—whether to see Mjölnir, two strangers on the throne, the destroyed statue, or the fact that Thor was having performance issues.

I heard a strange noise and glanced over to see that Gunnar was snarling under his breath, between growls.

"Daddy will *never* let go, Calvin."

And my heart threatened to break while somehow lighting on fire.

"Daddy will make him pay, Makayla. No one hurts your mother," Gunnar snarled, his feet sliding a few inches as he maintained his death grip on the hammer. White fur began to sprout from his arms, but he didn't fully shift.

And I released my restraint on my ichor, having been holding it the entire time so as not to give anything away until the right moment. My veins suddenly began to glow with golden light, and I heard some of the Asgardians gasp in horror, recognizing it immediately.

A godkiller was here, and rather than killing every god within eyeshot, he was letting his friend collect justice from just one god.

The hammer began to crackle with electricity, wild arcs snapping out to stab at the columns, the walls, the other statues.

Thor's face was a sheen of sweat, and he was gritting his teeth, panting desperately as he reached out, his hand like a claw.

I felt the air begin to tingle in warning, so I threw up a shield of air. With a concussive explosion that obliterated the other statues and knocked over the throne, Thor sagged to his knees with a wheezing groan.

Gunnar, on the other hand, maintained his stance, glaring down at the God of Thunder, panting furiously. His lone eye rippled with liquid gray, and he let out a roar that sent the hardened warriors of Asgard fleeing from the room, giving up their lifelong vocations as guards.

Because shit had just gotten real.

Gunnar wasn't finished, though.

He suddenly leapt high into the air, closing the distance to Thor in one jump, swinging the hammer down with all his strength—and some strength he definitely shouldn't have had. Whether that was the Nemean Lion Cloak or Geri and Freki, I had no idea.

Thor flung his arms up in an X, but the force of Gunnar's blow cracked the marble floor in a ten-foot radius, sending Thor flying into a nearby column. He struck it with his back, cracking it, but landed on his feet. He squared his shoulders, glaring back at Gunnar with pure hatred.

Hurt and humiliated, but otherwise still in the fight. Because as strong as Gunnar was, Thor was a god.

Which meant it was my turn to tag-in to the fight. Gunnar had made his point. He was going to go down in the history books as a legend of the highest magnitude. The werewolf who humiliated Thor.

Except I didn't jump in. Without knowing exactly what I was doing, I pointed one hand at Gunnar as I clenched my other fist—the one with the Temple Crest branded into my palm.

And I murmured a binding in a language that I didn't know.

An arc of wild, golden lightning struck Gunnar in the spine, and he arched his back with a roar of pain.

I panted frantically, trying to release my power, not understanding exactly what I was doing, but seeing that it was only hurting my best friend.

Gunnar screamed—one long breathless roar.

Thor chose that moment to hurl a dark, violent, lovingly-crafted bar of lightning at the man who had stolen his hammer.

It was a cheap shot, cowardly play, since Gunnar was obviously weakened. My golden bar of lightning winked out upon contact with Thor's own lightning.

Gunnar flew across the room and through one of the stone columns before slamming deep into the wall hard enough to make a crater. He fell to the ground, a section of the wall collapsing on top of him, burying him almost instantly.

Thor laughed—a harsh, cruel sound. "Stay down, dog."

Other than that, the room was deathly silent.

Thor turned to me, setting his jaw. "I wasn't supposed to kill you until the wolf died. To inflict maximum pain." I blinked, shaking my head. What the hell was he talking about. Thor was working for someone? "Let me just tell you how truly excited I am about this next part. I've been dreaming about it for quite some—"

The rubble burying Gunnar shifted, and a large rock tumbled down the pile. Thor froze, glancing back with a frown. Everyone watched in silence. My heart raced, begging for Gunnar to have survived the fall. His Nemean Lion Cloak *had* to have helped somewhat.

But five seconds later, nothing else happened.

Thor grunted, turning back to me. He opened his mouth to speak just as Gunnar exploded from the rubble with a roar that made the hair on my arms stand on end.

He clenched Mjölnir in one fist, and locked eyes on Thor.

And he was blazing with golden veins.

I gasped, staring down at my own arms. They no longer glowed. Was that what I'd done? Transferring my godkiller power to Gunnar, just like Odin had done with his wolves? I knew I had been thinking about power transfer quite a bit, but I hadn't consciously chosen to do it with Gunnar.

Seeing how much pain I'd caused him, it suddenly made more sense. I hadn't been killing him. I'd been hurting him, just like when he'd had to prove himself to earn the wolves.

Gunnar had also been made to swear an oath to Odin beforehand.

But Gunnar and I already had such an oath with the werewolf rune my parents had given him in his youth—to help him control his shifting cycles.

And I remembered how when I had first put on my Horseman's Mask against the Greeks, Gunnar and I had bonded in some strange way—his eyepatch turning to the quartz-like stone of my Horseman skin.

Had I transferred my power to him then, too? Or was that something different?

Regardless, I was simply relieved to see him alive.

He stomped down the pile of rocks, his face set with grim resolve as he advanced on the God of Thunder with calm, measured steps. Thor rapidly began hurling bolts of lightning at him. They struck Gunnar's Nemean Lion Cloak and fizzled out, having no more effect than a water gun.

Thor's eyes widened in horror, and he began shimmering with rainbow light. Gunnar lunged, closing the distance in a blur, and picked Thor up by the throat, slamming him into one of the columns. Thor gagged and gasped, the rainbow light winking out as if nullified by Gunnar's touch—just like my experience in Niflheim.

Thor had been forced to put some distance between us in order to run away. Gunnar leaned forward, his face blank as he stared into the terrified god's eyes without blinking.

"Fear me, God of Thunder. Wulfric has come to claim your soul. *No one* messes with my family," Gunnar snarled.

And he lifted Mjölnir high, still gripping Thor by the throat in the other hand. Thor began clawing at Gunnar's wrist, begging for forgiveness.

Instead, Gunnar gave him the hammer of justice.

Gunnar brought Mjölnir down—releasing his stranglehold at the last possible second—on top of Thor's head in an explosion of blood and golden lightning.

Thor crumpled lifelessly to the ground. Gunnar calmly knelt down over him and checked his pulse.

But a sudden blast of yellow lightning zipped out from Gunnar, slamming into my abdomen and sending me falling off the pedestal, into an innocent bystander—a large, bulky man. I shook my head, dazed. I stared down at my hands to see my golden veins back online.

There had to be a better way to trade power than to taser each other repeatedly. Recalling how Gunnar had almost had his arms bitten off, I decided a little shock was preferable.

The man I had bowled over helped me to my feet, glancing nervously at my glowing arms and being exceedingly gentle with me, as if to reassure me that he wasn't a threat. He was a tall, bulky man with white-blond, close-cropped hair, and a short beard. "I am Heimdall," he said, taking a polite step back when he was certain I could stand on my own. Surprisingly, he dipped his chin respectfully. "Thor had gone too far, Rainbow Maker," he said, eyeing the staff still clutched in my hand. I had to physically pry my fingers off, deciding that they'd locked up when the bolt of power hit me.

Heimdall dipped his head, and then turned his back on me, letting me know he wanted no part in our quarrel with Thor.

For shits and grins, I reached out to pinch his ass before jogging away. He gasped, hopping away in surprise. "That's from Freya!" I cackled over my shoulder, remembering my flippant comment to her back in Niflheim. And then I ran up to Gunnar to make sure he was alright.

I found him seated in a pool of blood, staring down at Mjölnir.

Asgardians formed a row facing him, but they were a healthy distance away, no one eager to be the first to address the man who had just killed Thor.

A god.

Then they saw *me*, glowing with my golden veins, and they recoiled in fear, not understanding my part in all of this but knowing I had been the catalyst for the chaos—the dude found sitting in their throne, taunting Thor.

Gunnar noticed my arrival and glanced up. "I did it," he whispered, and I saw that through the mask of blood painting his face, a streak of clear skin stretched down from his eye. A tear.

I knelt down, pressing my forehead against his as I gripped the back of his head. "Hell yeah you did. Calvin and Makayla have a fucking godkiller for a dad."

He shook his head wondrously. "I don't know how you did that, brother, but I will never forget it." He reached out to grip my forearms, tight enough to hurt. His eye danced with barely restrained emotion. "Never," he promised, his voice cracking as he stared at the golden light in my veins.

I nodded, smiling faintly. "That's what you two were talking about, wasn't it? Odin gave you Mjölnir."

Gunnar nodded with a slight grin. "Only after I promised to keep you safe. He cares more than you know, Nate. That was the only reason he let me borrow his wolves. To keep you safe. He told me afterwards."

I blinked at him, my internal self-righteousness wilting. "Oh."

"But I couldn't have done it without your help, brother."

I sighed, hanging my head. "Alright, you big brute. Let's get out of here. We did what we came to do. Odin and Freya are safe to take care of Ashley. They can come back and clean up this mess themselves. The way I see it, our work here is done."

"Let's go give the Allfather the good news."

I winced. "You sure he's going to take it well?"

Gunnar nodded adamantly. "I spent a lot of time with him while you were in Fae with Callie," he said, tapping Mjölnir suggestively. "In his eyes, Thor died long ago. It just took until today to bury the body."

I glanced down at the bloody mess a few paces away. Not exactly buried, but I knew what Gunnar meant. "Eye," I said, reaching into my pocket for something I'd transferred there from my satchel earlier.

He frowned at me. "What?"

I pulled out an empty glass vial and held it up to the light. "You said *in his eyes*. He's just got the one, remember?"

He grunted "I get it," he said dryly.

"Heh. I."

He growled, shaking his head in frustration. "Don't make me use the hammer on you, Nate. Things were going so well—hey! What are you doing?" he hissed, trying to shield my actions from the other Asgardians.

I stoppered the vial, holding it up to study Thor's crimson blood. Except it wasn't just blood. The moment I—a godkiller—had set the vial in front of it, I had felt a sudden thrum of power, just like when I had killed Athena.

I had just bottled up Thor's soul.

But Gunnar didn't need to know that. "Call me paranoid, but I want proof of death. Or insurance so I can find him if he decides to come back to life later."

I pocketed the vial and climbed to my feet.

"Bloody Funday," I said, shaking my head.

"What?"

"It's a new holiday at Chateau Falco. The Sunday you killed Thor. Bloody Funday." I glanced over at him. "It is Sunday, right?"

He shrugged.

I furrowed a brow. "We'll roll with it."

He shook his head. "Let's go, man."

I nodded. "I'm driving this time. I know how to leave. I just didn't know how to get here."

Gunnar let out a sigh. "Good, because I'm exhausted," he admitted, hefting Mjölnir in his hand.

I rolled my eyes. "I did all the work here. You were just a glorified cheerleader." Before he could respond, I grabbed his sleeve, waved at the baffled Asgardians, and Shadow Walked us back to the Armory.

Now it was time to take down Mordred.

If I decided to let Gunnar join me, I'd have to throw him into the healing pool first so he could regain his strength.

And I wasn't going to warn him ahead of time.

I also wasn't going to warn Odin. Because all my thoughts about his story had come to a head. Hearing Thor's claim about how he wasn't supposed to kill me until Gunnar was dead had changed things for me.

Thor had been working for someone, or on their behalf.

It had never been about Ashley, although I wasn't going to tell Gunnar that. Maybe when he cooled down a little and set Mjölnir down—somewhere far from reach.

Thor's statement had both confused and clarified some things, leading me to a sneaking suspicion. And only Odin had the answer.

And after what Pandora had told me about time, I was thinking I needed to jump on things fast, because if my suspicions were true…

We were all in more trouble than we'd initially thought.

CHAPTER 42

*P*andora was waiting for us when we arrived in the usual balcony area I had designated as my traveling spot. She took one look at me and blurted out, "How long were you in Asgard?"

Gunnar and I froze.

"An hour?" I guessed.

Pandora swore. "I figured as much. It's been five hours for us."

I gritted my teeth, shaking my head. "Damn it. Why is this all happening right now?" I demanded. "I thought only Fae was messed up."

Pandora shrugged. "It's all connected somehow. I don't have any answers, but I'm keeping track of it all," she said, showing me the notepad and pen in her hand. She scribbled something down and then looked up, noticing the panicked look on Gunnar's face. Because a large chunk of time had passed and a whole lot of things could have happened to Ashley in that window. "Oh. Your wife is fine. Freya is working hard to keep her comfortable, and she thinks the babes will come tonight."

Gunnar let out a shaky sigh of relief to hear that he hadn't missed it. "Thank you."

Odin entered the room at that exact moment. His eye immediately locked onto the blood-stained Mjölnir. "It is done," he said with a sigh.

"Yes," Gunnar replied.

Odin looked back up at him with a hollow smile. "Thank you. I will miss the man he once was, but that man died long ago. If there had been any way to sway him, I would have never had to steal Mjölnir in the first place."

I frowned. "*That* was why you stole his hammer? Because he'd turned bad?"

Odin pursed his lips, motioning for us to follow as he resumed his walk. Pandora left, flashing me a sad smile on her way by. I scooped up my satchel from against the wall and shared a long look with Gunnar as we approached Odin.

Gunnar looked just as confused as me, though.

Odin spoke over his shoulder, first glancing left and right to make sure we were alone. "I would like to explain," he began, speaking softly. "But I am forced to speak in generalities so that we do not attract the wrong sorts of attention." He looked at me. "This is one reason your parents never left you a detailed explanation of your own past, or their plans for your future. And it is why they hired gods to assist you. Merely *talking* about such things out loud can get you killed—even here, in your Armory. There is only one truly safe place where these things can be discussed—Solomon's Temple." I stared at him, shaking my head. So that was why my parents had chosen Last Breath for their landlord.

"Okay," I replied, biting my tongue from asking the dozens of questions on my mind.

Odin dipped his chin in gratitude for my agreement. "Many years ago, Thor got involved with the wrong crowd. I later learned that it was the same crowd your parents fought so tirelessly against."

My eyes widened, but I remained silent.

"When it became obvious that I could not dissuade Thor, I decided that I could at least diminish his power, so I stole Mjölnir and his other possessions. And then I fled." He locked eyes with me. "Yes. I, Odin, fled, disguising my identity as a butler to hide behind a man named Calvin Temple. *That* should tell you something about what kind of man your father was, Nate."

I shook my head. My parents had given Odin *sanctuary*? That was why he'd chosen to become my butler? Holy crap. I was beginning to comprehend the full scope of this nefarious group. If it was enough to scare someone like Odin—and entice someone like Thor—I was pretty sure I wouldn't like them, and that I should be terrified of them.

Maybe this was why Callie had been so cagey while talking to me in Fae. Maybe she had learned of this group.

Odin cleared his throat. "There is much more to discuss, but it should wait. I believe Alex will soon need you in Fae. I only spoke now in hopes to remove any concerns you had about my motivations. I know I have lied to you Nate, and I was never as good of a man as Pan. But I tried, in my own limited ways, to teach you what I thought you needed to learn. I can swear to you that I've never had anything but good intentions for you. Strike me dead now if you doubt me. I will rest easy knowing that at least my cursed child, Thor, can no longer destroy everything I spent my entire existence trying to build."

He held his arms out, waiting. Not as a dare, but with his eye closed and his breathing calm.

I studied him for a few moments, thinking.

"I'm not going to kill you, Odin. I'm not sure I entirely forgive you—I have too many questions to make that kind of decision right now. Which leads me to something important. I do have two questions that I need to ask you, and I believe you can answer them very easily. Even if you do not want to. Consider them an olive branch."

Odin had opened his eye, listening attentively as I spoke. "What are your questions?" he finally asked me.

"I'll start off with a statement. Just nod if I'm right."

"Okay."

"Gungnir was stolen about six months ago, right? When you caught the Knightmare snooping around your hut in Niflheim, you assumed it was him. But you never found evidence of his theft, or evidence that he had a partner, right?"

He nodded, knowing he'd already told me all but the timeframe. Internally, I cursed, trying to keep my breathing steady.

"Is the Bioloki in Niflheim, by any chance?"

Because out of all the realms Odin could have chosen for a safe refuge, he had picked Niflheim. A place that weakened gods with its toxic mist. What better place to deter any assassins from coming to find you when your cover as a butler had been blown?

And what better place to put a prison for a god? Even if they escaped, the very realm was poisonous.

Pandora had been upset that Odin had taken Ashley to Niflheim. He had to have known it wasn't a good environment for an injured, pregnant woman, yet he'd still taken her there. He knew all about my Armory, and he hadn't suggested it. Which meant he had a strong reason to want to be in Niflheim. Why else would he have given most of his powers to his pets— who were apparently immune to the effects of Niflheim. Odin hadn't been weakened from losing Gungnir, he'd been hiding his godly powers in his pets.

With his precious Gungnir gone, the only item worth protecting that I'd been able to think of had been this Bioloki.

Odin had stiffened. "Yes," he finally admitted. "But the only people who know where I stored the Bioloki are now dead."

I stared back at him, my mind a million miles away as I laid out the facts, trying to find a pattern. "You know who spent a considerable amount of time with dead people?" I asked softly. "And who recently hired a bunch of Knights?"

Odin's lone eye widened. "We…need to go. Right now."

CHAPTER 43

*G*unnar yanked open the door to the hut in Niflheim, still wearing the Nemean Lion Cloak. Odin shoved his way past to enter the back room where I had first seen Ashley. He stared down at the bed, clenching his jaws. Then he bent down and, with one hand, flipped it over to send it crashing into the wall on the other side of the room.

Holy crap.

Odin reached out and opened a trap door that had been covered by the bed. It opened up to reveal crude stairs, wider than I would have thought necessary. I shared a look with Gunnar, and he shook his head, letting me know he hadn't known about it. We followed Odin down several flights of stairs to find a large metal door.

Except it was wide open, the locking mechanism simply a knot of twisted metal, leaving a gaping hole where it had once been.

I gave Odin a very flat look. "I'm guessing this isn't supposed to be open." Odin shook his head, pursing his lips. We followed him through the opening to enter a small room the size of a prison cell, and in the center was a large chest the size of a coffin.

And the Knightmare's missing sword was lying on the floor. Gunnar scooped it up with a growl, sniffing it. "It's the same as the set from Hugin and Munin, but what is it doing down here?"

I glanced back, remembering the busted hole where the lock had been on the door. "Looks like an impromptu key to me."

Odin had walked around to the opposite side of the coffin and flung the hinged lid open. I watched as he stared down in stunned disbelief. His eyeball looked like it was in danger of popping out from the socket.

I made my way over with Gunnar to see for myself.

A man was inside—hogtied and gagged from ankles to wrists with a thin, delicate ribbon—and his eyes were wide as he tried to scream at us in muffled panic. He wore only his boxers and the side of his face was covered with dried blood.

My brain sort of shut down for a moment, unable to comprehend any of what I was seeing. Because my brilliant powers of deduction had never considered anything like this. I'd expected to find a book missing from a shelf. Not a dead man's sword, a coffin, and a hostage.

"Impossible," Odin hissed. "This is not *possible*." He was glaring at the ribbon and panting. I frowned at it, wondering why the man hadn't broken free of such delicate restraints. "That is Gleipnir!" Odin cursed.

I turned to him with a blank look and his cheeks darkened.

"Fenrir's bindings!"

Okay. *That* name I had heard before. Fenrir was the giant wolf that was foretold to kill Odin in Ragnarok—the Norse version of the Apocalypse.

Oh, and—fun fact—Fenrir was Loki's kid.

To prevent the prophecy—and Odin's death—the Allfather had commissioned the dwarves to make a restraint that not even the giant wolf could break free from—a silken ribbon made of six supposedly impossible things —the breath of a fish, the sound of a cat's footfall, the roots of a mountain, the beard of a woman, the sinews of a bear, and the spittle of a bird.

It was stronger than *any* chain or metal.

And I was looking at it.

My heart began to palpitate.

If this man was here, then that meant…

Loki, the God of Mischief, was in the Armory.

Gunnar snarled, pointing at the insides of the chest, which were covered in glittering, white stones. "Moonstones?" he demanded.

Odin shook his head, speaking in a monotone. "Not Moonstones. These are very different. They have the power to conceal auras and energies. I call them Sensates—for their ability to deceive your senses."

I watched as his eye suddenly flashed quicksilver. He was calling on his ravens to search the Nine Realms for what we should have found inside the coffin—the Bioloki.

Gunnar reached down and ripped the man's gag down. "How long have you been down here?" he demanded, already working to untie the ribbon.

The man gasped in a lungful of air, panting as he watched Gunnar work. "I don't know. I was watching you bond Geri and Freki when something hit me in the back of the head," he admitted, obviously ashamed and furious. "I woke up here. I've been screaming—"

"We need to go. RIGHT NOW!" I snapped, cutting him off. Gunnar finished with the ribbon, yanked it away, and then lifted the man out of the chest. I tore open a Gateway in the opening where the door had been, and then I reached back inside the coffin to grab the ribbon while everyone was distracted. Other than that, the chest was empty. I shoved the ribbon into my pocket as I grabbed Odin by the shoulder, snapping him out of his daze.

Gunnar led the hobbling man through the Gateway, supporting his weight since his legs were probably cramped up to hell. And I shoved Odin ahead of me to follow them.

Things had just gone from bad to worse.

❀

I stepped into the Armory, trying not to panic as I closed the Gateway behind me. I quickly stepped out in front of everyone and held out my staff to block them from stampeding, even though I felt like having a voluntary seizure.

Although we knew Loki was here, we didn't know what it meant. The conflux of events that had led me to assuming the Bioloki was in Niflheim had not led me to any outcome like this. I'd expected to find the Bioloki stolen to possibly be leveraged as a bartering chip against one of the players in this whole mess—probably Odin.

So what the hell was *really* going on? Because if Loki was free, it seemed like the original evil plan was blown to hell, and that Loki was here on his own agenda.

"Okay," I said, quietly and calmly. "No one else knows. Act normal and follow me."

In varying degrees of bad acting, they all complied—each person having their own reasons to be terrified out of their mind.

We each had friends or loved ones here, and Loki was strolling around in disguise, using his mastery of illusion in some manner that had fooled every single one of us. Whatever he intended, it couldn't be good.

I walked down the Hallway and found Pandora and Alice on a bench in the center of the room with the open balcony. Part of me felt a tremendous relief to find them unscathed, but I had other friends here who were still in danger. Pandora was braiding Alice's hair, but she paused as soon as we entered, flashing us a dazzling smile.

My eyes danced about the room, searching every corner as discreetly as possible. "How is Ashley?" I asked lamely, motioning with my hands for them—especially Alice—to play along.

Because Alice was a Seer, which meant she was already seeing something in my aura that told her we were all in grave danger. Her eyes widened in horror, but she didn't give us away by screaming or crying or anything.

"Ashley...is fine," she stammered.

Pandora was no longer able to read my mind, though. She frowned quizzically at my strange hand gestures, not understanding what was happening. Then she glanced to my right and noticed the man in boxers holding a sword. Gunnar had given it to him, preferring his new hammer.

She frowned harder. "Weren't you just in the hot tub—"

She cut off, her eyes abruptly widening as she seemed to finally read his mind. She jerked her gaze from face to face, as if needing to verify what she had seen.

She pursed her lips, her eyes growing hard, and the wooden brush in her hand snapped in half. It had been a very thick brush.

"Stay here with Alice," I whispered, hoping to keep her calm. "Where is—"

A scream echoed through the halls of the Armory. Gunnar's shoulders bunched up and fur exploded down his arms at the familiar voice—his wife.

Alice promptly gasped and then passed out, overwhelmed by the torrent of emotions she was seeing from the Alpha werewolf. Pandora caught her and pulled the child close to her chest in a protective gesture. "Go!" she hissed, baring her teeth at the invasion of her most sacred place—her home.

We all ran, Gunnar leading the way, but I was a close second.

We skidded to a stop in front of Ashley's door to find Drake nervously pacing back and forth, running his hand through his hair, obviously distressed about the sounds coming from beyond the door he was guarding.

Ashley.

He saw us and let out a gasp of relief. "I think it's happening—" he cut off abruptly, his eyes darting over Gunnar's shoulder to see his best friend. He cocked his head in utter confusion. "Wait a minute…"

Because the Cowan he'd been working with since Niflheim hadn't been the real deal.

Cowan lunged past me and grabbed a fistful of Drake's shirt. "Where is Cowan? The imposter!" the giant, muscular man growled, his face close enough to bite Drake's nose off.

Drake looked too startled and confused to use words, but his eyes flicked towards the door he had been guarding.

Gunnar reached for the handle and simply ripped the entire door off—hinges and all—before flinging it back behind him.

I used that tiny window of opportunity to cover my head from falling debris and darted through the opening before anyone else could beat me to it.

Thick, pungent incense filled the air, and strange, wild magic danced all around me—enough to give me a sudden, mild buzz. So, it took me a moment to process what the fuck my eyes were seeing.

Ashley—still wearing her blindfold—was lying on the bed, panting and screaming as she rode the pain of her contractions all by herself. And those contractions were close together, because I wasn't sensing much of a break between them. The babies were coming.

Now.

Her midwife, Freya, was on the ground, the side of her head bleeding heavily, and she was trying to scoot back as fast as possible.

Because Imposter Cowan held a very familiar spear high above his head, and he was already pulling it down to stab Freya in the chest.

Gunnar threw Mjölnir from over my shoulder, striking Imposter Cowan in the back hard enough for his deathblow to miss Freya by an inch. He lost his grip on the spear, and he flew into the far wall with a thunderous crash, bouncing back onto the ground.

Although I already held one of my own, I dove for the spear, recognizing it for what it was.

Gungnir—Odin's missing spear. Sweet baby Jesus.

Gungnir was rumored to never miss its target, so Imposter Cowan had to be the worst warrior ever born.

In his fall, Imposter Cowan accidentally dropped a familiar white stone —one of the Sensates from his prison—and he suddenly shimmered, revealing a different man entirely. He was tall, had long dark hair, and was built like an endurance athlete.

In midair, my skin suddenly began to glow with golden light, pretty much confirming everyone's running theory.

It really was Loki.

The Sensate was more powerful than I had been able to believe when Odin first described it. The stone had fooled everyone—Odin, Freya, Gunnar, Pandora, and even Alice, a Seer.

Either that, or Loki was way better with illusions than I had believed possible. He'd shifted into a werewolf in front of Gunnar and still hadn't been caught. God of Mischief indeed.

The only thing I knew for certain was that he wasn't a mama's boy, because he'd definitely been trying to murder Freya. The question was why?

Loki recovered quickly, though. He lunged out to grab the end of Odin's spear and rainbow lightning began to form over his hands. He'd pulled Gungnir out of my reach, but I managed to grab hold of his pants. If I'd managed to touch his flesh, I might have stopped him from teleporting altogether.

Every voice was screaming something different as I winked out of the room with Loki.

CHAPTER 44

We landed in a tangle of limbs, and luckily, I was on top. I reminded Loki of this by elbowing him as hard as I could, right in the nose.

I felt cartilage crunch—thanks to my godkiller juice—and he gasped in pain. I used the moment of distraction to jerk my staff and satchel clear, scramble to my feet, and get a quick scan of our environment before Loki could recover.

We were in a large clearing with three car-sized boulders. A huge Medieval castle loomed before me, and I noticed a field of very familiar glass grass less than a dozen yards away. My eyes widened, putting two-and-two together as Loki climbed to his feet between me and the castle.

Fae. Camelot.

I reared back and kicked the God of Mischief right in the nuts—hard enough to lift him an inch off the ground—grabbed Gungnir, and then took two long strides before using both spears to pole vault over the nearest boulder.

Because I remembered what Alex had told me about Mordred's alarm system, and I was betting that system had a violent deterrent.

Molten fire splashed into the ground behind me, hot enough to boil the very air. The force of the blast hit me at the apex of my leap and sent me flying to safety behind the boulder. I crashed to the ground, tumbling and rolling as I tried to maintain my grip on both spears.

I stared down at them in my hands, shaking to see that I was still alive, and that I had Gungnir. It was a long way from a win, but it was also a long way from a loss.

The game was still on.

I waited a few more moments for the air to cool down before peering around the boulder. Scorched, glowing earth smoldered where I had been standing with Loki. Mordred stood just outside the ring of fire, glaring at the howling creature in the center of the blast radius.

Loki was severely burned, his skin simply missing, cracked, or a melted smear on more than half of his body. He'd been hit with a Lokitov Cocktail.

But the bastard was still alive somehow. Damn.

"Where is my spear?" Mordred demanded.

I punched the ground angrily as my worst suspicion was confirmed. They *had* been working together from the start! The *how* eluded me, but all that really mattered right now was what I was going to do about it.

"Heal me and I'll tell you!" Loki rasped, kneeling in the embers.

Mordred considered the request for a second and then shook his head. "Too weak to heal yourself, God of Mischief?" He asked snidely.

Loki snarled, climbing to his feet. "I've been locked in Niflheim, in that cursed book, for *centuries*! My full power will take time to return."

Mordred nodded knowingly. When he'd escaped Hell, he'd stolen the Nine Souls to power up, so he knew full well what Loki was going through. And still, he showed no remorse.

Loki took an aggressive step forward. "Speaking of, where is my book? My prison?"

Mordred waved a hand. "I sold it to a bear for safekeeping in case you tried any of your usual tricks."

Loki snarled, clenching his fists hard enough that more of his ashen flesh simply crumbled away.

I frowned at Mordred's answer. A bear? That was random as hell.

"You are six months late, by my estimation," Mordred said. "My Knight never returned. Explain and I may heal you. I may even expend some effort to retrieve your book."

Loki cursed and took a threatening step forward.

Mordred grunted, holding up a hand in warning. "That's far enough. I do still have your son, Fenrir. Do not do anything rash. I'm sure you kept the ribbon and have clever plans to use it on me."

I blinked in horror. Fenrir wasn't a puppy for Mordred to just *have*, as he so casually put it. Without Gleipnir, how in the world was he restraining Fenrir?

Loki shook his head. "My opportunity to escape did not give me time to grab Gleipnir. I've never been the sentimental type, and I have no need for the ribbon anyway," he said with a horrific-looking smirk.

I licked my lips nervously. So it really had been Fenrir's leash, and it was currently tucked into my pocket.

It was sounding like Mordred really had granted Loki his freedom in exchange for Gungnir. Because Loki had known exactly where to take Gungnir once he acquired it.

And, as added leverage, Mordred had taken Fenrir hostage in case Loki did what Loki was famous for—mischief.

Loki obviously hadn't known about Mordred's alarm system. Then again, Mordred had said Loki was six months late, so Mordred must have changed his plans when Loki never showed up.

So, where did that leave me?

I glanced down at the spear in question, wondering if I should run away while I had the chance. But...Mordred was all alone. No Knightmares to contend with.

I noticed smoke in the distance and grimaced. Mordred's Knightmares attacking the Summer Queen? Were Alex and Talon and Grimm really that close?

I had no way of knowing for certain. Mordred must have taken time out of his busy schedule to come check the alert on his alarm system. A rare opportunity indeed. Once finished here, he would go back to the fight in the distance.

If I could kill him now, Alex could get some of his old Knights back. Hell, maybe the Knights would simply stop fighting in the distance, and I would win the whole war right here, right now.

I remembered how Odin had once said he could sense Gungnir, but he obviously hadn't been able to do so since it had been stolen. And Loki had dropped a Sensate back in the Armory before we'd fled here.

It must have been masking Gungnir's location from Odin.

I glanced up at the sky, praying for a fleet of Valkyries to come to my aid, locking onto their boss's spear like a homing beacon.

They didn't.

Which meant...Odin was busy.

Probably taking care of his wife. Or helping Freya deliver Ashley's twins.

Either way, it was looking like I was on my own.

Because if I went back right now, I'd miss an opportunity. Mordred could flee back to his Knightmares any second. I had to keep him *here*, by *myself*.

Me staying also meant Gunnar had the excuse to remain with his wife during the most important moment of their lives—the birth of their children. He wouldn't be in danger. We'd already killed Thor. He was safe. Ashley was safe. Calvin and Makayla would be safe.

I made my decision.

Loki's sudden shout drew my attention, almost making me cut my finger on the tip of the spear.

"Rot in hell, the both of you," he snarled, and I managed to lean out fast enough to catch a glimpse of him disappearing in a crackling, multi-colored flash. And that's when I recalled Pandora's absent comment back in the Armory—her thinking that Cowan had been in the hot tub.

The healing pool. Damn it. He'd regained enough of his power to run away. But I was still impressed he'd had the physical endurance to pull it off, especially burned half to death as he was. Then again, he was a god, and Mordred wasn't a godkiller.

Mordred had stiffened at Loki's parting words. "The both of you," he mused, gritting his teeth. I quickly ducked back, taking a moment to stare down at Gungnir's blade—a Devourer. As usual, vapor steamed off the gem in the center of the blade. If Mordred had risked this much—freeing Loki—to get it, I was going to do everything in my power to stop him. I set Gungnir down and whispered a word.

The grass rapidly grew over it, concealing it from view. I left my satchel propped up against the boulder and stood up, checking to make sure Gungnir wasn't noticeable.

"Which one of my good friends is it?" Mordred demanded, his voice booming out, loud enough to echo off the boulders. "Alex or Nate?"

I took a deep breath and stepped out from behind the boulder, gripping my rainbow staff in one hand.

"Hey, Mordred," I said, with not a hint of friendliness on my face. "I've missed you," I lied, thumping my rainbow staff into the ground.

CHAPTER 45

*M*ordred glared at me and then my staff. "Where is it?" he demanded.

"Don't tell me you actually *believed* him," I gasped. "Loki is long-gone with Gungnir by now. Remember, he's the master of illusions. How else do you think he held onto it for the past six months right under Odin's nose? Hell, he was probably holding it the entire time you were just talking to him." I scratched at my chin. "In fact, what if he wasn't even really burned by your fire?" I asked, chuckling.

I locked eyes with him, moving in a slow, methodical, circular walk, forcing him to turn in order to keep me in his line of sight. He looked furious and...wary of my questions. They had struck a nerve. I kept walking, loudly thumping my staff into the ground with each step, making sure I didn't do anything that would make him instantly react with direct force.

Because I was trying to get into his head.

Halfway through my walk of the perimeter, I slowed, furrowing my eyebrows. Then I slowly turned to look at him, cocking my head quizzically. Mordred now had his back to the boulder I had first been hiding behind. Perfect.

I kept the strain from my face as I called upon my Fae magic again—in hopes that he wouldn't have the ability to sense this particular flavor of power. I knew Mordred had mastery over at least several different forms of magic. He'd even eaten one of the Nine Souls, so he was no slouch in power. Hell, he might even border on demigod status.

I had no idea.

But he hadn't been born in Fae like me. He might know some Fae magic, but there was no way he knew it like I did.

"What if...*we are Loki?*" I whispered in an overly creepy tone.

I snapped my fingers, and there were suddenly twelve Nate Temple's for Mordred to contend with, all of us standing in a row. We didn't rush around trying to trade places. We just stood there smiling at him. He kept his eyes focused on me, ignoring the others, because I'd made no move to disguise that I was the first.

I gave him a slow, evil smile, and shrugged my shoulders. "Am I me?" I asked, and then I let out a harsh laugh. The other versions did the same a half-second later. Then I sort of let them start doing their own thing. Some began twirling their staff. Some began stretching. One was grinning, another was angry, another looked terrified. I began tossing my staff from one hand to the other as I watched him.

It was chaos.

Mordred paled, his eyes darting from face-to-face, analyzing and second-guessing himself. He would lock onto the original me most often, but I watched as the self-doubt crept in.

Maybe the first one was an illusion the whole time...

Because when emotions took over, the rational mind kept stubbornly trying to exert its influence. And none of the other illusions had made any attempt to switch places or anything, so...

It was so easy to point me out as the original that...it felt *too easy.*

Watching Mordred slowly taste insanity was a delicious moment for me, but I had to be careful not to push him so far that he ran away.

Which was why a *thirteenth* replica of me had been slowly creeping up behind Mordred this entire time.

And Number Thirteen held Gungnir.

"I command you to stop!" Mordred snapped. "If you don't cease these games this instant, I will kill Fenrir. If I die, Fenrir dies. Mark my words, Loki," he warned ominously. I forced myself not to cackle with glee upon seeing that I had fooled him.

Number Thirteen was finally close enough to stab Mordred in the back with Gungnir, and Mordred had no idea he was there.

"Do you promise?" Number Thirteen hissed.

Mordred jolted in surprise, but his reflexes were good. He spun while leaning to the side and hurling a fireball.

I, the overly obvious original, had closed the distance in silence, already halfway through my staff thrust at Mordred's spine. He realized his mistake when his fireball sailed through his opponent and splashed into the grass.

Still, he managed to move enough to save his life. Instead of severing his spine, my staff tore through his side, cracking a couple ribs on the way out of his abdomen.

He tried to swing a fist at me, but I ducked and gave him two powerful punches straight to the cracked ribs, hoping to break them off entirely so that they might pierce an internal organ when he tried moving again. He gasped in surprised agony, swinging wildly, but I had already moved ahead of him to grab the tip of my staff and yank it the rest of the way through his body.

He wheezed, clutching at his side, but I could tell he was already recovering—healing somehow. I saw his hand begin to glow as he used it to apply heat to the wound, cauterizing it.

Holy crap. Was that some power from him eating one of the Nine Souls?

He gritted his teeth, staring at me. "Hello, *Nate.*"

I bowed, brandishing a pretend cap. "Clever, right?"

He grimaced. "Unfortunately, yes."

"Now, hear me out before you start shooting lightning out of your eyes." I cleared my throat. "Loki knows illusion like no one I've ever seen before, and trust me, the Fae know illusion. Loki was under Odin's and Freya's noses, walking around without a care in the world—and they never had any idea. Their own *son.* Not only that, but he was impersonating a werewolf—even shifting when necessary—and none of the other werewolves knew. There were also two Seers who didn't see a thing."

I let that sink in, watching his anger fade somewhat. "Why are you telling me this?"

"Because he just left. And if Loki leaves your sight, it's only so he can get closer to you—by becoming someone you trust. One of your Knights, perhaps."

I took a step back and thumped my staff into the ground, waiting a few moments for him to process that. Because I wanted him to doubt his own men. Maybe not even doubt, but to feel paranoid. That had actually been the main reason for my little illusion charade. If I'd been able to kill him, all the better.

But I hadn't relied on that.

I'd wanted him to see—and fall for—illusion magic up close, and then for him to hear the person who'd just fooled him talk openly about how much *better* Loki was.

Because it was actually true, and it was another lever point I could manipulate to keep Mordred apart from his Knightmares.

To be honest, the thought had crossed my mind that maybe Loki had used his illusion magic to stage the argument with Mordred for *my* benefit —that the man in front of me right now might not actually be Mordred at all.

But that it might be Loki playing a long con on *me*.

I kept this thought to myself, but I was ready for it to become a reality— and at the worst possible moment.

"Shall we finish this?"

I smiled. "We shall."

CHAPTER 46

$\mathcal{F}$ ocusing on my Fae magic, I reached behind me and grabbed onto my shadow. I whipped it over my head and cracked it at Mordred, encasing him in a bubble of darkness. He struggled blindly, trying to ignite a ball of flame so he could see, but I was already aiming my staff at him and unleashing a bolt of lightning.

It ripped through the shadow and struck Mordred in the chest, slamming him against a boulder.

I ran towards him, dodging two blasts of air before his third hit me like a baseball bat in the thigh, sending me tumbling. I slapped the ground with both palms, freezing it solid before I hobbled away, trying to shake some feeling into my leg. Mordred tried to pursue but ended up slipping and sliding all over the place.

The sky abruptly turned to night, and I grinned as I heard Mordred crash to the ice with a curse. Fae didn't have sunrises and sunsets. One moment it would be day, the next it would be night.

I managed to climb to my feet with the aid of my staff, using my other hand to massage the muscle in my leg. I suddenly realized that Mordred was not making any noises, so I glanced up sharply, scanning my surroundings.

I heard a faint whisper before I cursed and grabbed my thigh at a flash of pain. Then another on my bicep and cheek. I hissed, Shadow Walking a dozen paces away and throwing up a shield in front of me—but using my magic was suddenly much harder, as if those cuts had zapped my reserves. While I was looking ahead, an incredible blow hit me in the kidney. I dropped my shield, swinging my staff at my unseen opponent. It connected with something I couldn't see in a flash of sparks that destroyed my night vision. I winced, realizing my staff felt much lighter.

I lifted it, frowning, only to realize that it was half as long as it should have been, ending in a jagged break that glowed like molten metal. I tried touching it with my Fae magic to flatten it out and recoiled as if shocked.

"I'm going to kill you, Mordred!" I hissed, trying to locate him.

"Do you promise?" he whispered my earlier taunt, also from directly behind me, and I grunted as my side suddenly screamed with fiery pain. I tried spinning to catch him but caught only air and lost my balance.

I hit the ground hard, and I felt a foreign object tear the wound in my side even wider. I reached down to check it and screamed as I grasped liquid fire. I bit my teeth, panting as I stared down and saw the other half of my rainbow staff sticking out of the side of my abdomen where Mordred had stabbed me.

Mordred shimmered into existence above me, stomping his heel on the hand holding my half of the staff. I heard a few of my fingers break, but I was too busy screaming to count.

Mordred had apparently been practicing his combat skills since Fight Club. Or maybe he'd been sparring with his Knightmares.

I tried throwing some magic at him, but I was in too much pain for it to be anything more than a weak slap, which Mordred batted aside.

He held a black blade, seemingly made of rippling liquid, in his fist. The blade he had used to cut me earlier, but I had no idea what it was made of. I tried calling out to it with my Fae magic, and I was firmly denied. Was it Fae or something else?

Mordred glanced down at me and then calmly lifted the black blade over his head. He'd already learned his lesson about granting me any last words. My unicorn had hit him like a dump truck last time—

My unicorn hit him like a dump truck this time, too.

It happened so rapidly that I flinched and let out a partial scream.

The two of them disappeared from view almost the moment that I recognized the familiar flash of red on black feathers.

I wheezed, trying to roll over to see them. Grimm was here!

Even though he was supposed to be helping Alex and Talon, I was grateful for his assistance, because I had severely misjudged Mordred.

I heard screams, curses, and heavy thuds of impact, but I couldn't make out anything in the darkness. Mordred wasn't using any kind of illumination in his attacks, so it just sounded horrifyingly violent.

I heard a loud cracking sound followed by a weary snort. Had Grimm wounded him? That wasn't enough. Not with Mordred.

I tried to raise my voice loud enough for my unicorn to hear me across the clearing. "Kill him—

A loud *thud* and *grunt* cut me off as something landed nearby. It skidded close enough to make me cough at a sudden cloud of dirt and debris. I could hear heavy breathing, but it was too dark to see what was happening. The edge of the rainbow staff sticking out of my stomach still had a faint glow, so I gritted my teeth as I rotated to get a better look.

And my heart stopped.

Grimm stared back at me. He was on his side, panting into the dirt. His horn had been snapped off at the base, and his chest was a bloody ruin.

I began to hyperventilate, shaking my head angrily, furiously, feeling a surge of hatred rise up from deep within me, momentarily dulling my pain. It wasn't much, but it was straight from the depths of my heart.

I grabbed the edge of the broken rainbow staff sticking out of my abdomen and hissed through the pain as it burned my hand. I yanked it out in one harsh pull, almost passing out in the process.

I used my feet to scoot me closer to Grimm. I heard Mordred steadily approaching, but I ignored him. I kicked my feet again, getting close enough to actually feel Grimm's labored breathing on my neck, and I realized I was sobbing.

"No, Grimm. I won't let this happen," I whispered.

He let out a long, high-pitched, but almost silent whine—a sound I didn't even know a unicorn could make. I gasped, openly crying and trying to blink through my tears. I set my hand on his nose, squeezing reassuringly, even though some of my fingers felt numb and stiff from Mordred breaking them.

"I love you, Grimm. Tell Alex that I tried," I whispered.

And I slammed the molten edge of the rainbow staff onto the nub of jagged bone where his horn had been. He kicked and bucked at the sensation of heat so close to his face, but I knew it wasn't touching his flesh. He was just in shock from his chest wound. I closed my eyes and focused on the rainbow staff, commanding it to do my bidding.

The molten edge fused to all that remained of Grimm's old horn, and the blood dripping down the staff bonded it all together with a flash of green smoke. When I pulled my hand away, excess grit cascaded down over Grimm's head and my wrist, leaving a long, jagged, gleaming point—larger than the original.

I scooted closer, and my free hand touched something on the ground. I grasped it as I heard Mordred drawing closer. But the most important thing in my mind was to wrap my other arm around Grimm's neck in a tight embrace as I pressed my cheek against his.

He whinnied weakly and I nuzzled my cheek harder against his as I felt Mordred stop just above me.

He grunted. "A boy and his unicorn. How sweet—"

A blast of multi-colored lightning hit him in the face from point-blank range, sending him flying at least fifty feet. I dropped the other half of the rainbow-staff I had accidentally found while crawling over to Grimm. That had been a fortunate find.

Knowing I had only moments to save him, I stroked Grimm's velvet nose. Then I slapped my other hand—and all the bloody rainbow grit left over from his new horn—onto his gaping chest wound. Then I poured my magic into him without mercy.

He screamed and began kicking his feet wildly, his eyes wide and spinning, but I held him down, funneling every last drop of magic I could into his wound, commanding the grit to heal and repair.

Because Grimm was one of my best friends. My brother.

My unicorn.

My magic flickered out and I collapsed onto my back, panting and seeing stars in my vision. I turned my head to face Grimm and stared in awe at his long, violently beautiful new horn. He was breathing steadier, and the wound on his chest was now just a big patch of semi-healed, glittering skin.

"Go," I whispered to him, trying my best to ignore the sounds of Mordred stomping our way again.

Grimm shed a tear, shaking his head violently. "No," he whispered. "Just hold on a little longer, Hope," he begged. "I need you."

I shook my head with a sad smile. "No you don't."

Because I'd tried tapping into my magic, and it had not been strong enough to Shadow Walk. I wasn't sure what Mordred's black sword was, but it had apparently leeched away my magic. Like it had spilled my blood, it had also spilled my magic reserves.

"Go, old friend. It's been my honor. And if Makayla ever wants a unicorn for her birthday party, you better fucking say *yes.*"

He snorted. "That's just not going to happen."

Mordred was suddenly towering over me again, and I saw a dagger of some kind racing towards my heart.

Grimm flung himself in the way, stabbing his new horn into Mordred's stomach.

But not before Mordred stabbed me in the upper chest near my shoulder and collar bone. I gasped at the flash of fire and pain. Grimm had deflected the strike somewhat, but combined with my other injuries, I was pretty sure this was it.

Grimm slammed Mordred to the ground, hopped in a circle, and then double back-kicked him into oblivion.

I reached my hand up to my chest, fumbling weakly for the dagger, but all I felt was a bone sticking out of my chest.

Grimm hissed. "That's my old horn!"

I shrugged, feeling dizzy and sleepy. "At least no one can see me now," I mumbled. "All beat up and lying around like a bum. Goddamned unicorn horn in my chest," I complained. "Ridiculous."

"Get up, Nate. grab my horn and I'll try to flip you onto my back. Maybe Pandora's hot tub can help you," Grimm pleaded, sounding desperate.

I shook my head, feeling suddenly nauseous and dizzy at the suggestion. "So I can fall off your back and plummet to my death? You want to get me killed *twice* by unicorn?" I muttered. "Ridiculous."

"I think someone is coming," Grimm said uneasily.

But something else he'd said caught my attention, making me frown. "Pandora…" It suddenly hit me. How had I forgotten that? "She can see me."

Like someone had flipped a switch, the scenery suddenly changed.

CHAPTER 47

I sat in a windswept desert of warm white sand. Colossal pyramids tipped in glass stabbed at the violet sky in the far distance, looking as large as mountains.

And I wasn't alone.

A black jackal god sat cross-legged no more than five feet away from me. Anubis. He looked up and sighed, holding his palm out in front of him. A glowing orb crackling with electricity hovered just above it.

"We have a problem," he told me by way of introduction.

I blinked at him, wondering if this was a hallucination.

I frowned. "I'm not here to pay my library fines, Anubis. I'm pretty sure they waive those after death."

"You're not quite dead yet. You have about thirty seconds left."

I arched an eyebrow. "Then what am I doing here?"

Anubis studied me for a few moments. And then he studied the orb in front of him. He sighed. "Remember the terms of your loan? You kill Mordred within two years, and I bring your pets back to life."

I narrowed my eyes. "They are not *pets*."

He nodded. "Sure. But they kind of are. Anyway. That's not my point. You still had time left, yet here you are."

I growled. "Gee. Thanks. I tried."

He nodded. "Yeah, about that. You see, in life, there are no participation trophies. Sucks, but it is what it is. You failed. Period. Loan due and payable—"

I leaned forward, cutting him off with a snarl. "You have *me*. You do not need Gunnar and Talon."

"—*In about thirty seconds*," Anubis said, completing his sentence with careful enunciation. Then he watched me patiently. His eyes danced as if he was desperately trying to tell me something, but I didn't know what it was.

I ran back through his words. I had thirty seconds before I failed, and then he would be forced to call his loan due?

"Okay," I said warily, not sure what he was getting at. "I still have thirty seconds before I break the terms of my loan. So…can we renegotiate?" I asked, taking a wild guess.

He let out a sigh of relief. "What an *excellent* idea!" he said. "Now, what can you bring to the table that I wouldn't already have in thirty seconds?" he asked urgently, seeming to lean forward.

I thought about it. "Um…" What did I have? I ran through an inventory of things in my satchel, but none of them seemed like they would be particularly valuable to Anubis. Not more than my soul.

I sensed him twitching out of the corner of my eye and looked up. He was facing me, but his eyes were rapidly moving from me to the electric orb in his palm. I frowned at it, obviously picking up on his hints that there was something special about this orb. And Anubis dealt in souls. So…this must be a soul.

I stared at the electricity and a sudden thought hit me.

"I can give you Thor's soul," I blurted out. Because it was inside the vial in my pocket. When I died, it would go to whoever emptied my pockets, and that *wouldn't* be Anubis.

He let out a sigh of relief. "What a valuable piece of collateral," he said, as if reading a script. "A powerful old god's soul instead of a powerful, adolescent godkiller." Was he being recorded or something? He was acting like he had the quality assurance department auditing our conversation.

I nodded. "Of course, if you *don't* think it's a fair trade, who knows where it might end up when I die. Any number of people could grab it. Like some of Thor's friends, the ones he was working so hard to impress—"

"Right, of course," Anubis cut in hurriedly, using his eyes to tell me to shut my goddamned mouth about *the group that shall not be named.* "You would be willing to give up Thor's soul to keep yours?"

"As long as you heal me from my wounds—"

"Ah. I cannot do that, but I can remove the damage from your fatal wounds. General wear-and-tear is not covered in our contracts. And, no offense, but you kind of got your ass handed to you back there."

This was worse than sitting down with an accountant and an aggressive life coach at the same time. "Heal my fatal wounds, and we have a deal."

"Splendid! If you could just sign here," he told me, whipping out a thick parchment and a pen, "then you can be on your way."

I took the contract and read over it carefully. I wasn't an idiot. Seeing nothing that looked concerning, I set it on my knee and signed it. Then I handed it back. "How do I give you Thor's soul?" I asked, frowning.

"When you return, smash it against something hard and repeat my name three times. That should suffice." He held out a hand. "Now, if you will please follow me, I will show you the way back."

I turned to see a gray door suddenly standing up from the sand about twenty feet away. It definitely hadn't been there moments before. I climbed to my feet and walked alongside Anubis, shaking my head.

"This is…unexpected," I admitted.

"Customer service is important. We aim to please."

I nodded very slowly. "Right."

"A Master Temple until your last breath," he said, shaking his head as if awestruck by his own good fortune. I glanced over at him to see his head facing forward, but his eyes were dancing intently.

"Thank you," I said carefully. Was he trying to tell me something?

He suddenly grabbed me to steady my balance—except I hadn't lost my balance. "Apologies, Master Temple. You looked about to fall," he said, staring deep into my eyes. "That would have been a bad end to a good night."

Numbly, I shook my head. "Just a stumble, I assure you."

And he winked.

There was no more discussion as he led me towards the door.

I walked in a trance, trying to understand what he was doing. It was an obvious reference to my father. Was he trying to tell me which side he was on?

"Remember," he said, opening the door, "do not forget to break the vial and repeat my name three times. That will complete our contract."

I nodded and stepped through the doorway into darkness. It clicked shut behind me, quite gently, actually—

Then the floor dropped out beneath me, and I was suddenly five-thousand feet in the air, free falling.

CHAPTER 48

I fell through the sky, but this time I did it much more gracefully.
Because although I was free falling, there was no wind whipping at my face, causing me to tumble and flip. Instead, it was as if I remained stationary while the Land of the Fae drew closer very rapidly.

And this time it was dark, showing me pockets of lightness here and there to signify cities, homes, and even a few bioluminescent environments.

I saw my mountain in the distance, cold, dark, and brooding.

But most of all, I saw the hot fires of war. Great, blazing flames surrounding a crystalline palace—the Summer Queen's home. It didn't look destroyed, but it was limping along. The battle had raged at her walls, causing much pain and heartache, yet she had not fallen.

Just stumbled, perhaps.

Another castle stood alone, surrounded by a lake of green, swampy, neglected water. The castle and surrounding city had seen its glory days long ago. It had thrived and prospered at one point, but now it was just a skeleton of its former self. Camelot.

I knew this, because my flight plan seemed to be sending me just outside it. Although still dark, my vision had started to adapt, growing accustomed to the lack of light.

So as I sailed closer to the ground, I noticed several strange things.

I saw my body—which pulled at me like a magnet, directing my free fall through the stratosphere.

I saw Grimm standing over me, but he moved slowly, as if underwater.

And I saw three glowing figures arrayed in a small arc approaching Grimm—who seemed to be guarding me protectively—although they were still some distance away. Enough time for me to warn him.

Knightmares were coming.

I didn't slow down as I slammed into my own body.

~

y eyes shot open and I gasped raggedly. The unicorn horn in my chest tumbled to my side, forced out of my wound. Grimm's eyes widened. "What the fuck?" he hissed incredulously.

The wound in my side burned with white fire as it sealed, the flesh knitting back together on front and back, and the muscles between spasmed and tugged inside me.

I wouldn't recommend it. Although the alternative was worse.

I urgently reached into my pocket and pulled out the vial of Thor's blood. I caught faint flashes of dim light within, as if his very blood was infused with lightning.

I slammed it against the ground, shattering it. "Anubis, Anubis, Anubis," I rasped. With a faint puff of smoke, the glass and blood was gone, leaving no evidence behind.

"What the *fuck?*" Grimm demanded, louder.

I propped myself up to a seated position, waving a tired hand. "I made a deal. I'll tell you later." He grunted unhappily, but he didn't press. I noticed my satchel sitting beside me.

"I figured you might want it," Grimm said.

I saw a flash of light and turned to look. Mordred stood about fifty feet away, staring at me. He glanced left and right, frowning momentarily, but then he shrugged it off. And took a slow, deliberate step towards me, his face determined to finish this once and for all.

Although no longer dying, my body was still throbbing in pain from my numerous injuries. And my reservoir of magic was pitifully low.

I subconsciously reached up and yanked the chain from my neck. The

Horseman Mask of Hope winked into existence, throbbing powerfully in my hand, hungry to be used.

I knew it was a gamble since it was already fractured, but if I could hulk out for just a *moment*, I could rip Mordred in half.

Removing all the curses on the Knightmares—especially the three I had seen making their way closer to me.

I lifted the Mask to my face, my hand shaking.

And it suddenly cracked loud enough to echo, scalding my fingers as two pieces fell to the ground beside me, smoking.

I stared down at them in stunned disbelief.

"You might want to see this," Grimm said.

I looked up to see Mordred frozen with one foot in the air, unblinking as he glared at me. I frowned.

Three figures stepped out from a copse of trees, the darkness repelled by some strange glow surrounding them. It wasn't actually a light, because everything around them remained dark.

It was more like...their aura was shining on a different spectrum that I was somehow able to see.

"How?" I whispered, suddenly recognizing them.

"Pandora told us it was time. Hope calls hope. You've been here two weeks, but she made us wait," Callie said, looking concerned at my injuries. A soft white light limned her body.

I choked, coughing as I struggled to prop myself up. Two weeks?

"Gunnar called us. Said you needed some sense knocked into you," Alucard said, sounding amused. "Figured he was probably right." A green glow pulsed warmly around him.

I turned to Gunnar, frowning at the golden glow outlining his massive frame. "Some sense knocked into me?"

He nodded, folding his arms. "You've been playing favorites, and Alucard and I now have hurt feelings. We're here to talk about that."

I blinked at him. Then I saw Callie grinning as she discreetly flashed me a view of the silver charm in her palm. The white light around her began to throb faintly, strengthened.

I narrowed my eyes. "You tattled."

"Damn right I did. Because I'm on their side."

Gunnar glared at me, his eyepatch glinting despite the darkness surrounding us. "When my friend literally throws his life away to prove how arrogant he is, I tend to not give a shit about his delicate sensibilities."

"Speaking of," Alucard said, stepping forward as he reached into his pocket to produce a metal flask. "You look like you could use a drink. I don't know what it is, but Pandora was insistent that you drink it."

I accepted it with a thoughtful frown. I tasted it, surprised to find it warm. And as the crisp, sweet water touched my lips, I felt a rush of warmth flow through me. I guzzled it, downing the entire thing.

Heat flowed through me, making my toes tingle.

I shuddered, taking a deep breath as I glanced down at my body. I was still beaten to hell, but the water had sped up the healing process, turning the sharp fresh wounds into the dull aches of injuries a few days old. Hot tub water. Yum.

It didn't do anything for my depleted magic, though.

It just made my current miserable existence slightly more tolerable.

"What happened here?" Alucard asked, squatting down to point at my broken Mask.

"I think Hope is dead."

"Hope *never* dies. Sometimes it is just hard to see," Gunnar said in a low growl. "You know how to fix it, Nate." I looked up to find him staring at my satchel.

Alucard was angling his head as if trying to peek inside it. "He's right, you know. Why else do you think Mordred suddenly froze? Almost like there's some cosmic force pointing out the obvious to you, Little Brother."

I narrowed my eyes, scowling. I'd had the same thought. Because when I'd first accepted the Mask of Hope, time had slowed, giving me a chance to talk with the Biblical Four Horsemen.

I looked over to see Callie now holding her actual Mask. "Go on, Nate. Stop standing in your own way. You think you're protecting them, but you're just robbing them of their dignity."

I flung open the satchel and grabbed the two remaining Horseman Masks. I held them in my hands, staring at them.

I cleared my throat. "The reason I didn't want to give them to you is because...I always meant to give them to you," I said. "It's like you found your Christmas presents early and opened them."

Alucard grinned widely. "I *knew* it!"

Gunnar grunted. "Could have fooled me. I remember asking very nicely and getting slapped the hell down."

I nodded. "I didn't want to put your kids in danger. I have issues when it comes to family stuff," I admitted with a shrug. "I didn't want to paint a target on your back."

Gunnar was silent for so long that I looked up. He was shaking his head with a sad smile. "Who cares if you paint a target on my back? No one will ever see it."

I frowned.

"I've already painted a target on my *chest*, Nate. I face my problems head on. Always. Who gives a shit about my back?"

I found myself nodding. "Yeah. Okay. You should write that one down. It's pretty good."

Callie was nodding.

I lifted the Masks. One was gold and one was green. Justice and Absolution. Both were made of the same quartz-like stone.

I handed the green one to Alucard. "Absolution," I said solemnly.

He accepted it reverently, his smile replaced by a deeply thoughtful expression as the Mask stuck to his fingers, making him gasp.

I had many reasons for choosing this Mask, but I didn't want to taint his own self-discovery. That was important. Just like I hadn't told Callie anything about Despair.

I'd picked that up from the Biblical Four Horsemen. They each had their own origin stories, something deeply personal that they could rely upon in moments of darkness.

We were a team, but there was a reason each Mask had its own name. I'd let them get familiar with the Masks before we held our first team meeting.

I flung the golden Mask at Gunnar. "Justice."

He caught it, grinning wide. I saw a sigh of relief escape his lips as it stuck to his palms. He trailed his fingers over it, grunting.

I absently wondered if Alice had known Gunnar would become Justice. Because she had tied golden ribbons in his hair in Fae.

And she had tied silver ribbons in Last Breath's mane, which was fitting if he became Callie's 'horse'.

"What do you need, Nate?" Gunnar asked, glancing down at my broken Mask. The two pieces seemed to be vibrating.

Before I could answer, Callie pressed her white Mask to her face. The white aura around her flared brighter, concealing her entirely.

When it faded, she stood before us in a white toga. Her arms were bare, but from the elbow down, it looked as if she had dipped her arms in liquid stone the same color as her Mask. Like she had diamond-encrusted, long-sleeved gloves. And from the knees down, she was simply white fog.

My broken Mask snapped together with a faint hiss of steam, and my eyes widened to see a diagonal white line across the face, stretching from temple to jaw.

Gunnar and Alucard didn't bother taking turns. They both slapped their Masks on at the same time. Green and gold light washed over us, making me wince. This time, I glanced down at my Mask first.

So I watched as a golden, jagged line spread over the face of my Mask— right beside the golden fracture mark. Then, a similar green line crawled across the Mask, sandwiching the two golden lines between the white and the green.

It flashed brightly and then began to hum. I grinned eagerly as I scooped it up. Then I turned to look at Gunnar and Alucard.

Other than their plain gold and green Masks, they...looked the same.

I remembered that Callie also hadn't changed when I'd first given her the Mask of Despair, but she also hadn't put it *on*. Gunnar and Alucard turned to look at her, and their body language let me know they were disappointed.

Callie shrugged. "I've used mine a few times."

They stared at each other like they were exes meeting at a Halloween party when no drinks had been served yet.

I laughed, shrugging my shoulders. "I think we all have different experiences. The Masks bond to you personally, so they need to get to know you. I had this thing forever before anything really cool happened," I admitted. "Give it time. Get to know it. Bond with it." And, with a deep, nervous, breath...

I put on the Mask of Hope.

A hundred fingers of lightning illuminated the skies as great tolling booms of thunder rolled across the Land of the Fae.

The darkness no longer impeded my vision—I could see clearly, but in shades of grays and greens.

A warm purr welcomed me, seeming to speak directly into my mind.

"Greetings, Horseman. Your family is complete and your Mask is healed, although your full powers are still recovering from the fracture. Much of that

strength comes from you, and you are currently injured and weakened. You should sit this battle out."

I nodded, knowing she was right. That's how I'd broken it in the first place—pushing too hard too fast.

Mordred abruptly looked like someone had just hit him in the gut with a baseball bat. He doubled over with a loud grunt and slammed into the boulder, no longer frozen in place.

I hadn't realized that I'd stood up, but I sensed my new brothers and sister standing beside me. And my unicorn. We watched him climb to his feet.

He stared back at us, his face pale and frightened.

"Destroy him," I snarled, lifting my hand.

And my Horsemen advanced in silence, their forms beginning to shimmer—

"HALT! Mordred is mine!"

And a lone figure stepped forward, holding a sword crackling with golden light. He held a familiar leather strap in his other hand.

Alex glanced back, seeming to acknowledge Callie, and dipped his head. "Thank you, Horseman. Thanks to you, Excalibur can now become whole."

Callie dipped her head politely, and I decided we definitely needed to have that talk. Soon.

Alex turned back to Mordred and touched the leather strap to the blade. The leather flared with white fire, burning away to ashes in seconds.

But Excalibur shone like the sun, making Mordred wince.

My Horsemen did not wince. We stared directly at the blinding light unfazed—probably the only people other than Alex who could do so without incinerating their eyeballs.

So we saw as white and gold armor suddenly rolled over Alex, decorated with exquisite details etched into the metal that I could discern even from this distance.

Excalibur slowly dimmed, and Mordred snarled, lifting his rippling black blade to his opponent. His eyes momentarily widened to see Alex now wearing armor.

But he recovered quickly.

The two kings clashed blades, and the nearby boulders cracked in half at the concussive explosion.

My Horsemen bore witness in silence.

CHAPTER 49

*M*ordred recoiled, lifting his blade in a wary guard.

Then they began to dance, and despite how good Mordred was with a blade…

Alex was easily *twice* as good. Twice as fast. Almost as if he knew Mordred's every move before even Mordred thought it.

The stunned look on Mordred's face confirmed this theory.

Alex lazily batted away three rapid strikes of Mordred's black blade as he spoke in a calm, authoritative tone. "You tried to steal something that was not yours." CLANG! "You corrupted twelve of the noblest men Camelot has ever seen." CLANG-CLANG! "And then you tried to murder your neighbors. You were sent to Hell once, Mordred, and I must admit, that I do not quite know what to do with you."

Mordred had backed away, panting heavily.

"You see, although I did not live in your time, I believe in chivalry. Nobility. Goodness."

Mordred snapped his fingers. Nine Knightmares suddenly winked into existence behind him.

Alex didn't even react to the new threat as he continued to speak to Mordred. "What I want to do to you is not chivalrous, Mordred."

He snarled back. "You are nothing, boy—"

"Which is why I have a friend who is definitely *not* a Knight. And…" Alex glanced back at me with a grin. Then he turned back to Mordred. "I'm beginning to think he has a point..."

I felt my heart begin to race, picking up on some of Alex's words.

I spoke hurriedly under my breath, talking to my Mask.

"Hey, you in there?" I whispered.

"*Yes,*" she replied, amused.

"How much juice do I have?" I asked, a sudden idea forming in my mind. "Enough for armor? I don't need to do anything fancy. I just don't want to take damage," I reassured her.

"*That...is acceptable, Hope. Be warned, you cannot last longer than one minute.*"

"Heard *that* before," I muttered. "It's going to be one crazy minute though. He's a big leaguer. You sure I can take it?"

Again, she sounded amused. "*You are a Horseman. When I say you can last one minute, I mean it definitively. One minute of whatever he throws at you.*"

"You sound *so* hot right now." She laughed delightedly.

I sensed Gunnar and Alucard staring at me nervously. I waved off their concern.

I turned to face Mordred, sensing the Knightmares beginning to surround Alex—who still did not look concerned.

"Call off your hostages, Mordred, or they will all die. MY HORSEMEN ARE HUNGRY!"

Lightning crackled across the sky as the four of us took a step forward.

"Take *me* instead," I snarled, walking towards him as smoothly as I could, which was difficult with my injuries.

I saw the hungry look in his eyes as he studied me and my Mask.

"Do I have your permission to obliterate this stain on humanity?" I asked, turning to face Alex.

He nodded. "Yes, Horseman of Hope." Then he turned to the Knightmares. "Behold the death of your king with honor. If he has the courage to accept," Alex said, turning to arch an eyebrow at Mordred.

He studied me, narrowing his eyes. I held up my hands, calling upon my Horseman wings only. They more resembled the bone spines of wings—with occasional long black feathers here and there—except they were made of the same quartz-like stone as my Mask, rather than bone.

They definitely didn't look capable of aiding in flight, although I knew that was their primary function. I wasn't intending to fly today, though. I wanted something more up close and personal.

Mordred nodded hungrily. "Stand down," he told his Knights.

And then I resumed my walk, using my wings to help support me as I moved. Mordred hurled a blast of air at me.

I easily batted it aside with one of my spines.

Mordred began running at me, hurling blast after blast of molten lava. Instead of slapping it away, I let it wash over me, running headlong into the carnage.

Mordred's eye's widened incredulously, but I still hadn't made any offensive moves other than closing the distance between us.

He hefted his sword, hurling the rippling black blade at my face.

I flung out my hand, using what little magic I had left to me.

Mordred's incredibly powerful blade—the one that had so efficiently kicked my ass earlier—ricocheted off my Mask.

I didn't even blink.

I felt something slam into my palm, but I didn't bother to look down before lifting it behind my head and hurling it as hard as I could at Mordred.

Gungnir screamed as it flew, faster than any lightning bolt.

I saw a cross-guard click out from the haft—as if it was a secret upgrade activated by the velocity of my throw—just before the long blade slammed through Mordred's heart and out his back.

The cross-guard prevented the Devourer from ripping entirely through Mordred's torso. Instead, the full force of my Horseman-fueled throw struck Mordred harder than even Grimm had hit him earlier, knocking him completely off his feet and carrying him towards Camelot's castle wall.

Gungnir slammed into the wall hard enough to crack stone, and I watched as the Devourer ate Mordred's soul, sucking it up with a slurping sound. Mordred dropped his head, hanging limp from the wall of Camelot.

As one, the nine Knightmares dropped to the ground in a metallic crash. None of them stirred, apparently unconscious.

I turned back to Mordred, verifying he was dead. Only then did I use a faint wisp of power to call Gungnir back to my hand. Mordred crashed to the ground in a wet thud as I caught the Devourer. I let out a breath, the brief use of magic making me lightheaded. I leaned on Gungnir as I pulled off my Mask, smiling down at it for a moment or two.

Then I turned it back into a coin and shoved it into my pocket. I felt a silk ribbon and pulled it out, smiling at a thought. Then I made my way over to Alex.

"Thank you," I told him.

He nodded. "I couldn't risk Mordred's soul getting into the wrong hands." He studied me thoughtfully. "I trust you to take care of it."

I nodded. "Of course. How bad was it with the Summer Queen?"

He sighed. "Not as bad as it could have been. Grimm was a big help. Until he disappeared out of nowhere. That's what started to concern me, because I saw him take off for Camelot."

I nodded. "He's a loyal friend," I said, wanting to change the topic. I glanced back at the Knightmares. "And none of them had to die."

Alex smiled faintly. "When I saw the lightning near Camelot, I came as quickly as possible. But when I saw that you had chosen your Horsemen, I thought all of the Knightmares were going to die today. Thank you for resisting the temptation," he said.

I nodded, handing him the silk ribbon. "You should tie them up before we can check them out and cleanse their armor. But I need to go to sleep, so the armor cleansing will have to wait. That will restrain anything, but I'm going to need it back when you're finished."

He nodded, accepting the ribbon. "Thank you, Nate."

I heard a lilting laugh and turned to see Callie and Alucard smiling at Grimm's new sparkly horn. Grimm, on the other hand, did not look pleased. The pair of fledgling Horsemen had taken off their Masks, but they held them in one hand, just in case any of the Knightmares woke.

I noticed Gunnar walking my way, but he had his head to the ground and his hands behind his back, looking as if he was in deep thought.

"Good luck with that," Alex said, walking away to deal with the Knightmares. Talon suddenly appeared beside him, wearing his white armor. I wondered how long he'd been hiding there unseen, ready to protect Alex in the event of a trap.

Or maybe Talon had been the trap—for Mordred.

I turned around too fast, and promptly lost my balance, still weakened from my injuries and use of magic. I landed on my ass with a grunt, gripping the ground with my hands to support my weight as my head continued to spin. It took a few seconds before I dared to open my eyes, and that was only because of a persistent, high-pitched yapping.

I opened my eyes to see two puppies growling at me, hunkered low as they prepared to vanquish me. Although their tails were wagging excitedly, so it would be a pleasant vanquishing.

I smiled, reaching out to pet the little fur balls. They attacked my hand—well, they tried to. It was harmless and fun to watch after the insanity of the last few hours.

I glanced up at Gunnar, about to ask who they belonged to.

He was grinning down at the puppies. He looked up at me, and I realized how freaking tired he looked. "Calvin, Makayla…meet your godfather."

I felt the world tilt and I fell back, banging my head on the ground.

As I faded into unconsciousness, I felt two tiny puppy tongues lapping at my face, as they hopped and climbed over me.

CHAPTER 50

J sat in one of the libraries at Chateau Falco, sipping some Macallan as I recovered from the long day. I watched, smiling as Gunnar and Ashley wrestled with their strangely mature pups, Calvin and Makayla. I had recovered from my shock to learn that she had given birth to actual freaking puppies—two weeks ago.

To them, it was old news.

But to me, it had only been hours before, thanks to the time distortions Pandora had told me about.

She had actually been my first stop after Gunnar had slapped me awake outside of Camelot, having handed off his pups to Ashley to take care of me. Pandora had taken one look at me before commanding Gunnar to carry me into the healing pool and toss me in.

Only then had Pandora brought me up to speed on everything that had happened in my absence. My fight with Mordred had encompassed two weeks in St. Louis time. Pandora was now keeping an eye on everything, making sure that time returned to its normal craziness rather than it's temporary extreme craziness.

I'd yanked her into the pool with me, wrapping her up in a tight hug, thanking her for sending my friends to me in Fae. She'd grown very still, seeming to melt into my embrace. And then the tears had come. Gunnar had left the room, and I spent more than an hour comforting her, reassuring her that I was okay. I even told her about my deal with Anubis and told her to hold onto Gungnir for me until I decided whether or not I wanted to hand it over to Odin.

The pool had helped my injuries, but to truly recover, nothing beat a glass of Macallan and a warm fire.

Except, maybe, two coked-out puppy werewolves.

I had tried to press Gunnar and Ashley on a full explanation about Calvin and Makayla, but they had refused, telling me that I had enough to process already, and that we would talk about it at length later. Since they were apparently fine with it, I had let it go. The mama and her pups were obviously healthy and happy.

And for tonight, that was good enough for me.

So I sipped at my drink before the fire, smiling absently as the puppies wrestled and tripped over absolutely nothing.

My thoughts drifted to my would-be abductor and our strange phone call. But that was a problem for a different day. Soon, but not today. I had much bigger things on my plate in the days to come.

Loki. Fenrir. My Horsemen. The mysterious, shadowy group—

I sighed.

My abductor could wait. Everything could wait. This was all that mattered tonight. Playing with werewolf pups.

I finished my drink and grabbed an old leather journal from the side table before sitting down on the rug. Then I cleared my throat.

The pups trotted over clumsily, their tails wagging as they panted. Calvin took after Gunnar, a white wolf pup with eyes so bright that they were chilling to look at.

Makayla took after Ashley, a black wolf with white paws.

"I don't know if you guys can understand me or not, but I want to make a habit of telling you fairy tales," I told them.

The pups settled down on the rug, resting their chins on my feet as they watched me, an almost-eerie intelligence dancing in their eyes. Ashley slid over to sit between Gunnar's legs, leaning back against him with a contented sigh. He wrapped his beefy arms around her, and the two of them smiled wistfully, listening in.

"I want to tell you about a man named Mallory, and a little troublesome boy named Wylde…"

With shaking fingers, I opened Pan's first journal, one of the many he had left behind for me after he'd died.

There were no words on the paper, just an amalgam of symbols and strange characters.

But I could translate them.

I cleared my throat and began to read. "Once upon a time..."

DON'T FORGET! VIP's get early access to all sorts of Temple-Verse goodies, including signed copies, private giveaways, and advance notice of future projects. AND A FREE NOVELLA! Click the image or join here: www.shaynesilvers.com/l/219800

*Nate Temple returns in **2019**.*

*Turn the page to read a sample of **UNCHAINED** - Feathers and Fire Series Book 1, or **BUY ONLINE**. Callie Penrose is a wizard in Kansas City, MO who hunts monsters for the Vatican. She meets Nate Temple, and things devolve from there...*

(Note: Full chronology of all books in the Temple Verse shown on the 'Books in the Temple Verse' page.)

TRY: UNCHAINED (FEATHERS AND FIRE #1)

$\mathcal{T}$he rain pelted my hair, plastering loose strands of it to my forehead as I panted, eyes darting from tree to tree, terrified of each shifting branch, splash of water, and whistle of wind slipping through the nightscape around us. But... I was somewhat *excited*, too.

Somewhat.

"Easy, girl. All will be well," the big man creeping just ahead of me, murmured.

"You said we were going to get ice cream!" I hissed at him, failing to compose myself, but careful to keep my voice low and my eyes alert. "I'm not ready for this!" I had been trained to fight, with my hands, with weapons, and with my magic. But I had never taken an active role in a hunt before. I'd always been the getaway driver for my mentor.

The man grunted, grey eyes scanning the trees as he slipped through the tall grass. "And did we not get ice cream before coming here? Because I think I see some in your hair."

"You know what I mean, Roland. You tricked me." I checked the tips of my loose hair, saw nothing, and scowled at his back.

"The Lord does not give us a greater burden than we can shoulder."

I muttered dark things under my breath, wiping the water from my eyes. Again. My new shirt was going to be ruined. Silk never fared well in the rain. My choice of shoes wasn't much better. Boots, yes, but distressed, *fashionable* boots. Not work boots designed for the rain and mud. Definitely not monster hunting boots for our evening excursion through one of Kansas City's wooded parks. I realized I was forcibly distracting myself, keeping my mind busy with mundane thoughts to avoid my very real anxiety. Because whenever I grew nervous, an imagined nightmare always—

A church looming before me. Rain pouring down. Night sky and a glowing moon overhead. I was all alone. Crying on the cold, stone steps, and infant in a cardboard box—

I forced the nightmare away, breathing heavily. "You know I hate it when you talk like that," I whispered to him, trying to regain my composure. I wasn't angry with him, but was growing increasingly uncomfortable with our situation after my brief flashback of fear.

"Doesn't mean it shouldn't be said," he said kindly. "I think we're close. Be alert. Remember your training. Banish your fears. I am here. And the Lord is here. He always is."

So, he had noticed my sudden anxiety. "Maybe I should just go back to the car. I know I've trained, but I really don't think—"

A shape of fur, fangs, and claws launched from the shadows towards me, cutting off my words as it snarled, thirsty for my blood.

And my nightmare slipped back into my thoughts like a veiled assassin, a wraith hoping to hold me still for the monster to eat. I froze, unable to move. Twin sticks of power abruptly erupted into being in my clenched fists, but my fear swamped me with that stupid nightmare, the sticks held at my side, useless to save me.

Right before the beast's claws reached me, it grunted as something batted it from the air, sending it flying sideways. It struck a tree with another grunt and an angry whine of pain.

I fell to my knees right into a puddle, arms shaking, breathing fast.

My sticks crackled in the rain like live cattle prods, except their entire length was the electrical section — at least to anyone other than me. I could hold them without pain.

Magic was a part of me, coursing through my veins whether I wanted it or not, and Roland had spent many years teaching me how to master it. But I had never been able to fully master the nightmare inside me, and in moments of fear, it always won, overriding my training.

The fact that I had resorted to weapons — like the ones he had trained me with — rather than a burst of flame, was startling. It was good in the fact that my body's reflexes knew enough to call up a defense even without my direct command, but bad in the fact that it was the worst form of defense for the situation presented. I could have very easily done as Roland did, and hurt it from a distance. But I hadn't. Because of my stupid block.

Roland placed a calloused palm on my shoulder, and I flinched. "Easy, see? I am here." But he did frown at my choice of weapons, the reprimand silent but loud in my mind. I let out a shaky breath, forcing my fear back down. It was all in my head, but still, it wasn't easy. Fear could be like that.

I focused on Roland's implied lesson. Close combat weapons — even magically-powered ones — were for last resorts. I averted my eyes in very real shame. I knew these things. He didn't even need to tell me them. But when that damned nightmare caught hold of me, all my training went out the window. It haunted me like a shadow, waiting for moments just like this, as if trying to kill me. A form of psychological suicide? But it was why I constantly refused to join Roland on his hunts. He knew about it. And although he was trying to help me overcome that fear, he never pressed too hard.

Rain continued to sizzle as it struck my batons. I didn't let them go, using them as a totem to build my confidence back up. I slowly lifted my eyes to nod at him as I climbed back to my feet.

That's when I saw the second set of eyes in the shadows, right before they flew out of the darkness towards Roland's back. I threw one of my batons and missed, but that pretty much let Roland know that an unfriendly was behind him. Either that or I had just failed to murder my mentor at point-blank range. He whirled to confront the monster, expecting another aerial assault as he unleashed a ball of fire that splashed over the tree at chest height, washing the trunk in blue flames. But this monster was tricky. It hadn't planned on tackling Roland, but had merely jumped out of the darkness to get closer, no doubt learning from its fallen comrade, who still lay unmoving against the tree behind me.

His coat shone like midnight clouds with hints of lightning flashing in the depths of thick, wiry fur. The coat of dew dotting his fur reflected the moonlight, giving him a faint sheen as if covered in fresh oil. He was tall, easily hip height at the shoulder, and barrel chested, his rump much leaner than the rest of his body. He — I assumed male from the long, thick mane around his neck — had a very long snout, much longer and wider than any werewolf I had ever seen. Amazingly, and beyond my control, I realized he was beautiful.

But most of the natural world's lethal hunters were beautiful.

He landed in a wet puddle a pace in front of Roland, juked to the right, and then to the left, racing past the big man, biting into his hamstrings on his way by.

A wash of anger rolled over me at seeing my mentor injured, dousing my fear, and I swung my baton down as hard as I could. It struck the beast in the rump as it tried to dart back to cover — a typical wolf tactic. My blow singed his hair and shattered bone. The creature collapsed into a puddle of mud with a yelp, instinctively snapping his jaws over his shoulder to bite whatever had hit him.

I let him. But mostly out of dumb luck as I heard Roland hiss in pain, falling to the ground.

The monster's jaws clamped around my baton, and there was an immediate explosion of teeth and blood that sent him flying several feet away into the tall brush, yipping, screaming, and staggering. Before he slipped out of sight, I noticed that his lower jaw was simply *gone*, from the contact of his saliva on my electrified magical batons. Then he managed to limp into the woods with more pitiful yowls, but I had no mind to chase him. Roland — that titan of a man, my mentor — was hurt. I could smell copper in the air, and knew we had to get out of here. Fast. Because we had anticipated only one of the monsters. But there had been two of them, and they hadn't been the run-of-the-mill werewolves we had been warned about. If there were two, perhaps there were more. And they were evidently the prehistoric cousin of any werewolf I had ever seen or read about.

Roland hissed again as he stared down at his leg, growling with both pain and anger. My eyes darted back to the first monster, wary of another attack. It *almost* looked like a werewolf, but bigger. Much bigger. He didn't move, but I saw he was breathing. He had a notch in his right ear and a jagged scar on his long snout. Part of me wanted to go over to him and torture him. Slowly. Use his pain to finally drown my nightmare, my fear. The fear that had caused Roland's injury. My lack of inner-strength had not only put me in danger, but had hurt my mentor, my friend.

I shivered, forcing the thought away. That was *cold*. Not me. Sure, I was no stranger to fighting, but that had always been in a ring. Practicing. Sparring. Never life or death.

But I suddenly realized something very dark about myself in the chill, rainy night. Although I was terrified, I felt a deep ocean of anger manifest inside me, wanting only to dispense justice as I saw fit. To use that rage to battle my own demons. As if feeding one would starve the other, reminding me of the Cherokee Indian Legend Roland had once told me.

An old Cherokee man was teaching his grandson about life. "A fight is going on inside me," he told the boy. "It is a terrible fight between two wolves. One is evil — he is anger, envy, sorrow, regret, greed, arrogance, self-pity, guilt, resentment, inferiority, lies, false pride, superiority, and ego." After a few moments to make sure he had the boy's undivided attention, he continued.

"The other wolf is good — he is joy, peace, love, hope, serenity, humility, kindness, benevolence, empathy, generosity, truth, compassion, and faith. The same fight is going on inside of you, boy, and inside of every other person, too."

The grandson thought about this for a few minutes before replying. "Which wolf will win?"

The old Cherokee man simply said, "The one you feed, boy. The one you feed..."

And I felt like feeding one of my wolves today, by killing this one...

∼

Get the full book ONLINE!

∽

*Turn the page to read the first chapter of **WHISKEY GINGER**, book 1 in the Phantom Queen Diaries, which is also a part of the Temple Verse. Quinn MacKenna is a black-magic arms dealer from Boston, and she doesn't play nice. Not at all...*

TRY: WHISKEY GINGER (PHANTOM QUEEN DIARIES BOOK 1)

*T*he pasty guitarist hunched forward, thrust a rolled-up wad of paper deep into one nostril, and snorted a line of blood crystals— frozen hemoglobin that I'd smuggled over in a refrigerated canister—with the uncanny grace of a drug addict. He sat back, fangs gleaming, and pawed at his nose. "That's some bodacious shit. Hey, bros," he said, glancing at his fellow band members, "come hit this shit before it melts."

He fetched one of the backstage passes hanging nearby, pried the plastic badge from its lanyard, and used it to split up the crystals, murmuring something in an accent that reminded me of California. Not *the* California, but you know, Cali-foh-nia—the land of beaches, babes, and bros. I retrieved a toothpick from my pocket and punched it through its thin wrapper. "So," I asked no one in particular, "now that ye have the product, who's payin'?"

Another band member stepped out of the shadows to my left, and I don't mean that figuratively, either—the fucker literally stepped out of the shadows. I scowled at him, but hid my surprise, nonchalantly rolling the toothpick from one side of my mouth to the other.

The rest of the band gathered around the dressing room table, following the guitarist's lead by preparing their own snorting utensils—tattered magazine covers, mostly. Typically, you'd do this sort of thing with a dollarbill, maybe even a Benjamin if you were flush. But fangers like this lot couldn't touch cash directly—in God We Trust and all that. Of course, I didn't really understand why sucking blood the old-fashioned way had suddenly gone out of style. More of a rush, maybe?

"It lasts longer," the vampire next to me explained, catching my mildly curious expression. "It's especially good for shows and stuff. Makes us look, like, less—"

"Creepy?" I offered, my Irish brogue lilting just enough to make it a question.

"Pale," he finished, frowning.

I shrugged. "Listen, I've got places to be," I said, holding out my hand.

"I'm sure you do," he replied, smiling. "Tell you what, why don't you, like, hang around for a bit? Once that wears off," he dipped his head toward the bloody powder smeared across the table's surface, "we may need a pick-me-up." He rested his hand on my arm and our gazes locked.

I blinked, realized what he was trying to pull, and rolled my eyes. His widened in surprise, then shock as I yanked out my toothpick and shoved it through his hand.

"Motherfuck—"

"I want what we agreed on," I declared. "Now. No tricks."

The rest of the band saw what happened and rose faster than I could blink. They circled me, their grins feral...they might have even seemed intimidating if it weren't for the fact that they each had a case of the sniffles

—I had to work extra hard not to think about what it felt like to have someone else's blood dripping down my nasal cavity.

I held up a hand.

"Can I ask ye gentlemen a question before we get started?" I asked. "Do ye even *have* what I asked for?"

Two of the band members exchanged looks and shrugged. The guitarist, however, glanced back towards the dressing room, where a brown paper bag sat next to a case full of makeup. He caught me looking and bared his teeth, his fangs stretching until it looked like it would be uncomfortable for him to close his mouth without piercing his own lip.

"Follow-up question," I said, eyeing the vampire I'd stabbed as he gingerly withdrew the toothpick from his hand and flung it across the room with a snarl. "Do ye do each other's make-up? Since, ye know, ye can't use mirrors?"

I was genuinely curious.

The guitarist grunted. "Mike, we have to go on soon."

"Wait a minute. Mike?" I turned to the snarling vampire with a frown. "What happened to *The Vampire Prospero?*" I glanced at the numerous fliers in the dressing room, most of which depicted the band members wading through blood, with Mike in the lead, each one titled *The Vampire Prospero* in *Rocky Horror Picture Show* font. Come to think of it…Mike did look a little like Tim Curry in all that leather and lace.

I was about to comment on the resemblance when Mike spoke up, "Alright, change of plans, bros. We're gonna drain this bitch before the show. We'll look totally—"

"Creepy?" I offered, again.

"Kill her."

∼

Get the full book ONLINE!

MAKE A DIFFERENCE

Reviews are the most powerful tools in my arsenal when it comes to getting attention for my books. Much as I'd like to, I don't have the financial muscle of a New York publisher.

But I do have something much more powerful and effective than that, and it's something that those publishers would kill to get their hands on.

A committed and loyal bunch of readers.

Honest reviews of my books help bring them to the attention of other readers.

If you've enjoyed this book, I would be very grateful if you could spend just five minutes leaving a review on my book's Amazon page.

Thank you very much in advance.

ACKNOWLEDGMENTS

Team Temple and the Den of Freaks on Facebook have become family to me. I couldn't do it without die-hard readers like them.

I would also like to thank you, the reader. I hope you enjoyed reading *KNIGHTMARE* as much as I enjoyed writing it.

Quinn MacKenna returns in 2019 with her Book 8 in the Phantom Queen Diaries, SEA BREEZE…

And perhaps a few new series will launch in 2019…

ABOUT SHAYNE SILVERS

Shayne is a man of mystery and power, whose power is exceeded only by his mystery…

He currently writes the Amazon Bestselling **Nate Temple** Series, which features a foul-mouthed wizard from St. Louis. He rides a bloodthirsty unicorn, drinks with Achilles, and is pals with the Four Horsemen.

He also writes the Amazon Bestselling **Feathers and Fire** Series—a second series in the Temple Verse. The story follows a rookie spell-slinger named Callie Penrose who works for the Vatican in Kansas City. Her problem? Hell seems to know more about her past than she does.

He coauthors **The Phantom Queen Diaries**—a third series set in The Temple Verse—with Cameron O'Connell. The story follows Quinn MacKenna, a mouthy black magic arms dealer in Boston. All she wants? A round-trip ticket to the Fae realm…and maybe a drink on the house.

Shayne holds two high-ranking black belts, and can be found writing in a coffee shop, cackling madly into his computer screen while pounding shots of espresso. He's hard at work on the newest books in the Temple Verse—You can find updates on new releases or chronological reading order on the next page, his website or any of his social media accounts. **Follow him online for all sorts of groovy goodies, giveaways, and new release updates:**

Get Down with Shayne Online
www.shaynesilvers.com
info@shaynesilvers.com

facebook.com/shaynesilversfanpage

amazon.com/author/shaynesilvers

bookbub.com/profile/shayne-silvers

instagram.com/shaynesilversofficial

twitter.com/shaynesilvers

goodreads.com/ShayneSilvers

BOOKS IN THE TEMPLE VERSE

CHRONOLOGY: All stories in the TempleVerse are shown in chronological order on the following page

NATE TEMPLE SERIES

FAIRY TALE - FREE prequel novella #0 for my subscribers

OBSIDIAN SON

BLOOD DEBTS

GRIMM

SILVER TONGUE

BEAST MASTER

BEERLYMPIAN (Novella #5.5 in the 'LAST CALL' anthology)

TINY GODS

DADDY DUTY (Novella #6.5)

WILD SIDE

WAR HAMMER

NINE SOULS

HORSEMAN

LEGEND

KNIGHTMARE

FEATHERS AND FIRE SERIES

(Also set in the TempleVerse)

UNCHAINED

RAGE

WHISPERS

ANGEL'S ROAR

MOTHERLUCKER (Novella #4.5 in the 'LAST CALL' anthology)

SINNER

BLACK SHEEP

GODLESS

PHANTOM QUEEN DIARIES

(Also set in the Temple Universe)

COLLINS (Prequel novella #0 in the 'LAST CALL' anthology)

WHISKEY GINGER

COSMOPOLITAN

OLD FASHIONED

MOTHERLUCKER (Novella #3.5 in the 'LAST CALL' anthology)

DARK AND STORMY

MOSCOW MULE

WITCHES BREW

SALTY DOG

CHRONOLOGICAL ORDER: TEMPLE VERSE

FAIRY TALE (TEMPLE PREQUEL)

OBSIDIAN SON (TEMPLE 1)

BLOOD DEBTS (TEMPLE 2)

GRIMM (TEMPLE 3)

SILVER TONGUE (TEMPLE 4)

BEAST MASTER (TEMPLE 5)

BEERLYMPIAN (TEMPLE 5.5)

TINY GODS (TEMPLE 6)

DADDY DUTY (TEMPLE NOVELLA 6.5)

UNCHAINED (FEATHERS... 1)

RAGE (FEATHERS... 2)

WILD SIDE (TEMPLE 7)

WAR HAMMER (TEMPLE 8)

WHISPERS (FEATHERS... 3)

COLLINS (PHANTOM 0)

WHISKEY GINGER (PHANTOM… 1)

NINE SOULS (TEMPLE 9)

COSMOPOLITAN (PHANTOM… 2)

ANGEL'S ROAR (FEATHERS… 4)

MOTHERLUCKER (FEATHERS 4.5, PHANTOM 3.5)

OLD FASHIONED (PHANTOM…3)

HORSEMAN (TEMPLE 10)

DARK AND STORMY (PHANTOM… 4)

MOSCOW MULE (PHANTOM…5)

SINNER (FEATHERS…5)

WITCHES BREW (PHANTOM…6)

LEGEND (TEMPLE…11)

SALTY DOG (PHANTOM…7)

BLACK SHEEP (FEATHERS…6)

GODLESS (FEATHERS…7)

KNIGHTMARE (TEMPLE 12)

Printed in Great Britain
by Amazon